Roses of Marrakech

Roses of Marrakech

Rachel Clare

The Book Guild Ltd

First published in Great Britain in 2018 by
The Book Guild Ltd
9 Priory Business Park
Wistow Road, Kibworth
Leicestershire, LE8 0RX
Freephone: 0800 999 2982
www.bookguild.co.uk
Email: info@bookguild.co.uk
Twitter: @bookguild

Typeset in Adobe Garamond Pro

Printed and bound in Great Britain by CPI Group (UK) Ltd, Croydon, CR0 4YY

ISBN 978 1912362 714

British Library Cataloguing in Publication Data.
A catalogue record for this book is available from the British Library.

In loving memory of my grandma, Sylvia Wynne

"But he, who dares not grasp the thorn
Should never crave the rose."

– Anne Brontë.

Prologue

December 1979

Ivy was born during a snowstorm. Building up to its crescendo, the wintry wind slammed stone-hard flakes against the hospital window to cruelly mimic the mother-to-be's agonising throes of labour. With a piercing cry, she mustered the strength to heave herself up on her elbows in time to see the slimy, pale creature slip from between her legs. For a brief moment, her newborn daughter was placed on her chest before a heavily built nurse scooped her up in a white towel and whisked her away. The squeak of rubber-soled shoes receding down the corridor, the new mother turned towards the window, averting her eyes from the pain etched on her husband's face. The first decade of their marriage afflicted by miscarriages, they'd desperately longed for this child but now the excitement, the plans they'd made, ebbed away just as the storm receded outside. They would all be stumbling in the darkness.

After hours of wakefulness, she wandered down the silent hospital corridor to the nursery. Bending over her baby's crib, she stifled sobs so as not to wake her as she gently stroked her daughter's silky, white cheek before tracing her finger down the left side of her face. In the grey, indistinct light of pre-dawn, she could see it was completely covered by a livid, red birthmark. Unable to recall much of what the consultant had said, one word forced its way back to the forefront of her mind as she stood there shivering. *Permanent.* At that moment, she saw her daughter's eyes flicker open seeming to meet her gaze. A spark of recognition igniting between the two, as the new mother looked into her striking green eyes the love she felt for her child overwhelmed everything else.

Knowing that their child would be born at Christmas, she and Daniel had already decided that if it was a girl, they'd call her Holly or Ivy. Careful now to avoid the name of a blood-coloured berry, they settled on the latter, not realising the irony in calling their daughter after a plant which, as it grows, covers and conceals what lies beneath. During those first few years, with her husband's unwavering support, Ivy's mum tried as best she could to cocoon her daughter in love, to shield her from the world's cruelties. But as her child outgrew her babyhood she knew it would be impossible to continue in this way if Ivy was going to lead a normal life. Her own mother having died many years before, she turned to her aunt Rose to help her guide her daughter down the treacherous road of childhood.

It was an astute choice. Growing up in Lavenham, with its picture-postcard, pink-thatched cottages and surrounding undulating countryside, Ivy needed to be given the tools to carve her niche in the outside world. A wise and caring woman, she quickly found Rose to be a kindred spirit. By the time she was seven, their relationship had grown so close that the little girl insisted on spending every moment she could with her beloved great-aunt. So every Sunday, after lunch, her mum dropped her off at Rose's cottage, where the two of them retreated to a low-beamed sitting room which, with its walls lined with shelves crammed with books, Ivy pretended was their secret library. Delving into the extensive treasury of classical literature, history books and poetry anthologies with their lovely tooled leather covers, they immersed themselves in the pages, losing all track of time. Ivy's irrefutable favourites were Charlotte Brontë's novels with their shy, strong heroines but she also enjoyed leafing through the great, hefty travel books with their entrancing colour pictures while Rose told stories of all the wonderful cities she'd visited. A boat ride on the blue ribbon of the Danube, the white points of the Fishermen's Bastion rising from Castle Hill in old Buda vying for her attention with the Neo-Gothic parliament building in Pest. Eating *Sachertorte* in the opulent surroundings of a Vienna hotel, meandering past painters on the cobblestone streets of Montmartre up to the magnificent white dome of Sacré-Coeur; these tales gave the little girl a wanderlust to visit such places herself one day.

"Will this mark on my cheek disappear when I grow up?" Ivy asked her great-aunt late one afternoon, an exquisitely illustrated *Tales of Arabia* propped on her knee. It was mid-January, a month after her eighth birthday and, looking out at the white pillows of snow which covered the sleeping winter garden, she was glad to be in the cosy lamplight of their library.

"No sweetheart, you remember we explained that it is part of who you are, just like your lovely green eyes?" the old woman whispered, stroking Ivy's cheek as they sat together in their favourite leather armchair. Apart from her parents, Rose was the only person she'd ever let touch it.

"But I don't want it to be part of me," she cried. "Some of the older boys at school say it's so ugly, that no one will ever love me. They call me horrible names."

Ivy watched as Rose carefully wrote the offending boys' names in her looping handwriting in a cerise silk covered notebook, "I'll have a quiet word with your teacher tomorrow. Miss Jones, isn't it?"

"Yes," Ivy muttered, knowing that her great-aunt would sort it out with minimum fuss.

"I realise it hurts now and it seems like you will feel this way forever but I promise you will grow up to be a beautiful young lady, you'll see." Rose said, with that enchanting smile which always made her great-niece feel everything would be alright.

The old woman then drew her into a warm embrace, engulfing her in that familiar smell of freshly baked cakes mingled with the flowery perfume she always wore. Ivy wanted so much to believe her and yet found it hard to imagine that anyone would ever see the horrible red mark on her face as beautiful. Scrutinising Rose's face, she saw that in old age she had lovely high cheek bones and porcelain-white, still smooth skin, while her eyes were an indefinable colour which changed from hazel to olive-brown in the shifting light. Smiling lovingly at her, it puzzled Ivy as to why she had never married, for she was so kind and gentle and had obviously been a great beauty in her youth.

Rose was true to her word and, after accompanying Ivy's mum to the headmaster's office, the boys never bothered the little girl again. But something in Ivy's attitude shifted that day. For the next few months every time she passed a mirror, she rubbed her hand over her birthmark, imagining she could wipe it away as she could a smear of spaghetti sauce. One day, she locked herself in the bathroom for over an hour, scrubbing the ugly thing with her mother's nailbrush. But instead of making it disappear it just became more livid and painful and she sobbed herself to sleep that night, believing the boys had been right all along.

By the time she left primary school, Ivy's sweet nature had drawn a small but loyal group of friends to her with Mei, her best friend since reception class, her best friend still. As Ivy progressed through secondary school, her academic work excelled. Although reading the books in Rose's library from a young age had fostered a keen interest in History and Geography, she found her talents lay in foreign languages and gained good enough A-levels to be accepted by the highly-rated French department at King's College, London. And for a while it looked as though she had put all her insecurities behind her, just as people shed their thick clothes when the chills of winter come to an end.

1

Spring sunlight streamed through the arching glass roof of Liverpool Street Station, burnishing the coppery highlights in Ivy's shoulder length, auburn hair as she stepped off the train that Friday evening. Barely five feet two and of slight build, she had difficulty manoeuvring her overnight case and carrier bags, which strained with gifts for Mei's children, through the oncoming tide of suited commuters eager to make their Whitsun weekend escape from the crowded capital. Taking advantage of a bottleneck ahead of the Underground station to adjust the bags' plastic handles which were cutting red rings into her wrists, Ivy's mind rewound to the first time she'd arrived there almost two decades earlier.

Mei's hopeful prediction that reading for their respective degrees at King's College would give them the opportunity to experience the city's bright lights together had meant they'd made the London university their first choice on their UCAS forms. But whereas Ivy's diligence in studying had resulted in her A-level grades surpassing the course's requirements, her friend's growing preoccupation with sixth form boys had led to her barely scraping passes and, after going through clearing, she'd ended up at South Bank University to study English and American Studies. And so, alighting a train that Sunday evening in late September with huge suitcases containing her clothes, crockery and course books, Ivy's stomach had roiled with apprehension as the reality of leaving her quiet Suffolk town for the vast city overwhelmed her.

Descending to the darkness of the Underground now, she subconsciously flicked her carefully cut fringe over the left side of her face, her olive-green eyes lowered to watch her step. Waiting on the platform with a melange of tourists and business people, she noticed a smartly-dressed man in his late thirties looking at her appraisingly. Even though specially formulated camouflage creams prescribed by her skin specialist had given her the confidence to face the world outside, the cruel comments she'd suffered from the boys in primary school had left their mark and she imagined the man guessing at what lay beneath her makeup. So, instinctively, instead of returning his smile, she pretended to rummage in her handbag for something until sensing he'd turned his attentions elsewhere.

Once on the tube Ivy wedged herself between loud groups of Spanish and German teenagers who, with their colossal backpacks, resembled giant turtles. As the train set off, their youthful exuberance brought back memories of her friends, or rather acquaintances, during her own student days. With universities separated by the brown snake of the River Thames, she'd rarely seen Mei during term time, their plans to room together unfulfilled. Instead, Ivy had remained in halls of residence for the duration of her degree, flanked by her neighbours, Alyssa, a straight-talking Geordie from her French classes and Caroline, an Art student from Berkshire, who'd floated around like a colourful butterfly in tie-dyed creations of her own making. They'd been nice enough girls, pooling food and taking it in turns with Ivy to cook meals for the three of them. Although unspoken, Ivy had always been conscious, however, that she was the third person in the friendship and had rarely accompanied the vivacious girls on their weekend forays to Greenwich and Hampstead Heath, giving the excuse that she had an essay pending or some reading to catch up on. Indeed, it had only been when her parents or Rose had visited that she'd been persuaded to leave her work for an afternoon at the V&A or Covent Garden. Following a disastrous stay at the Université de Poitiers at the end of her second year, as her finals had approached, Ivy had pared down her life to the familiarity of her living quarters, lecture theatres, library and a weekly shop at a nearby supermarket. Unfortunately, by keeping the dangers of the city at a distance, she'd also failed to expose herself to its vibrancy and diversity, meaning that whenever she visited now, she still felt like a tourist.

Meanwhile, Mei's failure to make the grade had set her life on a divergent course in more ways than one. At a party to celebrate the end of her first year she had met Philip, a serious young man, who'd just graduated with a first-class degree in architecture. After spending every waking moment together during that long, hot summer, they'd fallen in love. With her parents' approval of Mei and Philip's relationship crossing ethnic boundaries, she'd moved into his dockside apartment the following September, as he'd embarked upon the first step in his career with a prestigious city firm.

Two years later and two months after her graduation, Ivy had been bridesmaid at their beautiful wedding at St Martin-in-the-Fields followed by a reception on a Thames barge. Watching the floodlit Houses of Parliament float past, resplendent beneath a canopy of stars, Ivy had glanced over at her friend dancing with her husband, her expression one of complete happiness. She'd met a boy and they'd fallen in love; it was something people did all the time. It seemed so simple and yet, as the song had faded on the warm summer breeze, Ivy had been unable to imagine it happening to her.

With a respectable 2:1, Ivy's French tutor had encouraged her to apply for translation jobs in various offices in London and the E.U. headquarters in Brussels and Strasbourg. When polite rejections had flooded her letterbox, part of her had been relieved that she'd have to turn her attentions back home. Although her mum's suggestion of French secondary school teacher training hadn't quite appealed to her, Rose had stepped in to suggest primary teaching and suddenly everything had fallen into place. She'd immediately enrolled on a course and, by the time she collected her P.G.C.E. certificate a year later, she'd already secured the Year Three post at St. Mark's C. of E. Primary School in Colchester and, fourteen years later, she was still there.

After negotiating changes at King's Cross St. Pancras and Euston, Ivy finally found a forward-facing seat and was able to submit to the train's hypnotic movement on the final leg of her journey. Seeing her reflection in the window as the train passed through Camden Town station, she knew that despite the dark shadows beneath her eyes, testifying to too many late night sessions of planning and marking, her mother had been right. Teaching suited Ivy. She adored children and they reciprocated the feeling. Constantly energised by their enthusiasm to learn new things, it was exciting to see the world through seven and eight year-olds' eyes, endless with its possibilities and dreams even though sometimes she had to remind herself it was *their* dreams and that she was merely the facilitator.

As for *her* dreams, dreams of travelling to exotic places where she could converse in French and various other languages she'd learned the rudiments of over the years, they remained unfulfilled. She momentarily wondered what it would be like to pursue them, but by the time she alighted the train at Belsize Park, dusk was falling and she'd convinced herself that her job as a teacher was more than enough for her.

Her mobile buzzed in her pocket, "Hi Mum."

"Hi love. I know you're on half term now and wondered whether you wanted to come around for Sunday lunch?"

"That would have been lovely but I'm staying the weekend at Mei's. I'm coming back Monday night though," Ivy stepped aside to let a group of youths pass.

Her mum hesitated, "Come round on Tuesday then. We can still have the chicken and I've got something I want to talk to you about concerning Rose."

5

"What?" Ivy queried, instantly sorry she'd asked for she knew her mum wouldn't discuss anything of importance on the phone.

"Oh, Ivy, we'll have a good chat when you come," her mum paused, "have a nice trip and give Mei and the children my love. Bye for now."

As she rang off Ivy's stomach lurched, knowing her mum intended to broach the sale of Rose's house, an issue they had been skirting around since her death in February. *Her death,* the words seared deeply once again as she pictured Rose's peaceful face on the hospital pillow. Her demise had come very quickly, from a seemingly fit nonagenarian to a frail and infirm shadow of herself. "I'm ready to go, that's all," she'd said, that last night in the quiet room off the ward, looking over Ivy's shoulder as though someone was standing behind her. "It's just that I've got more people waiting for me there than I have here now." She'd smiled her familiar sweet smile, "I don't want to leave you or your mum but it's time… "

"Auntie Ivy, Auntie Ivy." Her reverie was interrupted by excitable shouts as she exited the Underground station. Ruth bounded towards her, shiny, black plaits leaping in the air. In her deep brown, almond-shaped eyes and her beautiful pale skin, Ivy could see the five year-old Mei, who had sat next to her on those tiny grey chairs and then shared her crisps with her at morning playtime on their first day of school over thirty years ago. Maybe it was because Mei was Chinese and therefore different from the other children too, but they had instantly formed a close friendship which had only deepened with the passing years.

"Ruth," Ivy smiled, catching the child in a bear hug, "how are you?"

"Great, now you're here. I've soooo been looking forward to seeing you. I was thinking about you all day," the little girl beamed.

"I hope you were thinking about what your teacher was saying, too," Ivy released the child, smiling into her lovely, heart-shaped face.

"You know she's your number one fan, Ivy." Mei stepped towards her, her willowy figure dressed in an immaculate burgundy pencil dress while her ebony, chin-skimming bob framed her neat face. Holding the hand of her small son, she embraced Ivy with her spare arm.

"Umm, try telling that to some of the children in my class!" Ivy laughed, lightly pinching Harry's chubby cheek between the soft pads of her forefinger and thumb, "and how are you, young man?"

The little boy had been regarding her solemnly. "Got for you," he smiled, sliding a girl fashioned from Play-Doh into the palm of Ivy's hand, "she got red hair like you."

"That's beautiful," Ivy lifted it to scrutinise it, "oh yes, I see. And you made this all by yourself?"

"Yep," Harry nodded, pride bursting from his puffed out chest.

"That's very clever of you," Ivy smiled, ruffling his black, spiky hair.

"Yes, it looks like I've got another architect on my hands," Mei gave her son an adoring look, "following in the footsteps of his father. Let's hope I see a bit more of Harry than Philip… "

Ivy let the comment float away on the warm breeze as Ruth tugged her towards the zebra crossing past cafés and restaurants, their tables and chairs spilling onto the pavement this early summer's evening. Watching her step as they cut onto a shady side street, Ivy took in the vast Victorian semis, with their scruffy gardens, the numerous doorbells with handwritten names beside them testifying to their seemingly endless subdivisions. She shuddered as she pictured the claustrophobic interiors of their dark, poky flats, so different from her own in Colchester and was glad their hefty prices had always defeated Mei's arguments of her moving there. As they passed horse-chestnut trees with clusters of pink-white flowers perched on the end of their branches like candles, the huge houses gave way to smaller, Edwardian villas. Set back from the road with manicured gardens in front, Ivy had liked the 'cottage feel' of them when Mei had first brought her there eight years ago, heavily pregnant and eager to put hers and Philip's city apartment and lifestyle behind them to set up a family home.

Ruth ran on ahead up the pathway to the house, pausing outside the glossy blue front door to catch her breath, the others following. Ivy noticed the cherry tree in the garden was in full blossom, the flowers clinging to the branches like swirls of pink candyfloss. Once ensconced in the spare room, with the overly enthusiastic attentions of Ruth, Ivy joined them all downstairs. Her presents of a bucket of plastic dinosaurs and *Frozen* book with a sing-a-long CD, proved popular as the three of them amused themselves while Mei disappeared into the kitchen. Tea was a simple tomato and basil pasta with garlic bread, which they ate in the gleaming, state-of-the-art kitchen. After finishing the washing up, while Mei took the children for their bath and bedtime story, Ivy retreated to the living room in the company of Paulo Nutini and a bottle of red wine. Although not to her taste, the room was stylishly minimalistic with its muted beiges and creams while oriental art adorned the walls with fiery bursts of red and orange. Sitting alone, she couldn't help but think that her friend had it all – a husband who doted on her, two adoring children and a charming house in a fashionable North London neighbourhood.

"So what's new?" Ivy asked as Mei eventually collapsed on the sofa next to her, having changed into a pair of elegant, red silk pyjamas.

"Not much, I'm afraid," Mei held out her glass, "just a top up, please."

"What happened to the nursing course you were thinking of applying for when we met up at Easter?" Ivy poured the wine as her friend grimaced.

"Well, I sent off for an application form, it came and… I didn't get around to filling it in," Mei took a sip of wine, shrugging her shoulders.

"Come on, Mei, I thought you said that when Harry starts school you'd do it," Ivy smiled at her friend, "have you talked to Philip about it?"

"Yes, and he's told me to go for it. The children's school is five minutes from the college so when Harry goes there in September… " her friend paused, as though searching for her next words.

"Then what's stopping you?" Ivy tucked some stray hair behind her ear.

"Just myself I suppose, it's such a massive decision," Mei sighed, "such an investment of time and money. I've never seriously considered having a career before. When Philip and I married, I just lurched from one temp job to another before the kids came along. I wanted to be a mother more than anything but now it's starting to sink in that soon I'll be at home on my own and I want… "

"You want more?" Ivy sat back, resting her glass on the arm of the sofa.

Mei nodded, "but I don't know. Going back to study at my time of life, I'm just not sure whether I can do it."

"Of course you can. You'd make a wonderful nurse. God, I remember you dressing up every day in the nurse's uniform in reception class," Ivy laughed, "I bet not many people can say they've had a career in mind since they were five."

"No, I don't suppose so. I think the prospect of me wearing the uniform is the main reason Phil's been so supportive," Mei laughed, "it's just so daunting though. It would be a huge adjustment for all of us. It would mean Phil changing his work patterns to fit in with me… "

"Promise me you'll give it some serious thought?" Ivy added, "you could still apply for the September intake, if you get a move on."

Mei nodded, folding her long legs beneath her, "what did you dream of doing when you were younger?"

"I don't think I had one specific dream," remarked Ivy, thrown off her guard. Not considering her hopes of travelling to be very practical, she'd come to believe at an early age that marriage and therefore children were probably off the agenda because of her disfigurement. She blinked momentarily as her friend leaned over to click on a free-standing lamp which was accompanied by an uncomfortable feeling she was about to be interrogated.

"You always had posters of Marrakech on your bedroom wall when we were teenagers," reflected Mei, looking intently at her, "you said that when you'd completed your degree you were going to take a trip there."

"I did, didn't I? It was my great-aunt Rose reading books to me that whetted my appetite to see the palaces and souks but I said lots of crazy stuff back then," Ivy waved her hand, dismissively, "and then I grew up and became a teacher, moulding children's minds," she laughed.

"Just think about it for a second," Mei folded a purple silk shawl around her as the night air grew chill, "you've got no commitments, you've got the six weeks' summer holiday coming up in less than two months. What's stopping you from just hopping on a plane?" she challenged.

"I suppose I even have the means. When Rose died earlier this year, she left me some money," Ivy processed her thoughts as she went along, "and whenever we talked of Morocco, she always implored me to visit it one day."

"Well then, if I can consider applying to study nursing at my age, you can at least think about it," Mei clapped her hands together, "there really is nothing stopping you!"

"Nothing, except myself," she muttered, draining her wine glass.

"Touché!" Mei smiled as Ivy conjured up a picture in her mind of the red city, low and tent-like beneath the dramatic peaks of the Atlas Mountains, where French,

West African and nomadic influences mixed together in an exotic melting-pot. The last outpost before the cooling waters of the Mediterranean gave way to the dry heat of the Sahara Desert.

2

"Summer is supposed to be the best time of year to sell a house," Ivy's mum came straight to the point as she removed a steaming pan from the Aga the following Tuesday, "so how about we contact an estate agent about putting Rose's cottage on the market?"

Feeling her chest constrict, Ivy focused on her mum's repetitive hand action as she mashed globs of melting butter into the potatoes, to avoid answering. Since her great-aunt's death, she'd been comforted by the knowledge that her cottage had remained untouched, waiting for her to take a trip down memory lane anytime she wanted. Selling it would mean breaking her final connection with Rose and she still didn't feel ready.

Noticing his daughter's crestfallen face, Daniel Fielding drew her into his arms, "I know… We both know how upset you are Ivy, but Rose wouldn't have wanted her cottage lying empty. And the longer we keep it like that, the costlier it will be to maintain, not to mention it could attract vandals."

"Then why don't you two move in?" Ivy surveyed the reclaimed beams, stone-flagged floor and latticed windows, realising her mother had tried to recreate the ancient rambling farmhouse kitchen of her childhood in a semi-detached house barely fifty years old on the outskirts of Lavenham. "You always wanted an old house at the heart of town, didn't you?"

"It was a pipedream I gave up on years ago," her mother shot her a puzzled look. "And besides, your dad and I have lived here since the day we were married. This house holds all our memories, we couldn't consider leaving now... Come on, help me with the vegetables before they go cold."

As her dad carved the chicken, Ivy ferried dishes of carrots, peas and sprouts to the table, contemplating the sense of what her parents were saying. She reasoned they had been retired for quite a few years now, and probably could do with a top up on their pension pot, even though they were too proud to admit it. While she would be happy to move into Rose's cottage and commute to her school in Colchester, there was no way she could ever afford to buy out her mum's share on her modest teacher's salary. She had no choice but to let it go.

"I know you're both right," admitted Ivy, her eyes filling with tears as they sat down to eat, "but before you speak to anyone or start emptying the house, I'd like to visit it to see it exactly the way Rose did the last time she was there."

Turning to her mother, she added, "and maybe we should start sorting through her things?" Hearing her own words, her insides contracted at the thought of looking through her great-aunt's private possessions as it didn't seem her place somehow. She'd been postponing it for months perceiving it as an intrusion, and yet now she conceded, it was something they'd have to do. Maybe it was better just to get it over with? "We could go over after lunch?" she suggested, forcing a weak smile.

"If that's what you'd like to do dear, we'll leave your dad with the washing up and I'll drive us down," her mother's hand briefly brushed Ivy's.

"Oh thank you, it's nice to know I have my uses. At least you don't think I'm too old to do that, Erin," her father cut in, the amused expression on his ruddy, round face instantly lightening the heaviness of the mood which had descended on them.

"If you're talking about yesterday, I don't think climbing a tree to chop down the top branches is something any middle-aged man should be doing. Honestly, Ivy it's just like living with a ten year old." Rolling her eyes, Ivy managed a smile, knowing how her dad's devil-may-care attitude often exasperated her mother but also liking the fact he'd never change.

Situated just off Lavenham High Street, Ivy had always considered her great-aunt's traditional Suffolk pink cottage, topped with its neat thatched roof, the loveliest in the village. Nothing altered her mind as, stepping through the creaking gate later that afternoon, she inhaled the sweet scent of the first roses of summer and noticed raindrops from the brief lunchtime shower glistening on the petals of delicate freesias and showy peonies. She recalled that her great-aunt, a keen gardener, had scattered wild flower seeds to make the rear garden into a meadow which reached back to a small orchard of apple, pear and plum trees. Remembering all those autumns of her childhood when they'd relieved the branches of their heavy loads, she felt sadness overwhelm her that she would never again get the chance to make delicious jams with her great-aunt.

"What are you thinking about?" asked her mum. With her thick, dark blonde hair tumbling towards her shoulders, barely touched by strands of grey, brilliant blue eyes, wrinkle-free skin and slim figure, it was hard to believe she'd celebrated her seventieth birthday earlier that year. But Rose's death, the last of her generation in the family, had somehow made them all older overnight.

"I was remembering the happy times I spent here with Rose, all our cosy afternoon teas by the fire in the winter, our picnics in the garden, surrounded by summer flowers," Ivy sighed. Noticing a tear escape down her mum's cheek, she realised too late that she hadn't often accompanied her on her visits here, that it had mostly been just her and Rose. Deciding not to continue on this track, she rested her hand upon her mum's shoulder, "are you all right, Mum?"

"Yes. It was only after Mum's death that your great-aunt and I became close." She smiled, fighting to regain her composure, "we wasted so much time. Throughout my childhood and teens there was always a distance between us. Rose rarely came to visit us on the farm. I often wish she had because she was so lively and I think she would have injected a bit of fun into our lives, but whenever I invited her over she always seemed too busy with her flower business."

"Looking back, I always thought it strange you didn't have the same relationship with Rose as I did," Ivy smiled, "she was such a warm person."

"No, I'm not really sure why," her mum shook her head, collecting her thoughts. "But I think it was down to Mum. She was a sober, pious woman and although she never said anything, it was clear she disapproved of Rose, of the way she dressed, the way she acted, the way she lived."

"Yes, knowing what Rose told me of Grandma Fran, I can see that," Ivy agreed.

"After Father died we had to sell the farm and we went to live with my grandma and Rose. I always thought Rose was so pretty, so fashionable and just wanted to be like her. But Mum predictably discouraged me from getting too close," her mum laughed, "but that's just the way she was. I suppose she was only doing what she thought was best for me."

"Probably, but it's a shame you and Rose missed out on spending time together because of her." Ivy turned as she reached the front porch just ahead of her mum.

Her mum smiled, "but Rose more than made up for it with you. She was absolutely besotted with you from the first time she visited you in hospital. And at first I was glad that you'd have a grandmother figure to look up to, but then, when you reached your teens, you'd spend nearly all your summer holidays at her flower shop. And I must admit to feeling a little bit envious, I wanted you to spend more time with me instead… "

"I'm sorry, Mum," said Ivy, putting her hand on her mum's jacket sleeve, "I never knew… "

"Oh, I don't blame you," she paused, searching for

the right words, "I just didn't feel ready to share you with anyone. I suppose I thought she saw you as the child she'd never had. It sounds silly and now she's gone, I… "

"Mum, I don't know what to say," Ivy swallowed hard.

"But that's my problem, not yours," her mum shrugged her shoulders, wiping her eyes with the back of her hand, "come on, let's get this over with."

As the front door swung back, they were greeted with a stale, shut-in smell. While her mum busied herself, opening downstairs' doors and windows to let in some fresh air, Ivy lingered in the hall in contemplation of the Constable reproductions of Rose's favourite Suffolk scenes, reflecting that they'd probably been her great-aunt's last view of her beloved cottage. Feeling the floorboards thrum beneath her feet with the rhythmical ticking of the grandfather clock, Ivy considered how it still marked time, long after the life of its owner had ended.

"I'm going to sort her clothes. I'll pack up what I can for charity shops," her mum produced several plastic bags from her handbag, "you could have a look through her jewellery if you like. I don't think there's much of any worth but there might be something of sentimental value you want."

"Maybe later," Ivy absently stepped towards the place which held her most precious memories of Rose as her mum headed up the stone staircase.

Lingering on the threshold of the room, her heart raced as she took in the volume and diversity of the books crammed onto the dark oak shelves; tantalising worlds waiting to be explored once more by the flick of a page… Her great-aunt's brown leather chair sagged as she sat down to snap on the green and blue Tiffany lamp, the refracted beams of light falling across the pale wallpaper like a peacock proudly fanning its feathers. Recalling that her conversation with Rose about her birthmark had taken place here, she realised this room and the novels within it had been her childhood sanctuary from school and its bullies. How could she bear to let it go? Within these walls, she'd admired and pitied Tess of the d'Urbervilles, had been entranced by the excessive hedonism of F. Scott Fitzgerald's damaged heroes and heroines and had lost herself in the dark, passionate novels of the Brontë sisters. She'd loved choosing a book from the vast array, deciding on it simply because a title had grabbed her imagination before easing it off its shelf watching other books expand into its place as though it had never been there. Settling in a chair beside her great-aunt, she'd flipped the pages, inhaling their mustiness before they'd read it together. She ran her fingers down the dusty spines now, rereading the titles before selecting and putting *Jane Eyre* into a cardboard box along with a dozen or more of their favourites. And as silence descended once more, she could almost hear Rose's strong, Suffolk vowels echoing through time, forever a part of the house, her heart sinking that soon it would all be lost to her.

A memory, returning in fragments at first, suddenly seized Ivy. She recalled rivulets of rain running down the window panes and the heat from the fire as they'd toasted crumpets on forks, the burnt edges countering the raspberry sweetness of the jam. Rose sitting in the corner, reading tales of her childhood from a notebook, its pages covered with her lovely writing. *Rose's diary.* Ivy sprang out of the chair to frantically scan the shelves. Presently her eyes rested on *Great Expectations*. Yes, now she remembered! Sliding the novel and its neighbouring ones from the shelf she reached her hand into the cool darkness behind.

The green cover was silky beneath her fingertips as she extricated it from its hiding place. Flicking carefully through its pages, Ivy noticed Rose had used several different inks and even writing styles, denoting she'd probably written the journal over a long period of time. Loose pages had been sewn into the notebook as if, having perhaps remembered something she'd missed out, Rose had made sure it was included in the correct place. Sometimes sentences had been scrawled out and pages even ripped out, their jagged white teeth still attached to the spine. Not quite knowing whether to read it or give it to her mum, Ivy slipped it into her bag, postponing the decision until later. After flitting from room to room, she climbed the steep stairs. Seeing Rose's single bed with its magnolia, candlewick bedspread and her hairbrush and Pond's cream laying forlornly on the heavy, oak dressing table, she felt tears spring to her eyes once again.

Her memories were interrupted by her mother's sudden appearance behind her. "Here, I know Rose would want you to have this." She slipped Rose's ring into Ivy's palm, the tiny gold crown sitting triumphantly on the heart at its centre, cupped by two loving hands, also fashioned from gold. Ivy had never seen it off her great-aunt's finger before and somehow it didn't feel right to put it on her own, so instead she attached it to the chain of the cross she wore around her neck.

"She has so little to show for such a long life," she sighed, regaining her composure enough to help her mother pack Rose's skirts and blouses into a black bin bag.

"You can't judge someone's happiness on just a few possessions," her mum smiled sadly, "your great-aunt had a lot going for her – she had a lovely childhood. My mother often told me stories of the happy times they shared as a family."

Ivy frowned as she neatly folded Rose's clothes. "It must have been dreadful for her and Grandma Fran to lose their elder sisters when they were so young. I can't imagine what they all must have gone through."

"No. I think not talking about it was Rose's way of coping," her mother smiled, "but she made the most of things too. She did a lot of good work as a town councillor after the war and then she built up her beautiful flower shop. She was so proud of it. She found it so rewarding, helping people through their lives; celebrating weddings, christenings, birthdays, anniversaries, Christmas. Even funerals… "

"I know, I just think it's sad that she spent most of her life alone in this house," Ivy felt the tension release the handle as she attempted to tie the bag, "damn, it's snapped."

"Here let me try. I've brought some string." Producing a ball from her pocket, her mum cut a long length and looped it round the bag in a triple knot, "there we are. Now I think we should get going, your dad will be wondering what has happened to us."

Wedging the bulging bin bags beneath her arms, her mum stepped towards the door and Ivy knew that their conversation was at an end, even though it felt there was

21

so much more to say about Rose. Clicking shut the garden gate a few minutes later she knew she would forever miss the house where she had enjoyed her great-aunt's company and where she had learned so much about herself. But she was also buoyed by the little green notebook nestling at the bottom of her bag, for it meant she was at least taking some part of Rose with her.

Dusk was falling as Ivy drove home to Colchester that evening. She managed to park in front of the house which, when it had been built a hundred and fifty years before, had been the home of a wealthy Victorian businessman but was now divided into three spacious flats. The top floor flat belonged to a divorced middle-aged man, James, who Ivy barely saw due to his considerable business interests abroad. The first floor flat had been empty since the young couple, Laura and Liam, had had a baby boy just before Christmas and had moved to a semi on a new estate on the other side of town. After renting a small property during her first two years in teaching, Ivy had secured a mortgage to buy the ground floor flat, which with exclusive access to the back garden, didn't feel like a flat at all. There she'd planted roses in an attempt to recreate her great-aunt's garden and, surrounded by their exquisite perfume, she loved to sit out there with a glass of chilled white wine on balmy, summer evenings.

Stepping into her flat, it struck her how far removed it was from Rose's cosy sitting room. Having been the drawing room of the original house, it was spacious with high ceilings, a polished oak floor and a large window which flooded the room with light giving it a nice airy feel. Over the years she'd made it home, choosing warm creams for the

22

walls, sofa and chairs, accented by cushions, throws and rugs in her favourite olive green.

Still unsure what to do with it, she placed her great-aunt's notebook on her bookshelf for safe-keeping and, feeling exhausted and emotionally drained from her visit to Rose's cottage, she went straight to bed, instantly falling into a dreamless sleep. Over the next few days she busied herself, catching up with her lesson planning for the forthcoming half term, washing, ironing and restocking her fridge, the notebook lying untouched on the shelf.

Early on Friday morning, Ivy was woken by rain thrumming like dice against her bedroom window. A couple of hours later she sat watching water run down the glass, smudging the grey street beyond, all possibility of her planned walk to the park gone. Padding around her flat, she was wondering how to pass the rest of the day when she caught sight of Rose's journal on the shelf with the other books she'd brought back from her cottage. Despite still feeling uneasy at the prospect of intruding into her great-aunt's personal thoughts, she was at a loose end and, cuddling beneath a fluffy blue blanket on the sofa, she began reading.

December 1989

"As I grow older and on the verge of a new decade, I feel a compulsion to write down the memories I have of the important people in my life and the events that shaped the person I am today. Although still lucid for my age, I realise my memory is not

23

what it was so I'm consulting diaries I made at the time as well as adding thoughts I have now about past events. It will not only serve as a reminder to me of all the joy and sadness I have experienced but also, I'm hoping, it will live on after I'm gone as you see that I always tried to make the most of my life. Even now as I sit here with my pen poised over the paper, I'm not sure where I will end up but I'll begin with my mother and father who influenced everything that I eventually became.

I was born in the room above my father's butcher's shop on Lavenham High Street at lunchtime on 28th June 1920. I'm told it was a scorching hot day and maybe that's why I have always hated the cold. My mother awoke to find that my father had filled every vase, jug and jam jar he could find with pink roses, and surrounded by their delicate fragrance, she named me after them. It was a quick, easy birth for her, following my three sisters, Violet and Eleanor, who were more than a decade my senior, while only a year separated Frances and I.

My earliest memory is threading daisy chains in the fields my father owned on the edge of town. I remember seeing women in the streets dressed in black, talking about the sons, husbands and brothers they had lost in the battles of the Great War. Everyone seemed to have lost someone dear and I thanked God that my father had been too old to fight and I had no brothers who could have been called up. Those were quiet, mournful days in the town but the confines of home were a safe haven where I laughed and enjoyed life with my family. It was other people's grief and not ours after all. But I learned a valuable lesson when I was very young, that I must never take anything for granted but make the most of everything that came my way. One of the many regrets I have is that I didn't always put this into practice in my own life.

How can I explain how much I loved my parents? My mother, Sarah Jane, was the daughter of farm labourers whose poverty necessitated her leaving school at just fourteen. When she was sent to work as a servant in the home of a local solicitor to supplement her family's weekly income, she initially saw it as a cut above farm work. But as the months passed she found it isolating, the chores physically demanding and the hours long and she soon realised she'd exchanged one life of drudgery for another. On one of her errands into town, she met and became friends with the greengrocer's son, Edward Endicott. Their friendship eventually blossomed into a romance and courtship. Despite his initial disapproval at Sarah Jane not being of their class, my grandfather eventually consented to their marriage and set up my father in his own butcher's shop. My father had the woman he wanted and my mother had the life she'd been dreaming of, a husband she adored, a home of her own and eventually a family.

My father was a good man, loving and kind. That`s not to say he didn`t enjoy a drink in the pub with his friends every Friday night, a flutter on the horses every Saturday afternoon and he was always on the lookout for the next big business deal. During their first years of marriage, he prospered, purchasing several more shops on the high street. He spent his money and indulged in the finer things of life. But he was also the rock upon which my family was built. His devotion to my mother, my sisters and me was unquestionable. I loved his sense of humour, his courage, his kindness, his ability to see the good in everything and everyone.

My father was to become the most successful businessmen in Lavenham in those economically tough times after the Great

War. He paid for my sisters and I to go to private school, for pretty dresses, for music, dancing and French lessons. When they entered their late teens, he even bought Violet and Nell a small sweet shop to run as a hobby. But my father's generosity touched many people's lives, not just ours, as his compassion set him apart from other men. During the depression of the 1930s, he helped his customers whenever he could, letting them run up credit for meat to feed their families, even though he knew they would never be able to repay. In time, his kindness would prove to be his downfall."

Ivy carefully closed the diary and replaced it on the shelf, trying to absorb it all. Although she'd known her great-grandfather had been a butcher in Lavenham, she'd no idea what he was like and found Rose's account of him illuminating. A respected man among his peers whose philanthropy had set him apart, she wondered why Rose had never spoken about him. Realising there was no one left who could tell her now, she hoped she'd discover more about him from the diary. Although the temptation was there to find out straight away, she reined herself in, comforted by the notion that her great-aunt still had things to tell her.

3

Switching on her computer later that evening, Ivy absently clicked through her emails. She was about to shut down when she noticed the last google search she'd made on returning from Mei's: *Marrakech riads*. Then she'd just had a cursory look at one or two websites but now, her great-aunt's words reverberating in her mind to make the most of life, it felt that she was sending her a sign. Never one to ignore them, Ivy refreshed her search.

That Sunday, with the heady aroma of sweet peas filling the car, Ivy negotiated the winding, narrow lanes to her parents' house, passing traditional pink thatched cottages, their gardens blooming with delphiniums, lilac and hollyhocks. "You're just in time for lunch," her mum took Ivy's flowers and inhaled deeply, "these are beautiful. Where did you get them?"

"I picked them from my garden this morning," Ivy kissed her, "I've always loved the scent and thought I'd try growing some this year. They've been quite a success."

"Apart from Friday, you've been lucky with the weather this half term," her mum smiled, wiping her hands on her apron, "lunch is nearly ready. Go and see your dad while I put these flowers in water."

Dominated by a massive sofa whose coarse cream covers were embroidered with faded red roses, Ivy's mother had extended the homely feel of the kitchen to the sitting room with its rough plastered walls and mismatched furniture. Next to her comfy old armchair, she had positioned an occasional table stacked with a toppling tower of well-thumbed historical novels while lamps with floral shades illuminated the dark corners of the room. On the far side of the log burner stove, Ivy saw her father sitting in his cream, leather chair, snoring softly, an open book balanced on his chest.

"Hi dad," she greeted him, touching him softly on the arm. Opening his eyes, it took a second for him to register who she was before a delighted smile lit up his face.

"Come and give your old dad a hug," he said, reaching his arms towards her, "looking forward to going back to school tomorrow?"

"Yes I am, as ever," she smiled, seeing the amusement in his eyes as he repeated the same question he'd been asking her at the end of a holiday for the last thirty years. Bending down, she whispered in his ear, "I just want to tell you first because Mum might get a bit upset. I've booked to stay in a riad in Marrakech for the entire summer holiday." She took a deep breath as her dad processed her words, "I know it will be a bit of a shock, believe me, it is to me too. But everyone keeps saying I should be more decisive and assertive and, well, I've been dreaming about visiting Morocco since I can remember. And then the other day I was reading… " she paused, "it's sort of Aunt Rose's memoir. She writes about her sisters and how her dad helped his customers after the First World War and well, I can't quite explain it but I booked the holiday there and then. I thought Rose would want me to do something special with the money she left me, although now I'm having serious second thoughts."

"Don't, you've done it and it sounds wonderful, just the sort of thing your mum and I should have done forty years ago. Don't worry about your mum. I'll break it to her gently," her dad slotted his bookmark in between the pages before snapping shut his Jack Higgins novel. "You know how she worries, but I'm sure she'll be really pleased for you, deep down," he winked.

"Can I have some help, Dan?" her mum's voice drifted from the kitchen, "the meat's ready for carving."

"Give me a minute, Ivy," her father muttered as he shuffled in his slippers, a little more stooped than she remembered. Sitting in her dad's armchair, Ivy considered her parents, how unlike they were in many respects and yet they somehow complimented each other too. Meeting when they were just nineteen at a midsummer dance, after a whirlwind courtship, they'd married in Lavenham church. Having just celebrated their golden anniversary and obviously still in love, Ivy wondered what their secret was.

"You're mum's really pleased you're planning a wonderful holiday, Ivy, " her father announced, winking as he set down their plates on the table. Ivy's eyes instantly flew to her mother, but she was met by an inscrutable expression.

"Of course I am, love. I would never stop you doing

what you wanted. But as you're going on your own, just make sure you keep in touch and take good care of yourself," her mother smiled, trying to disguise the anxiety in her voice.

Enjoying their spring lamb dinner, they settled into an easy conversation about Ivy's work and her parents' eighty year-old neighbours, Edna and Ernest, who were planning on having a swimming pool installed in their garden ahead of the summer. It wasn't until they were on to the strawberry and rhubarb tart that the conversation turned to Rose.

"What's this you were telling me about Rose's memoirs?" her dad asked as a puzzled expression crossed her mother's face. Scooping clotted cream onto her spoon, Ivy shifted uncomfortably on her chair, wondering where to begin.

"When we were at Rose's cottage, I found a notebook. I remembered her starting to read it to me when I was very young and I found it was still in the place she'd hidden it. I haven't got very far with it. At the moment she's just talking about her family, her parents and sisters." Ivy paused, unsure what else to add. "She didn't write it at the time, she started it in 1989."

"She never showed it to me so I'd be quite interested in reading it," her mum smiled, "as you know, my dad, Albert, died not long after I left primary school and Mum and Aunt Rose were always so tight-lipped about the past so I didn't press them but now… well I'd be interested to discover more about them all."

"I'll bring it over when I've finished it," Ivy answered, wondering whether she should have reached the end before telling her parents of its existence.

"No, don't rush through it on my account," her mum waved her hand, "if it has waited over a quarter of a century, it can wait a little while longer."

Afterwards, Ivy suggested a walk to help them digest the not inconsiderable lunch. Her father politely declined, preferring to read the Sunday supplement.

"Roughly translated as dozing in your chair with an open newspaper on your knee," laughed her mother, slipping on her jacket. They strolled down the lane in a comfortable silence, the hedges on either side full of butter-coloured honeysuckle, infusing the air with its sweet smell. It was a pleasantly warm day, the white vapour trails of airplanes soaring in the cerulean skies overhead. In seemingly no time at all, they reached the end of the high street, where Tudor houses leaned against each other as though in quiet conversation. Passing the *Crooked House* tea-rooms, Ivy almost suggested popping in for a pot of tea. But something tugged her away.

Instead they continued on, the black and white half-timbered building of *The Swan* creeping into view, the ochre tiles of its gabled roof glinting in the early summer sun. It was a familiar place for Ivy, somewhere synonymous with her great-aunt Rose who'd regularly brought her for Sunday lunch whenever she'd stayed for the weekend at her cottage and she wanted to see it once more. Reading Ivy's unvoiced thoughts, her mother linked her arm and led her through the heavy oak door. A few years since her last visit, Ivy saw its interior had changed considerably from her memory. And yet, taking a seat in the corner of the bar, she thought that it had been sympathetically refurbished, the exposed beams and sash windows enhanced by the modern, monochrome decor.

"So, Marrakech?" her mum jolted her from her thoughts to hand her a glass of chilled white wine.

"Yes," Ivy hesitated, setting her drink on a mat, knowing she was about to learn her mum's real opinion of her impulsive trip abroad.

"I'm glad you finally booked it," her mum smiled, wrong-footing Ivy who wasn't quite sure what to say.

4

For Ivy, the second half of the summer term raced ahead in a whirl of school trips to the countryside and coast, the children's overwhelming favourite being a rain swept visit to Colchester Castle when they'd all got soaked to the skin. The dull task of writing end of year reports filled her evenings, while each weekend she plunged into her planning for the forthcoming academic year. Faced with such a momentous task which she usually spun out over the summer holidays, she began to regret her spur of the moment decision to spend five-and-a-half weeks in Marrakech. But, paradoxically, her busyness meant time passed quickly and the final day of term came around in seemingly no time at all. After a tearful leavers' assembly, Ivy said goodbye to her own class, sending them home with goodie bags and good wishes. Then, as was the custom to celebrate the end of the school year, she and her colleagues congregated in the staff room for drinks and nibbles.

"I think I'll be spending the first few weeks of the holidays catching up on my sleep," commented Sara, her young face looking drawn as she tucked into a sausage roll with gusto, "my class have been such a handful since the SATs, I only hope they settle down when they start secondary school in September, for their sakes and their new teachers."

"Oh, don't even mention September! All I'm thinking about is my trip to Crete," commented Naomi, flicking her thick fringe out of her eyes as she helped herself to quiche, coleslaw and crisps before sitting down and addressing her next words to Ivy. "I know I'm getting a difficult class from you in the autumn, you must be so relieved this year's over."

"There are some challenging children, true," said Ivy diplomatically, knowing she'd be in for a far easier ride with the children coming up to her next term, "but there are some lovely kids in that class too."

"The class I'm inheriting from you aren't exactly angels either, Naomi. You'll be fine," said Kate, loading her plate with crackers, hummus, carrot and celery. "I think we all just need a well-earned break. Things will look different in September."

"Did you book a holiday in the end, Kate?" asked Clare, the head teacher, who had brought strawberries and clotted cream to put atop her ever popular home-baked scones. With her work and toing and froing her daughters to university, Ivy often wondered how she found the time to fit everything in as well as always looking as fresh as a daisy with her perfect skin and silky, black, shoulder-length bob.

"Yes, a fortnight in Florida. We're flying out on Sunday.

Liam and Freddy already have every day planned – Disney, Universal Studios, Epcot, a Hawaiian themed Crazy Golf course. I'm not sure Pete shares their enthusiasm for it all," Kate pulled a face, "how about you?"

"Rob managed to get time off work so we're going to Lake Garda next week. The girls go away with their friends now so we can just please ourselves. We're just going to enjoy some boat rides to different villages on the lake, relax, eat pasta, drink wine," replied Clare, turning to Ivy, "and of course, you're going to Marrakech, aren't you?"

"Yes, tomorrow," she said, taking a bite of a scone, "these are delicious."

"She's been fretting about her trip all week," piped in Amber, Ivy's forever upbeat young teaching assistant, "thinking she should've asked someone to go along with her."

"Oh, you'll be fine, Ivy. I visited Morocco with a group of friends to celebrate our A-level results. Being on a strict budget, our riad was very basic but it had a certain charm," commented Clare, "and I had the time of my life sampling the street food and shopping in the souks, I didn't want to return to England. You'll absolutely love it, Ivy!"

"That's what I've been telling her," Amber smiled, helping herself to some succulent strawberries, her carb-free diet not permitting her to indulge in a scone. "I wish I was going with you, Ivy. I'll just have to make do with two weeks on the Amalfi coast with my parents," she sighed.

"I'm sure you'll cope," Ivy replied, excitement suddenly coursing through her that she was on the brink of her trip of a lifetime. That night, after completing her packing, clearing

35

the fridge of any perishable food and having a quick tidy around, Ivy finally found a quiet minute to herself. Taking Rose's journal from the top of the bookcase, she was looking forward to discovering more about her family's past.

"It upsets me now that I always found it difficult to talk about my two elder sisters, and it grieves me that people in the town saw them as tragic women, their lives curtailed by suffering and illness. In truth there was so much more to them than that, and I now feel able to tell something of their story. I had three sisters, Violet the eldest, Eleanor, a year younger, who we called Nell, and, of course, Frances. I grew up in awe of Nell, for she was beautiful and vibrant with the most wonderfully positive outlook on life. Her lively, cheerful personality ensured she had a wide circle of friends, and being the leading light in the local amateur dramatics group, she had dreams of carving out a career for herself on the stage. She was everything I wanted to be. Whenever Nell and I spent time together, she always made me feel confident that I could do anything I set my mind to. Now that I grow old I reflect on the wasted opportunities in my life, and wonder if things would have turned out differently if she had been around to inspire and advise me as I grew up.

Violet was our eldest sister, just a year older than Nell. Whilst possessing the same gentleness, slender figure and beautiful honey-coloured hair as Nell , she was altogether more serious with a fiercely strong maternal instinct towards Frances and I. For, I think Violet had decided when she was quite young that her future happiness depended on getting married and having children of her own. In their different ways, I adored both Violet and Nell, the former giving me a shoulder to cry on

36

and motherly advice whenever I needed while Nell taught me life was a gift to be grabbed with both hands.

Several years passed before Fran and I were born, and as with her first two daughters, my mother gave birth in quick succession to her youngest two, first Fran and the following year to me. Being so close in age to Fran, I suppose it was expected we would follow in Violet and Nell's footsteps and grow up the best of friends. But the truth was we never really got on. I think she resented me for usurping her place as the baby of the family, a position she had occupied all too briefly. What made it harder for her was, whereas Violet, Nell and I had inherited our height, honey-coloured hair and hazel eyes from our mother, Frances took after father's side of the family. Always small for her age and with a tendency to plumpness, to make matters worse when she was seven she was found to be short-sighted, a condition which required her to wear glasses. Looking back I realise what I was too young to see then – how unhappy she must have been. But then I only saw that the two of us didn't share any interests. Frances preferred to be at home, sewing dolls' clothes or helping with the household chores, which in my eyes made her a boring playmate. I'm ashamed to say I would rather spend time with any of my friends than with my sister, and even when Violet found her crying one day and discovered she was being bullied in school, I didn't try and help her, I just left her to fight that battle on her own. There are so many things I wish I could change and that is one of many, but children can be selfish and uncaring and I was no better than most.

When Fran and I began senior school, the differences between us became clearly delineated. Fran had always been quite religious, attending church every Sunday, often on her *own I have to admit, but when she entered her teens, she began to throw herself more and more into all the other activities connected with it. She joined the choir, became a Sunday schoolteacher and was ever-present at fundraising activities. In short, the church became her primary interest, which initially I thought a good thing as it got her out of the house, meeting new people. Unfortunately as time went on she opted out of many of the social events in town to pursue her bible studies with fervour, and in doing so the judgemental side of her nature began to emerge.*

In the meantime, my thoughts began to turn toward the opposite sex. In the darkness of our bedroom, I told her about conversations I'd had with boys in school, confiding the names of those I liked. In turn, she'd reply I should spend more time with my prayers talking to God so after a while I stopped telling her as her disapproval dampened my excitement."

Ivy's plane touched down at Marrakech Menara Airport exactly twenty-four hours after she'd closed her classroom door behind her. After standing patiently in lengthy queues at passport control and the baggage carousel, she stepped out of the air-conditioned building to inhale her first deep breath of hot African air. Relief washed over her that, after so many years of dreaming, she had finally arrived on this strange, new continent.

She immediately put on her wide-brimmed straw hat and her huge sunglasses to protect her face from the sun's fierce rays. Wheeling her cases across to the taxi rank, she was glad she'd dressed practically in navy cotton trousers, green stripy tee-shirt, pumps and a thin jacket to cover her arms. Inside the taxi, the heat of the black leatherette seat seeped through her trousers as she told the young driver her destination. French, once familiar, felt foreign on her tongue. In her guidebook she'd read the two main languages in Marrakech were Tashelhit, a local Berber dialect and Darija, a Moroccan derivation of Arabic. But French was also freely spoken due to Morocco's history as a French protectorate and, whenever she'd imagined visiting, she'd always pictured herself having conversations in the language she was once fluent in. She only hoped that she would soon shed her rustiness.

After fifteen minutes, they left the bare, flat landscape of the Moroccan countryside and the expensive, sprawling hotels on Marrakech's outskirts behind as the taxi cab snuck through an imposing gate in the pink-pigmented city walls. "C'est si belle, la cité en rose," sighed Ivy, folding her jacket into her red holdall.

"Yes, it was the French who decreed that all buildings should be pink. The pigment comes from the local soil," replied the taxi driver, thankfully speaking slowly to give her brain a chance to translate from French to English. As they crawled down a narrow street bustling with women in pastel-hued robes doing their daily shopping, Ivy glimpsed his kind, brown eyes in the rear view mirror and exchanged smiles with him.

She wound down the window, eager to breathe in the scents of this new continent, where Berber, Middle Eastern and French cultures collided in a melting pot of spices, noise and heat. Donkey carts loaded with fresh vegetables, men on mopeds weighed down with boxes of oranges, glistening orbs in the late afternoon sun, passed by. Taxi drivers, imagining they were driving sleek Formula One cars instead of rusted Fiats, managed to squeeze through non-existent spaces in the dusty streets of the souks.

"It's quiet now," her driver remarked as the alleyways continued to narrow with seemingly each turn he made, "everyone will be having their afternoon siesta."

"It's just as I imagined it would be," smiled Ivy, as they approached a shady street with high-walled buildings on each side, "I've wanted to come for so long."

"My brother moved to France with his family but I could never imagine leaving. Marrakech is in my soul," he patted his heart dramatically with his hand as he drew to a stop, "your riad is just down here. But this is as far as I can go."

"Thank you," smiled Ivy, tipping him ten dirhams, as her guidebook had recommended, before he removed her luggage from the boot.

"Bon voyage," he waved. And then he was gone and Ivy found herself alone in the shut-up, silent street. Panic pulsed through her as she looked in vain for signs, either written or indeed of life to guide her, as a stream of sweat traced the line of her backbone. Then, from seemingly nowhere, a little boy appeared. In the coming months, she would look back at this moment and wonder whether Mustapha running into her was a mere coincidence or something more. But, as the child smiled beguilingly up to her, she only took in his long white tunic and trousers, masses of curly, jet-black hair and his tiny face which made his brown eyes look huge. He seemed small for his age, which she gauged to be nine or ten as she compared him with children at her school.

"Madam, Madam," he danced around her before slipping his hand unnoticed into the handle of one of her suitcases, "I will take you to my father's riad."

"Attendez, I've already booked in at a riad, Riad El Alaqui," she started, but the boy just smiled as he hared off, pulling her case, with Ivy struggling to keep up. Feeling her hot breath catch in her throat, she had no choice but to carry on as with one wrong turning, she feared he, and her luggage, would be lost forever. She kept spotting glimpses of his tunic as he rounded corners, his sandals clattering on the cobbles, before a long wail suddenly sliced through the stifling air, blocking out all other sounds. Continuing on, Ivy pictured the Muezzin atop the minaret as his voice echoed over the pink city for the fifth time that day.

Rather than opt for a luxury hotel in the suburbs with a sparkling-turquoise pool and all-inclusive meals or the Mamounia Hotel, with its illustrious clientele list, way beyond her price range, Ivy had always had it in mind to stay in a riad. Meaning 'garden house', a riad was a traditional mud-brick guesthouse built around a courtyard, with high walls blocking out the noise of the Medina the minute you walked through its doors. She liked the contradiction of an oasis in amongst the frenzied throng of the souks and TripAdvisor had only corroborated her romantic notions, telling stories of calming pools and cool tiled walls and floors.

Sitting by a rose-petal strewn fountain, with a refreshing glass of mint tea to hand while classical music played in the background sounded just the antidote she needed after the final frantic weeks at school. As one guidebook succinctly put it, "*Marrakech has its riads just as Florence has its art galleries and Greece has its ancient ruins.*" During her internet search, the Riad El Alaqui had attracted Ivy because it was family-run with just a dozen rooms, the perfect place for her to wind down and so she was still intent on staying there, once she'd retrieved her luggage...

"C'est ici," the little boy stopped at a door with no signage, not even a nameplate but Ivy had no breath in her lungs left to protest. Clenching his fingers into a tiny fist he knocked three times on the large, ancient, wooden door, which looked like it had not been opened in years, as Ivy felt her apprehension heighten.

"Bonjour et bienvenue," smiled a man a moment later as the door swung open, "I am Khalid Hassan." He was wearing a silk shirt tucked into black trousers and had bright eyes and a kind smile peeped from beneath a bushy beard. He was perhaps in his early forties, Ivy thought as she stepped in.

"Merci beaucoup," she murmured, as nervousness immediately drained from her. Feeling she'd entered another world, the light spaciousness of the cool courtyard took her breath away as its beauty invaded her senses, a stark contrast to the dark, dusty street she'd left behind. It was indeed the restful retreat she'd dreamed of with its burbling fountain and quiet music playing in the background. Breathing in scents of fragrant jasmine, it was everything she'd read about and imagined.

"I'm sorry Sir, but I haven't booked here," Ivy pointed

42

out, reluctantly, "I just met this little boy in the street and he brought me here. I was on my way to Riad El Alaqui."

"Mustapha," the man admonished as the little boy backed sheepishly into a corner, "I'm sorry Madame, my son is a bit zealous. But my sister, her husband and I co-own the El Alaqui and this riad, El Amrani. So you are welcome to stay here or Mustapha can take you there if you choose?"

"You stay here, Madame, s'il vous plait?" the boy entreated, his brown eyes bigger than ever.

Ivy looked up to the billowing, white canopy which dissected the azure sky above into quarters. Birds, hidden in pomegranate trees, tweeted happily, their sweet singing amplified in the close confines of the courtyard. Low tables, with soft easy chairs clustered around, were positioned in dappled, shady spots. Terracotta walls and columns gave the riad a warmth while the blue, aqua-marine and green mosaics, shades of sky and sea, simultaneously gave the enclosed space a feeling of the natural world. She noticed Mustapha staring at her intently, with the most imploring look in his great eyes, and felt her heart melt.

"Yes, I will be happy to stay here," smiled Ivy, as the peace of the place enveloped her, "c'est si belle."

"Merci beaucoup, but I must apologise for my son's behaviour," the man said, as Ivy saw the little boy flash his smile once more, "it's good that my sister, brother-in-law and I jointly own the two riads, otherwise they would be out of business by now."

"Mais, j'aime beaucoup Madame. Elle est très gentile," the little boy interjected, slipping his tiny hand into Ivy's.

"Don't try and get around the lady that way," his father added sternly.

"It's okay," Ivy laughed, "as I said I'm very happy to stay here."

"Alright then," the man turned to address his son in rapid French, "just don't tell your uncle. As it is he can't understand why half his guests book and then never show up."

They all laughed as Ivy considered the thought that luck rather than judgement had found her the perfect place to stay in Marrakech.

"Here we have a small library, gallery and a restaurant where all the meals are freshly prepared. How long are you staying?" the man enquired, hastily completing a form.

"Five and a half weeks," Ivy found herself slowly tuning into his heavily accented French, "I've wanted to come here for many years. And as I work in a school I have a six week holiday so I'll have the chance to immerse myself in Moroccan culture."

After sorting the payment, explaining the meal arrangements and other details of day-to-day living at the riad, Khalid Hassan handed her the key for room 23 which was attached to a carved wooden orange and would subsequently be impossible for anyone to lose, even Ivy. "I will get someone to take your luggage up to your room, but should you need anything else, just ask. I hope you have a wonderful time in Marrakech, Madame."

"Thank you and see you later, Mustapha," Ivy smiled at the little boy before he retreated down the corridor as his father continued to lightly chastise him.

The calming ambience of the main courtyard extended to Ivy's room, with its white walls, white duvet and diaphanous-white curtains which fluttered in the cooling breeze coming in through the open window. All this whiteness lightened the effect of the heavy, carved wooden furniture which was traditionally Moroccan; a bed, small bedside table, wardrobe and an ornate dressing table-cum-writing desk. Sitting atop the latter was a clear bowl of water, the floating pink roses permeating the air with their sweet scent which Ivy inhaled deeply before busying herself with unpacking her suitcases.

Finding places for her clothes and shoes, arranging her face creams in the pristine bathroom with its walk-in shower and stacking the novels she'd brought on the desk, it soon began to feel like home. She'd chosen her books carefully because she wanted to submerge herself in Africa in her reading at night and she placed her great-aunt's notebook carefully at the summit of the pile so it was easily accessible whenever she felt like delving into it again. After a quick shower, she changed from her clothes, dishevelled from her journey, into a simple jade-green sundress and sandals. Relaxing into holiday mode, she took some time to explore the riad. Its rooms laid out around charming small courtyards, Ivy noted the location of the small spa room before discovering a secluded rose garden, albeit just past its best now in late July. Then, heading out beyond the riad's safe confines with her map, excitement bubbled within her at the prospect of seeing Marrakech's main square at sunset.

In centuries gone by, all Moroccan cities from Agadir to Tangier, had a main square where musicians and storytellers entertained crowds but Marrakech's Jemaa el Fna was the only one left now. Her heartbeat quickening, Ivy followed the maze of winding alleyways until they opened out onto the square, where she found herself entranced by dozens of food stalls emitting exotic smells, twisting up on spirals of smoke into the dusky-pink sky. Aromas of cooking meat and frying fish mingled with spices, caught in her nostrils as she strolled past charcoal grills where locals and tourists queued for their supper. Normally worried about eating street food at home for fear of contracting food poisoning, she threw caution to the wind and tried some spicy broth and stuffed lamb, which tasted even more delicious than they'd been described in her guidebook.

Sated, she took in the snake charmers inducing cobras to sway in tune with their flutes while tooth pullers flexed formidable pliers above trays of extracted teeth. Turning towards the crowd's cheers, she watched one acrobatic team after another enter, cart-wheeling and somersaulting as the square became an impromptu stage. They were followed by a carnival of belly-dancers in elaborate gold costumes, as hawkers and soothsayers charmed the expectant crowds. In another corner, Ivy spotted *Gnawa* musicians who Rose had once told her of, thumping out tunes on *ginbris,* a type of banjo. As she drifted from one part of the square to another, Ivy could see why this was considered Marrakech's heart and soul, why it had enchanted visitors for over a millennium as she too became caught up in its magic.

"Madam, Madam!" Children's voices pierced Ivy's thoughts. Looking down, she saw two local boys she estimated to be no more than eight. Draped over their arms were scores of plastic circles, illuminated with coloured LED lights.

"Look, I show you," the smallest boy proclaimed, whirling one of the bright circles around on a stick before whipping it up high into the night air to create a pretty effect of light and colour, "you buy for just ten dirhums."

"And you go home now, it's very late," she told him, pressing a note into his palm for far more than he'd asked.

"Thank you, Madam," he smiled before the crowd swallowed him up again. Ivy shuddered at the risk he was running, approaching strangers every night in an attempt to make a sale. She didn't want to reflect on it now though, as the long day of travelling finally caught up with her. Instead, following her map, she retraced her footsteps to the riad and within twenty minutes she was lying in bed, thinking of how her first evening in Africa had been everything she'd imagined it would be. Reaching out, she took Rose's diary from her bedside table and began to read.

5

"When I was twelve, Mother took Violet and Nell to France. I can still remember the disappointment I felt at not being able to go with them, but Mother explained that it was a kind a pilgrimage she was undertaking and that Frances and I were too young. Violet, knowing how upset I was, promised to write often and describe what they were doing so that I could see it all through her eyes. I kept her wonderful letters which created vivid pictures in my mind of places beyond the sea and I'm sticking them into this journal so that they will always be remembered.

August 17th, 1932.

My Dearest Rose,

It already feels like a lifetime since we left you, Father, Frances and Suffolk behind. I do not know where to begin. Maybe I should start at the quayside where we waited to board the ferry? The excitement was palpable in the air as people loaded their luggage onto the gangplank. I reflected how that small strip of water was all that separated me from the patchwork quilt of European countries, with their exotic languages and cultures and beyond that, Africa and Asia – places which I can scarcely imagine.

Mother spent the entire journey in the lounge, feeling rather sick from the movement of the boat. Nell insisted that we go on deck however, and we watched full of excitement, as the harbour walls receded behind us. Once onto the open Channel the water became choppier, a myriad of blue and green shades as the sun glinted on it. Oh Rose, you would have loved it. The fresh smell of the sea, the cooling spray on our skin; the only sounds were the chugging of the engine below deck and the screaming of gulls in the flawless blue sky. It was exhilarating!

I've a funny story to tell you. At one point a man's boater hat flew off his head and Nell and I watched it being carried away on the waves. I know it would have made you scream with laughter but we had to show decorum, although it did make us smile! At Le Havre we caught a packed train which took us through beautiful countryside. The fields of blood-red poppies stretched for miles. It is difficult to imagine that this peaceful place was a scene of such violent and bloody battles just fourteen years ago. I find it reassuring that, despite the actions of men, nature always seems to find a way to restore itself, and this is particularly true of northern France.

At Amiens, hungry from our journey, we lunched in the station restaurant. Just imagine I ate my casserole du poisson where the Prince of Wales frequently dined when he was stationed in the city in 1916! Then we found a porter to transport our luggage across the square to the Carlton Belfort Hotel, where we were due to spend the night. Amazingly the ornate, white facade suffered little damage during the war and I even spotted a sign left from that time, "No lorries through town," written on the wall!

Early next morning we caught one of the hourly buses taking families to visit their loved ones' last resting places on the battlefields. We chatted with widows, sisters and parents, their lives changed irrevocably by events that took place in the now verdant fields our bus skirted around. There was a kind of camaraderie between them as they talked about their losses, which I wasn't privy to. Without warning, a vast cemetery with hundreds of white gravestones stretching into the distance came into view, an awesome but most terrible sight. The bus came to a stop and half a dozen people bearing wreathes or bunches of flowers alighted in a hushed silence, which was repeated at two more cemeteries in quick succession. Eventually, Mother signalled we'd reached our destination. This time, there were only the three of us who climbed down from the bus. The cemetery here was much smaller than the previous three, giving the feeling that the men who rested here may all have known each other. A fanciful idea I know, but strangely comforting. Now Rose dear, I know how much you wanted to come with us so I will try my best to capture this place and the feelings I experienced.

The bus pulled away in a cloud of dust and a silence descended upon us. Cream coloured stone walls stretched like protective arms around the graves of the young men who, having died in such horrific circumstances, have at least been granted a peaceful and beautiful place to rest for eternity.

I paused to read the inscriptions on the first few graves. So little really to mark their passing... name, rank, regiment, date of death and sometimes their age. I hadn't expected them to be so young, so many much younger than I. I imagined all the lives that had been affected by the deaths of these men and boys, all the happiness they and their families had been denied and all the talent and potential the world had lost. I lingered at each grave, resting my hand on the stone while I read their names out loud, my own act of remembrance for their sacrifice.

Presently, I looked up to see Mother and Nell a few rows ahead standing with heads bowed beside one particular grave. Mother slowly bent forward, placing her hand on the top of the stone as if resting it tenderly on her brother's shoulder. I approached slowly to read the name carved upon it; Corporal J Mattheson, Suffolk regiment. Our uncle aged 21, forever younger than I am now.

Sometime later, we withdrew to sit on a stone bench in the shade of the wall to wait for the return of the bus. Suddenly becoming aware of the overwhelming perfume of roses and lavender, blossoming at the foot of every stone, I watched as a gardener moved slowly along the rows, deadheading the flowers. The heat of the day bore down on us, the only sound the humming of the bees. I became lost in contemplation in this beautiful but terrible place.

Your loving sister,
Violet xx"

6

Ivy woke to find her room flooded with morning light which seemed to possess a sharper quality here in Africa. Stretching out like a starfish over her double bed, she felt the knots in her neck and shoulder muscles, tightened by the plane journey, unravel. After a few minutes, however, she sprang out of bed. Her appetite whetted by her nocturnal visit to the Jemaa el Fna, she was eager to experience its first incarnation of the day.

She showered and dressed quickly in white capri pants, lavender sun top and sandals, leaving her towel-dried curls tumble over her shoulders. After spending time getting the balance of her camouflage cream and sun cream just right, she wound her way down the spiral staircase to join the other riad residents in the spacious courtyard where she breakfasted on black coffee and croissants smeared with apricot jam.

"Bonjour Madam," beamed Mustapha, tilting the coffee

pot to pour her a cup. This morning the little boy wore a long, black tunic, his bare feet peeping through sandals beneath it, and the same cheeky grin on his face. "You have a nice time so far?"

"Yes, thank you," nodded Ivy, closing her well-thumbed guidebook, before continuing in French, "I visited the Jemaa el Fna last night. I've never seen anything like it. It was simply wonderful."

"Madam, you must watch out for pickpockets," he advised, his brow suddenly furrowed with concern. After a few minutes' chat, beckoned by his dad to serve coffee to a loud Australian couple, Ivy watched his diminutive figure reluctantly retreat. He reminded her of how vulnerable the little boys who patrolled the square were, with their beautiful big brown eyes and beguiling smiles. Downing her black coffee, she sighed in relief that Mustapha had an over-protective father keeping an eye on him within the confines of his riad, even though the little boy's body language told her the feeling wasn't mutual.

Stepping onto the Jemaa el Fna at just after 10am, Ivy saw that the open-air food stalls and entrancing entertainment of the previous night were gone, a silver streamer and a lost red tassel the only traces of their existence. In their place were a dozen or so juice vendors, pulling their carts piled high with pyramids of glossy oranges, into the exposed centre of the square. Thinking their flimsy umbrellas provided inadequate protection from the already relentless beat of the sun, Ivy hugged the square's shady edges, careful to avoid the henna tattooists, who she'd read, grabbed tourists' arms, and began their work before you could protest! She was fascinated, however, by the wrinkled, wizened men purveying potions for such whimsical things as healing a broken heart to an instant cure for acne. When approached by them, however, she shook her head, thinking it unlikely any of them actually worked! So bold were their boastings, if there was any truth to them, they would surely have taken the medical world by storm.

Moving on, she was persuaded, for a small payment, to have her photo taken with a water seller in traditional costume which included a wide, blue-fringed hat, before watching him lug his antiquated, metal dispenser over to the fruit carts to set up an impromptu refreshment station. With beads of sweat clustering around her throat, she browsed the stalls on the south side of the square, buying a large glass of chilled grapefruit juice and filling bags of dates, dried figs, almonds and walnuts for evening snacks at the riad.

The square shimmered in the intensifying heat as it nudged towards midday, the signal for Jemaa el Fna's second incarnation as snake charmers appeared from the dark warren of alleyways. Drawn by the discordant sounds of the men's oboes and flutes, Ivy found herself spellbound as the snakes slowly lifted their heads from their baskets to sway to the rhythm of the high-pitched notes. Around the edge of the square, tracksuited acrobats tumbled in an attempt to rouse the café crowds with their dizzying back flips but it was the Gnawa musicians who stole the show, once again, for Ivy. Playing ancient Moroccan Islamic songs on their strange looking stringed instruments, she found the sound haunting as it entranced both her and the crowd. She hardly knew where to look next in the square, for something exciting and entertaining seemed to be taking place in every corner. Normally very self-contained and content with her own company, Ivy suddenly wished she had someone with whom to share these new experiences. Had she been too impulsive in embarking on this long trip on her own? A cloud momentarily passing over her, she managed to shrug it off. No, she was determined to enjoy herself.

After enjoying a savoury crêpe with a deliciously spicy vegetable filling, she headed down an alleyway. Looking up, she saw shafts of sun spilling through the palm-frond roof to illuminate a lute maker hard at work as the sweet resin of filed wood hung headily in the air. Possessing no artistic talent whatsoever, she had great admiration for these skilled artisans who worked so industriously. Moving slowly past the carpenters and blacksmiths, she wondered how the latter could bear to work in front of their furnaces in such extreme heat. Around the corner, carpet weavers toiled at large looms side-by-side hatters and cobblers, and she found herself amazed that these cottage industries still used the tools and techniques inherited from their great-grandparents, barely changed for centuries. Peeking into their stiflingly hot workshops, her mind rewound to rainy summer holidays of her childhood when she'd visited open-air folk museums where tour guides had re-enacted the skills and professions of their ancestors. But this was real; the clang of metal against metal, sparks flying to produce a horseshoe or cutlery for people to use in their everyday lives. The thought of these craftsmen plying their ancient trades for a living, thrilled her; the past still living and breathing on these streets.

"Madam, Madam, voulez-vous un sac?" shouted a man with a long, grey beard. Emboldened by the freedom that being in a foreign country afforded her, Ivy did something then she never did when a market holder called out to her at home; she approached his stall. After all, she had come to Marrakech for new experiences and the souks were a quintessential part of that.

"Oui, bien sûr," she smiled, surveying the rainbow of leather handbags suspended from the ceiling of his cubbyhole. There were indeed several that she liked but she settled on an olive-green one, "le vert s'il vous plait? Trois cents dirhams?" she ventured.

"Quatre cents, s'il vous plait?" he muttered, a slight smile playing on his lips as he unhooked it. Having read it was bad form to pull out of a deal once bartering had commenced, Ivy considered her next move.

"Trois cents cinquante," she suggested, at which point the old man offered his hand as gnarled as leather and they shook on it. As she emerged, blinking, into the sunlight, she was pleased with the deal she'd struck on her first purchase and her mood lifted. Ploughing deeper into the tangled cobweb of the souks, she looked up to see a wonderful array of carpets and handmade rugs hanging from makeshift 'washing lines'. From the number of tourists haggling over them they were obviously much sought after souvenirs, and no wonder for they were beautiful! However, she quickened her step, not wanting to purchase heavy or bulky items she couldn't take home and in a matter of moments unexpectedly found herself in the Souk Sebbaghine.

Everyone she'd spoken to who'd visited Marrakech had

recommended the dyer's souk as a place not to be missed. Although she conceded the dye pits looked and smelled like hell, the aroma was easy to ignore, distracted as she was by hanks of wool hanging in coloured swathes from the rafters like a man-made rainbow. Snapping her camera, she captured these and the vibrant skeins of freshly dyed saffron and vermilion, drying against the pink walls. Surveying the scene, she noticed several stallholders having a nap and considered how the pace of life here was so different from home where everyone was rushing from A to B, never pausing in either for too long.

By contrast, the Souk Smarine felt as cramped and crowded as Regent Street on a Saturday afternoon. The main thoroughfare, it sliced through the Medina's heart and was, disappointingly, principally a tourist bazaar, selling cheap, mass-produced souvenirs. Not wanting to linger, Ivy hurried to the fork at its northern end to escape down a dark passageway which brought her to the Rahba Kedima where, she couldn't resist peeping into one of the old apothecaries. The cool darkness welcoming, she scooted in amongst a group of baseball hat and sneaker-wearing Americans and scanned the traditional cosmetics arranged in neat rows. She noticed the principal sellers were lip rouge in a range of shades and kohl eyeliner in only the blackest black, which all the Moroccan women she'd seen so far seemed to favour, while the third product, profuse in the shop, was henna. Ivy smiled as the shopkeeper, his big, black beard hanging over a flowing, white robe, beckoned her over.

"Come and see our demonstration. You're under no obligation to buy," his eyes crinkled into a friendly smile.

Feeling safe among the party of middle-aged Americans, she dutifully followed the man up a few flights of rickety stairs and into a bright white room, edged with glass cabinets full of lotions and potions for cosmetic and medicinal purposes. She took her place on a bench next to a young, hot-faced French couple who were fanning themselves with brochures in the absence of air-conditioning. On her other side, however, was an American, who, due to the combination of his weight and the heat, was sweating profusely. The effects wafting beneath her nose, Ivy could only hope the presentation included testing some sweet-smelling samples.

As the salesman launched his patter, Ivy perused the leaflet he'd pressed into her palm. Containing a description of oils manufactured in the apothecary, made from plants grown locally, including argan, almond, orange blossom, coconut, rose and lavender, she noticed they were only a fraction of the price of similar products at home. When people had tried and tested the products, which thankfully went someway to counteract her neighbour's pungency, Ivy noticed the man turn his big sell up a notch. Unsurprisingly there were no takers for the acne, haemorrhoids or warts ointment, or at least no one admitted to such afflictions in public. Ivy opted for a pot of moisturizer, a beautiful pale-pink cream smelling of sweet summer roses, which took her back to idyllic days in her great-aunt's garden. She added a jar of lavender foot cream to her basket, which she thought would provide a welcome antidote to tramping around the souks.

"C'est belle," purred the young woman seated next to her, as the man massaged some jasmine oil onto the palm of her hand.

"Maybe you could get your boyfriend to buy you some?" suggested the demonstrator, looking at the attentive young man at her side. Smiling indulgently at the young couple, Ivy paid for her purchases and, feeling the heavy atmosphere of the airless room bearing down on her, slipped unnoticed through the door, down the stairs and back out into the street.

As yet unaccustomed to the Moroccan heat, she suddenly found herself drained of energy so, on returning to the cool comfort of her riad, she showered before settling onto her bed for a siesta. Woken by the Muezzin's evening call echoing across the rooftops, she whiled away the next hour or so sitting at the desk and, against the background of street noises rising up through the open window, she wrote her experiences of her first day in her notebook. As night fell quickly outside, she had no inclination to venture out again. But realising she was quite hungry, she laid out her purchases of dried fruit and nuts from the market on her bedcovers, supplementing them with some crisps she'd bought in the airport and water and fruit thoughtfully provided by the riad. Comfortably arranging the pillows behind her, she took Rose's diary from the bedside table and resumed reading Violet's letters to her sister during her trip to France.

7

"Paris, August 23rd, 1932.

My Dearest Rose,

Paris must be the most beautiful place in the entire world! I feel I will swoon on the spot! It is as though I have been waiting for my whole life to come to this elegant city.

Yesterday we visited the Eiffel Tower or the Tour d'Eiffel as the French call it! I swear I have learned more French words in two days than I did in two years at home with our tutor! I can hear you laughing, little sister. From the top of the Tour d'Eiffel I could see the city climbing to the white domes of Sacré-Coeur in the north and descending to the green waters of the River Seine to the east. Every direction I looked there was a sight I had read about in a book – the Jardin de

Tuileries with the Louvre glittering beyond its dense trees, the Arc de Triomphe proudly poised at the end of the Champs-Élysées and the mysterious green darkness of the Bois de Boulogne which sprawled beyond the white buildings as far as I could see. I felt like a bird perched atop the tower, breathing in the clear, cool air, as I tried to commit everything to memory.

The streets here are wide and tree-lined with lots of elegant white buildings. They make Lavenham High Street seem like a toy town. The Parisians call them boulevards and they are filled with cafés where people sit at tables out on the pavement and watch the world go by. Everyone here seems to have more free time to enjoy themselves than they do at home. And, you should see the women's elegant clothes! Our dressmaker would be enraptured! It really does seem that fashion is the religion here even though there is a proliferation of churches which Mother seems intent on us visiting!

This evening, we enjoyed a delicious meal in a tiny restaurant in the Marais. I've never tasted Jewish food before. Then we strolled around the Place des Vosges, the rays of the dying sun catching the pretty pink buildings. The square was full of families, great-grandparents down to tiny babies. We must have been stopped half a dozen times by people wishing us a pleasant evening. It was almost like a village within a city, where everyone knew each other.

My eyes are tiring as I sit here in the lamplight of my hotel room, I must stop now. But I felt compelled to tell you of these wonderful sights and experiences before they fade from my memory. I hope you will come one day to see them for yourself!

Your loving sister,
Violet xx

Paris August 26th, 1932

My Dearest Rose,

Our hotel in the Marais is run by a lovely Jewish couple, Monsieur and Madame Jastrow. Madame Jastrow is the kindest lady, she has a friendly round face, wears her silver-white hair in an old-fashioned chignon and, at all times, has a pair of half-moon glasses perched on her nose, as though they are about to fall. But they never do! Nothing is ever too much trouble for her. She clucks around Nell and I like an old mother hen! After a morning marvelling at the wonders of Da Vinci at Le Louvre, we retired to the hotel. While Mother and Nell went to their rooms for an afternoon nap, I found Madame Jastrow crocheting in the cluttered sitting room, a huge, ginger cat lazing at her feet.

All I can say is that more French must have rubbed off on me from Miss Kirkbride's lessons than I previously thought! Although I was extremely rusty at first, with a bit of miming, Madame Jastrow and I managed to have a conversation. As we talked I noticed the late, afternoon sun glinting on a gilt frame in pride of place above the mantelpiece. The face of a young man with laughing eyes smiled back at me. Somehow, I managed to understand it was her only son, Samuel, who'd been killed at Verdun in 1915. As she spoke, I looked at his photograph, so proud and so handsome in his uniform. But what struck me most was how young he looked. I'd always assumed soldiers to be older, experienced men but, on this trip, I'm learning, many of those who fought the war were younger than I am now, and not much older than you, dear Rose.

Sitting next to Samuel's picture, the silence interrupted only by the tick-tock of the clock, got me thinking of my own life and that we really must make the best of each and every day because we truly never know what is around the next corner. Even though I may never visit this enchanting city again, this trip has made me clear about certain things. When I get home I'm going to marry Frank, and hopefully, if we are so blessed, we'll raise a family together. That is what I want from my life.

See you in a few days,
Your loving sister,
Violet xx"

8

Disturbed by bad dreams, Ivy overslept and consequently it was after ten when she made it down to breakfast. Sitting at a table for two next to a striking painting of the desert, Mustapha's father, Khalid, served her today, setting down a tray of delectable, glazed pastries before performing the theatrical ceremony of pouring the mint tea she'd ordered. As she'd witnessed at teahouses in the souks, he lifted the silver teapot high into the air in one fluid movement before tilting it downwards and she found herself mesmerized watching the pale-green, translucent liquid gracefully arcing from the long, curved spout into her glass.

"You're enjoying your stay here so far?" he smiled, bringing the teapot to a rest on her table which gave Ivy the opportunity to admire its intricate craftsmanship.

"Thank you, yes," she replied, her fingers hovering over the faded, flowery notebook she'd planned her trip in these past months, "except I want to go to Essaouira and

I haven't seen any travel companies in the city that offer the trip."

"Leave it to me, Madam, you're here for over a month aren't you?" he asked, scribbling something onto a piece of paper. "Let's see what we can do."

As he retreated she savoured the delicate taste of an almond pastry, while contemplating the temptation to spend the day in the riad. But, just as she pictured herself quietly reading, the hurried clatter of shoes on the tiles interrupted her thoughts as Mustapha appeared, his clothes dusty from the streets. Tucked beneath his arm were some battered cardboard boxes.

"Good morning, Madam," he made himself at home in the wicker seat opposite Ivy, which creaked loudly in protest. With his elbow, he nudged her tea tray slightly in order to put the boxes on the table and smiled, his engaging eyes as big as saucers, "how are you, Madam?"

"Very well, thank you, Mustapha," she smiled, realising he'd taken a shine to her and that chatting to him would provide further practice in honing her beleaguered French skills, "what have you got there?"

"Games," he smiled, spreading out the boxes to reveal a choice between snakes and ladders, chess and backgammon. "Do you play?"

"Yes, snakes and ladders," Ivy said, seeing from the little boy's disappointed expression that this was clearly not his first choice. Nevertheless, he assembled the board without protest and gave her the dice to roll. Ivy might not have had a busman's holiday in mind, but as they passed the dice back and forth, she was pleased to have a companion to alleviate her loneliness and surmised the feeling was mutual.

"Hey wasn't that a five?" Ivy exclaimed during their seventh game, as the boy moved his counter to reach the bottom of a ladder which took him nearly to the top of the board.

"No, Madam," he answered, his mischievous grin telling her otherwise.

"Mustapha," his dad's stern voice echoed across the courtyard, "you're not cheating are you?"

"No Father," the little boy looked from Ivy to his father, imploringly.

"Come on, I've put the T.V. on for you in the back. You've played long enough, you need to leave the poor lady in peace," he smiled.

"It's no trouble," smiled Ivy, watching the little boy reluctantly slouch away.

"See you tomorrow, Madam, for another game?" he turned, his face expectant. He waited to see her nod before finally disappearing to his father's office, his precious games safely tucked beneath his arm.

Ivy settled back in her wicker chair, absorbing soothing scents of jasmine drifting from a large pot behind her table. Tilting her head to the canopy above her, she became entranced by its diaphanous material rippling in the breeze. She reflected how fortuitous she was that Riad El Amrani was situated in a beautifully renovated 16th century townhouse since that was what had initially attracted her to Riad El Alaqui. There was much more to it than that though and she took it all in now: its exquisite woodwork, its carved plasterwork, its white marble pool, the neutral shades broken up every now and again by a bright splash of colour – from the terracotta columns to the intricate blue and green mosaics. With its enclosed, homely atmosphere and hues of the natural world, it was difficult to say whether she was inside or out.

The soothing effect of the mint tea taking hold, she finished off the sweet pastries while admiring the Berber portraits and other desert landscapes displayed on the walls. Sauntering across the courtyard to examine their finer details, she was impressed by the high standard of the exhibition by local artists. In the far corner, she noticed a tiny library and stepping in, it took her eyes a moment or so to adjust to the darkness. Although the pale, pine furnishings could not have been further removed from the rich oak of Rose's library, perusing the shelves gave her the same expectant feeling. Perhaps the books themselves, closed and collecting dust, waiting to be read and brought to life again, created the ambience, she mused, picking up an over-sized, hard-backed tome about the Atlas Mountains. Taking a seat on the soft sofa, she slowly leafed through its pages, skipping through the lyrical descriptions in flowery French to linger on the dramatic black and white photos.

"What brings you to Marrakech?" a voice enquired, almost an American accent but underscored with softer undertones. Ivy looked up to find the speaker leaning forward from a dark alcove into a shaft of light. His face was not good-looking in a conventional way but rugged with a day's worth of stubble while a wide smile lit up his brown eyes. With dark hair flecked with grey and fine lines etched around his eyes and mouth she guessed him to be a few years older than her. Smartly dressed in a navy shirt and slacks, he didn't look like the average tourist she'd seen out and about on the streets. Usually possessing an inbuilt radar to detect strangers looking at her, she wondered how it was she'd been sitting for a quarter of an hour in such an enclosed space without sensing his presence.

"A holiday. I've wanted to come for as long as I can remember," she smiled, relieved for a break from speaking French. It was either this or something in his demeanour which made her continue, she wasn't sure. "When I was a little girl my great-aunt told me stories of snake charmers, the desert and the Atlas Mountains topped with snow. It's a place that has always intrigued me."

"I understand," he nodded, closing the thick, leather-bound book he was reading, to give her his full attention. There was a stillness and quietness to him and she sensed that in the library he had found his perfect place. Taking his silence as an invitation, she went on.

"I read French at university, and in fact my final dissertation was about Albert Camus' writings on Algeria so my interest in North Africa grew. My great-aunt died recently and since we were both interested in Morocco I decided it was time I experienced the souks first hand rather than just reading about them... " she trailed off, suddenly regretting that, in her relaxed state, she'd begun to ramble.

"I'm sorry about your great-aunt," he replied, a shadow momentarily passing over his expression, "I read Camus' novels years ago in school. I'm French-Canadian so I grew up bilingual too," he smiled, the skin at the edges of his eyes crinkling as he did.

"I wouldn't say I was bilingual, not any more anyway," she stated matter-of-factly, tucking her long, swept over fringe behind her ear.

"A few weeks in Morocco and you'll be speaking French like a native again," he smiled. There was something about him that she found reassuring, not a feeling she was accustomed to experiencing with a stranger, as she sensed her usual reserve melt away.

"What are you doing here?" she enquired, after a moment, suddenly curious to know more about him.

"Searching." Finding the man studying her face intently, she instinctively looked away. "For inspiration. I was lecturing in Art at the University of Toronto and decided to take a sabbatical. I've been here almost five years now, trying to find a new way of expressing my own art. It sounds prosaic, doesn't it?"

"Not at all, what sort of things do you paint?" The book weighing heavily on her knees, she leaned over to put it on the table, conscious her coral sun top was of a lower cut than she would have liked at this moment.

"Everything really – landscapes, portraits, realistic, impressionistic. Maybe that's my problem, that I paint everything pretty competently instead of painting one thing brilliantly," he sighed, smiling.

"Those are your paintings displayed in the courtyard?" she ventured, as he nodded. "But they're wonderful, so atmospheric, you're a really talented artist…"

"Jacques Deschamps," he offered, his eyes meeting hers,

holding them. He proffered his hand and taking it, she felt his skin warm against her own.

"I'm Ivy, Ivy Fielding," she murmured as he continued to look at her.

"Ivy," he repeated to himself, a smile briefly illuminating his face.

For the next hour or so, they sat on adjacent low cream sofas, in the half-light of the little library, enveloped by the silence of shelves full of books. They talked of literature, of poetry, of nature and of beauty, of everything that mattered to both of them, switching between English and French. They didn't mention anything specific about their lives and despite that or maybe because of it, Ivy felt liberated to connect with Jacques on many levels. For the first time since Rose's death, she felt she was talking to a like-minded soul who shared her interests and outlook on life. This sudden realisation both surprised and pleased her.

"I have an appointment in town this afternoon," he announced eventually, replacing his book on the shelf, "but are you free this evening?" A hopeful smile played on his lips.

"Yes, I am," replied Ivy, the words escaping from her before she had time to consider.

"We could go for a meal, if you wanted?" he offered, uncertainty slowing his voice. "It's just that with you being on your own I thought you could use a friendly face?"

"Yes, I would like that," Ivy formed an uncertain smile, her heart sinking that in spite of their long conversation he merely saw her as a girl on her own in need of some company.

"I'm sorry, that didn't come out how I'd rehearsed it in

my head," his eyes sparkled, "I meant to say, *I've enjoyed talking to you and would like to continue our conversation over dinner.*" She saw his expression was serious now, his strong features appearing to be carved from granite.

"So would I," she nodded, musing she could happily talk to him all evening, intrigued by what he said and what he didn't say in equal measure.

"Good, I'll meet you here at 7pm?" he smiled, standing up hastily. Nodding in assent, her eyes followed him across the courtyard. He was over six feet, taller than she'd expected him to be, his shoulders and chest broad, as though he worked out in his spare time, tapering down to a slim waist. Feeling warmth rise in her as she watched his long, fluid strides, she could not deny the first stirrings of attraction towards him. But at the very moment these feelings demanded acknowledgement, she suppressed them. She definitely was not going down that route. However, unlocking the door to her room later, she was sure of one thing – she wanted to discover more about him.

9

In her room, Ivy's stomach fluttered with anticipation and trepidation in equal measure. It had been well over a year since she'd been on a date, an ice-skating disaster with a Maths teacher called Graham, who she had met on a first aid course. Within half an hour she'd realised they had absolutely nothing in common and she had hastily drawn the evening to an end, pleading a mountain of marking waiting at home. Despite knowing or perhaps because she'd already connected on a much deeper level with Jacques, the intimacy of a dinner date began to worry her as she wondered whether she could bear the scrutiny of sitting opposite him for hours. Her concerns escalating, she showered and teased her hair into soft curls before laying out her chosen outfit on the bed, to save panic later. She opted for a midnight blue top, sparkling with silver thread which she teamed with white, skinny jeans, hoping she'd struck a happy compromise between casual and a touch of 'dressy'. Unable to contemplate a heavy lunch, she finished off some softening kiwi fruits and bananas she'd bought in the market.

Gazing at her birthmark, which hadn't adapted well to the heat at all, she laboriously went through her makeup routine until she was satisfied that every inch of purple was safely concealed. And then she put on another layer. But still her nerves refused to quell. The echo of the Muezzin's call to prayer signalling she still had hours until she was due to meet Jacques, she settled into a wicker chair, rearranging the white cushions to make herself comfortable, as she sought escape in Rose's diary.

Finding her place, Ivy carefully unfolded a yellowing newspaper cutting, the brittle paper feeling fragile in her fingers. As she took in the dateline – Tuesday December 27th, 1932 – in the top left hand corner, she realised it was just a few months after Violet and Nell's pilgrimage to the First World War battlefields.

"Prominent Lavenham Wedding. Successful businessman's daughter married. Miss Violet Beatrice Endicott, daughter of one of Lavenham's best known tradesmen, Mr Edward Endicott and Mrs Sarah Jane Endicott, was married at Lavenham Parish Church on Saturday to Mr Frank Staveley, son of Mr Thomas Staveley and Mrs Laura Staveley of Victoria Road, Lavenham.

The wedding aroused a great deal of interest in the business community in the town and the church was well filled for the ceremony. The bridal group presented a very pretty spectacle. The bride, who was given away by her father, wore ivory duchesse satin overlaid with silver lace and pearl trimmings, and carried a handsome sheaf of lilies and carnations, the colours of which blended happily with her dress. There were three bridesmaids, Miss Eleanor Endicott, sister of the bride, and the bride's two little sisters, Frances and Rose Endicott. These were dressed alike in pale-pink crêpe-de-chine, with silver trimmings and carried baskets of pink carnations."

Reflecting upon the article's description of her great-grandfather as a successful businessman, Ivy mused Rose must have inherited her acumen to run a successful flower shop for so many years, from him. She reread the report several times, marvelling at the way the journalist had cleverly captured the essence of this charming bridal group. She didn't require a photograph to see Violet standing before her, a vision in ivory and pearl, her pretty-in-pink bridesmaids, Frances and Rose, showering her in flower petals scooped from their baskets and, the image strong in her mind, she refolded the cutting carefully along its creases.

"In the end my fear of losing Violet when she married was softened to some extent by witnessing her joy. That Christmas Eve when she wed Frank was the happiest moment of her life, indeed a joyful day for all of us. Violet looked radiant in her wedding dress scalloped around the neckline by our clever dressmaker's intricate beading. The skirts fell to the ground like swirls of snow as Nell, Frances and I dressed her. To me she looked like a fairytale princess that day and I remember wondering whether my wedding would be as beautiful. My only regret, as I left for church, was that Violet would no longer be at home, to laugh and joke and sing and as the day progressed

through the lovely ceremony and the wedding breakfast, my sense of loss began to cut deeper.

I sensed that Frances felt the same, for that night in our bedroom she was unusually quiet. Not even her prayers seemed to have the power to uplift her spirits. Rising from her knees, she climbed into bed without uttering a word, her usual refrain, 'have you said your prayers yet, Rose?' left unspoken. I remember trying to get her to talk to me, to offer me words of comfort I suppose, but it was clear we were growing ever more further apart as another chance for us to draw closer was missed.

My abiding memory of that day though is watching Father waiting to enter the church with Violet on his arm and his pride at giving away his eldest, most treasured daughter. It was as though she gave him the strength to do anything. But that was the effect my sister had on us all. She was generous, beautiful and radiant. Later, when the darkness came, I clung to that light."

10

In an attempt to calm herself, Ivy focused on shafts of sunlight as they spilled across the trickling fountain, refracting into rainbows in the air. After a few minutes she spotted Jacques crossing the courtyard; a bright smile playing on his lips. As he approached, she noticed his hair was slicked back and darker than before, as though he hadn't been long out of the shower and had rushed to be with her. Observing he'd changed into a smart white shirt and steely grey suit, she was glad she had also made an effort with her appearance.

"You look lovely," he smiled as she stood up, her head barely reaching his upper chest. As he leaned down to kiss her on each cheek in the French custom, she inhaled his expensive aftershave with its citrus undertones and shivered involuntarily. Drawing back, she was glad he appeared not to notice. "Shall we go?" he offered, his deep brown eyes holding hers for a moment.

"Yes," she replied, surreptitiously tugging her top down over the waistband of her jeans before linking his proffered arm. Secretly pleased at his compliment on her appearance, she realised how unaccustomed she was at provoking such a reaction in men, if that's what it was.

Leaving behind the riad's serene atmosphere, they traversed a network of busy, narrow alleyways. Aside from her blossoming attraction to him which frightened her somewhat, Ivy felt safe in Jacques' company as shadows clung to the sides of buildings and people pushed by them in a hurry. Their easy conversation continued after its hiatus of seven hours as they talked of Moroccan culture and art, passing by shops displayed with brightly painted ceramics, exquisite leather bags and towers of colourful spices, all of which was a welcome distraction for her.

Night time, as was its way in this part of the world, cast down its black veil without the precursor of a lingering summer twilight. As they walked, Ivy marvelled at how the souks transformed into the colourful show she had witnessed on her first night. Approaching a babouche shop, with its Moroccan slippers artistically displayed outside in lustrous hues of silver and gold, pink and orange, blue and green, she lightly tugged Jacques' arm, drawing him to a halt.

"Fancy bartering for a pair?" Jacques suggested, his tanned face glistening slightly with perspiration. "It's part of the fun!" Feeling her own face moisten in the still very hot night air, Ivy worried her concealing makeup might run and made a note to herself to check in the Ladies as soon as they arrived at the restaurant.

"Alright," she smiled, sensing his enthusiasm and not wanting to gloat about her previous success with the leather bag. His fingers lightly entwined in hers, they slipped into the Aladdin's cave of slippers.

"C'est combien?" Jacques presented the middle-aged Moroccan man who'd appeared from the back of the shop with the red pair threaded with green she'd selected. Behind him, Ivy noticed a crumpled mattress and thought maybe it wasn't such a good idea to ruffle a big bear of a man when he'd just woken up.

"Cent vingt dirhams," the man stated, to which Jacques laughed and offered him fifty. After a few minutes of to-ing and fro-ing, in which time, despite the rapidity of their French, Ivy understood they were getting further apart rather than closer together, she decided to take charge.

"Quatre-vingts dirhams," she threw in, to which the man smiled and, a proffered and welcome glass of mint tea later, Jacques and Ivy continued down the souks, a polythene bag containing the babouches swinging between them.

"I didn't mean for you to buy them for me," Ivy noticed that Jacques' drying hair had flopped over his forehead to give him a boyish look, "especially as I ruined your bartering."

"I know you didn't," he laughed, an enigmatic smile playing on his lips, "but I wanted to get them for you anyway."

"Thank you." She felt herself flush, considering how much she was looking forward to having dinner in his company before returning to the reality that she knew next to nothing about him.

Rounding a corner, her nostrils were assailed by the intoxicating scent of leather. In front of them was a tiny space, no more than ten feet square, where three men crafted shoes and bags. Ivy paused to watch them as they swiftly and skilfully cut the beautiful leather into different shapes. Aware of Jacques' presence behind her, she closed her eyes and inhaled deeply.

"As you can see, the artisans congregate in their own quarter. This is the quartier en cuir," clarified Jacques as they arrived at a courtyard with twinkling fairy lights suspended from every possible pillar and balcony. Rickety stalls displayed exquisite leather bags in an array of colours and styles and Ivy couldn't help but notice the expert craftsmanship was at odds with the dilapidation of the place. Hanging from the balconies, washing flapped in the slight breeze, testifying to the fact that families lived here which was confirmed when Ivy heard a baby crying, the sound rising above hammering emanating from the workshop below. Old doors and discarded materials stood against the pillars, contributing to a general air of unkemptness.

"A lot of men learn their craft in workshops like this while living in small apartments with their wives and children above. It's something we wouldn't contemplate but it seems to work for them," Jacques smiled. As they walked on in contented silence Ivy briefly wondered why Jacques wasn't married as, despite her inexperience with men, something told her that was the case. Taken by his engaging personality, she deduced it was almost certainly a choice he'd made, most probably linked to his unpredictable career as an artist. Although intrigued, she didn't feel it was her place to broach the subject as it might seem intrusive or force her to impart her absence of a love life to him, both of which were equally mortifying.

"Breathe in deeply," Jacques whispered, doing so himself, "when I do so I imagine the Mistral wind making its way from the desert, picking up scents of the spices, incense and freshly cut wood, carrying them onwards. "

"Umm," sighed Ivy, noticing how long his dark eyelashes were, "thank you for bringing me. It's wonderful. I would have definitely lost my way if I'd come alone."

"A lot of people are frightened of getting lost here. But for me, that's the special thing about it. It is a place made for losing yourself in with its maze of crooked streets and winding alleyways," he smiled, as they continued on, "the Medina is housed in 12th century walls where there are so many ancient mosques and Quranic schools. Whenever I take a stroll here I can feel those nine hundred years of history bearing down upon me," he turned to face her.

Looking into his dark eyes, she decided that he had an artist's lyrical soul, something she admired. But as they continued deeper and deeper down ever darkening alleyways she pondered whether there was something else that moved him to speak this way. Momentarily distracted by a man crafting exquisite birdcages, Jacques voiced the thought uppermost in her mind.

"I always think birdcages are sad things, don't you?" he uttered, placing his hand in the arch of her back as a man in a long, red robe roughly pushed past her.

"Me too," she nodded, returning to her previous thought but not daring to explore it now. "If God had intended birds to be in cages he wouldn't have given them wings to soar in the sky."

"No, he wouldn't," agreed Jacques, giving her a strange look but saying no more.

"We'll follow the Rahba Kedima," he remarked as the souk suddenly forked off in different directions.

Time nudged on regardless as they browsed and chatted and presently the sky turned inky black. The air became thick with smells of spices as Ivy noticed plumes of smoke rise into the night air and her stomach somersaulted at the prospect of seeing the Jemaa el Fna again, in all its night time glory. They dodged a couple of scooters buzzing by like bees before Jacques suddenly pulled her off the bustling street into a deserted hall.

"Where are we?" asked Ivy, slightly breathless, her voice echoing in the cool darkness.

"It's the oldest bakery in Marrakech," whispered Jacques, leading her into a dark room lit only by the flicker of flames where Ivy could just make out the silhouette of a man who was pushing loaves of bread into the primitive looking oven.

"It's wonderful," Ivy inhaled the fresh bread. They remained for just a few minutes before the suffocating heat hastened their emergence into the cooling night air as they took the final few steps to the Jemaa el Fna.

For a moment or two, Ivy tried to take in every detail, before finding it was easier to simply submit to the full frontal assault on her senses. It was the most incredible scene, with men and women cooking up a feast of Moroccan delicacies. As they passed the stalls, Ivy noticed that each one seemed to have its own speciality – from spicy broth to the stuffed lamb she'd tasted the previous evening to aromatic couscous. She wanted to try and taste every one.

"I've always imagined it to be like this," she breathed, "but never actually thought it would surpass my expectation."

Turning towards Jacques, his eyes were full of fun as he saw the scene as though for the first time through her eyes before the expression vanished to be replaced by another, unreadable emotion. Although slightly unnerved by it, she neither blushed nor felt the need to look away.

"We could eat on the stalls but I did ask you out... " he hesitated, looking around, "and there's a nice restaurant I go to up there," he offered, pointing his hand heavenwards into the swirling smoke. "It's your evening so I'll leave it up to you."

"The restaurant sounds good," decided Ivy, thinking that after her time in the sweltering souks and the teaming square, somewhere cooler, quieter and hopefully air conditioned, sounded very appealing. Her misgivings about sitting under his close scrutiny evaporated too, allayed by their growing familiarity.

She followed Jacques through a non-descript room with just a few tables and a soft drinks refrigerator humming in the corner, before they climbed a wrought iron spiral staircase up to a quiet terrace. As they waited to be seated, Ivy excused herself to go to the Ladies where, leaning over the sink to the mirror beyond, she detected the faint trace of her birthmark beginning to appear. She carefully touched up her camouflage makeup until she was satisfied that in the candlelight of the rooftop restaurant, Jacques wouldn't notice anything untoward. Emerging to find him waiting on the spot she'd left him, she gave a reassuring smile, and followed the waiter as he led them to a table on the edge of the balcony where a candle gutted in a red glass holder.

"You really do get a bird's eye view here," remarked Jacques as Ivy, from their lofty position, surveyed the Jemaa el Fna in its entirety, noticing ornate columns on buildings and women walking around in beautiful robes, small details not visible when they'd been in amongst it.

"There's so much going on in every direction you look," gasped Ivy, captivated by everything that was unfolding just a few yards below. "You don't really believe it until you see it."

"No, you don't. The theatre and the food have been non-stop attractions ever since this square was used for public executions in about 1050. Its name – Jemaa el Fna – literally translates as 'assembly of the dead'," he hesitated suddenly. "Sorry, just nudge me if I'm slipping into tour guide mode!" Ivy smiled. "No, please go on, it's fascinating."

Sensing her genuine interest, Jacques continued, "I like to think of it as a stage, with the massed crowd eating and drinking while they are being entertained. All of life is unfolding down there," he smiled with a wide sweep of his arm, "locals making a living, holidaymakers enjoying themselves, couples on their honeymoons. It's life magnified by a thousand. I'll never tire of seeing it, of breathing it in as long as I live."

Ivy smiled, moved not just by his words but the emotion resonating in his voice as the slow notes of oboes cut through the quicker rhythm of drums below them. Perusing the menu, they decided to share a few dishes and eventually the waiter set out a veritable feast in front of them. As they dug into a selection of local tagines, pita bread and salad, Ivy's attention remained focused on the square below as storytellers spellbound crowds of locals with what she could only imagine to be Arabic legends, although their gestures needed no translation. From her vantage point, she saw all the tales she had read about the Jemaa el Fna come to life.

"I could sit here from dusk until dawn," Jacques finished off some spiced vegetables, "and I have, on many occasions!"

"I can certainly see why you chose Marrakech to inspire your painting," Ivy nodded as Jacques smiled. Silence descending on them, she let herself become immersed in the scene below, suddenly feeling very small but part of something bigger at the same time.

For dessert they ordered bite-sized pastries filled with orange blossom infused crème pâtissière. After the spiciness of the main course, Ivy found they cooled and soothed her palate as their conversation encompassed everything that was happening around them, before eventually returning to the specifics of their lives.

"You said you're a teacher in an elementary school?" he asked, his Canadian accent pronounced as he uttered 'elementary', soft and melodic.

"Yes," she watched the candle gutter in its glass. "The children in my class are seven and eight years old. I've taught younger and older years but I prefer Year Three. They are at the age where they know the rudiments of Literacy and Maths, most of them anyway," she grinned. "It's interesting teaching them new subjects like French and Science, seeing how they react, their enthusiasm. I find every day is different."

"It must be rewarding," he stirred his blacker than black coffee as shadows played on his face, "to know that you're making a difference in children's lives?"

"Yes, it is. Sometimes it's great when you can get through to a child, give them the extra support and confidence they need and change their life in some small way," she smiled, savouring the sweet orange blossom cream on her tongue. "But at other times it can be very frustrating. I want to do everything I can to give them the chance of a better life, but sometimes it's just not possible," she sighed, not wanting to sour the evening's mood.

"I can relate to that in my work at the University of Toronto. I found that I was always held back with red tape, with all the admin. In the end you can only do your best for your students, within limits," he trailed off and Ivy guessed that she was unwelcome to pry any further. Instead, their conversation returned to the more comfortable subject of French literature, focusing on Albert Camus and Emile Zola, whom they discussed in French, as both of them had studied them in the mother tongue and it seemed more natural that way. Then, Jacques unexpectedly diverged back to the personal.

"When I lived in Canada, I always kept my dream of becoming an artist in the background. I think most people's dreams remain just dreams but I had some money saved and I initially came out here for a month's travelling to see a new country and get inspiration," he paused, watching as the crowds began to disperse in the square below. "I was approaching my fortieth and I needed a break, a change. Some friends were already here so I crashed at their place.

Three weeks later I realized that I had found my spiritual nexus in Marrakech. Maybe I hadn't been running away from my previous life but in pursuit of this one all along? Anyway I applied for a Visa, arranged a sabbatical from university and the rest is history, as they say. Of course I couldn't impose on my friends indefinitely, so I now rent a small room at the riad which Monsieur Khalid lets me have for a reasonable fee. He says it isn't suitable to let because of its size and lack of view but it suits my purpose just fine!"

"How brave, just to drop everything and start a new life," mused Ivy, feeling the strong coffee burning her throat.

"There wasn't that much to drop, in the end. My parents were dead," he paused, noting Ivy's sad look. "They were in their midforties when I was born and after my mum passed from cancer eight years ago, my dad followed six months later. He couldn't go on without her, I guess. They were lucky, they had a long life together. I suppose it was inevitable one would follow the other even though it was difficult for me being left behind," he sipped his coffee, his serious expression giving way to a smile as his eyes held hers. "Anyway, I had no siblings, no ties. I had skills in art which I thought I could use over here just as well and I'd grown up speaking French so even the language wasn't a big deal."

"Even so, I'm not sure I could do that," sighed Ivy, thinking that even if she didn't have her parents, her job and responsibilities at home, she could never contemplate such a move.

"But you already have, in a way, haven't you?" he looked at her, his expression quizzical. "To come here for the summer on your own, that takes guts. Some of the tourists I meet won't venture out of their hotel unless they're on an air conditioned, escorted bus tour."

"I think I've seen some of them in the Jemaa el Fna," laughed Ivy.

"See what I mean? You've done something most people wouldn't have the courage to do. Travelling here alone," he replied, the warm night air ruffling his hair so it fell over his face in an informal manner. With that illuminating smile of his, he suddenly looked years younger as she glimpsed the boy he'd once been.

Ivy had numerous questions working their way to the front of her brain but in the end she didn't ask any of them. She figured Jacques was a complex and complicated character and that what he was telling her was just the tip of the iceberg, just as she omitted important details about her life. And so it suited her to leave it that way as prying would probably encourage the same from him. Instead their conversation reverted back to friendly banter, pondering how the acrobats learned their daring and dangerous moves, whether henna painting had health implications, where the tradition of snake charmers originated from and how snakes' venom was extracted. Time passed quickly and it was approaching midnight by the time they paid the bill. Returning to the riad, a chill cut through the alleyways and Jacques gallantly handed Ivy his jacket. Warmed by his body, she gratefully pulled it close to her own.

"It's because we're on the edge of the desert," he explained, clearly retracing their footsteps from memory as the dark alleyways all looked identical to Ivy, "that the temperature drops so dramatically at night."

Ivy was disappointed their walk back seemed much quicker than coming. Maybe she had just imagined the first to take longer or maybe Jacques had taken a shortcut back because it was almost midnight? Either way he was soon pushing back the heavy door to reveal the familiar courtyard, the scent of roses lingering in the cooling air.

"Thank you for a lovely evening," smiled Ivy, keeping her tone casual and friendly, unaccustomed to the maelstrom of feelings bubbling inside her, "I'm not sure I would have been brave enough to venture out to the Jemaa el Fna so late at night without you."

"My pleasure," Jacques leaned forward into the charged space between them, his lips touching hers briefly. "I've enjoyed myself, too," he murmured, his eyes searching for approval in hers as the silence hovered between them before she managed a shy smile.

"Will I see you at breakfast?" she asked, feeling flustered despite the coolness as midnight approached. Jacques' kiss, although light, had taken her unawares, filling her with longing to see him again.

"I'm not sure. I have an early appointment tomorrow," Jacques hesitated, shifting his weight from one foot to another. Realising he was floundering over what to say next, Ivy opted to give him an easy way out.

"Good night, Jacques," she extricated her fingers from his. As she climbed the stairs up to her room, she sensed his eyes following her and knew she'd abandoned him too soon. But it was too late to turn back.

11

In the still darkness of her room, she peeled off her outer clothes, damp with perspiration, before removing the now melting makeup from her face. In the harsh light of the bathroom her birthmark seemed more vividly red than usual. Maybe it was the heat, an allergic reaction to the sun cream she'd been wearing or a combination of both? Either way, as she snapped off the light, it amounted to the same conclusion: she had done the right thing leaving Jacques before things had progressed. Even if he liked her, which it seemed he did, did he like her enough to see past the livid mark which covered half of her face? But something told her there were many hurdles to mount before they reached that point in their relationship, if indeed, she dared to clear any.

After an hour or so and still unable to find sleep, she switched on the lamp and fumbled on the bedside table for Rose's diary.

"I remember my 13th birthday clearly, six months after Violet's wedding. The countryside shimmered in the heat that scorching summer. We went for a picnic by the river. When I say 'picnic' I'm not referring to a few soggy sandwiches and crisps. Mother's idea of a picnic was a sumptuous spread of large pork pies, cuts of cold meats and chicken legs. There were fresh bread rolls, cheeses, pickles and strawberries. But it was the trifle in the cut glass dish and my birthday cake, elaborately decorated with marzipan roses, that set it apart from other birthdays. I recall my sisters' calf-length, white dresses soiled with grass-stains, our wide-brimmed straw hats and my mother's parasol. I recollect the rowing boats moving slowly up the river making the most of the perfect summer day, the feel of the parched grass cutting between my toes and the cold of the water circling my ankles, as I hitched up my dress to take a paddle. I remember my father on a rare day off from work, falling asleep, exhausted from his new business venture and my mother reading Tess of the d'Urbervilles, her favourite novel, while I lay with my head in Violet's lap. I can still smell the strong, sweet scent of wild garlic and I can see the white stars of Queen Anne's lace nestling among the greenness of the river bank. I can hear the reeds brushing against each other as a soft breeze stirred them and I can hear my sisters' laughing. Their laughter drowns out everything now.

Soon after that picnic, in late July I think, Violet became unwell. I cannot be sure of the exact day or date. It didn't seem significant at the time. None of us knew what time had in store that day by the river. Maybe it's as well. The doctor quickly diagnosed consumption, or TB as it would be called today. With hindsight it's easy to look back and say: "If I'd have known how things would work out, I would have done this or that." But I think that hindsight can be a bad thing. People did what they thought was best, not with hindsight, but with hope.

My father did everything he could. She was his first daughter after all, the only one of the four of us he had led up the aisle. He paid for her to go to a private sanatorium on the coast where she sat day after day, with all the other women, breathing in the cool sea air. However, my sister's condition deteriorated and in late September, with her husband Frank's approval, she came home to us. I ran through the hallway, flinging my arms around her, trying to ignore how thin she'd become, her translucent skin and the dark shadows beneath her beautiful eyes. The rooms had been so quiet and empty without her, I was just glad to have my sister back, her beauty and kindness lighting up the house once again. I didn't realise what her return home to us meant.

It was a few days later that my mother explained gently that there was no chance of her recovering. With tears in her eyes, she told us Violet's condition was rapidly advancing, that she maybe only had a few weeks left. Young, beautiful, gifted and kind, she should have been planning her future with Frank, she should have been at the beginning of her life, with years of happy family times stretching out in front of her. She should not have been lying in a dark, silent room, her body growing weaker, wracked with violent coughing fits. It was so unfair. I knew that God was going to take her away from us. And I knew that there was nothing any of us could do to stop it. I was angry with Him, angry with everyone, angry with the world. I know I must have made things much worse for my parents and looking back I feel ashamed of my young self.

Violet, in her quiet, gentle way, seemed to accept her fate, something I knew I never could have done. I would have railed against it with my last breath. We would all sit around the sofa where Violet lay in the daytime, talking, reminiscing, making plans and laughing, just as we had always done. We talked of our childhood together, of dances my older sisters had been to and of a time when Frances and I would be old enough to go to our own grown-up dances. During the day when Frank and Father were working, that room was the domain of us women. Everything was as it always had been before Violet married. And everything had altered and was about to change again irrevocably. The inescapable knowledge that she would leave us soon made each moment we spent with her more poignant. Whenever Violet fell asleep there always seemed too much left to say.

She often read books from her shelves, books she had read when she was younger and had been saving to read to her children. In her unselfish way she accepted that she would now never get the chance. It was during this time I realised the simple beauty of my sister's dreams: for her marriage and children. But that in turn made me realise that I had my own ambitions to fulfil. I wanted to have a career of some kind if Father would let me, or travel abroad as my sisters had done. I knew I had too much to fit in to my life even if I lived to be ninety. But what I wanted most was to love someone and be loved in return, just as Violet was.

Over the next few weeks Violet seemed to become more and more peaceful. I never saw my sister complain and if she did, she did it silently. But there were times she'd have violent coughing fits when her whole body would shake uncontrollably, and it was then when Fran surprised us all. She was always on hand whenever Violet was overcome with one of these unpleasant episodes, catching the coughed up blood and mucus in a bowl, gently washing our sister's face and making her comfortable. Frances was always good at providing practical help and I think it was a comfort to her that there was still something she could do for her beloved sister.

As the days went on Violet slept more and more and when she awoke was too tired to even sit up in bed. I willed her to find the energy to talk to me, not wanting to waste those final precious days. I took it in turns with our mother, Nell and Fran to sit with her, with Frances opting for the long night shifts. Our days together were punctuated by the thud of farm labourers' heavy boots on the cobbles of the street as they walked to work before daybreak and back home after sunset. But with the curtains drawn all sense of time passing in between was lost in that room. We felt as though we were living in a bubble. It was a twilight world where the edges between day and night were blurred. It was almost as though the five of us held some special power in that room: that we were trying to hold back time."

12

Ivy endured a fitful sleep, her waking thoughts and dreams alternating between her embryonic feelings for Jacques and the confused signals she was receiving from him. By the time dawn light filtered through the curtains, although she'd managed to put them aside, Rose and Violet preyed on her mind as she pondered whether her great-aunt's loss of her sister at such a young age had made her such a sympathetic shoulder to cry on during her own teenage troubles. Needing to speak to someone, she rose early but she found the breakfast room deserted. With Jacques and Mustapha nowhere to be seen, she lingered only long enough for a quick coffee and croissant before grabbing a fresh apple and setting off for the Koutoubia Mosque. A Moorish minaret towering above the old town, it was high on her list of places to see in Marrakech and she hoped it would provide a diversion from her circling thoughts.

The rising sun intensified the pink hue of the houses and

shops as Ivy wound her way through the Medina. Her white shirt damp with perspiration, the iconic minaret spurred her on, just as she imagined it encouraging weary travellers in times gone by, no doubt relieved to catch their first glimpse of the city after an inhospitable desert trek. Completed in the 12th century by Almohad Sultan Yacoub el-Mansour, it had become the city's principal place of worship. Its name, meaning Mosque of the Booksellers, had derived from the many book stalls which had clustered around its base, long gone now, of course.

Her walk into the sun continuing, Ivy fretted over the effect it would be having on her face, particularly in the light of the developments in her friendship with Jacques. So, instead of attempting to cross the road in the grip of rush hour, she ducked into a traditional Moroccan coffee house for some respite. Enticed by the aroma of freshly baked bread, her stomach rumbled as she climbed to the rooftop, which had a homely ambience with its long, green divans strewn with ruby-red scatter cushions and low, mosaic-tiled tables in dark blue hues. A white canopy fulfilled the purpose of a sunshade while wafting the cool breeze it caught above the heat of the street.

"Are you open yet?" Ivy asked the young waiter in traditional Muslim dress emerging from the kitchen, a tray piled with pastries perched on the palm of his hand. After just a few days, she was already hooked on them, their delicate melt-in-the-mouth choux pastry combining with the sweetness of African confiserie and she was on the lookout in the souks for a cookery book to repeat the experience on her return home.

"Yes," he smiled, his dialect difficult to understand, "you want a nice view of the Koutoubia Mosque?"

Ivy nodded as he led her to a table at the front of the terrace with an uninterrupted vista of the sand-coloured minaret, soaring heavenwards from the lush, green gardens at its feet. Far beyond it, she glimpsed the high peaks of the Atlas Mountains for the first time, rising like a line of jagged teeth. With such a scene before her and out of earshot of the roaring traffic, it was the perfect place to while away the morning – and many others in the coming weeks, she decided.

"You'll hear the Muezzin in twenty minutes or so as he makes his second call to prayer of the day," the waiter handed her a menu.

Even though his manner was relaxed, Ivy wondered what he must make of her, a Western woman travelling alone. It had never crossed her mind that her single status might be more of an issue in Morocco than at home. Or maybe he wasn't judging her at all? As she ordered mint tea and pastries, she remembered the previous evening when she'd felt so comfortable walking through the streets with Jacques, passing people who would have certainly taken them for a couple. It had been a welcome feeling, even though she conceded it was unlikely to happen again.

After a refreshing sip of tea, she bit into an intriguing green and white confection. The consistency of butter cream, it had been dipped in coconut and chopped nuts and, although a little sweet for her taste, the sharpness of the mint in her mouth made it palatable. Turning her attention to what was immediately below her, she found the contrasts interesting, too.

Palm trees, pink flowers and wrought iron lanterns, which would not have been out of place in a fashionable resort in the south of France, lined the broad boulevard. But while the promenades of Nice or Cannes would be quiet, laid back affairs by mid-morning, the rush hour extended a little later here. Bikes, carts laden with farm goods, expensive looking cars and women in hijabs carrying their wares on their heads; all jostled for their place here. Albeit in an organized chaos, it somewhat diminished the boulevard's elegance.

Her thoughts unexpectedly moved back to Violet. Realising that her trip to France had been her one and only visit abroad, she pitied her. It was sad to think that much of her trip, apart from a few days in Paris, had been haunted by suffering and death. She could only hope that seeing all those First World War soldiers' desperately curtailed lives had helped Violet when illness had struck her a few years later, giving her a measure of comfort that God had granted her a bit more time to fall in love and marry. But maybe this had just made it more difficult?

Unbidden, the memory of Jacques' brief kiss came flooding back. Trying to interpret it, she found she couldn't. It seemed incredible it was only twenty-four hours since their first meeting. So much had happened between them already, although she couldn't begin to attempt to define her feelings for him. And yet, recalling their conversations, so easy and unforced, it felt as though they had already connected on a much more intimate level than just two travellers who had ended up in the same riad. There was definitely something with the potential to develop between them, if she'd let it and if, indeed, he wanted it to.

They certainly shared many interests. But there was something else to her attraction to him, something lying just beneath the surface that she couldn't quite put her finger on. He was an emotional, passionate man, an artist; qualities which should bring him happiness. And yet she recognized that at his core there was also a vulnerability with which she could identify. She sensed that something had damaged him, sending him halfway across the world to find a new life for himself in Marrakech. The question she had to ask herself was; did she have the strength to help Jacques when she had trouble steering her way through her own problems?

Unable or unwilling to face such a searching question at that moment, Ivy fished in to the dark depths of her handbag for her great-aunt's notebook. It was the only way she could stop thinking about the dilemma of the present – to escape to the past once again.

"Some days while Violet slept I would help Nell in the sweetshop. Originally meant as a hobby for us, we were now making a fair profit from our labours and I seemed to have developed a talent for arranging the window displays. Looking back I can see the seeds were sown for my future business in floristry, but of course that was still a long way off. That year the warmth of summer lingered into late September. One particularly humid day I had spent the morning rearranging the window display, moving fancy chocolate boxes out of the sun's reach and replacing them with rock, boiled sweets and gums, which were less likely to melt. During that time Nell made up ice cream sandwiches which were particularly popular with the endless stream of local children who came through our doors.

I had just finished piling up the rock in rainbows when I saw my friend Margaret waving me over to the other side of the street, her blonde hair framing her delicate face like a gilt picture frame. The same age as I, Margaret was the daredevil friend I would have liked Frances to be. Needing no further encouragement, I removed my apron, picked up two ice cream sandwiches and ran out, much to the consternation of the queue in the shop. In seconds we were racing past the tobacconists and up the high street to her dad's farm. It was a relief to breathe fresh air into my lungs after being cooped up in the stifling shop all day.

Margaret's father owned one of the biggest farms in the area. He kept pigs, cows, sheep and chickens as well as cultivating a variety of crops. Margaret and I climbed to the top of one of the haystacks, our fingers sticky with melted ice cream. Bathed in the hot midday sun, the yellow hay making a soft bed for us, we ate them quickly. The light was white up there and, after dark weeks spent in my mother's sitting room with the curtains drawn so Violet could sleep, my eyes had become unaccustomed to such brightness as I squinted in the strong sun.

It had only meant to be a half hour break from the sweet shop but a day later, it was still the talk of the high street. One of the farm boys came to chat with us, Jack I think he was called, indulging in a surreptitious smoke. Everything happened so quickly after that – a discarded match, the crackling, the heat far stronger than the sun, the dancing flames.

Margaret, Jack and I managed to escape down the side of the haystack, grazing our legs on the coarse hay as we slid down. But despite the attempts of Margaret's dad, burly Farmer Tom, and useless buckets of water thrown at the escalating flames by Jack and two other farm hands, the haystack was reduced to ashes in a matter of minutes. A vain attempt to beat back the inevitable, it failed miserably to quell the flames.

And in the meantime my sister's life was running all too quickly to its end. Whenever I went into town it became clear that everyone loved Violet. The milkman, the baker, the kindly old woman who ran the teashop three doors down, all asked me how she was, sending their good wishes and presents including flowers, fruit, cakes, chocolate. Even the cantankerous widow Mrs Moore who normally never shared more than pleasantries with anyone gave me a beautifully embroidered cushion to make Violet more comfortable. Although she was my dearest sister I was surprised at how many others' lives she'd touched. I often wondered whether people would have acted the same if it'd been me. I somehow doubt they would.

As we grasped every moment we could, time marched on regardless. As the year drew to its close and the last leaves fell from the trees so our time together was also nearing its end. When it finally came though, it crept up behind us, unseen. After a violent coughing fit in the late afternoon of that dull Friday, Violet became calm. Her face, ravaged by her illness, suddenly brightened and her eyes sparkled as of old. I remember feeling a surge of happiness course through me as I truly thought she had overcome her illness. Her voice as she spoke to me was strong and firm and I recall that last conversation almost word for word.

"Hold my hand, Rose," she reached hers out to mine and I grasped her fingers gently.

"I want to say I'm glad I was your sister, even though I wish it could have been for longer," she whispered, stroking my hand. I pleaded with her not to say these things, claiming it would tire her. But it wasn't that. I didn't want to say goodbye. I didn't want that moment to have come already. It was too soon.

She then told me in her calm and gentle manner that even though I was the youngest in the family she knew I was the strongest. She asked me to help our parents after she'd gone for she realised how much they would grieve all their lives for her. She reminded me of the letters she'd written to me from France when she'd seen how parents' grief over the deaths of their sons was undiminished even after fifteen years. She told me to keep an eye on my sisters too, perceiving that Nell, although outwardly confident, had a sensitive and fragile side to her nature and implored me to be kind to Fran. Knowing we were not close friends, she explained how much of her awkwardness was down to insecurity and low self-esteem. Finally, she told me to follow my dreams and find happiness for myself, wherever and whenever I could and most importantly to find someone to love. She then got me to promise to do what she'd asked, which I did, not quite understanding what it was I was pledging.

As my parents, Frank and Nell entered the room, I retreated, trying to commit to memory my sister's smile, knowing I would never see her again. In our bedroom, I found Frances weeping, her body shaking uncontrollably. I put my arms around her, feeling her body tense as it flinched from my touch. I remember she'd told me when the time came she didn't want to go and say goodbye to Violet, so I didn't press her.

Instead as she drew away she asked me to kneel beside her and pray. In my usual fashion I prayed, no demanded, God not to take my sister, if only she did not die, I would never

102

ask Him for anything else, ever. Frances of course, in her pious way, prayed for Violet's soul and for their reunion in heaven. I remember feeling so angry with Fran. I didn't want Violet to go to heaven, I wanted her here with me. It was just her way of coping with it I realise now, and I hope that her prayers gave her some solace. But at a time when we should have been united in grief, we couldn't even agree on that.

The end came quietly just after 4am, an hour before we heard the first dawn chorus. In that moment, my childhood abruptly came to an end. The war had left so many families devastated and mine untouched but in those dark hours I realised that we were just as vulnerable as everyone else. When my sister died I sat by the open window listening to the noises of the night: a fox barking in the distance, the scratching of branches against the window, the creak of the floorboards beneath unseen footsteps.

I couldn't cry or sleep or think – so I just listened."

13

"You want to buy one?" Mustapha bounded into the library the following day where Ivy was struggling through Camus' *La Peste*, while her lamb tagine lunch digested. Slightly out-of-breath from running or excitement, or both, he brandished some suspiciously plastic-looking bracelets in lurid greens, pinks and yellows, his smile seemingly as wide as the horizon.

"Let me see," she draped them on her fingers, her initial dislike for the colours giving way to admiration for his entrepreneurism. "How much are you charging for them?" she smiled.

"Two dirhams each," he declared, producing yet more from his pockets like a magician in the Jemaa el Fna. Ivy couldn't help but laugh for he had managed to undercut the souks by almost 50%.

"Yes, I'll take one of each," she smiled, slipping them over her hand, so they splayed out on her wrist like a fluorescent rainbow.

"Mustapha… " his father's voice echoed across the courtyard. As the little boy shrugged his shoulders, Ivy had just enough time to slip a folded ten dirham note into his hand for payment. Smiling sweetly, he stuffed the note into his back pocket. Watching Mustapha's slight figure recede across the courtyard, Ivy reflected how he'd restored her equilibrium after learning the harrowing details of Violet's death. Sated by the satisfying stew and enveloped by the silence of books, she whiled away the sultry early afternoon hours continuing to read the existential novel.

The heat and humidity had dipped considerably as she headed to the Ensemble Artisanal at just after four. Although desperate for a spot of retail therapy, despite Jacques' helpful tips on bartering, she still felt daunted by the prospect of going alone. The artisan's complex, however, appealed to her wish to take something home which had been handmade in Morocco, and being state-run, all its goods were authenticated and priced. Knowing this gave her the confidence she needed to buy some good quality souvenirs. Even though haggling was viewed as an exciting experience by tourists it just didn't suit her.

The main road seemed more manic than ever as carts stacked with crates of unsold goods trundled alongside Mercedes with blacked-out windows and every sort of vehicle in between. Ivy breathed a sigh of relief when she left the fumes and horn-peeping behind to step into the shopping complex. The place was deserted, the more seasoned shoppers no doubt putting their tired feet up on hotel sun loungers dotted around swimming pools. In the entrance, she paused to peruse paintings of horses running through the desert sand before the passageway opened out into a sunny courtyard, shaded with trees and dotted with plants in huge blue pots. Strolling around the set-price boutiques, she admired the ceramics, clothes and jewellery on sale.

As it was only a short walk back to the riad, Ivy decided to make the most of the security of the fixed prices and quality goods. Thinking a tagine cooking pot would make a good gift for her culinary-loving mum, she located a shop in a quiet courtyard with some lovely earthenware ones on display. Smiling at the girl who looked to be about eighteen or nineteen, her pretty face framed by a fuchsia hijab, Ivy selected a pale-blue cooking pot, her mum's favourite colour.

"Did you make these yourself?" Ivy passed the pot to the girl to wrap, eager to engage with her and feeling more confident with her French after her long conversations with Jacques.

"My brother made them. He is a potter," she stated matter-of-factly, "I paint them with my mother."

"It must be lovely to work with your family," Ivy noticed her beautifully flawless skin.

"Yes, it is," smiled the girl, shyly, "but I want to be an artist. Those are my paintings in the entrance."

"I was admiring those," Ivy handed her a wad of small denomination dirhams, "I like the way you've captured the horse's movement kicking up the sand."

"Thank you," the girl blushed slightly as she twisted turquoise tissue paper around the funnel, "this is what makes the money though. Is it a present for someone?"

"Yes, my mother," Ivy replied, regretting the girl's predicament.

"Ah, then I'll do it extra special," smiled the girl as her fingers worked fast and furiously to pleat the paper around the pot.

"That's beautiful," smiled Ivy, stepping back into the sunlight of the courtyard. "But make sure you don't give up on your painting," she added, feeling her mood lift as she offered her words of encouragement. Ivy was careful not to disturb the black and white kittens sleeping in slats of sunlight as she explored the other workshops and stalls. She found the atmosphere relaxing if a touch sanitized after the alchemy of the souks. Next she ducked into a workshop where a young man was fashioning a chair and asked him about his woodcarving.

"My grandfather taught me the craft when I was a very young boy," he explained as she hungrily inhaled the scents of resin and wood, "I can't remember not working with wood."

"It is such beautiful work," Ivy admired the intricacies of the birds and flowers he was creating so effortlessly, "but how come you charge so little for it when you're so skilled?"

"I still make a profit," he smiled, his caramel eyes warm, "the government stipulates we charge fair prices so everyone's happy."

"I'll take this," Ivy remarked, picking up a box and tracing the minutely carved gardening tools on its lid, "my dad will love it. He likes to dabble in woodwork as a hobby although it's nothing like your work."

"Thank you," beamed the man, suddenly looking even

younger. "I am very proud to be able to sell my own work to tourists. Here, I give you these too, one for you and one each for your parents." He reached under the counter to retrieve three key rings. Laid on the palm of her hand, Ivy saw they were miniature, Moroccan leather slippers, two green and one yellow, about the length of her little finger, "they are symbols of good luck but the yellow ones are the luckiest so I give this one to you," he smiled, pointing to the one in the middle.

"Thank you very much," smiled Ivy, handing over the money for the box, "you are very kind."

"I hope you enjoy the rest of your stay in Marrakech," he proffered, as she put the small parcel into her shopping bag. "And remember to keep the yellow babouche for yourself. It will bring you good fortune."

Her earlier sober mood after reading Rose's diary had now completely dissipated and, smiling, she entered a studio where an old man was painstakingly embroidering flowers in vibrant shades on white blouses. While looking through his work, Ivy instinctively switched to French, not conscious she was doing so.

"Je voudrais l'une avec rose et vert, s'il vous plait," she pointed to one with panels embroidered with roses in various shades of green and pink.

"C'est tout?" he said, carefully extricating it from the display so that he didn't crease any of the others.

"Non," she stated, thinking how her mother would like one too, "Je voudrais celui aussi," she said, pointing to one with a similar design in blue and yellow.

"They are the shades of the sand and sea," he remarked,

folding them neatly into an expensive-looking, cerise cardboard bag with cord handles.

Outside his shop, putting her change into her purse, she noticed he'd only charged ninety dirhams for each blouse. Feeling an uneasiness engulf her, she half turned back before realising that to do so would be an insult. Completing the quartet of shops in this area was an artist selling oil paintings of the souks and a silversmith; an engaging young man who spoke excellent English. Ivy admired his craftsmanship attractively displayed in glass cabinets as he explained how he'd mastered the intricate working on bracelets, earrings and pendants where he combined silverwork with semi precious stones.

Deciding to treat herself to some earrings, after substantial deliberation, she settled on a pair in the shape of silver disks, the size of old half pennies. The man had skilfully cut out a circle in the middle of each one before decorating them with the tiniest loops and plaits fashioned from silver. Three silver strings, threaded with tiny turquoise beads, dangled from the circles, each one finished off with what looked like an exquisitely minute bunch of grapes. Ivy imagined an ancient African princess wearing such jewellery and decided she'd have to wear her hair off her face to show them off, if she dared.

Weighed down by guilt at having blown her budget, Ivy wended her way back through the souks, vowing she wouldn't be tempted into buying anything there for the remainder of her trip. After the sleepy silence of late afternoon, the streets were coming alive again as night approached and she contemplated heading back to the riad to see if Jacques was there. But when her mind wound back to their parting words, she realized that he had intimated nothing about another meal, maybe deliberately so. So, feeling more confident tonight, she headed to the Jemaa el Fna once more, where the curtain would be going up for the evening's performance.

Enticingly rich aromas of cooking meat wafted through the warm air as the charcoal grills crackled with heat. Even though she had eaten a substantial lunch in the riad she suddenly felt famished. Seeing the food being cooked right there and then, served on paper and eaten with the fingers, with Western tourists who spoke no Arabic pointing to items they wanted, she was tempted to try it again. However, feeling tired and overheated from her walk, she opted for the cool Terrasses de l'Alhambra and the familiarity of a vegetarian pizza. She enjoyed her meal looking out over the square, remembering the intimacy she and Jacques had shared in a restaurant just a few metres away, wondering whether or not it would be repeated. For dessert she was a bit more adventurous, ordering cinnamon-laced oranges which she ate slowly, savouring each mouthful. Her attention was caught by a white stork which was nesting on a nearby rooftop, before she descended to the hub of entertainment and excitement once more.

But tonight, maybe exhausted by her exertions, she felt the atmosphere oppressive, the crowds and the cacophony of noise stifling; things that hadn't bothered her with Jacques' comforting presence by her side. Yearning for the cool sanctuary of the riad, she berated herself for doing too much in the heat of the day. She must pace herself until she'd acclimatised.

Reaching the riad she went straight to her room, longing for a cool shower and the comfort of her bed. Eschewing any thoughts of reading more of Rose's memoirs, which she had found very upsetting, she drifted straight off to sleep as soon as her head touched the pillow. However, she experienced a series of disturbing dreams, of Violet's cruel death, of snake charmers draping snakes around her neck, of menacing crowds encircling her. At 4am she awoke in a cold sweat and, although she felt neither revitalised nor restored by sleep, try as she might, she could not find it again.

14

Ivy drained her coffee cup, leaving only the bitter dregs behind. From her secluded corner of the courtyard, she watched other guests eat their breakfast, her hopes of Jacques joining her this morning, fading fast. Sighing, she realised this was what being let down lightly felt like and, seeking a refuge from her disappointment, she retreated into Rose's diary.

"But somehow after Violet's death, life went on. There was shopping to do, meals to plan, the Christmas of 1933 and what would have been Violet's first wedding anniversary to endure. Come summer there would be strawberries and raspberries to pick and boil into jams, plums and blackberries to bottle in the autumn for winter pies, and all year round there was sewing to do and all manner of other activities. But most importantly for me, I discovered I could find my escape from all this in the different worlds of my books.

In those solemn, winter months the distance between Frances and I widened as her life became more and more focused on the church. I missed Violet terribly, my protective big sister, in whose shadow I'd always felt safe and so, despite the ten year age gap, Nell and I found solace in each other's company. I admired Nell greatly – she was elegant, witty and charming; all the things I quite obviously was not. She was the sort of person who made friends effortlessly, who seemed to draw people to her and I envied her all these things. But in the weeks following Violet's death her warmth and friendship were my greatest comfort. Unable to sleep we'd talk long into those dark nights. Nell was in love with and engaged to Charles, who absolutely adored her, and she confided in me about their plans for the future. But life had other ideas for her."

Wiping the tears from her face, Ivy closed the diary. The pain Rose had endured losing Violet was almost unimaginable for one so young. As she reflected on her own childhood, the name-calling and bullying in the playground at primary school and never having a boyfriend to dance with at school discos as she grew older, she remembered how on each occasion, she'd always turned to her great-aunt. Rose had always seemed to empathize with her, instinctively knowing the right words when she most needed them. Maybe, she realised now, it was because Rose's childhood had been every bit as difficult as hers, albeit for very different reasons.

As a means of distraction from the tragic story emerging from Rose's diary, she turned to her guidebook. Flicking casually through the pages, they eventually came to rest on the Saadian tombs. Listed as a Marrakech must see, she discovered the Saadians had been a forceful dynasty during the 16th and 17th centuries, defined by Edith Wharton for its '*barbarous customs but sensuous refinements*'! Reading on, she found they'd originated from Taroudant, to the south of the Atlas Mountains but, eager to extend their influence, they'd vanquished the Merenids of Fes and had formed their court in Marrakech, from which they'd ruled for almost 120 years, re-energising the city in the process. At a loose end, Ivy decided it was as good a day as any to visit their graves and arranging her diaphanous wine-red scarf around her shoulders and setting her sunhat on head, she stood up, glancing around one last time for Jacques.

"Ah, Madam," she heard the patter of footsteps on the mosaic tiled floor as Mustapha caught up with her, "you still enjoying your holiday?"

"Very much. It's a beautiful city," she replied, as he pushed back the unruly black curls falling into his eyes.

"Thank you, Madam," he beamed, evidently taking it as a personal compliment and she found herself wondering what sort of life it was for a child living with his father in the riad, an endless stream of visitors passing through but never the same ones staying for any length of time.

"Where are you going today?" his teeth were seemingly luminescent against his dark skin.

"Les tombeaux Saadiens," she pulled down her sunhat so its big brim shaded her face.

"Ah, our royal family. Very interesting, Madam," his eyes implored her, "I could show you the way? And then do a tour for you, I know a lot about Morocco's royal family."

"Mustapha!" His father shouted in exasperation from behind the desk.

"Maybe another time," she said softly before leaving the father and son locked in a heated discussion. She mused that Mustapha was certain to grow up to be an entrepreneur of some sort, adding tour guide to his possible career options which already included salesman, translator and professional backgammon player. But she didn't envy his father the job of keeping a rein on his son until such a time. As she cut down the warm warren of alleys, she decided to make it clear to Monsieur Khalid on her return that his son wasn't bothering her in the slightest and in fact was injecting a lot of fun into her stay.

Although not a long walk, the exertion soon began to take its toll. Feeling her skin prickle in the heat, Ivy was unsurprised when she saw the temperature of forty degrees flashing on an electronic billboard. The highest since her arrival, she fretted about the effect it was having on her birthmark. A circle of shade beneath a street vendor's tatty umbrella gave her a moment's reprieve as she purchased a bottle of water, its icy exterior nicely cooling her fingers. Although crowded, she found the wide, airy streets and cleanliness of the Kasbah more agreeable than the souks off the Jemaa. Here, she passed food stores, clothes shops and convenience stores, their open doorways giving glimpses of the treasure troves of delights inside. The beautiful red buildings the city was famed for were more visible here too and, surrounded by people going about their everyday lives, Ivy got a feel for the real Marrakech, away from the tourist hot spots.

"C'est combien pour les petaux en rose?" she enquired, stopping at a grocers, the heady scent of pink, red and white dried rose petals, rising to meet her.

"Vingt dirhums," replied a boy of about fifteen, sitting in the shade of the shop's awning. Immediately breaking her vow not to buy anything today, Ivy purchased two large mixed bags, deciding to give one to her mother and to display the other as a pretty pot pourri on the chest of drawers in her room for the rest of her stay. The riad was, after all, beginning to feel like a home from home, something as unexpected as it was welcome.

The street becoming increasingly rubbish-strewn, she was glad to spot a small, handwritten sign, *Tombeaux Saadiens,* so inconspicuous she almost missed it. Taking final greedy gulps of her warming water, she abandoned the bottle to join a line of people down an alleyway so narrow her shoulders almost brushed the warm walls on either side. But shuffling along, her anticipation overrode any claustrophobic feelings she had. Her guidebook described the first room as a former prayer hall, housing centuries old tombs, the ceiling held up by ancient columns. But tagging onto the back of a tour group of Americans, it was the shafts of light that caught Ivy's attention, spilling down the columns onto the alternating cream and blue tiled floor. In the enclosing darkness she could just make out, every few metres, a grave marked out by smaller tiles in different patterns, some with intricate, ornate designs topped by pedestals of different heights. The higher the pedestal the loftier position held in life, she overheard the cap-wearing, impossibly tall, American tour guide explain. Whichever way you looked at it though, kings, ministers, servants and even royal children, they were all long since dead, whatever they had been or done in life forgotten with them. Perhaps it was still being caught in the raw grief of her great-aunt's death but she suddenly felt her throat constrict as she was overwhelmed by a profound feeling of sadness.

The crush of people in the room was making it difficult to breathe, and she knew she needed to get outside. She quickly backtracked, apologizing for going against the tide of people crowding into the darkness behind her. Outside, she rested on a low wall which separated the path and flowerbeds, and as the warmth from the stones seeped through her clothes, she closed her eyes to concentrate on regulating her breathing to prevent it from escalating into a panic attack. Beads of perspiration stung her eyes with saltiness.

Her breathing slowing, she watched as a tiny, stray, black cat ventured out of the shade of the tree, where six others were sleeping, to weave in and out of her legs in a figure of eight several times. Once acquainted, it lay down on its back and submitted to her tickles on its tummy. As it purred gently Ivy felt herself relax too, the knots in her muscles unravelling as the tension slowly subsided. After a few minutes, she'd calmed enough to return to the tombs, followed by her new, feline friend. The cat's attempt to make a break into the building, however, was quickly thwarted by the attendant, who shooed it away. Ivy watched with amusement as the creature turned around, purring with annoyance, before disdainfully retreating back to the shade of the garden.

She found the Hall of Twelve Columns impressive with its intricate cedar wood and stuccowork, the graves of Sultan Ahmed El Mansour and his family carved from Italian Carrara marble. Looking up in awe at the walls she admired their intricate carvings and honeycomb archways, gilded with pure gold.

"They say you can't take it with you?" remarked an American woman behind her, her loud voice echoing around the hall, "well, these guys have had a helluva good go!" A large lady, she wore a white, baggy tracksuit, which Ivy assumed made up in comfort for what it lacked in style.

"He's a Marrakechi Midas," agreed the younger man with her. While other tourists glanced disapprovingly at him Ivy laughed in agreement. She felt uplifted that, instead of fearing death, this Sultan had embraced it, much as he had done everything during his life. It was a state of being to which Ivy aspired.

"He also redefined the term 'family man'," Ivy commented, to the chuckles of the Americans as they skirted his final resting place. Surrounded by his many wives, children (whose graves were significantly smaller) and his servants (whose graves were tinier still), he kept them as close to him in death as had been in life. Leaving the Americans behind to take photos of the Sultan's grave, she shuffled into the main chamber where she extricated herself from the line of people to admire the exquisitely emerald-tiled roof with its three soaring portals and stucco frieze of eight-pointed stars.

Walking back through the Kasbah later, Ivy felt her spirits oddly uplifted. She had expected the experience at the tombs to be a somewhat sombre one, which of course it had been. But whether it was the beauty of the surroundings or the fact that the family still rested peacefully side by side after half a millennium, she felt a strange comfort. At that moment she felt maybe life didn't feel so daunting and hopefully death not so final, as it crossed her mind that she may see Rose again one day. Arriving back at the riad, she was greeted by an oasis of coolness. Her tongue, furry from slight dehydration, she settled in the courtyard with a pot of mint tea and Rose's diary. Certain she had guessed Nell's fate, she nevertheless felt a compulsion to read on to discover the truth.

15

"It was the spring of 1934 when Nell became sick and I immediately knew the shadow of death was hovering over our family once again. She was twenty-four years old. My father paid for her to go to a private sanatorium as it was still thought that fresh air could help, if not cure, people suffering from consumption. On the Suffolk coast, the sanatorium consisted of fifty or so wooden chalets where we would visit her at weekends. Her fiancé, Charles, always took us in his smart, black Austin car and, under other circumstances, I would have enjoyed those drives. But as the low-lying land of the coast beckoned, a queasiness always overcame me at the prospect of my sister's further deterioration since our previous visit. We would take little treats hoping to tempt Nell to eat something and try to update her on all the news from Lavenham. I remember being impressed by the nurses who cared so lovingly for their patients, covering the beds with heavy tarpaulin before wheeling them outside to breathe in the cold air.

The treatment did help some of those women. Louisa and Jane, in neighbouring beds to my sister, both went home with clear prognoses. But it was to our despair that my sister didn't share their good fortune. My father spent a lot of money, more money than he could afford as it turned out, on the best treatments for her. But Nell became weaker and weaker. At the end of July, as the weather turned hot and humid and the roses were coming into their second flowering, my father brought Nell home. This time I needed no explanations from Mother. I cried myself to sleep that night as did Frances, for once united in our all-consuming grief.

Nell's death came one night in late September. A few days before, our neighbours had covered the high street with straw just as they had done for Violet. However, although the muffled sound of horses' hooves and car wheels on the straw might have been the same as the night Violet had died, everything else was different. There was no quiet acceptance of death as it came through our door for the second time in twelve months. The doctor visited Nell for the final time that evening.

"It shouldn't be long now. The end will probably come before the morning. Goodnight, sir," he tipped his hat to my father. I took a short intake of breath, at once expecting the news and yet not accepting it. It seemed only a heartbeat away since he'd said the same thing about Violet.

Returning to Nell's bedroom, a light rain had begun to fall outside and the covering of cloud cast it in a soft, lavender light. Nell was sitting back on the pillows, exhausted after a violent bout of coughing. The white sheets splashed red, Nell, sapped of energy now, closed her eyes, the final convulsion having pulsed through her body like an electric shock. Maybe, that was it, I thought to myself as I sat on the end of her bed, maybe the end would come peacefully to her now? But I was so wrong.

To my dying day I will never forget what unfolded next. As Nell tried to heave herself up Mother wrapped her in her arms, attempting to soothe her. But, with coughs wracking her poor emaciated body, my sister used every ounce of her remaining strength to push Mother away, while cries of fear, terror and anger echoed around the room.

As clearly as if it was yesterday I see that awful scene being played out again before me. Not allowing any of us, not even Charles, to touch her, I watched in mounting horror as Nell's transparent fingers grasped the sheets, twisting and turning them as she tried with every part of herself to beat back death and cling onto the life she loved, the life which she should have only just been beginning.

Eventually her tense, pain-wracked body relaxed and falling back, her eyes wide with terror, she let out a final voice of protest, barely a whimper. That night there was a great storm. As the rain slashed down against the windowpanes, it was as though the elements had come out in support of my sister's outcry against the unfairness of her life and death.

The night Nell died I lay in bed, willing sleep to find me but instead the image of my sister's tight, white knuckles grasping the crumpled blood-splattered sheets refused to leave me. When things get me down I always remember how desperately she tried to stay with us. As the thunder became a distant growl and sleep beckoned, I knew I would grieve for my sisters for the rest of my life. And yet if that's all I did, that would have been a waste of my life too.

So, I vowed to make the most of each moment remaining to

me, to try to fulfil my dreams where my sisters' had been cruelly snatched from them. It had been devastating not only to lose my dear Violet and Nell but also to witness my parents' grief for their first and second born. Yet, whilst I would always carry my sisters' memory with me, I was determined that it would not be in a maudlin manner. The following few years passed peacefully in our household, the next significant event occurring in 1937, the summer I turned seventeen, the summer I attended my first dance.

A sultry, sticky night, I recall standing before the mirror, admiring my pale-pink gown which fell around my ankles in satin swathes. I noticed Frances momentarily look up from her reading to shoot me one of the disapproving looks I had become immune to. I had long since abandoned attempting to recapture the bond I'd shared with Violet and Nell with her and yet part of me pitied Frances. I knew she'd adored them too and grieved them terribly but she would never let me become the confidante she needed or she mine. She withdrew further and further into her religion, which in recent months had manifested itself as sullenness and criticism of my attempts to get on with my life. So I neither wanted nor asked Frances to accompany me to my first dance. I believed my friend, Margaret, would make a much livelier companion.

It was the first of dozens of dances I attended that summer and the next. My father insisted Mother's skilled dressmaker, Miss Doubleday, hand stitch all my gowns. I realised later that their cost must have been another nail in the coffin as his financial problems spiralled out of control. But I don't believe he was reckless with money, he simply wanted to put some enjoyment back into my young life after everything I had lost.

My friendship with Miss Doubleday blossomed too. The day after each dance, she insisted I go to her shop where she asked me all about my evening, what the dance hall had been like, if people had complimented my dress, who I had spoken to, who I had danced with. As she listened intently, I described how I'd felt like Cinderella, whirling around in the arms of a young man, although rarely the same one. A lot of children in the town made fun of Miss Doubleday which was a shame because she was such a kind-hearted woman. Born without a voice box, she talked through a big, black contraption she wore around her neck which produced a harsh, mechanical sound. She was always interested in hearing every single detail of the dances and after a while I wondered whether she had ever been to a ball herself, realising that probably her only experience was through my second hand recounts. So, I made them as detailed as possible, adamant she wouldn't miss out on a single thing."

16

Engrossed in *Le Figaro*, Ivy spotted Jacques, smart in a black suit and open-necked, white shirt, sitting at the table nearest the fountain. What struck her was his tranquil stillness in contrast with the group of Australian backpackers in the far corner of the courtyard who were clearly in some kind of competition with their American counterparts on the adjacent table as to who could make the most noise. Their accents in particular grated on Ivy, making her realise just how refined Jacques' French-Canadian lilt was. Taking in his dark hair, chiselled features and tanned skin, he was more handsome than she remembered, and she allowed herself a secret smile at the memory of their evening together.

But that had been a few nights ago, and since then he'd definitely made himself scarce, leading her to believe he didn't want a repeat of their date, if indeed that's what it had been. Self consciousness creeping over her, she was grateful for a pillar to sneak around to the continental breakfast buffet. Loading her plate with warm bread rolls and assorted jams, she was making her way to a secluded table when suddenly he looked up from his newspaper. Not merely foiling her chance of escape, it was as though he'd been aware of her presence all along.

"Ivy," his cheerful voice carried across the courtyard, "won't you join me for breakfast?"

Walking towards him, she was pleased she'd decided to wear a pretty peach and cream polka-dotted print dress as the noise level in the place reduced an octave and she felt the eyes of other diners settle on her.

"That came out louder than I intended, sorry. I just wanted to get your attention," he smiled, seemingly aware of her predicament as she pulled in her chair. Thankfully, however, he left it at that as a waiter poured her a coffee and topped up Jacques'.

"I'm sorry I didn't see you yesterday. I'm trying to find somewhere to display my artwork and I had a few appointments to view gallery spaces around the city," he smiled, his words accompanied by hand actions as was the French way. "I was hoping to be back in time for us to dine together but my final meeting overran."

"I understand," she smiled, the regret in his dark eyes and tone of his voice telling her he was speaking the truth. The weight of her doubts falling from her, she realised he hadn't been avoiding her at all. Acknowledging he wasn't on holiday and had business matters to attend to, she vowed silently to stop jumping to the worst possible conclusions all the time. "Did you find anywhere?"

"Nothing within my price range I'm afraid, but I've

lined up a few more places to view today," his brow crinkled as he took a sip of his coffee, "at the moment I rent space at the Galérie de Luc a few streets away. It's owned by some Canadian friends and they only charge me mates' rates."

"That's good of them," Ivy said, smearing a roll with apricot jam. Although a little confused why he'd want to be burdened with the overheads of his own place when he had such a favourable deal with friends, she elected not to broach the subject. Being adventurous and creative as well as a bit of loner, she supposed it was understandable he'd want to branch out on his own.

"Yes, only I'm never quite sure whether they display my work because I'm their friend and they feel sorry for me or whether it actually has artistic merit," he laughed, his hair flopping over his tanned forehead, his eyes animated.

"I'm sure it's the former," Ivy smiled, taking a delicate bite of her roll, "having seen your work on display here."

"Umm… thank you," he sighed, rolling his eyes, "I clearly have my work cut out with you, Ivy, but I suppose honesty goes a long way."

"I mean the latter! That it does have artistic merit!" Realising her mistake, she broke out into a giggle, "actually I was contemplating one of your paintings yesterday – the colours and the movement of the sand and sky, the overwhelming vastness threatening to consume the tiny, dark figure in the foreground," she looked down at her plate, suddenly embarrassed. "I'm sorry, I'm no expert on art. That's probably not what you were trying to convey at all."

"That's exactly what I had in mind, thank you for the compliment, Ivy." His smile this time didn't reach his eyes as she watched the now familiar shadow pass over his face. In a heartbeat, though, it was gone, and when he smiled again it was as if the sun had emerged from behind a cloud. His dark eyes met hers once more, holding them in his gaze, "it means a lot, coming from you."

"I'd love to see the rest of your work sometime," Ivy added, sipping her coffee, "it's at the Galérie de Luc you say, where is that?"

"Or I could show you around tonight, if you wanted?" Seeing her puzzled expression, Jacques continued, "my friends have an apartment adjoined to the gallery. Louise is an excellent cook."

"Louise?" Ivy repeated, her stomach suddenly twisting at the thought she'd read the signals wrongly and that he might actually have a girlfriend, after all.

"Yes, and her husband, Patrick. He is my oldest friend and the best one I'm ever likely to have, for sure," clarified Jacques, downing the rest of his coffee in one gulp, "I'd love for you to meet them. They are both very… " he paused, as though struggling for a word, "dynamic."

"I don't want to put them to any trouble," she hesitated, instantly daunted by the prospect of turning up at the house of strangers, expecting them to cook her dinner. She felt comfortable with Jacques because he made her feel so, but being subjected to the scrutiny of his best friends was something else entirely and she was frightened she wouldn't measure up in some way.

"I'll give them a ring, if it makes you feel better," he assured, reading the anxiety on her face and clearly wanting to alleviate it.

Ivy pretended to become quickly immersed in her guidebook while he scrolled through his contacts on his iPhone. But she didn't manage to read a single word as, with her interest piqued, she couldn't help eavesdropping his conversation. She noticed Jacques spoke in rapid French to his friend, and was slightly taken aback for they had always talked in a mixture of French and English. Pondering it, she realised that he clearly preferred the former, but took care to switch back to English when he wanted to clarify something she didn't quite understand.

"Is it okay if I bring someone to dinner tonight, Lou?" Jacques' voice remained even as he listened to his friend's response. After a prolonged moment, he continued.

"Yes, she's staying at the riad. She's English but she's pretty fluent in French too, you and Patrick will like her a lot, I'm sure," he winked before there was another long pause while Ivy fidgeted with a loose thread on her cuff, unable to imagine what Louise's reply was.

"No, there's no need to go to any trouble. Just do your usual, it will be wonderful, as it always is," he protested and a long pause followed.

"Ok, we'll see you then. Bye Lou," he ended the call. Putting his phone on the table, he looked up at Ivy, his eyes crinkling with a smile, "there, you're an invited guest."

"I don't really think she had much choice," Ivy pointed out, seeing Jacques' eyes were filled with merriment.

"Oh, she's fine with it," he laughed, putting his papers into his file, "she'll be brushing up on her English as we speak to impress you tonight."

Ivy thought he was going to say something more about

his friend but instead he ventured. "What are you doing in the meantime?"

"I thought I might visit the Ali Ben Youssef Medersa," she revealed, disconcerted he wasn't going to provide her with a few more details about his friends, who she wanted to impress for his sake, "it sounds a fascinating place."

"Ah, the Quranic school? I'd definitely recommend it. I don't think the city's palaces can compare with its religious architecture but you may disagree. The local mosques and shrines are closed to non-Muslims but luckily the Medersa isn't," he scanned the website on his phone, "yes, it's open today."

"You've convinced me," she smiled as he stood up to leave.

"I'll meet you here at 7.30 tonight? It's only a short walk from here to their apartment," he concluded, bending to kiss her, "enjoy your trip to the Medersa." Taken aback by the sudden but surprisingly intense feel of his lips on hers Ivy found herself momentarily lost for words.

"Yes. And happy gallery hunting," she called as he turned away, his leather file wedged under his arm.

Watching him recede across the courtyard, Ivy sensed that this second kiss, coupled with Jacques' invitation to dine with his friends had moved them on from casual acquaintances keeping each other company at the riad, to something more. But as she brooded over Jacques' friendly familiarity with Louise, she felt her stomach twist. She had always been uncomfortable under the scrutiny of other women, fearful that she wouldn't measure up in some way. Heading out to the dusty streets later that morning, she wished it was just the two of them dining together before resolving there was nothing she could do except to take the evening as it came.

Hot from the exertion of walking, Ivy took a moment to admire the Ben Youssef Mosque. With its sparkling-green pyramidal roofs, it brought a much-needed splash of colour to the dusty plaza with its predominant shades of cream and ochre. Although the adjacent Medersa where she was headed was admittedly less grand in comparison, Ivy thought its courtyard exquisite, with its mosaic floor tiles in beguiling patterns of sea-green and sky-blue.

In the entrance hall she admired the exquisitely carved cedar cupolas and wooden-latticed screened balconies. As she strolled around, she felt it a shame the school had closed in 1962, eclipsed by another, much larger one in Fez. Visiting a former bedroom, still set out with a sleeping mat, writing implements, a Quran bookstand and hotplate, she preferred to think of the place in the days when 900 students had wandered the rooms and corridors, engrossed in their studies. Running her fingers across the carved bookstand, she couldn't help think how different it was from her spacious modern room at university. Being claustrophobic, she couldn't imagine what it would be like to live here with no windows and just three square metres of space. And yet somehow, in its simplicity, it had fulfilled all the needs of its students.

By the time Ivy arrived back at the riad, her head was pounding due to the heat. Although the pain subsided over a quiet, courtyard lunch of a pita bread filled with various cheeses and salads, she decided not to venture out again as she knew the temperature wouldn't start dropping until sunset and she wanted to be on best form that evening for Jacques and his friends. Instead, she filled nine pages of a brown, leather-bound notebook she'd purchased in the Ensemble Artisanal with details of her trip so far, concentrating on the scents, sights and sounds of the souks and her meetings with Jacques. When she had committed all she could remember to paper she called the waiter to order a pot of mint tea. After the customary pouring ceremony, he withdrew, leaving the remainder of tea for her to deal with though not from such a dizzy height. Although her fuzzy head meant she wasn't in the mood for reading, Ivy extricated Rose's diary from her bag and she found herself tracing her fingertips over the pages, roughened by time. Reaching the inside back cover, her nail suddenly caught on a paper pocket, secured with several strips of Sellotape. Gently, she peeled them back, her heart skipping as a sheaf of old photographs dropped to her knee.

Luckily Rose, or someone else as the writing seemed less embellished than that of the diary, had helpfully penned the names on the backs. All the photos were in black and white, placing them many decades ago. But despite this, the faces were somehow familiar to Ivy and her initial guesses as to their identities, proved correct. By reading her great-aunt's diary, she somehow already knew these long-lost family members and was able to recognise them.

The first was of her great-grandmother, Sarah Jane. In a posed studio shot, beneath an arbour wreathed in flowers, Ivy thought she looked the typical Edwardian girl. Although not dated Ivy guessed it was likely taken round the time of her marriage in 1905. She was dressed in a floor-length, dark skirt and white lace blouse with a decorative white stole around her shoulders. Her dark hair was swept back beneath a hat decorated with flowers while her face wore an expression of self-assured confidence. Ivy was stunned at her great-grandmother's striking physical resemblance to her own mother at that age and, indeed her own graduation photos.

The second photo had a dedication written diagonally across the bottom left hand corner: "With my love from Nell," but even without it, Ivy would have guessed who the young, beautiful girl was. Wearing a low-waisted, white, sailor-style tunic over a dark, knee-length skirt, dark stockings, her flat shoes with low heels and narrow straps across the insteps, Nell's vivacity shone through. She appeared to be stepping forward out of the frame, the photographer capturing her youthful exuberance perfectly. Her light-coloured hair hung loose around her shoulders, framing her lovely face with its straight nose, wide eyes and a kind smile as Ivy thought her even more striking than her great-aunt had described. It was heartbreaking to think of her just a few years later clinging onto the bed sheets, in a vain attempt to beat back death as it claimed her for its own.

The next two photographs featured wedding groups. Ivy instantly recognised the first photo to be of Violet's wedding party in December 1932, so vividly described in the newspaper cutting Rose had kept. Her eyes perused the group, picking out Violet, Nell, and flower girls Rose and finally Frances, a little detached from the others but smiling sweetly. She thought of Violet, who would be dead less than two years later and of Nell, newly engaged, who would never reach her own wedding day. The next photo was familiar to her as her mother had it on display at home. Ivy's grandparents, Albert and Frances, smiled back at her on their wedding day.

In the final photo, the people were further away from the camera and difficult to distinguish, with no writing to identify who they were. There was a prosperous looking man wearing a formal three piece suit, a watch chain strung across the front of the coat, holding the hand of a little girl, who looked no more than five in a frilly, white apron. Ivy realised that it could have been any one of the sisters, probably with their father, *my Great Grandfather*, she thought. Standing proudly in a large shop doorway, Ivy could make out large slabs of meat hanging in the window. She lost track of time, gazing at it as Rose's writings came to life in front of her eyes. Then she flitted from one photo to another, as she got to know the faces of her family that had been lost to her for all these years. Intrigued by the photos, Ivy turned to the page where she had broken off last time and resumed with the next instalment.

"I can't recall the exact date but sometime in the autumn of 1938 my father was declared bankrupt. It was a culmination of circumstances; economic fortunes had been on a downward trend since the Wall Street Crash and for many years he had been giving his customers credit or extra meat to feed their families. The only trouble was, they never recovered to a good enough financial position to pay him back. So he allowed their

debts to slide at a time when he also had to pay the bills for my sisters' expensive but ultimately fruitless medical treatment. The combination caused the business he had spent years building up to crumble to its core but I also think that the deaths of Violet and Nell had hit him much harder than we realised. He literally lost the will to carry on, making him indifferent when he lost his shops and eventually our home. I don't think he regarded those things as important anymore and of course compared to what had befallen us they weren't, but we all still had to live somehow and it was left to my mother to try and pick up the pieces.

Mother found a small terraced house we were able to rent for a reasonable sum taken from the money we had left over from the auction of the contents of our old one. She persuaded my father to take on a job in a local warehouse, an assistant manager in the packaging department, I think. My heart bled as I watched him trudge out every morning and return each evening, exhausted and humiliated, hardly speaking while we sat together, eating our meal. He began to lose weight and became a shadow of himself, his spirit broken. I often wondered why he couldn't be brave and live for the wife and daughters he had left, but he seemed intent on joining Violet and Nell.

While Mother and I tried to help him, Frances, as she always seemed to, removed herself from the situation, preferring the sanctuary of the church and Women's Institute meetings. It was at the autumn fair that year that she introduced me to Albert, a farmer and widower who was twenty-five years her senior. Balding and rather overweight, I couldn't at first see my sister's attraction to him but as the winter chill blew in, Albert began to call around, bringing her thoughtful gifts of eggs, butter and bacon, all the things that were suddenly in short supply in our house. It was then I began to see what a quiet, kindly soul he was and how deeply he cared for Frances. "

17

Getting ready for the dinner party, even though the idea of spending the night under the scrutiny of strangers somewhat unnerved her, Ivy was eager to make a good impression on Jacques' friends. Sensing they would be arty, creative types like him, she opted for a full-skirted, sunflower-yellow dress she'd picked up at an antiques' market a couple of summers ago, which up until now, she'd never found an occasion to wear. Teaming it with a wide emerald-green belt and black patent pumps, she carried through the fifties feel of her outfit to her hair, sweeping it into a French plait, which not only looked elegant but also kept her neck cool.

A new air of confidence sweeping over her, she found Jacques waiting in the courtyard. Dressed in his smart navy suit, his eyes told her he was more affected in the transformation in her appearance than the words he spoke. "Ready to go?" he said quickly, placing his hand in the small of her back, the warmth from his skin causing her to shiver involuntarily.

"Yes," she replied as a smile suddenly lit up his face, making him even more handsome. And the questions as to why he'd want her to meet his best friends at such an early stage in their relationship, gnawed at her once more.

In the warren-like alleyways of the Medina, locals eager to get home jostled against tourists set for a night out. Ivy, however, found herself enjoying the experience, happy Jacques was by her side as they swam against the tide. "You're positive your friends don't mind you bringing me?" she enquired, feeling his warm fingers thread hers as he led her down a particularly dark stretch.

"Not at all, as I said Patrick and Louise are some of the nicest people you will ever set eyes on." Despite the darkness, she could tell by the lilt of his voice that he was smiling, "by the end of the evening you'll feel like you've known them for years."

"How did you meet?" she ventured, her pumps' soles slippery on the smooth stones. Arming herself with a little more information might help put her at ease.

"We were on the same course at art college, twenty-five, no, twenty-six years ago. We took the same classes and encouraged each other in a sort of friendly competitive way. The Berlin Wall had fallen the previous November and the three of us did a collaborative project on its graffiti," his voice was undercut with nostalgia. "We were just kids really, but in those days we thought we could make our mark. We were idealists. The world was changing around us and we wanted to make sure we were going to be part of it. Sounds silly now, I know," he said. Although Ivy found herself making encouraging noises, what he spoke of was beyond her realm of experience. All her life, she'd seemed to have had restrictions on who or what she could be, imposed by other people and, of course, herself.

"Here we are," he announced eventually, stopping to rap his knuckles on a large, oak door. The building beyond was shrouded in darkness but presently sounds of someone stirring inside made Ivy's heart pump faster. Her hot breath caught in her throat as the prospect of meeting two people who were clearly very important to Jacques became imminent. Closing her eyes, she reasoned she was intelligent, lively and, if given a chance, could hold her own in conversations on a number of topics. She was also confident she looked good tonight but nevertheless as the door swung open, she bit her lip apprehensively. Her eyes drawn to the beam of light cutting through the dark street, she heard a male voice speak in the same soft accent as Jacques.

"Come in, Ivy. What a lovely name!" A man well over six feet tall, with a kind face stooped to kiss her on both cheeks before standing aside to motion them in. "Enchanté."

"Thank you for inviting me, Patrick," she said, suddenly sorry she hadn't tried to pick up a bottle of wine as was the etiquette on such occasions.

"It's our pleasure," Patrick said, greeting Jacques with a friendly hug as he entered the hallway after her, "when Jacques mentioned you, I had a hunch you'd be someone special."

Feeling herself blush a violent shade of crimson, she took a moment to study Jacques' friend. With his thick, steely grey hair and laughter lines crinkling around the eyes he appeared to be in his late forties even though Jacques had implied they were the same age. Bespectacled and tall to the point of being bean-pole like, he had a kind, humorous air about him and Ivy immediately sensed why he and Jacques were such good friends.

"Pat's always considered himself the smooth-talker," smiled Jacques, flicking stray strands of hair off his perspiring forehead.

"When I could get a word in," Patrick winked, turning to Ivy, "Lou and I think Jacques would find his perfect profession as a tour guide, getting paid to talk to his heart's content."

"Speaking of Lou, let's go meet her," Jacques smiled, taking Ivy's hand in his. Whether he wanted to present them as a couple or sensed her anxiety, Ivy couldn't tell. Following her host down a narrow passageway, she noticed the encroaching walls were entirely covered with framed paintings, mostly of mountains and the sea but she was particularly drawn to the haunting face of a Berber woman, the only non-pastoral picture. Descending three stone steps, she found herself in a stylish dining-cum-living area with terracotta-washed walls surrounding a large, curved settee covered in colourful throws and filled with soft cushions, the natural colour scheme soothing her slightly. There were yet more paintings of Moroccan scenes adorning the walls while intricately-woven rugs were strewn over the wooden floor, of a much higher quality than those in the souks. Suspended from the ceiling were metal fretwork lanterns, which diffused soft light over well-worn easy chairs. Through an exposed, red-brick archway was a large table. Although big enough to seat at least a dozen people, she noticed only four places had been set at one end. With delicious spiced cooking smells emanating from the room beyond, the relaxed, Bohemian atmosphere put Ivy at ease.

"Can I get you some drinks?" proffered Patrick, as Jacques steered Ivy to the sofa, taking his place next to her.

"Surprise me with your wines," replied Jacques, turning to Ivy, "Patrick makes his own, although I must warn you, they are not for the faint-hearted."

"Maybe a white wine spritzer?" the host turned to her, his head grazing the low ceiling.

"Thank you. That would be lovely," she smiled, watching as his long legs took him to the drinks cabinet on the other side of the room in three easy strides.

Bending close, Jacques whispered, "are you okay?" As she nodded, he came even closer to whisper in her ear, "I should have said before, you look beautiful tonight."

Smiling, his eyes held hers for a long moment until she saw their focus move to something beyond her. As though on cue, Louise appeared promptly from the kitchen and in just a few fluid movements she reached Jacques, who got to his feet, to partake in the customary French welcome of two kisses on each cheek. By his side, Ivy stood speechless, taking in the woman's crimson dress which hugged her slender figure and long legs, her thick hair falling past her shoulders in glossy, brown waves. She seemed to exude elegance from every pore and Ivy felt herself flush at her own perceived inadequacies as this seemingly ethereal beauty greeted Jacques. With a rustle of silk she suddenly turned to face

Ivy who found herself looking into a pair of inquisitive grey eyes.

"Ivy, welcome," she exclaimed, pulling her into a tight, perfume-infused embrace, "I'm so glad you could come." She had the same soft accent as Jacques, and, putting her first perceptions of inferiority aside, Ivy felt herself immediately warm to her. Releasing Louise, she took in her high cheekbones and flawless, unblemished skin and was momentarily seized by a ripple of jealousy that she herself hadn't been blessed in this way.

"I told Ivy what a wonderful cook you are," Jacques smiled but Louise brushed his comment aside with a dismissive flick of the wrist.

"I'm so glad to be here. You have such a lovely home. Thank you for inviting me or being cajoled into it by Jacques," Ivy added as Jacques grinned. Louise joined in, her laughter a breath of fresh air before her expression suddenly turned serious again.

"Jacques has never brought anyone here for a meal before. Patrick and I were beginning to think he never would," Louise commented as the men looked on. "You're from England?"

"Yes I am, not too far from London, actually. It's a small but very old city called Colchester, its origins go back to the Roman times." Retaking their seats, Louise pulled up a footstool to perch on. As nerves made Ivy gabble on about her hometown, she felt a little uncomfortable beneath her gaze, even though there was nothing to suggest it was anything but benevolent.

"Oh, I adore your accent!" Louise suddenly exclaimed,

the lamplight catching her dangling earrings and lip gloss, making them sparkle, "I'd love to be from some place that was so ancient. I grew up in Québec and it has got its old buildings, fine, but nothing older than a few centuries. That's one reason I came to Marrakech. I feel immersed in its history here every time I step onto the streets."

"It certainly is an extraordinary place. I've wanted to come since I was a child," Ivy continued, comfortable on the sofa, with Jacques' elbow gently brushing her side, "I visited the Ben Youssef Medersa this morning and I have never seen such exquisite tiling anywhere."

"I love going there with my sketchbook. In fact one of the patterns there inspired the painting I'm working on at the moment," Louise paused as Patrick set a tray of glasses onto the low table, "perhaps you'd like to see my studio later?"

"I'd love to. Thank you," Ivy smiled, surmising Louise's paintings would be highly skilled.

"I thought you might like to try this local apéritif, Ivy," remarked Patrick with a smile. As Jacques handed her a glass of the amber liquid, she noticed her hands were clammy, and concluded it was because she sensed Louise's glance still cast in her direction. She tried to guess what she was thinking, coming to the conclusion that it was probably something to do with the status of her relationship with Jacques as he'd told her very little during their phone conversation. Unable to imagine whether she approved or not, she turned her attentions back to Jacques. As he did with his coffee at breakfast, she noticed he proceeded to swallow his drink in one and, following his lead, she took a large gulp, as scents of orange blossom dancing on her tongue were followed by the slow burn down her throat.

"Wow!" she remarked, smiling at Patrick, "that certainly packs a punch."

"Doesn't it? But I find it delicate at the same time," he replied, his wide smile revealing a mouth full of white teeth.

"Of course Jacques is the talented painter among us," Louise continued with her conversation, seemingly oblivious that it had moved on from art.

"Yes, I've seen some of his paintings at the riad. They are excellent, I love his use of light and shade," Ivy glanced over to him, his dark eyes intently focused upon her while the ghost of a smile on his lips told he was pleased by her assessment.

The conversation continued to be light and fluid, touching on Ivy's first impressions of Morocco and her hosts' seasoned views on being North African residents. Jacques chipped in now and again, and soon Ivy realised that while she considered him practically a native of the city, Louise and Patrick still thought of him as a tourist, it being, she estimated, 2009 that they had emigrated to *la cité rose*. The dynamic between Jacques and his friends both surprised and intrigued her, so different from the one she shared with him. The spicy cooking aromas gathering potency, Patrick and Louise eventually excused themselves to dish up the meal.

"What do you think?" enquired Jacques, his eyes expectant, clearly wanting her approval as the subdued lighting softened the contours of his face, giving him a vulnerability once more. Seeing he was clearly loved and admired by his friends, she realised too that, each time the conversation had threatened to veer off to a mutually exclusive topic between the three of them, he'd steered it back to a subject in which she could participate.

"I can see why you count them amongst your best friends. They are lovely people. Very engaging," she smiled sincerely, sensing how she responded was important to him.

"That's why I knew you'd like them and vice versa," he replied, a smile reaching his eyes as he paid her the compliment. Ivy noticed that he had been careful not to tell her too much about them, guessing now it was to allow her to get to know them herself and formulate her own opinions and she silently thanked him for it.

"The starters are ready," Louise smiled, having somehow crept up on them. Passing through the low brick archway, Ivy's eyes were drawn to the walls of the dining room beyond, lined as they were with shelves crammed with hundreds of well-thumbed paper and hardback books. It gave her the impression of dining in a library, a notion which appealed to her, reminding her of Rose.

"You've gone to so much trouble. It looks stunning," Ivy removed her gaze from the books to take in the table, laid out impeccably with midnight blue plates and shining silver ware on a deep red damask cloth. White candles guttered in glass holders while the centrepiece was a silver dish which spun around so everyone could easily access the salads displayed on it.

"It only took Lou today and most of yesterday to prepare," interjected Patrick as his wife gave him a playful dig in the ribs.

"Looks like we're in for a treat," smiled Jacques, skirting the table to take the seat opposite Ivy. Having eaten with him in the Jemaa a few nights ago, she felt at ease being in his eye line.

"Thank you, Jacques. It's nice to know somebody appreciates my cooking," Louise rolled her eyes at her husband as he set down the drinks. "Now, we have slow-cooked smoky eggplant, salads and tangy-sweet beets," she explained, taking her seat between Ivy and Jacques, "and this is pastilla."

"Pastilla is a parcel of filo pastry. This one is filled with shredded pigeon cooked with onions and dusted with cinnamon to give it a distinctly Moroccan flavour," Patrick revealed. Ivy thought they looked like little golden pillows, almost too perfect to eat.

"They are delicious," she enthused, biting through the crispy pastry to reach the tangy filling. She glanced at Jacques, feeling overwhelmed by the trouble these two strangers had gone to for her. Their chat about art continued over the starters, with Louise insisting they each try all of them. Ivy's firm favourite was a fresh mint, lime and cucumber salad and she requested the recipe so she might try it at home. When they'd finished, Louise loaded the table with tagines and dishes of steaming herb-infused couscous and saffron rice dotted with ruby-red pomegranates.

"Once a month we find something to celebrate with this meal," commented Jacques. "Moroccans call it a diffa which means feast. It is a way of getting families together: grandparents, parents, sons, daughters and friends. It changes depending on the time of the year with seasonal delicacies served. The desired result is happy taste buds, harmony among humankind and the sleep of the dead," he laughed.

"Yes, and today we are welcoming our new friend, Ivy," Louise, tipped her glass against hers, "and I can definitely vouch for the latter, Patrick's snoring could wake the whole of the Medina after a dinner party," and they all laughed, setting the tone for the rest of the evening, their conversation flowing as heartily as the wine as they enjoyed the succulent meat and fruit tagines.

"Couscous is a staple food across North Africa," Louise explained, "tiny grains of semolina that are cooked by steaming so that they swell and turn light and fluffy."

"I think I like the beef dish best," smiled Ivy, deducing her three companions were serious foodies, "the meat just melts in the mouth."

"That's my favourite too," agreed Patrick, "closely followed by lamb. Lamb with prune and roast almonds, lamb with dates, lamb with pear and artichokes, in fact anything with lamb. Of course, when we stayed in Essaouira last summer we enjoyed lots of fresh fish tagines."

"I hope to visit there while I'm in Morocco," commented Ivy, dabbing her mouth with her serviette. Suddenly feeling Louise's eyes on her, she flicked her side fringe over her cheek in response.

"Maybe we could all go?" Louise chipped in. "It would be such a relief to get away from the never-ending heat of the city, to feel the soothing sea breeze on my face. Oh, it is so agreeably languid there! The town only seems to stir in the late afternoon when the fishing fleet returns. Oh, it would be so wonderful to visit again. Can we?" She looked imploringly at Jacques, the candles' flames reflected in her eyes.

Clearly unhappy at being put on the spot, Jacques busied himself by scooping another spoonful of the pomegranate-jewelled couscous onto his plate, "what do you think, Ivy?" he said quietly, his eyes meeting hers.

"Yes it would be lovely," she responded, after only a flicker of hesitation, which she saw from their expressions, went unnoticed. She realised she was being swept along with Louise's enthusiasm, but felt a sincere hand of friendship was being held out to her and whilst usually distrustful of strangers' motives, for once in her life she decided to "go with the flow." The earth wouldn't tremble beneath her feet, the sky wouldn't fall down over her head, she suspected.

"That's settled then," concluded Louise, "Patrick will drive us there. There's so much to see, the city ramparts, the beach. Oh, to inhale the fresh, sea air again! We'll have a lovely day." She paused for a minute, her brain whirring so quickly it was almost as audible as the ceiling fan circling over their heads. "I've just had a better idea, why don't we make a weekend of it? Stay in the Villa Maroc again? Oh Ivy, a night away would give us much more time to explore. You'll adore it there," she enthused.

As they reminisced about the riad in Essaouira, for the first time in the evening Ivy felt on the outside of the group who had shared so much together. Her heart sank with disappointment as she longed to be part of it once more. Later, as Louise and Patrick cleared away the plates, Jacques turned to Ivy, his expression anxious, "I'm sorry about that, the last thing I wanted Lou to do was bamboozle you into a trip. She can be a little overenthusiastic once she gets an idea into her head."

"Yes, she can be a touch overpowering," Ivy nodded her head, "but, I don't mind. I like her."

"I hoped you would," he broke out into a smile, his hand clutched in hers across the table, "but I don't want you to feel pressurised by her in any way. If you don't want to go on the trip, I'll break it to her gently in the coming days."

Part of her, the overly-cautious part, told her not to get deeply involved with Jacques' friends, that it would be easier to extricate herself from the whole situation when she flew home. But she found her resolve wavering by the friendliness and hospitality they'd shown her, "I think it's a lovely idea."

She watched as relief washed over Jacques' face and some other emotion she couldn't discern. "I'll book it for this weekend then," he smiled, his voice rising to include his friends in the kitchen beyond, "if I can't get us in at Villa Maroc, I'll try for something similar."

"Wonderful!" Louise clapped her hands, rejoining them, "it will be like a holiday. It's funny but since we moved out here, Ivy, we've had fewer holidays than we had in Canada."

"That's because our entire time here is a sort of holiday," Patrick added, stooping to top up their wine glasses. As they discussed details of their proposed trip, Ivy reflected that as she'd had it in mind to visit the pretty, white coastal town to see Morocco from another perspective, she should be pleased to have a trip arranged by people she trusted. Yet, seeing Louise's eyes glitter in the candlelight as she held court, she knew she and the men had been outmanoeuvred by her. Unable to pin down the reason, she realised Louise was a woman used to getting her own way.

"It'll be so much fun, Ivy." Louise leaned forward to take her hand, as Jacques watched, "the souks are a lot quieter there. I'm sure we'll be able to lose our men for an hour or two."

"Yes, I expect we will," Ivy smiled, noticing how she referred to 'our men' and not knowing quite what to make of it. But what she'd told Jacques was true, she did like Louise. Seemingly ridiculous considering her beauty and the confidence she exuded, there was something about her, on another level, with which she identified.

"Was that your artwork in the hallway?" Ivy asked, eager to discover more about her intriguing hostess.

"Yes," replied Louise, topping up her wine glass, "I lost my mojo when I was in Toronto but since we moved here, I've found so much inspiration, I've been painting almost non-stop. It's been so liberating in Marrakech. I've been able to lose myself in its streets and my artwork."

"You've done enough to fill our gallery next door three times over. I have to make sure there's space for our paying artists," Patrick added, his eyes meeting Jacques', "some with mates' rates though."

"Do you paint too?" Ivy asked Patrick, suspecting Jacques hadn't informed them of his decision to go it alone yet and feeling privileged he'd taken her into his confidence.

"Not since art college, unfortunately. One day, a year after we graduated, I had this epiphany that I could never hold a candle to Louise and Jacques no matter how much I honed my technique," he smiled. "But Toronto is a big film-making city so I went back to college and, on finishing my course, I got a job as a set decorator on *Murdoch Mysteries.*"

"I love watching that," exclaimed Ivy, "there's so much humour in it that you just don't get in British detective series."

"The cast and crew get on so well and I think that really shines through on screen," Patrick nodded, "I miss the closeness of it all, feeling part of a community. Now I just flit from film to film over here, working with different people all the time. It's not the same at all."

"You work on Moroccan films now?" enquired Ivy, remembering mention of a vast complex of film studios on the edge of the desert, in her guidebook.

"Yes, in Ouarzazete," Patrick drained his wine glass before topping it up again. Although not big drinkers, he and his wife made Ivy feel virtually tea-total in comparison and, not wanting to embarrass herself in front of Jacques' friends, she decided to spin out her current glass. "Many international film companies work there too. *Lawrence of Arabia, Gladiator* and *Kingdom of Heaven* were all shot there. I've done a few French films and you might have heard of *Game of Thrones?* I did quite a lot of work on that."

"Really? I love *Game of Thrones.* Can you visit the sets?" Ivy asked, seeing Jacques smile at her out of the corner of her eye.

"Yes, many of the sets remain in place after shooting has finished so the studios operate guided tours," smiled Patrick. "As you may imagine, Biblical films are particularly popular as the landscape is similar to that in Israel and Jordan, but they are a whole lot cheaper to film here!"

"We could all take a trip there too while Ivy is here?" Louise suggested excitedly, turning to her, "oh you must see the Tizi'n'Tichka pass which leads through the Atlas Mountains, and maybe Patrick could arrange for us all to have a tour of the studios? How long are you here for, Ivy?"

"Another month." She'd already been there over a week, which had flown by. She feared her five-and-a-half weeks in Morocco, which had seemed like an age when she'd booked them, would in fact pass in the flicker of an eye. The realisation dawning on her, something in Jacques' body language as he shifted in his chair told her he'd had the same thought.

"Maybe we should let Ivy decide before foisting all these trips on her?" Patrick interjected, as Ivy noticed a flash of fury in Louise's eyes, but then just as quickly it was replaced with light from the guttering candle and she wondered whether she'd imagined it.

"We'll let you know," Jacques winked at Patrick, surreptitiously glancing at his watch, "surely it's time for dessert?"

After the heavy tagines, the sweet was mercifully light with tiny, flaky pastries filled with cream and almonds. "They're easy to do. It's just filo pastry covered in nuts and piped with crème anglaise," explained Louise, "you'll see Moroccan pastries in every café you visit. Honey cakes called chabakia are popular with locals. They are deep-fried and dipped in honey and are served a lot during Ramadan to give an instant energy boost, at the end of the day."

Later, when all offers of helping their hosts clear up were

rebuffed, Ivy and Jacques retreated into the lounge with a pot of mint tea.

"I think I've just understood that Moroccans drink such copious amounts of this to aide digestion," smiled Ivy, patting her stomach, "I can't remember the last time I ate so much."

Jacques shifted his weight slightly and the sofa springs threw them together, "I'll put some music on."

"Lady Antebellum, please," shouted Louise from the kitchen. Ivy flinched, glad she hadn't said anything to Jacques she didn't intend to be overheard, for it seemed her hostess had eyes and ears everywhere. The lateness of the hour combined with the soothing effects of the mint tea made Ivy feel sleepy and she lay back, careful to avoid leaning on Jacques despite their close proximity. Eventually, when Louise and Patrick joined them, Ivy noticed a subtle shift in her manner. Her previous lively good humour over dinner had given way to a quieter, more reflective mood causing Ivy to briefly wonder whether she and Patrick had an argument in the kitchen.

"I think we'd better be heading off soon," announced Jacques, either sensing how tired Ivy felt or eager to make a move himself, she couldn't decide on which.

"But you haven't seen my paintings yet," protested Louise, suddenly regaining some of her previous enthusiasm. She put her hand, cold from her chilled wine glass, in Ivy's, pulling her to her feet, "come on."

Ivy and the men followed her dutifully up a spiral of stairs, as Louise scooped up her floor-length skirt to avoid tripping. On the roof Ivy felt the coolness of the night air wash over her skin as Louise threw a switch to light up rows of twinkle lights, hanging like silver stars in the inky sky above, and illuminating her outdoor artist's studio. Beyond them sparkled the lights of the sleeping city, the floodlit Koutoubia Mosque soaring above the tightly-knit buildings of the Kasbah.

"This is your studio? It's incredible," remarked Ivy, noticing Louise's desk, easel and painting palette, while wondering how she could work out here in the sun.

"Yes, I mostly paint at night from my sketches or else memory. Patrick will tell you what a rotten sleeper I am," she grimaced.

Ivy perused the paintings, squinting in the uneven light emitted from the fairy lights to detect the nuances of colour. Some were very dark and shadowy which she assumed had been inspired by the souks but the majority were of white buildings, luminous against the turquoises and azures of the sea and sky. Ivy was no expert on painting but she could see Louise's skill was on a par with Jacques'. But where he tended to use the faces of people and animals as his subject matter, Louise's focus was on glorious landscapes with tiny, indistinct figures in the foreground, when indeed they had people in them at all.

"Are these of Essaouira?" queried Ivy, stepping over to the cluster of seascapes to view them more closely. Louise smiled, her eyes glittering in the moonlight as she spoke.

"Yes, I always feel particularly inspired to paint there. I don't know if it is the colours of the sea which remind me of Lake Ontario or because whenever I see the Atlantic Ocean I imagine they are the same waters that hit Canadian shores thousands of miles north-west," she hesitated, glancing to Jacques, before finding her thoughts again, "but I think these are among my favourite pieces. That's why I have them in my studio so that I can see them every day."

"They are so striking," murmured Ivy, filling the silence vacated rather awkwardly by the two men, who lurked in the darkness behind them. "You are so talented. Painting is something I've always wanted to do but I'm completely useless. I always got F grades in art at school."

"We all have to be good at something," assured Louise, shivering in the midst of the steeply plummeting night temperature, "and bad at other things. My Achilles' heel is any kind of sport." Ivy smiled, grateful for her hostess' attempt to put her at ease.

"Come on, we'd better go down. It's getting quite chilly up here," implored Patrick, enveloping a protective arm around his wife, "and I need to be at work early tomorrow."

The four of them retraced their steps down the spiral stairs, Patrick stopping at the front door, a signal that the evening had run to its end. Ivy stood slightly back while Jacques hugged Louise, thanking her for the sumptuous meal. Whatever he whispered into her ear made her hostess smile as Ivy felt her stomach twist with unexpected jealousy at their closeness formed over many years. But then, an instant later, he'd released her and it was Ivy's turn to make her farewell.

"The meal was delicious, thank you so much. And I'm grateful to you for showing me your studio. I love your work," Ivy commented as Louise gripped her tightly, seemingly unwilling to let the evening, which she had crafted so perfectly, slip from her grasp.

"I've enjoyed every minute of it," she announced with a frozen smile as she released Ivy, the joy she'd embodied earlier having disappeared from her eyes, "and we must arrange that trip to Essaouira. How about on Sunday? Are you free Jacques?"

"I'll be in touch about it," Jacques countered, Ivy noticing his face was flushed with frustration as he ushered her out of the door. Their exit seemed a bit rushed but glancing at her watch, Ivy saw it was after two and realised the men must be fatigued after their working day while all the effort she'd put into the evening to make it a success had surely tired Louise too.

"Looking forward to it. Sleep well tonight," Louise shouted before the heavy, wooden door swung shut on her smile, plunging Ivy and Jacques into near darkness. Resting his arm on her shoulder, Ivy felt the warmth of his skin against her own as they walked back, reaching their destination disappointingly soon. Standing in the riad courtyard facing each other, the warm air thick with the scent of late summer roses, Jacques spoke softly, "thank you for such a beautiful evening."

"I think that was mainly down to Louise. She is the most wonderful cook and a perfect hostess," Ivy responded, sensing the heightened emotions of the moment and instinctively wanting to deflect attention away from herself.

"She is," Jacques moved closer, so close that she could feel his warm breath on her face, "but that isn't what made tonight so wonderful for me."

Her heart thudded as, cupping her chin in his hands, he moved in to caress her tenderly on the lips. Although it only lasted a matter of seconds, it was long enough to taste the promise of his passion. Drawing back, his eyes searched hers, requesting permission to continue. All evening Ivy had been hoping Jacques might kiss her again but now she was caught in the moment with him, she suddenly felt flustered and unprepared for whatever came next. "Good night," she smiled instead, kissing him softly, conscious only of the fountain trickling somewhere in the darkness.

Her room stiflingly stuffy, Ivy found sleep difficult to come by. At first she relived their goodnight frame by frame, basking in the knowledge that Jacques desired her but it was soon subsumed by regret she'd curtailed it. She knew a holiday romance was on offer with him, if she wanted it. Hugging the spare pillow, she realised she did and that it would probably be possible to conceal her birthmark from him for the short amount of time she had left in Marrakech, as she'd done in past relationships. But paradoxically what held her back was that her feelings for Jacques already ran so deep she was unsure whether she'd be able to emerge unscathed from such an affair to fly home in a just a month's time.

Unable to ponder it any longer, she turned her thoughts back to the fine food, sparkling wine and conversation and how she'd felt so at ease in the home of Jacques' friends. But as the hours wore on and sleep still avoided her, Ivy was unable to discard the notion that there was something about her hostess that was a little too perfect to be true.

18

The clear light of late morning was filtering through the blinds when Ivy woke. Despite this, her limbs were lethargic as she lay against the soft pillows, lost in the memory of the previous night. Nobody had ever looked at her the way Jacques had in the courtyard. As she remembered his kiss, her body tingled with the feeling he wanted more. Simultaneously expectant and yet daunted over the prospect of a next time, she turned her thoughts to her vibrant hosts. Patrick and Louise had been exactly the sort of friends she'd expected Jacques to have, with their creative careers and irrepressible sense of adventure. Why then, as she replayed the dinner party, did she feel a sense of uneasiness creep up on her, as chilling as a winter frost? Rising from her bed, she immediately shrugged off the notion, vowing to break her habit of needlessly worrying about everything.

The tiled floor cold beneath her bare, bed-warmed feet,

she was padding over to the bathroom when she noticed a note had been pushed beneath the door.

Ivy,

Had a wonderful time last night, hope you did too. I am going to Ouarzazate Studios with Patrick this morning as he has asked my advice on one of his film set designs. I'll probably be back too late tonight to see you, so don't wait up. But I have a trip planned tomorrow I think you'll enjoy.

Jacques.

Rereading his words, disappointment flooded through her. Ivy chided her foolishness for lingering on their parting just minutes earlier when Jacques had been up for hours, his thoughts having certainly moved on to his work for the day ahead, leaving no space for her to occupy. But he was also planning to meet her tomorrow, she thought optimistically, before the situation became even blurrier in her sleep-soaked brain.

She dressed quickly in an above-the-knee navy sundress and plaited her hair, as it needed washing. While applying her makeup as thickly as ever, it dawned on her that these past few days she'd taken extra care with her appearance to impress Jacques. Knowing he wouldn't be waiting for her in the courtyard, she took Rose's diary down with her to read over her late breakfast.

"The first week of September 1939 was momentous for me for two reasons. On that bright Sunday morning in the parlour, we listened as Neville Chamberlain announced that Britain and her allies were at war with Germany, and on a personal level, on the 6th my father collapsed on his way home, passing away in hospital two days later, officially from a stroke. But I knew he'd died a broken man.

After his funeral we were faced once more with the problem of what to do next. For the past few years, we'd been renting a small cottage on the outskirts of Lavenham, which, despite its poor state of repair, had been all we could afford. It was a good thing Frances and I had found employment before father died, my sister behind the counter of the sweetshop we had once owned and I doing little jobs in the florist, mainly cleaning up, although Mrs Walker did allow me to do simple arrangements. That autumn, we also planted fruit and vegetables in the tiny garden behind the cottage and kept chickens as there would likely be shortages of eggs once the war began to take its toll.

As the clock struck midnight on New Year's Eve 1939, Albert proposed and Frances accepted. The following day, Mother cooked a lovely roast beef dinner, the meat thoughtfully provided by Albert, to celebrate. We chatted for hours and learned more about my soon-to-be brother-in-law. He'd been married before, to his childhood sweetheart, Agnes, in a hastily-arranged ceremony in 1915, just before he'd left for France. There he'd been involved in the thick of the fighting at Ypres, the Somme the following year and then Ypres again. He'd been reunited with Agnes for just a few short months when the war ended before she'd succumbed to Spanish 'Flu. "But Frances has given me a second chance of happiness," he smiled at my sister. And for once in her life I saw her eyes were smiling with happiness too.

On January 31, 1940 Frances and Albert were married in the church where they had sung together for so many years in the choir, and where their quiet courtship had slowly progressed. The snow was falling thick and fast as my sister and I left the house in the bridal car. I walked behind her into church, her dress and veil austere, but still giving her a beauty she didn't normally possess. After a short reception in the village hall with their friends from church, and as the snow continued to softly fall, we waved the happy couple off in one of Albert's carts decorated with white ribbons. Whenever I saw Frances that spring and summer, she was always smiling. In Albert, she'd found an attentive, indulgent husband who cared for her deeply but, although very pleased for her, I couldn't help think that I wanted more than that for myself.

When Frances moved out of the cottage after her wedding, leaving just my mother and I, I had to get a proper job to help support us. Growing up, I'd always harboured dreams of becoming a nurse or Father setting me up in my own little business but they were dreams that would remain unfulfilled now. I was fortunate that the war suddenly offered lots of opportunities for girls like me; even though I soon learnt that I wasn't actually qualified to do anything. Even training to be a nurse, my chosen career, would have taken far too long to have been any real use to the war effort.

Of course I could have joined one of the women's armed forces and I wish I'd been brave enough to follow Churchill's rally to the British people 'to wage war, by sea, land and air, with all our might and all the strength God can give us: to wage war against a monstrous tyranny.' But I'd always been a home bird and Mother needed me more than ever now. So, after a short but intensive secretarial course, I succeeded in securing a job in Colchester Magistrates' Court as a file clerk and minute taker, my shorthand speed being the best in my class by some margin at over 120 words per minute. It was steady work and, at a time when the world had been turned upside down, it felt I was restoring some order to my life.

So, I whiled away those first years of the war sitting in dusty, old courtrooms with even dustier, old judges, taking meticulous notes, secretly horrified at the depths to which people could plummet. There were some serious cases of course, but mostly they were small-time criminals and I'm sorry to say that I soon became insensitive to them. I had always been so in tune to other people's misery but now I deliberately stayed coldly detached as I scribbled in my notebook. I suppose it was trying to deal with my own problems which made me act like that, and I'm glad it passed with time. I've always loved being able to help others and still do but there were changes coming in my life that I was ill-equipped to deal with.

My mother also looked for a job to improve our finances. Being good friends with the postmistress for many years she was offered a part-time position recently vacated by a young woman who saw a future in the Wrens as a better alternative. After being at home raising my sisters and I, it gave her a new, if enforced, lease of life. It afforded her a sense of purpose as people needed her again and it helped her forgot her grief, at least during the daylight hours.

In December 1941, Japanese aircraft attacked Pearl

Harbour and America entered the war. Listening to President Roosevelt describe it as 'a day that will live in infamy' gave me renewed hope that, with America fighting with us, it would all be over very soon. But as 1942 progressed into 1943, with all the rations and restrictions becoming increasingly severe, hopes of a victory still seemed as distant as ever. Luckily, we had no men in our family to be involved in the fighting, and although there were food shortages elsewhere we became largely self-sufficient, growing our own fruit and vegetables and our chickens producing a steady supply of eggs. As far as our lives in Lavenham were concerned, the war touched us quite lightly, except for the arrival of evacuees.

Since the first autumn of the war, children had been appearing in the village as bombs mercilessly fell on London night after night. For the first few weeks, the children were housed in the old school before people took them into their homes. In the spring of 1943, Mother and I looked after a little boy called James until a distant cousin of his father's in North Wales sent for him. Frances was in no state to take in a child though, recovering from the second of several miscarriages that were to blight the early years of her marriage. Frances and Albert so wanted a child, but each time, less than three months into her pregnancy, she would come around, her eyes red-ringed, to say she'd lost her baby. As time passed she lost hope, and whenever I saw Frances and Albert together, she was increasingly short-tempered with him, as though he was to blame for their childless state.

Then, in September 1943, an airfield was set up just over a mile to the north of Lavenham. My interest piqued, I often went for walks that autumn, each time noticing new buildings had sprung up; huge hangars, control towers, regimented rows of barracks to hold hundreds, maybe thousands of men. The runways, according to well-informed gossip, were built from the rubble of buildings destroyed during the London bombing raids. Although I knew it was necessary, all this activity destroyed the peace which had pervaded the town and, with military bases now surrounding Lavenham like the points of a star, every time I went out, I felt fearful for my safety.

I had one close friend during those years; her name was Sophie. A court usher, we barely spoke during work hours, but living on her family farm just down the road from us, we caught the same bus every morning and evening. Over time, we got to know each other; talking about everything from our families, our work, and in her case, her latest boyfriend. In many ways we were like chalk and cheese, she had luscious, dark-brown hair and tanned skin to my fair hair and complexion. But it wasn't just in appearance that we were different. Sophie loved going out socialising – to dances, the cinema and the pub while I spent the evenings with Mother, reading, sewing or playing board games with the wireless playing in the background. But then, one warm Friday evening in May 1944, with the acceptance of an invitation, everything changed."

19

Not fancying struggling through the scrum of the souks, Ivy decided to treat herself to the relaxation of a hammam. Flipping through her guidebook, she considered several options before eventually deciding on the city's most historical one – the Hammam Dar El-Bacha. The only problem was, the 1pm to 9pm opening times for women meant she'd be at a loose end for the morning, something that was quickly remedied as Mustapha came bounding across the courtyard.

"Madame Ivy, Madame Ivy," he cried, a game of snakes and ladders beneath his arm, "you play with me?"

"Yes," she grinned, noticing the delight on the child's face. And so they whiled away the remainder of the morning playing and laughing, with Mustapha eager to learn a few more words of English.

"So in English, 'hello' is 'bonjour' and 'goodbye' is 'au revoir'?" he enquired, mid-way through their seventh game.

"That's right," smiled Ivy, sliding her red counter down a snake's back to the bottom of the board.

"Can you teach me some more? I would love to go to England, one day," he gave her one of his lovely, bright smiles.

"I'm sure you will," replied Ivy, thinking that although it was unlikely, hopefully Mustapha's entrepreneurial spirit would carry him a long way. They continued playing companionably, if a little competitively until Ivy saw her watch nudge past midday.

"I have to go now," she announced, seeing disappointment shadow the little boy's eyes, "we'll play again soon, I promise."

Entering the bustling souk, she realised that due to Mustapha's insistence of playing two extra games and her easy submission, she didn't have time for a lunch stop. Instead, with the Moroccan sun at its hottest at this hour, she made sure the wide brim of her sunhat completely shaded her face as she cut across the Jemaa el Fna, picking up a quick pitta stuffed with spicy chicken which she ate en route to the hammam.

Stepping into the cool oasis of Hammam Dar El-Bacha, her eyes drawn to the rich blue and gold ceiling, Ivy smiled, content she'd made the right choice. Walking through the entrance hall, tiled in the now familiar soothing sea shades of blue and green, she reflected this had been the case throughout her holiday so far. At home, she always seemed to stay with the safest option but in Marrakech, feeling unfettered by people's opinions and giving herself free rein to go with her instincts, she had been rewarded with some memorable experiences.

Her tebbaya, a slight woman in her twenties, was dressed in a smart, dark uniform while a neat, black veil covered her hair and the edges of her pretty face. Smiling, she led Ivy into a small room with pegs and white cabinets wrapped around the walls. Ivy sat on a bench while the woman asked questions about her health and noted her answers in her file. As she went on, Ivy's stomach twisted at the prospect of broaching the subject which had subconsciously held her off visiting a hammam during the first week of her holiday.

"I'm not allergic to any oils but I have a birthmark on my face," she said eventually, her hand instinctively lifting to where it was.

"What kind of birthmark is it?" asked the tebbaya, her expression inscrutable.

"A port-wine stain," Ivy struggled, realising that she'd not actually considered its definition for years, just living with the effect it had on her confidence, instead. "It's caused by abnormally formed blood capillaries in my skin. I've had a bit of eczema there in the past and over the last year or so, I've noticed it darkening and the skin around it thickening slightly. It completely covers the left side of my face."

The tebbaya calmly made some notes, before looking up, "I think I won't use any products in that area then."

When the young woman had left the room, Ivy stripped down to her turquoise swimming costume. Then she delved into the bottom of her bag for her makeup remover. Soaking some on to a piece of cotton wool, she dabbed gently until the layers slowly peeled off to reveal what lay beneath. More self-conscious than if she'd been naked, Ivy gazed in the mirror, unable to remember ever seeing her face so red and inflamed. She hoped it was due to the effects of the Moroccan heat and would calm down when she returned to cooler climes. Pulling the hood of her pink towelling robe as far down over her face as it would go, she walked down the corridor to the room where the tebbaya was waiting. As she passed a woman emerging fresh-faced from her treatment, Ivy realised she'd not revealed her naked face to a stranger for a decade or more. Closing the door to the treatment room behind her, silence bore down on her as she walked slowly across the bare room towards the tebbaya, her breath held. After what seemed an age to Ivy, she looked up from the oils she was preparing. Noticing her eyes drawn to the left side of her face, Ivy inhaled sharply.

"It's a lot smaller than you described," the young woman remarked, with a kind smile.

"What?" replied Ivy, surprised. Having anticipated a whole host of comments the tebbaya could make, that was the very last thing she'd expected.

"Yes," she stepped forward, "the way you described it, I thought it would cover the whole of the side of your face but in fact it starts way below your eye."

"I suppose it does," replied Ivy, tracing the curve of clear skin beneath her eye socket that she no longer saw whenever she looked in the mirror.

Feeling her muscles unknot as the tension drained away, Ivy looked up to the high, blue patterned ceiling, noticing it gave the impression of the sky. "Now, shall we start? If you hand me your robe, lay down and make yourself comfortable?"

The first part of the hammam was the gommage, which

consisted of an exfoliating treatment with a waxy black soap made from natural palm and olive oil and pore-cleansing essential oils. As the tebbaya gently massaged them into Ivy's skin with a kessa, a rough-textured glove, as she'd promised she was careful that none of the products touched her face. As the process went on, Ivy felt herself relax, safe in the woman's capable and caring hands.

"How did you learn to do this?" Ivy asked, after ten or so minutes, already feeling invigorated. Thinking of it in metaphorical terms, she imagined herself shedding who she had been, as the tebbaya removed all the dead skin that had been clogging up her pores for the past years. Now she felt she could breathe again.

"It's a tradition which comes from Berber culture, dating back to the 7th century," the tebbaya paused to scrub Ivy's heels a little harder, "it is a beauty routine developed because of my people's proximity to the Sahara. They needed extreme measures to keep their skin in good condition and they have stuck to the regime for over a millennium. My mother taught me and her mother before that and hers before that. Family traditions are very important in our culture," she added.

"I think that's wonderful," commented Ivy, as she reflected on the close family ties required to make what the woman described possible, "I've just been reading my great-aunt's diary and I don't think I have anything in common with my great-grandmother or my grandmother who died long before I was born. I don't feel any connection with them, in fact I hardly know anything about them at all. It's quite sad really."

"But our generation, we have the freedom to choose

our own way in life, don't we?" the tebbaya shrugged her shoulders. Ivy smiled, pleased with the compliment but estimated she was well over a decade older than this woman.

"Yes, I suppose so," Ivy replied, realising that in spite of everything, she had tried to do that throughout her life, albeit within certain limits.

Having completed the exfoliation, the tebbaya went on to pour jugs of rose water over Ivy's body to wash away all remains of the soap before handing her a fluffy, white towel to dry herself. While she was doing this, the girl indicated Ivy move to a towel-padded table, where she had chosen oils scented with rose and lavender for a relaxing massage.

"I use the healing oils of argan for stressed out skin," the tebbaya explained, pushing deeper and deeper with her rhythmic massage technique.

"I've never used argan oil before. I've seen it for sale at home of course, but it's quite expensive," Ivy commented, feeling her body relax further.

"The argan trees are found only in south western Morocco, and nowhere else in the world." She gently probed the muscles on the back of Ivy's neck and shoulders, "they are similar to olive trees. They bear a fruit from which oil can be extracted by splitting, roasting and pressing the nuts. I used to help my grandfather with the whole process when I was a small girl."

"I'll have to get some before I go home," muttered Ivy, feeling herself drift away on a cloud of sleep as the tebbaya gently but firmly continued massaging in hypnotic, circular motions.

"Wake up, Miss," the tebbaya's gentle voice dragged Ivy

from unrecalled dreams. "You must sit up slowly now, put on your robe and drink this," she set a cup of steaming tea on the small table beside her, "then when you feel ready to go, tell me."

As instructed, Ivy took her time, her head spinning slightly as she slipped her robe over her now-smooth shoulders. Feeling the warmth of the rose petal tea settle on her stomach, after a few minutes she got to her feet. Peering into the mirror, she was taken aback by the smooth, white skin on the unaffected side of her face, which she had never seen look so bright and refreshed. Turning cautiously, she noted that even her birthmark appeared less red than it ever had at home.

"I can't believe how clean and relaxed I feel," Ivy turned to face the tebbaya, who was busy writing something in her file, "what an amazing experience, thank you."

"As I said, they are skills passed down through generations so they are proven to work," she demurred, "I'm glad you're pleased with the results, now I'll leave you to get dressed."

Alone, Ivy carefully examined her face up close in the mirror and there was no denying her birthmark was less inflamed. She also realised that even though it had been on view to a stranger for almost an hour, she hadn't once felt self-conscious. Dressing, she knew it was down to the girl's reassuring nature as a confidence she'd never felt before surged through her reinvigorated body.

20

Emerging from the coolness of the hammam into the lethargic lull of late afternoon, Ivy found the streets deserted. She eventually stumbled over a shop selling argan-based oils, lotions and soaps, perfumed with a variety of flowers and she selected bottles of rose, lavender and jasmine oil, hoping to recapture the soothing effects of the massage she'd just enjoyed when she got home. Smiling to herself as she made her final few steps back to the riad, she imagined the latter's translucent yellow liquid to be the decanted Moroccan sun, which would provide a welcome antidote to the darkness of coming autumn and winter months. Arriving back just after six o'clock, Mustapha greeted her with a welcoming smile. "Hello, Madame Ivy, you had a nice day?"

"Yes, thank you, Mustapha. I had a lovely, relaxing time at the hammam," she smiled, scanning the courtyard forlornly for Jacques. Recalling he'd said he didn't expect to be back from his trip to the film studios until late, it unexpectedly hit her how much she'd missed him and she longed to see him.

"Ah! Very nice. Do you want dinner tonight?" Seeing the little boy smile sweetly at her forced her to regain her composure.

"Yes I will, please," she smiled, taken aback once more by his uncanny knack of reading her thoughts. "Can I have the little table by the fountain at seven?"

"Of course," he nodded, making a note in his big writing in the leather-bound book residing on the desk, "I could join you if you like and we could practise English together?" he ventured, his brown eyes as big as saucers.

"Okay, then," laughed Ivy, admiring the little boy's bare-faced tenacity while grateful that she wouldn't have to dine alone, after all. Back in her room, relaxed and drowsy from her treatment, she kicked off her shoes and fell onto the bed for a short siesta, succumbing to the slower rhythm necessitated by the African heat. Carts clattering on the cobbles below soon lulled her into a deep and satisfying sleep. When she woke, although the room had significantly cooled, a languid drowsiness still held her limbs in its grasp but standing beneath the shower, the cool water running in rivers down her body, soon revived her.

In preparation for her dinner arrangement with Mustapha, she slipped into a full-skirted, red dress adorned with white butterflies which the children in her class had been taken with during the forties dress up day to celebrate the anniversary of V.E. Day back in May. Applying the finishing touch of red lipstick, her vibrant look matched her light-hearted mood, buoyed as she was by the tebbaya's reaction to her birthmark. At its most vivid in the Moroccan heat, the young woman hadn't been shocked or disgusted by it and Ivy began to wonder whether what she saw in the mirror each morning and night was how other people perceived it after all.

Against the calming backdrop of the trickling fountain, Ivy enjoyed the most delicious meal with her charming little companion. To her amusement, the first part of the evening doubled as a competent English lesson on food and drink vocabulary as Mustapha insisted on knowing the words for all the items they ate, but as he began to tire, he slipped back into French.

"I like having you here, Madam Ivy," he smiled as they bade each other goodnight, "you are kind like my mother was."

Noticing his referral to his mother in the past tense but not wanting to prise open a potentially painful memory, she left his comment hanging in the rapidly cooling night air. "A demain, mon petit," she smiled instead, before heading to her room. Having showered earlier, she quickly slipped into her pyjamas and into bed, eager to resume Rose's diary. After skipping over pages filled with ramblings about rationing and blackouts, it suddenly became very interesting.

21

"In late April 1944, the war literally landed on our doorstep, when the 487th Bombardment Group USAAF established a base on the outskirts of Lavenham. Most people seemed pleased when the Americans arrived and we definitely felt safer knowing they would be flying raids over Germany. I began to notice the airmen out and about and they seemed captivated by our pretty town, intent on photographing every half-timbered building and ancient church they set eyes upon. No-one could fail to admire their smart uniforms, which made each and every one of them look like an officer. But in other respects they appeared, in my eyes anyway, to have a more casual approach than our boys. Caps often worn at jaunty angles, hands in pockets, chewing gum, they looked to have stepped straight off a film set. But time would soon alter my initial observations.

I remember my first encounter with them was one balmy Friday evening in early May when Sophie and I were returning home from work, our bus wending its way down the country lanes. To alleviate the stuffiness, I wound down the window, inhaling deep breaths of fresh air, most welcome after the traffic fumes which hung over Colchester like low cloud.

Sophie usually got off a couple of stops before me at the end of the lane leading to her parents' farm, but that evening she suggested we go into Lavenham together to start the weekend with a drink in The Swan. She joked there were always plenty of handsome, American airmen waiting at the bar to smooth talk local girls. At first I refused as I had never set foot into a pub in my life or spoken to men outside of my parents' presence and I knew my mother would certainly not approve. I'd had a sheltered upbringing, you see, in part due to my parents' need to cocoon me after the tragedies which had befallen Violet and Nell.

Sophie, looking crestfallen, then explained the real reason for her suggestion: apparently on an errand into Lavenham the previous Saturday she had struck up a conversation with three young Americans in the grocer's shop. One in particular, handsome and dark-haired Luigi, had caught her eye. She had arranged to meet him this evening in The Swan, but as her parents were in their sixties and set in their ways, she had told them that she was coming for tea to my house. Sophie then admitted her tales of boyfriends were not exactly true, something I had long suspected, and that even though she liked Luigi she was nervous about seeing him again and she begged me to accompany her.

I have often wondered how things might have turned out if I'd refused my friend's request and turned for home but as my skin wrinkles with age, I've come to realise it was at this moment *my life set on the course it was destined to follow. As I see my twenty-three year-old self standing in the dark street, Sophie's perfume hanging heavily in the air, knowing all the happiness and heartache that followed, I would have no hesitation in linking my friend's arm once more to head through the oak doors of The Swan.*

With an air of nonchalance we didn't feel, we entered the pub and, despite it being crowded with airmen, Sophie immediately spotted Luigi, who waved us over. Despite her earlier nervousness, they were soon chatting animatedly. From an Italian immigrant family living in Chicago, he looked pleasant enough but I have to admit, I found him rather loud and over-confident. Feeling like a gooseberry, I furtively glanced around as the bar began to fill up with girls I had never spotted in the village before. Wearing bright lipstick and nylon stockings, they chatted and flirted with the off-duty servicemen and I suddenly felt shabby and down at heel in my grey cardigan and navy skirt, while smells of sweat, beer and perfume mingled unpleasantly in the enclosed space. Reluctant to leave Sophie on her own I indicated for her to follow me to the toilet, where I told her we ought to be going, for apart from anything else, I was tired and hungry after the long day at work. Unable to persuade her to leave, I got her to promise she would return home soon, before her parents noticed it was getting late.

Feeling light-headed, I fought through the crush of bodies to the door. In the warmth of the late spring evening, groups of girls and airmen had spilled out onto the street, their behaviour of a more intimate nature than I'd been privy to inside. Flustered, my memory of what happened next is blurry. I recall one of the flyers who, a little worse for wear with drink, began shouting in my direction in a harsh, resonating voice.

It was then I heard a gentle drawl, exhorting my unwanted admirer to leave me alone. I watched as the owner of the voice emerged from the shadows, gauging him to be about my age, maybe a little younger. In his uniform, he too was tall like the others but not as thickly set as his broad shoulders and chest tapered down to a slim waist. His hair was in the same short style as the others but whereas theirs was dark, his was the colour of ripening wheat. As he stepped towards me, I saw his face was finely-featured, his eyes the blue of the ocean he had crossed to get over here. I felt my heartbeat quicken but just as he was about to reach me, another inebriated flyer waylaid him, grabbing his arm and speaking in a rapid way I couldn't understand. While he was distracted, I took the opportunity to beat my retreat, consoling myself with the notion that my rescuer was probably just as brash as the others. But later that night, listening to the nightingale sing softly outside my window, I found I could not drift off to sleep for thinking about him.

I saw the airman again the following Wednesday. I was on my way home from work, carrying some provisions I'd picked up from Sophie's farm. I struggled down the lane running parallel to the airfield balancing my bags of potatoes, carrots and leeks which I thought would make a nice stew. Suddenly I heard the heavy tread of footsteps behind me, and a little alarmed, I turned to see the airman with wheat-coloured hair catching me up. For some reason, all these years later, I remember almost word-for-word that very brief, first conversation.

"You're the girl from The Swan!" he exclaimed, slightly breathless in that soft accent of his. He looked at me intently

178

with his deep blue eyes, causing me to forget the weight of the vegetables.

"I don't think I introduced myself the other night," he removed his cap, his long legs awkwardly falling into my walking rhythm, "I'm Ryan."

"Rose," I said, unaccustomed to the intense scrutiny I was receiving from this complete stranger.

"An English Rose," he exclaimed, smiling as I contemplated what exactly his idea of an English rose was.

"I'm sorry," I said, the handles of my bags cutting painfully into my arm, "but I must get home," and I continued on my way, heeding Mother's warning about associating with these young men.

"I'll see you in The Swan on Friday evening!" he shouted as I felt his eyes follow me down the lane. I just about managed to fight the urge to look back."

22

Ivy stared blankly at the swirling sands of the Sahara, oblivious to both them and the growing numbness in her knees beneath the weight of the glossy travel book. Alerted by footsteps, she looked up, nodding courteously as the group of young backpackers from New Zealand walked across the courtyard. Unable to concentrate she closed the book and leaning back, pondered the developments in her great-aunt's diary. It was clear to her that Rose's second encounter with Ryan had obviously had some special significance else why would she bother to recount it almost fifty years later? Remembering her own instant attraction to Jacques, she wondered if something similar had happened to Rose. But clearly nothing had come of it or she was sure she would have heard something, either from her mother or from Rose herself? With a warming sip of mint tea, she nipped such thoughts in the bud and, re-opening the travel book, managed to lose herself in the pictures of golden desert which seemingly stretched for miles and miles.

"Ivy, I was hoping to find you here," Jacques' cheerful voice pulled her from her musings. Looking up, she saw he was dressed smartly in black jeans and a light-green polo shirt. His bright smile melting her insides, she was relieved that despite having no arrangement to see him, she'd put on a flattering full-skirted dress in a pale shade of olive green and blow-dried her hair prettily around her face.

"Jacques." Easing the book off her knee onto the table, she averted her eyes so he wouldn't notice the confused emotions pulsing through her. Sitting down beside her on the sofa in the library, to her surprise, he took her face in his hands and kissed her gently. When he finally pulled back, she felt instantly calmed by his loving expression.

"I'm sorry I didn't see you yesterday. Pat wanted me to take a look at some work he is doing for an action movie; it was all quite sudden and it took longer than I wanted. It was gone midnight when we got back," he apologised, his leg warm against hers; both comforting and disturbing at the same time.

"You don't have to explain it to me, Jacques. I wasn't expecting to meet you," she said, seeing something akin to sadness cloud his expression, "I mean I hoped I might, but I know you have work to do."

"Not today I don't," his tone brightened, as he stared intently at her, "do you want to go somewhere together?"

As she nodded, a wide smile transformed his face once more and her heart pumped faster with the realisation that she could have such an effect upon him. "Yes, I'd love to," she replied, picturing all the places she still had to explore in this enchanting city.

"How about we go see the Jardin Majorelle?" he proposed. Agreeing to his suggestion with a smile, she felt flattered he'd want to take her to such a romantic spot. As his dark eyes held hers, she noticed how the sunlight streaming through the skylight picked out olive-green flecks in them. Clasping her hand, he continued, "the garden is Majorelle's masterpiece. In the 1980s, Yves St Laurent fell in love with it, rescuing it from certain ruin. For me, it is the most beautiful place in Marrakech, an inspiration for any artist."

Something in the timbre of his voice told her then that he hadn't picked the place by chance. He clearly wanted to take her there, to share its beauty with her, a notion which caused her to shiver imperceptibly. Pleased she'd chosen to wear a pretty dress that both flattered her petite figure and was appropriate for walking around elegant gardens created by the legendary French fashion designer, Ivy excused herself, lingering in her room just long enough to collect her sunglasses and an emergency tube of camouflage makeup. The latter she secreted in a zipped compartment at the back of her handbag in the eventuality that the effects of the ferocious heat may require a touch up. Clutching her broad-brimmed straw hat, her heart was light with excitement as she clattered down the spiral steps, to where Jacques waited.

Strolling through the Medina, hand-in-hand, they enjoyed a companionable conversation about their exploits of the previous day. Never having taken the time to relax in a hammam, Jacques hung on her every word, interested in the different stages of the process while Ivy was intrigued to learn about the fusion of art and technology in film making. Around them people shouted and haggled, but engrossed in their conversation, Ivy barely noticed them, content to be caught in a bubble with Jacques.

"I find Jacques Majorelle's description of his garden particularly poignant," said Jacques. "Vast splendours whose harmony I have orchestrated. This garden is a momentous task to which I give myself entirely, it will take my last years from me and I will fall, exhausted, under its branches, having given it all of my love."

"I suppose the discipline is similar to painting, isn't it?" Ivy continued as Jacques remained silent, "creating something of great beauty from light and colour."

"You're sure you're not an artist?" Jacques said, an inscrutable expression passing over his face as he steered her down the wide, busy thoroughfare of the Rahba Kedima.

"Most definitely not. The children in my class can testify to my stick men drawings on the whiteboard. The majority of them draw better than me," Ivy laughed, suddenly wanting to know what it was about the garden they were headed that moved him so. "Jacques Majorelle inspires you?"

"Yes. His father was Louis Majorelle, the celebrated Art Nouveau furniture maker," he explained, his soft Canadian tones more pronounced as his English became more practised. "Born in Nancy, France in 1886, Jacques honed his painting skills at the Academie Julian in Paris. He travelled to Marrakech in 1919 to recover from the heart problems which plagued him and to pursue his career as a painter. What is it?" he asked, noticing Ivy's focus drifting.

"I'm sorry I don't mean to be rude, but when you said

1919," she said, passing a butcher's shop where slabs of meat hung in the window, putting her in mind of the photo of her great-grandfather standing proudly outside his shop, "well, these past few weeks I've been reading my great-aunt's diary. She was born in 1920 and, as I told you, was in my life up until a few months ago. I always thought the First World War so long ago, something I studied in History GCSE twenty years ago when, in fact, it still seems within touching distance," she paused.

He smiled, giving her that strange, admiring look of his as they sidestepped a thin, red river of blood from the animal carcasses, finding its way in the cracks in between the paving stones.

"Anyway, you were telling me about Jacques Majorelle's story, which sounds fascinating," she linked his arm.

"Do you really mean that?" Jacques lifted his eyebrow.

"Yes, really," she affirmed, as he pulled her gently back as a cart rattled past, having just delivered its load at a shop.

"A few years after his arrival in Morocco, he acquired some land around his painting studio to landscape a garden. It opened to the public in 1947 and became famed as one of the world's most mysterious gardens. His trademark style complements rare flora with vivid touches of colour," he paused.

"The lush green cacti and pale-green reflecting pools contrasted with terracotta pathways, the cobalt-blue walls of the studio?" she enquired as they continued, "and the sunshine-yellow plant pots?"

"You just forgot the fuchsia bougainvillea but other

than that, you could set yourself up as a rival tour guide," he grinned, his eyes widening with surprise.

"Er no, I just got it straight out of a guidebook and happen to have a good memory," she giggled. At that moment, in the quiet, back alleyway, darkened by the closed-up buildings and high, pink walls, they came across a group of small children, squealing with excitement as they kicked a football in clouds of dust. "Is this a shortcut?" she enquired.

Jacques laughed, "No, we're here," he announced, taking in her confused expression, "and even people who think they're immune to natural beauty have told me that the contrast on the other side of this wall takes their breath away."

"Yes," replied Ivy, remembering her feelings whenever she stepped into the riad's quiet courtyard away from the mayhem of the souks, "the one heightens the experience of the other."

"Exactly," agreed Jacques. As he gently pushed the blue door open, Ivy felt a surge of happiness with the realisation that her feelings were in total harmony with this man next to her. Following brick-red paths, over-spilled by plants collected from the four corners of the earth, Ivy was entranced by the strange-shaped cacti and soft fall of coconut palms and weeping willows, by white water lilies floating on shining pools and bright bougainvilleas and ferns clustering around the bright blue pavilion at the garden's heart.

They continued on past murmuring fountains and burbling streams, the delicate sound of trickling water accompanied by birdsong. For Ivy, the simplicity of nature and the complexity of art unexpectedly collided here in a way she had never experienced before or even thought possible. She certainly understood why Jacques seemed so at home here.

"Depending on the time of day you can hear the song of many different birds. At this stage of the summer before dusk falls, there will be blackbirds, house sparrows, robins, blue tits, grey tits, warblers and turtle doves. But if you come in the evening you will hear oriental nightingales and collared doves," he stopped for a moment and, as if on cue, the sweet song of a blackbird resonated in the air.

"I've been here many times in the evening to hear scores of croaking frogs too," he continued, his expression bright, "it's quite a musical chorus."

"I'll have to come back one evening," she smiled, deliberately using the first person singular. Immersed as she was in Rose and Ryan's romance, she took care not to attribute such feelings to her and Jacques. They were just two travellers enjoying an afternoon in Marrakech's ornamental gardens.

"Yes, we will," he countered, smiling at her.

Continuing on, the bamboo forest gave way to peaceful pools, where lotus flowers and water lilies floated on mirror-like surfaces while Ivy watched baby turtles dive into the murky waters below. The striking pavilion with its mixture of Moorish charm and Art Deco design, stretched up in more exaggerated shades of yellow and blue than the sun and sky above. Hidden down a side path they soon discovered the memorial to Yves Saint-Laurent, a discreet, grey stone obelisk standing about seven feet tall and they paused at the bench before it.

"What a beautiful way to remember someone," Ivy whispered, as sunlight filtering through the trees, played on the stone, "I didn't know he had such a strong connection to Marrakech."

"He loved it and made it his home," he turned to her, his eyes holding hers. Shaded by the foliage from tourists' prying eyes, Jacques lowered his head until his lips lightly brushed her own. Then, putting one hand on her back, he drew her closer whilst his fingers tangled in her hair as his kisses became more urgent. But even as Ivy felt her desire reciprocated, she sensed some other emotion in him: a loneliness and longing which mirrored her own. As two small children came running down the path, they reluctantly drew apart. Looking at one another, they spoke no words but were aware they had stepped over a threshold from which they would be unable to return. Slipping his arms round her waist, Jacques silently led her to the blue pavilion, its dove-grey balustrade exquisitely carved to give the impression of intricate lace. "I love the idea that he placed the artist's studio in the centre of the garden he created," Jacques smiled, "and it's now a small museum devoted to Berber art."

They lost track of time exploring its cool interior, admiring Majorelle's lithographs which depicted the kasbahs of the Atlas Mountains, used as posters to entice early 20th century travellers. "I didn't realise Morocco had been a tourist destination for Europeans for well over a century," Ivy commented.

"Oh yes," Jacques nodded, "especially for the French of course, but also the British. For them, it was the best of both worlds here – exotic Africa but also not too far from Gibraltar."

On the upper floor, Jacques became engrossed in the display of objects from the Rif Mountains, in the beaded jewellery and the intricate craftsmanship of the leather goods, basketwork and woven textiles, seemingly forgetting Ivy was with him. Guessing he was searching for inspiration for his own work in the diversity of the vibrant Berber culture, she found herself wondering what this man could offer her when such a substantial part of him seemed lost at all times to his art. Squinting as they emerged into the sun some time later, Jacques stood patiently while Ivy photographed the blue Art Deco building. Beckoning Jacques into shot, she clicked away, wanting to capture his smile and how he looked the day she acknowledged her feelings towards him.

"Voulez-vous un photo ensemble?" asked a Frenchman, with a small goatee beard, who looked to be in his mid twenties.

"Oui, merci," said Ivy, handing him her camera, explaining which button to press.

Standing in position with Majorelle's blue masterpiece towering behind them, she felt Jacques' hand rest lightly on her hip. She imagined, as the young man clicked the photograph, that he must assume they were a couple. And for the first time, the thought that they could be, crossed her mind. Smiling at the camera, she tried to commit the sensations of the moment in time to memory so that, whenever she perused the photo in future, she would be able to relive them.

"Pouvez-vous prendre un autre pour moi, s'il vous plait?" Jacques asked, leaping forward to press his phone into the man's hand. And then he was back at her side, drawing her ever closer to him. As the man snapped an almost identical image, Ivy's instinct, as always, turned the afflicted side of her face away from the camera.

"There is a lovely courtyard café here, if you fancy some lunch," suggested Jacques. Ivy smiled in agreement as they followed another sun-dappled path which wound its way around the back of the lily pond to a clutch of modern buildings to the side of the garden. On their way, they ducked in Galérie Love, housing all the 'love' posters, which were in fact collages Yves Saint-Laurent had designed annually for his family and friends.

"I can certainly see why people appreciate these," whispered Jacques, out of earshot of a loud-speaking middle-aged British couple, "but if I'm honest, I don't really like them."

"I know what you mean," Ivy replied, pleased when the couple retreated back into the afternoon heat, leaving them alone, "they are not really my cup of tea either."

"What is this obsession Brits have with tea?" Jacques laughed, taking hold of both of her hands, before pulling her towards him once more.

"Let me see," she smiled, inhaling his musky aftershave, "probably because we're the only nation who knows how to make it properly."

"Oh, I think you'll find the Canadians could give you a run for your money," he said, a smile playing on his lips.

"Is that a challenge?" she narrowed her eyes.

"If you want it to be," he playfully kissed her, "or maybe I'll just have to visit England sometime soon and see how it's done by the experts."

Unsure whether he was joking or not, she left his comment hanging in the humid air as they made their way to the cafe. The Café Bousafsaf, named after Jacques Majorelle's original house, was in a shaded corner of the garden. Finding a secluded table in a back corner, they ordered a carafe of iced water, a chicken tajine and a Majorelle salad to share. There, they chatted and laughed, revelling in each other's company, with nothing else they would rather do. Losing all track of time once more, it was 5pm by the time they paid the bill. They found the food shops of the Kasbah were teaming with people on the hunt for fresh ingredients for their evening meals as they made their way back to the riad.

"I want to take you to one more place. It's just around the corner," Jacques looked down at her thoughtfully as they passed a herbalist shop.

"Where?" Intrigued, she arched her eyebrows as they dodged a family weighed down with parcels.

"You'll see!" His mouth tweaked into a smile. As Jacques led her through the streets, Ivy noticed the air had cooled by a few degrees since they'd been in the garden. The side street he took her down had a more residential feel to it with houses nestling behind locked gates and, foraging in his pocket for a rusty looking key, Jacques stopped in front of a three-story building, its pink stone crumbling with age.

"This is the Galérie Rose, Mind your step," he cautioned, taking her hand and leading her up a dim staircase, which creaked in protest with seemingly each footstep. Peeking around the corner, Ivy saw a large chamber with sepia close-ups of Berber people displayed on an exposed brick-and-concrete wall. "Its exhibitions vary from straightforward travel photography to more interpretive works like this one. They are mostly by Mediterranean artists with local themes," he explained.

At the summit of yet another flight of stairs, he unlocked a further door, swinging it back to reveal a large, light and airy room. Ivy walked around it, her footsteps resounding on the terracotta tiled floor, before she paused at the window, drinking in the view of the city, a pink kingdom turned vibrant red by the rays of the sinking sun.

"Louise and Patrick have been kind enough to let me store my paintings at their gallery for the past year or so, but as you know, I want my own space," he paused, walking over to the large windows which covered one wall, to where Ivy stood. "And this came on the market a few days ago. I could put on my own exhibitions here in conjunction with the main gallery downstairs and there is even a small space where I could work and live," he opened a door revealing a kitchen-cum-living room with the same city view, adjacent to a bedroom and bathroom. "What do you think?" His eyes were wide with expectation.

"I think it's wonderful," smiled Ivy, touched her opinion mattered to him, "there's plenty of light and you can even see the green of the Majorelle Gardens from this window."

"Just about," he grinned, standing so close she felt his breath brush her hair, "I think it's the best studio space I've seen in Marrakech."

At that point, his phone buzzed with a text. "Oh, it's

Louise again," he said, with a slight frown. "She wants to know if you want to come to Essaouira with us next Friday?"

"I'd love to," Ivy smiled, thinking it would be a chance to see the coastal resort and spend more time with Jacques. Even though Louise could admittedly be over-controlling, Ivy's liking for her overrode any misgivings she had.

While Jacques texted his friend back, her great-aunt's volition to seize the moment, echoed in Ivy's mind and as Jacques replaced his mobile in his shirt pocket, she said, "I think you should go for this place, Jacques. I could just see you working here. It seems perfect for a studio."

"I will. I've kept putting it off and I don't know why. Thank you," he declared, looking at her intently, his thoughts unreadable to her once more, "I've enjoyed today more than any I can remember in a long time."

"Me too," she took his hand as, surrounded by silence and stillness, they watched the red ball of the sun sink below the horizon. Later as they enjoyed a candlelit dinner at a neighbouring roof restaurant, Jacques excitedly outlined his studio plans, the flood-lit city around them keeping the darkness of night at bay.

23

Later that evening, Jacques' goodnight kiss fresh on her lips, Ivy forged ahead with Rose's diary by the window in her room, the cool night air fluttering the pages every now and again.

"Over the next few days, whenever I had a moment to myself, I found Ryan crept into my consciousness. He was nothing like the over-sexed, over-paid Americans my mother had warned me about but even so, I concluded, it wouldn't please her that he was occupying my every waking thought. But the more I pushed him away, the more stubborn he became in refusing to budge from my mind. Knowing it was unacceptable to go to The Swan alone but wanting to see Ryan again, I persuaded Sophie to let me go with her the following Friday. She agreed on condition I gave Luigi and her time together, which I did gladly for I could see she was smitten by him too. I put on my best blue dress, which had belonged to Nell, and lying to my

mother that I was going to the cinema with Sophie, I set off for *The Swan*, excitement welling inside me at the prospect of seeing Ryan again.

The bar was again filled with smoke and airmen drinking, laughing and flirting with the girls like the last time. Sophie immediately spotted Luigi and retreated to the snug, leaving me in a quiet corner, to scan the sea of faces to no avail. Whenever an airman approached, I checked my watch, to give the impression I was waiting for someone and wished to be left alone. As the clock struck nine, I scrambled for my bag which had fallen between my feet, stopping to tell Sophie I had a headache and was going home before pushing my way through the raucous crowd of off-duty American flyers.

"Rose!" I looked up to see Ryan, weaving his way towards me. I took in his pristine flying uniform, his blonde hair slicked into a quiff, his strong, angular jaw, ocean-blue eyes and that quietly confident air which I found so attractive. I felt my heart flutter in my chest but before he reached me, he was intercepted by another airman. I overheard the young man asking Ryan if he wanted to join them on a night out at the Athenaeum in Bury St Edmunds for a change. Ryan took the final step towards me and asked if I wanted to go with them, his eyes imploring me to accept. I trembled with anticipation as I considered the prospect of being held in his arms as we glided around the dance floor. I knew that he would keep me safe but I also realised that my mother would be expecting me home before too long so I reluctantly refused. As Ryan's eyes turned from me to the soldier and then back to me, I could see him mentally debating what to do next. I told him that Friday night at the Athenaeum would be far more exciting than in Lavenham and wished him a good time, trying to stop pictures of the pretty girls he would meet from racing through my mind.

Disappointment welled in me as I watched Ryan's tall, slender frame disappear into the warm night. I retreated to my corner and for five, uncomfortable minutes observed other couples until the realisation sank in that I would never see him again. When I could bear it no more, I pushed my way through to the door, bouncing off the sturdy frame of an airman on the other side. Sent off balance I found myself hurtling towards the ground when, out of nowhere, I felt a pair of strong hands grab me, pulling me up.

"Thank you," I raised my eyes to my rescuer, only to see Ryan's handsome face smiling down at me, "but I thought you'd gone."

"Decided not to. How about you show an American boy the delights of Suffolk?" his speech slow and steady, he flashed that white smile of his. Taking hold of my hand, he said he'd waited at The Swan for me every evening and wanted to get to know me. For a girl of my upbringing, going to a pub with a girlfriend was risky enough but walking down dark, country lanes at this time of night with a man I barely knew, particularly an American serviceman, was unthinkable. But there was just something in Ryan's demeanour which allayed my fears and I somehow knew with certainty that I would be safe with him.

He fell into step with me as we took a stroll, the fragrance of honeysuckle drifting towards us on the warm evening air. Even now, after all this time, its perfume takes me back to that moment, back to him. Commenting on its sweet smell, Ryan said the climate where he lived in the southern U.S. was too hot for a plant like that to survive. As we talked, he seemed captivated with Lavenham's timber-framed houses and pretty gardens, saying his folks thought he exaggerated their quaintness in his letters home. The 16th century guildhall particularly impressing him, I explained how the town had become rich on the medieval wool trade when merchants invested their fortunes in properties and he was incredulous that many of the buildings were over three hundred years old.

When I told him about the 500kg bomb dropped on Bolton Street by a Heinkel in November 1940, which had fortunately failed to explode, he recalled seeing newsreel of Coventry, its medieval streets reduced to rubble. Wanting to fight back, he'd joined the military and, attracted by their motto, 'Fly and fight with the greatest team in the world,' he'd chosen the Air Corps. After primary and basic navigation training in Virginia, he'd completed his transition training at Nashville, Tennessee followed by B-24 training in Savannah, Georgia where his current crew had come together for the first time. From the far flung corners of the U.S. with their different backgrounds and dialects, he said they'd quickly formed deep friendships. On their arrival in Lavenham, they'd converted to B-17s, something he was glad of as he explained it was an easier aircraft to handle, particular during inclement weather. As we talked, Ryan's youthful enthusiasm touched me deeply as after nearly five years of war, our villages were depleted of men my age and the ones left were worn down, old before their time. Ryan, in comparison, seemed so full of confidence, doing his job and his duty, convinced he'd return safely from each and every mission.

Although touching on difficult topics, I was grateful for this chatter, a welcome diversion as stirrings of desire rose in me.

Eventually though, our conversation petered out, and sensing his eyes upon me, I was powerless to prevent a blush engulfing my cheeks. As I raised my eyes to meet his, he shyly looked away.

Surprised by his reaction, it suddenly dawned on me: he was experiencing the same feelings as I and was unaccustomed to them too. As I led Ryan through the cornfields, the moonlight bathing us in its silver light, it felt as though we'd stepped into a magical kingdom, which countered the regret I was feeling for unwittingly choosing a shortcut. I watched him climb the stile in elegant strides before he took hold of my arm. My body tingled once again as the heat from his hand seeped through the flimsy sleeve of my summer dress.

With the corn scratching at our legs and the trees touched with the light of the rising moon, Ryan commented how the landscape reminded him of his home in Virginia although it was much greener. Closing his eyes, I sensed he was imagining himself back there far away from the war. It somehow fitted that he was a country boy, confounding my expectations that all American servicemen lived in sophisticated cities crammed with buildings reaching for the sky, the neon-lit streets far below teaming with automobiles and streetcars.

He went on to tell me all about his family back home, how his grandfather had emigrated from Ireland at the end of the last century and his family had farmed in Virginia ever since. Ryan was expected to take over one day, but for the moment he was studying at Richmond University where he was halfway through his engineering degree which he hoped to complete when his work here was done. He pulled out a crumpled photograph from his pocket, a wistful smile playing on his lips as he handed it shyly to me. In the background was a solidly built farmhouse with a white veranda wrapped around it in the style of Tara in *Gone with the Wind* but not nearly as grand.

In the foreground stood a middle aged couple I took for his parents, smiling good humouredly into the camera. As I handed it back to him, Ryan studied it for a moment. Lost in memory, he only noticed a cowpat at the last second and as he lurched forward to avoid it, I felt his leg brush against mine. "Sorry," he murmured, stepping back, our eyes meeting and holding until the moment dissolved on the cooling, evening air.

As we approached the second stile I put my hand in his once more. Feeling his fingers entwined with mine, I trembled, which he couldn't have failed to notice. He kept my hand until our walk brought us to within sight of my mother's cottage where I knew we must part. As reluctant as I to do so, Ryan extracted a cigarette from his top pocket before asking if he could see me again. And so we made plans to meet at the church's lychgate at six o'clock the following evening, but as he stubbed out his half-smoked cigarette beneath his boot, he still made no attempt to leave. Instead, his eyes locking with mine, he bent his head to kiss me gently on the lips as thunder rumbled over the distant wheat fields.

I walked the last few hundred yards on my own, worried that my mother might be watching out for me, my mind filled with conflicting emotions. Although my head warned me of the foolhardiness of falling for a man whose life was in constant danger or at the very least would soon have to return across an entire ocean to his homeland, I'd already felt my heart connect with his. And I knew that if my feelings were reciprocated by him, I would be powerless to resist."

24

Ivy looked up to find Jacques heading across the breakfast room. Taking in his hair darkened by gel, his crisp, white shirt, narrow burgundy tie and navy suit, she felt her stomach somersault. However, noticing his briefcase, her desire was quickly quelled. Having business to attend to meant he wouldn't be spending the day with her.

"Sleep well?" he bent down to give her a lingering kiss, his fingers mercifully stroking her unafflicted cheek.

"Very, although I didn't fall asleep for a long time. Reading Rose's diary with all its revelations is definitely not conducive to dozing off as soon as your head hits the pillow," she smiled as he dipped a pain au chocolat into his coffee. Taking his silence as an invitation to continue, she regaled to him the details of Rose and Ryan's blossoming romance.

"You can understand why there were so many G.I. love affairs during World War II, can't you?" he absently took her hand. "Constantly being thrust into life-or-death situations heightened feelings and emotions. I suppose people had to find happiness where and whenever they could."

"Yes and I know Rose and Ryan were parted in some way, almost certainly not through choice," she paused, buttering a baguette while she considered her words, "I almost think I should stop reading their story while they're still happy."

"But happiness is only a part of love," he continued, his expression intent and serious. "It is all the times it is tested which determines whether it endures or not, whether it becomes stronger, or in some cases, weaker."

Ivy nodded but remained silent, realising a man as charismatic as Jacques would almost certainly have been in love before, probably on more than one occasion. And yet she didn't press for details, preferring to remain in the bubble of knowing he was attracted to her and the anticipation of what would occur next between them.

"Busy day ahead?" she enquired, instead.

"Yes, I took your advice on seizing the moment and phoned the estate agents about leasing the studio," he neatly arranged his paperwork in a brown leather zip-around file which had seen better days.

"And?" she said, excitedly.

"And I've got a meeting with them at 11am," he smiled, glancing at his iPhone.

"That's great news, Jacques. I hope it works out for you," Ivy said, sincerely, "is there anyone else interested?"

"I don't get that impression. But it only came on the market recently and property in the Medina gets snapped up fairly quickly which means I'll have to strike while the iron's hot," he paused, his eyes holding hers, "the only disappointing thing is I was looking forward to spending the day with you." Leaning across he lifted her hand, gently touching it to his lips.

"Don't worry about it," she smiled, his casual assumption they'd spend the day together somewhat making up for her disappointment that they wouldn't.

"If the meeting goes well, it'll mean I'll be tied up most of the day because I'll have to sort things out at the bank, but we could have an evening meal together?" he suggested, downing his coffee in one.

"I'd like that," smiled Ivy, her fingers still curled around his, reluctant as she was to let go.

"Shall we say eight o'clock?" his expression was expectant, "I'll meet you here?"

"Yes," nodded Ivy as he stood up, his departure imminent.

"Have you anything planned for today?" he lingered, evidently not wanting their conversation to end either.

"I'm going to explore the Ville Nouvelle. I thought it extremely elegant with its wide, white boulevards when we briefly passed through it yesterday," she smiled, "and I fancy a break from the souks."

"Oh the Guéliz district! It's lovely there," he smiled, picking up his briefcase. "You'll see such a contrast to the narrow streets of the Medina. I only wish I could come with you," he bent down, his lips briefly but firmly touching hers, "but I'll look forward to tonight instead. À bientôt!"

"Bon chaunce!" Watching him walk away, her heart tugged. She couldn't help but compare her arrangement to have dinner with Jacques at the end of his working day with Rose's snatched meetings with Ryan, heightened by the uncertainty whether they would see each other again as he flew his plane into mortal danger on a daily basis. On a romantic scale, they seemed at opposite ends, her relationship with Jacques safe and comfortable. The feelings welling inside her, however, told a different story and she couldn't escape the fact that their time together was fast running out, just as it had, she suspected, for Rose and Ryan.

After waiting all these years to feel a deep attraction and connection with someone, who seemed to reciprocate her feelings, how could she possibly bear it? Returning to her room, she collected her essentials – sunhat, sunglasses and long-sleeved blouse, putting thoughts of Rose and Ryan and Jacques firmly to the recesses of her mind.

Heading through the souks to the Ville Nouvelle, she recalled that the French had first moved beyond the crowded Medina walls in the early 20th century with aspirations of a more comfortable lifestyle. There, they had built their new city on a hill of broad avenues, detached houses and ornate parks to resemble ones they'd left behind in their mother country. Clinging to the shade, Ivy could almost have mistaken Guéliz's wide roads, lined with restaurants and upmarket shops, for Parisian boulevards, although the tall, palm trees wafting in the warm wind, gave them more of a flavour of the promenade in Nice. To her relief the air was noticeably cooler as she joined Avenue Mohammed V, considered the spine of Marrakech, connecting the old and new cities. Passing smart boutiques, she was content to window shop, certain she'd break her budget if she ventured into their dark interiors.

Crossing the exposed Place de la Liberté, the sun beating on her head, she fought the urge to cool off in the turquoise waters of a large fountain, where a group of tourists bathed their feet, evidently not possessing her resolve. She hurried on to the Place du 16 Novembre, noting the imposing white building which housed the city's main post office more than merited its mention in her guidebook. After the warm ochres, reds and pinks of the Medina, her eyes were refreshed by the paleness and clean lines of the buildings as European architectural styles fused with Moorish influences.

Pushing on, she soon reached a small, shady square with a restful garden at its centre. Perspiring profusely now, she retreated beneath the yellow and white awnings of a pâtisserie, where she gratefully ordered an iced jasmine-infused tea and tarte aux framboises. She pictured Jacques at an estate agents' office nearby, recalling the passion in his eyes when he'd spoken about purchasing his own studio and prayed that it would work out for him. Conflicting thoughts crowded her consciousness though as she realised that achieving his dream of setting up a studio and gallery would surely keep Jacques in Marrakech forever, and barring the odd holiday, she was doubtful she'd ever see him again.

After a trip to the cafe's luxurious and mercifully air conditioned powder-room, Ivy retraced her footsteps down the boulevard. The noise of rattling cutlery and cooking smells emanating onto the street signalled lunch preparations were well underway in the many fancy restaurants. Happily drifting along, Ivy abruptly felt herself pulled up as the heel of her sandal snagged in a crack in the pavement. Embedded as it was, it took a minute or so to extricate it and when she finally managed to set it free, she saw it was discoloured by the cement which had begun to melt in the intense heat. Hopping beneath the awning of an upmarket-looking shop, she dug into her handbag for a wet wipe.

As she did, a woman exited the shop, roughly pushing past her. Squinting as she looked up, Ivy was struck by the woman's dishevelled appearance which stood out among the well-dressed French-Moroccan women who frequented this swish part of the city. A willowy figure wearing a battered, holey straw hat, dirty jeans and a paint-splattered tee-shirt, her attire seemed at odds with the expensive looking bags she was carrying. It was only when she had taken half a dozen steps across the pavement it struck Ivy who she was.

"Louise," she yelled, but Jacques' friend appeared not to hear despite the street being relatively quiet. Slightly bemused, Ivy watched her cross the wide boulevard and winced on seeing her dodging the traffic haphazardly with scant regard for her safety. The confident, elegant woman Louise had presented at her dinner party was greatly at odds to the vulnerable figure she cut now and Ivy's brain welcomed the plausible conclusion that, having had a productive morning painting, she had decided to reward herself with an impulsive spot of retail therapy. Her eyes followed her until satisfied Louise had safely reached the opposite pavement before she turned to the shop she'd left. As she did, she almost collided with a woman pushing a pram who tutted loudly before retreating into the cool shade of *Bébé et Maman*.

Disparate thoughts raced through Ivy's mind as she leaned against the wall, the warmth of the bricks permeating her damp shirt. Louise being pregnant would certainly explain a few things she'd noticed at the dinner party: firstly her fragility which provoked such a protective instinct in her husband and, to a lesser extent, Jacques. Thinking back, she recalled Louise had politely excused herself to go to the bathroom on numerous occasions at the meal which would corroborate her theory. And yet Ivy was sure that she'd seen her drink quite a few glasses of wine to the point of being tipsy, which seemed to refute the idea she was with child. Something about it all didn't quite add up, and more than that, it gave Ivy a slightly uneasy feeling.

Returning to the old city she found the souks quiet, with locals taking siestas as the rigours of Ramadan began to take their toll. As she wasn't eating until after eight, she stopped at her now familiar rooftop café overlooking the Jemaa el Fna to while away the afternoon hours. Enjoying a light salad, she once again studied the view of the sandy-pink Koutoubia Mosque as it soared into the sky, pale blue with a heat haze at that time of the day. She watched mesmerised, as horse-drawn carriages with their sparkling-green bodywork, pink interiors and pristine-white canopies, weaved in and out of the tourists. At home, Ivy had read in her guidebook that they were popular with couples wanting a romantic evening ride around the edge of the Medina and out to the Palmeraie, a former oasis on the outskirts of town, where the rich escaped the heat in their secluded villas. At the time she had dismissed such a trip, knowing that she wouldn't want to do it alone. But now, her pulse began to race as she considered the possibility of taking a ride with Jacques, one evening.

Turning her attention to the open-air market, she was fascinated by the people who traded and bought here, of the colourful vibrancy of their stalls, their clothes and their characters. It was as though after sleepwalking through her life for the past few years, reading her great-aunt's diary and learning what had happened to her sisters, had opened her eyes. She no longer wanted to live a safe life stifled by the fear of what may or may not happen. Instead she would try and grasp every opportunity that came her way with both hands, relishing the joyful immediacy of it and cherishing the satisfying memory of it afterwards. She had been too cautious for too long. She must begin to take chances as they presented themselves; to truly live.

At just after five she returned to the riad to shower in preparation for meeting Jacques. In the bathroom mirror, her birthmark seemed as angrier a shade of crimson as she'd ever seen it and she let out a deep sigh, imagining that it would soon be visible even through her thickest layer of makeup. And all the taunts she'd been subjected to in school, all the doubts which had crippled her when she'd attempted to date boys at university came flooding back to her. She questioned yet again the wisdom of getting physically close to anyone, especially a man with whom she suspected she was starting to fall in love. Her mind raced as she imagined Jacques' reaction to her disfigurement, the sense of betrayal she had kept it a secret from him when he'd been so open with her from the start.

Finding these thoughts emotionally draining, she lay down on her bed. Despite the pillow's welcoming softness however, she was only able to drift into a shallow, rather fitful sleep. Later, preparing for dinner with Jacques, she dressed in an ankle-length, emerald-green dress which accentuated her auburn hair, beautifully. Seeing her reflection in the mirror, for a moment, she didn't recognize the woman who smiled back at her. A woman who looked happy. A woman secure in the knowledge that Jacques would never see what lay beneath her perfectly applied makeup. No, she would never have to tell him. She would go home, he would stay here, but she would make the most of their time together and, like Rose, keep those memories for a lifetime.

25

Jacques was late. Waiting for him in the riad library, Ivy flicked through a wedge of leaflets she'd found on one of the shelves, trying to quell the butterflies fluttering in her stomach. After a few minutes she stumbled on one with lots of glossy photos of the Guéliz area of Marrakech. With its array of designer shops and restaurants she'd seen that afternoon, she was unsurprised to discover it was considered the up and coming district in the city, a fact which made Louise's shabby appearance there all the more perplexing.

Reading on, she thought it a sad shame though that the Marché Central, developed over the centuries as a place for locals to grocery shop and gossip, had been deemed obsolete and pulled down to make way for the new, impersonal complexes in stainless steel. She recalled that, towards the end of her life, Rose had bemoaned that people didn't talk to her on the bus as they used to; a sad symptom of technological advances as people found their iPhones far more interesting than their fellow passengers.

Looking up, her breath caught in her throat as she spotted Jacques crossing the courtyard. Clean shaven, his spiky hair dark with gel, he looked smart in an open-necked, black shirt tucked into black jeans and she was struck by the effort he made with his appearance every time he saw her. Or maybe he was just naturally stylish.

"You look lovely. Your dress brings out the green in your eyes," the skin around his eyes crinkled as he smiled, taking the seat beside her. Feeling his warm hand grasp hers, his kiss was slow and lingering and Ivy found herself relaxing into it. "How was the Ville Nouvelle?" he enquired after a moment or so, his graceful fingers brushing hers.

"Interesting," she answered, breathing in his spicy aftershave. She was about to tell him about seeing Louise, but something held her back. Her instincts told her that her revelation might be a bit awkward and in any case it was really no concern of hers, "how was your trip to the estate agents?"

"All sorted. It took a bit of negotiating as in the end there was another party interested but I managed to secure the lease on the studio," he pulled her into a warm, tight hug, "thank you for giving me the shove I needed. What you said really spurred me on. Thank you," he whispered in her ear. As he released her, she smiled but remained silent. Looking into his dark eyes, she noticed how tired he suddenly looked and realised it was an effort for him to appear wide awake and sociable, an effort he was making for her.

"So shall we celebrate? I thought we'd have a meal in the

Spanish quarter?" he kept hold of her hand, intertwining his fingers in hers as they left the coolness of the riad, "I know a little restaurant there which serves good food, mainly Italian, ironically."

"It sounds delightful. At home, I virtually live on pasta and I'm getting withdrawal symptoms," she said, the air stifling in the back street. For a few minutes they walked on in silence when unexpectedly Louise came into her thoughts once more.

"What's wrong?" his eyebrows knitted together as he noticed her sudden frown.

"Maybe nothing," she sighed, relieved he'd picked up on the anxiety that had been niggling her, "but when I was out earlier, I saw Louise."

"In Guéliz?" The surprise audible in his voice confirmed Ivy's suspicions that she was indeed a creature of habit who didn't usually stray far from the Medina, if at all.

"Yes, she didn't look her normal self. I mean, I don't really know her, but the other night she looked so beautiful and confident and yet today." Seeing concern flicker in his eyes, she wished she hadn't mentioned it after all as she searched for the right words, "she looked somehow, 'lost' is the only way I can describe her."

"Would you excuse me a moment?" he whispered, his tone tense as he let go of her hand suddenly so it dropped down by her side, "I just have to give Patrick a quick call, check that she's okay."

While he took his iPhone from his back pocket, Ivy walked ahead to afford him a degree of privacy. She surmised it was Patrick he was speaking to, Jacques' questions and statements followed by long silences, filled by his friend on the other end of the line. Ivy wondered whether she should mention the babywear shop she'd seen Louise exiting before concluding it was the woman's private business which she might not want Jacques – or her – to know about. As Jacques' silences lengthened, the conversation evidently growing more serious, Ivy worried that telling him so soon after leaving the riad had sent their evening spinning off kilter, the good mood with which he'd greeted her just a quarter of an hour before, irretrievable.

"Is everything alright?" she enquired when he replaced his phone in his pocket.

"Yes, Pat says she's safe and sound in bed. She forgets her medication sometimes and as a result suffers these episodes," he explained, his previous agitation gone as his breathing deepened.

"You don't have to tell me if you think you're breaking a confidence," Ivy replied, giving him an easy way out but instead Jacques stepped in front of her, his eyes holding hers.

"You're so sweet," he sighed, his fingers brushing her face as she inwardly winced, hoping he couldn't feel the coarseness of the skin beneath her foundation.

"She's still grieving for her son. He died when he was just three; drowned in Lake Ontario," he paused, his expression darkening as he struggled to find the words. "It was winter so the lake was frozen. Everyone in the city skated on it. And Luc was so light but he stepped on a thin layer of ice and he fell under. There was nothing Louise could have done but, of course, she'll never accept that. Patrick's been her rock but she's suffered from depression and anxiety ever since. She has a medical cabinet full of anti-depressants which help her to some extent but there's nothing to heal her heart."

"Poor Louise. That's dreadful," reflected Ivy, thinking of her great-grandmother losing Violet and Nell within a year, barely able to imagine how it would feel to lose a child.

"Yes, that's why she came to Marrakech, to escape the memories of the accident but I don't think it's possible," he reflected, a dark shutter slamming across his emotions before they threatened to get the better of him.

"No," Ivy tried to take it in as her shoes clattered on the cobbles, visibly shaken by his words. "How do you ever get over something like that?"

"I don't think you do. Not Louise, anyway," added Jacques and, not knowing what else to say, Ivy left the conversation there. As they continued on, negotiating the darkened streets in silence, she gradually felt his hand clasp relax as he let go of the tension the memory of his friend's trauma had stirred in him.

Presently they veered down a street with no lighting at all, off to the right and then one off to the left until they came to a lane, barely wide enough for a cart, lined with single-storey houses. In the evening gloom, from what Ivy could make out, they resembled a row of English terraced cottages, picturesquely planted with flowering trees to cast a welcome shade during the daytime heat. The elegant contrast to the chaos of the Jemaa el Fna and the souks struck Ivy, "so this is the Spanish quarter?"

"The heart of it," smiled Jacques, clearly trying hard to restore his buoyant mood from earlier. "This is the Rue de Yougoslavie. Those are mulberry trees," he added as she followed his eyes up into the dark mesh of branches stretching above them.

"It has a nice ambience here, relaxed in comparison to the Medina. I like it," Ivy had already decided she would revisit the area in the daytime to steal a better look at the architecture, obscured now by the rapidly fading light.

"It is one of my favourite areas of the city. The houses here are of an unusual design and they used to be brightly coloured," he paused as they came to the end of the street, "but then a few years ago they were painted in the uniform Marrakech pink which I think is a bit of a shame. I still come over here once a week though. Out of all the quarters of the city this place has probably given me the most inspiration in my painting."

"It definitely has a surprise at each turn," nodded Ivy, as they negotiated a particularly tight passageway.

"It does, even for me, despite my many visits over the years. Which reminds me, I must show you my favourite art supplies shop in the universe," he enthused, stopping outside *Couleurs Primaires,* an old-fashioned little shop with a wooden sign swinging over the door, seemingly more at home in a Dickens novel than a North African street. Peering into the gloom, Ivy could just make out that it was stacked with shelves of easels, paints and implements. "I called in just last week. I buy all my raw materials here. I'm registered as an art teacher with them and so is Louise," Jacques added, cheerfully.

Their conversation then centred on art once more as they strolled on until eventually they reached a row of brightly lit restaurants. "This doesn't sound very Italian," Ivy remarked as Jacques stepped in front of her to open the door of one, an aged-looking sign *Le Chat qui Rit* swinging gently above it.

"Appearances can be deceptive. It serves the best pasta in town, al dente tossed in fresh herbs and drizzled with a fruity olive oil," he raised his eyebrows as he put his hand on her shoulder, following her in, "totally delicious!"

As an Italian girl in her early twenties, her dark hair knotted in a loose chignon at the base of her neck led them to a table, Ivy thought the dining room had a rustic charm with its red distressed chairs, green and white tablecloths and subdued wall lighting which wouldn't have looked out of place in the Tuscan countryside. She noticed it was packed with locals enjoying pasta, against a backdrop of sunny yellow walls stencilled with images of the laughing cat which only enhanced the cheerful atmosphere. Feeling relaxed in their secluded corner, Ivy ordered tortellini in a creamy asparagus and cheese sauce while Jacques opted for the seafood linguine.

"All the fish is brought in daily from the coast," he explained, as they clinked glasses swirling with burgundy-coloured wine, "the chef Leonardo is originally from Sicily and insists on freshly caught fish. He'll be out later to ask you how your pasta was with a glint in his eye as he already knows the answer."

Their conversation then seamlessly moved from one topic to another, interrupted only (as Jacques had predicted) by the effervescent octogenarian Leonardo, his suspiciously thick, jet-black hair in a style reminiscent of Elvis, checking they were satisfied with their food and,

Ivy suspected, relishing the profuse praise they gave him. She thought the evening was progressing delightfully until the waiter brought over the dessert menus, "no, I'll just take the bill, please," cut in Jacques, abruptly. Ivy looked at him, trying to mask her disappointment, immediately worrying what she'd done wrong to make him want to curtail their meal.

"There's a wonderful ice cream parlour on the corner I want to take you to," Jacques smiled, reassuringly, as optimism flooded back into her body. Next door but two, *Dino's* was a gleaming little establishment serving delectable Sicilian gelato. After their stroll in the humid night air, Jacques enjoyed a cream Piedmont hazelnut while Ivy refreshed herself with a Sicilian lemon and mango sorbet.

"This tastes better each time I have it," he commented as they resumed their walk.

"It's definitely authentic." It put her in mind of one of the few holidays she'd had abroad with her parents, in Sicily, 'the football' kicked by the 'boot' of Italy, her dad had described it. Her sorbet melting in her mouth, she recalled dragging them to an ice cream parlour on Cefalu harbour twice each day, mesmerised by the rainbow array of colours and flavours. After an unsuccessful date on the first morning with a bright-blue bubble gum, she had eventually fallen in love with a pale-green pear-flavoured one which she'd sampled for the remaining days of her stay.

"What are you thinking?" Jacques eventually enquired, surveying her in that slightly amused way of his she'd begun to get used to.

"Just about a holiday I had in Sicily years ago with my

parents," she said, the sorbet's sharpness playing on her tongue, "we stayed in a delightful town on the northern side of the island called Cefalu."

"Really? I stayed there once," Jacques said matter-of-factly. "It was while I was doing my degree, I must have been about twenty."

"I think I went at the end of my second year at high school," laughed Ivy, doing the calculations and coming to the conclusion that, as Jacques was seven years older than her, it was possible they could have been there the same summer. It briefly crossed her mind what would have happened if they'd met then, whether they would have got along as they did now or whether she would have been so inhibited and shy she wouldn't have dared talk to a handsome, Canadian boy a few years her senior?

"I thought it was a lot less touristy than Taormina, although we did go there too," he paused, crunching his cornet. "Of course the amphitheatre sloping down to the sea there is dramatic but I preferred Cefalu."

Although eager to know who he'd travelled with, somehow she couldn't find the courage to ask. Instead, they continued talking about their respective memories of the Mediterranean island before an easy silence stretched between them. Hearing him yawn in the darkness above her, she remarked, "you'll sleep well tonight."

"Definitely, and whatever dreams I have will be happy," he turned to face her, the moonlight casting his face in a bluish light, making his strong features even more striking, "I meant what I said before. It was you who inspired me to take the plunge with the studio. I've been wanting to break out on my own for a while but I just never did anything about it until now."

"But I didn't do anything," she protested, wiping her sticky hands on a twist of paper.

"Sure you did," he eyed her thoughtfully, "the encouragement you give without even knowing it, it's probably what makes you such a great teacher."

"How do you know I'm a great teacher?" she smiled, shyly.

"Because I know you," he replied, the moonlight catching the white glint of his teeth.

The streets became quieter and presently they reached the final stretch of dark alleyways where he took her hand once more, leading her home. As she fumbled for her key in her bag in the alleyway outside the riad, he leaned against the warm stones of the wall. Catching him looking at her, Ivy turned towards him.

"Thank you for tonight," he murmured, pulling her near and tracing his finger over her face as though trying to commit the contours of her features to memory in the darkness. She was caught with the urge to pull away before he felt the different texture of skin on her cheek but something kept her there as he cupped her chin in his hands and slowly moved her face towards his.

When his lips finally met hers there was no hesitancy this time. The urgency of his desire became apparent in his breathless kisses and Ivy felt herself responding to a need as great as his own. After a few minutes he managed to stop as though pushing away a tidal wave of emotion. His expression was serious as he whispered, "come to my room tonight, Ivy?"

Standing in the darkness with his breath warm on her face, Ivy knew the easiest thing in the world would be to say 'yes'. She realised he wanted to be with her as much as she wanted to be with him. And yet she knew once they had set on that road she'd have to come clean about her birthmark. Her mind skipped to the moment she'd be forced to reveal it which would perhaps sour their fledgling romance before it had had the chance to take off the ground. She couldn't take that risk, not just now – and yet she knew time was something they didn't have. Her stomach turned with uncertainty at the quandary before her. "I want to," she bit her lip, "I just think maybe it's a bit soon."

"I understand," his eyes held hers, his expression hopeful and yet confused. How could he possibly comprehend her feelings though, with all the mixed, muddled up messages she was sending him, when she couldn't make sense of it herself? Her eyes followed him as he walked down the corridor before turning at the last moment to smile back at her. Arriving back at her room, Ivy didn't want to contemplate what had just occurred or how she was going to adapt to their ever growing feelings. So, yet again, she found sanctuary from the confused thoughts tumbling through her mind in her great-aunt's past.

26

"During May 1944, events at the airfield were gathering apace in anticipation of an Allied breakthrough. Whenever we had the chance, Ryan and I took walks together in the lanes and sun-dappled woods or, on wet days, we'd meet for afternoon tea in the guildhall, where, beneath its white-washed beams and low ceilings, we'd talk for hours. As we got to know each other, we realised how many interests we shared as our likening for each other slowly began to develop into something deeper. I discovered Ryan was two years younger than me, and like me, had had a sheltered life, mostly at home on his family's farm. I sensed he missed them greatly, much more than he ever told me.

Other than Luigi, he had many friends in his crew, attracted no doubt by his outgoing, friendly manner and whenever we joined them for a drink I saw how popular he was. I loved Ryan's optimistic view of the world which matched my own as we discussed our individual plans for the future when the war was over. As I'd sensed at our first meeting, he had an incredibly sensitive, caring side to his nature, showing concern for his other crew members, always feeling he must never let them down. During this time while he was still waiting to be deployed, we saw each other almost every day. Either Ryan would wait by the stile each morning and walk me to the bus or else he'd be waiting at the bus stop when we pulled into Lavenham at 5:30pm every evening to accompany me on my walk home.

How do you write about happiness such as ours? Sadness breaks things down into easily examinable pieces as it moves from its beginning to end, but happiness encompasses the whole and is far harder to pin down. For me, during the spring of '44, it was just a state of being that I never wanted to end. There are fragments which remain all these years later – his smile that was just for me, a tender word in his slow, southern drawl, so different to the harsh accents of some of his fellow countrymen, the warmth of his skin against mine as he held my hand. Ryan never took me for expensive meals, never treated me to nylon stockings as Luigi did Sophie. He didn't need to. I was enraptured when one day Ryan began to talk about 'our' future together in Virginia. In quiet moments alone, I often pictured myself sitting with him, the sun setting on the porch of our elegant house. At night in the darkness of my room, I dreamed about marrying him and raising a family together. It was a feeling I had never known before. I was in love. And I knew I would never feel this way for anyone else.

In an extract of a diary I kept that year, I recorded on 14th May that Ryan was walking me home through the dark lanes when suddenly he turned, pulled me in his arms and held me tightly for a long time. I asked him what was wrong and he whispered that he was frightened of what lay ahead. As he stepped back, I remember seeing something in his eyes that made me fearful too. He looked so young, so vulnerable, he was still just a boy in many ways. I tried to reassure him, reminding him his group had been rigorously drilled in New Mexico, a training I knew would stand them all in good stead when they were deployed into action. My words seemed to do the trick as he visibly pulled back his shoulders and told me firmly that everything would be okay.

He didn't tell me then but that night was the eve of his first mission and in the coming months I realised it was also the last glimpse I would have of the carefree and confident boy I was coming to love. Just a week later when we met at the church gate, I sensed that something in Ryan had subtly altered. His normally easy, laid-back manner had been replaced by an edginess as he looked round anxiously while we talked. We strolled to The Swan in silence as, for the first time our conversation ran dry, a slight awkwardness hovering between us. I was worried I had done something wrong and although he assured me this wasn't the case, he refused to be drawn any further. We settled into a corner with our drinks and he slowly seemed to emerge from his mood, and for the rest of the evening, appeared to be back to his old self.

Although I didn't know it at the time, Ryan's group was heavily involved in bombing airfields of northern France as part of the Eighth Air Force's campaign as they geared up for the invasion of Normandy on 6th June, 1944. Ryan himself was a navigator in a Boeing B-17 flying fortress and, although he didn't tell me much during our meetings, I did some research after the war and found that his group had targeted coastal defences, road junctions, bridges and locomotives during

221

the invasion. It was an important job and one which suited his gentle nature towards his fellow men, the loss of civilian life being kept at a minimum. I also discovered that just 21 missions was the average life expectancy of a crew, a fact which no doubt preyed on all their minds. But at the time I didn't know that – I only knew that Ryan was flying into danger and there was nothing I could do except bide my time and pray for his safe return."

27

"Where exactly are we going?" Ivy enquired, feeling as elegant as a fifties film star in a cream linen full-skirted dress, her hair pinned up beneath her wide-brimmed straw sunhat. Sitting next to Jacques as his Fiat Punto competed with Marrakech's Monday morning rush hour traffic she felt excited at the prospect of finally spending a full day with him.

"The Atlas Mountains," he smiled, his attention focused on a moped buzzing in and out of the sedate SUVs, "although I haven't settled on a route. I think we'll just go where the mood takes us today."

"Sounds like a good plan not to have one," Ivy smiled, noticing how the sun picked out the fine, golden hair covering his forearms, his elegant fingers clutching the steering wheel.

"Yes whenever I make one, chances are I break it," he added. Ivy watched as he skilfully pulled across four lanes of traffic before turning onto a quieter road. Although Jacques didn't bat an eyelid, it all seemed quite chaotic to her and vindicated her decision not to hire a car herself as there was no way she'd find the courage to drive these roads where the Highway Code clearly didn't always apply.

The breeze from her open window gently keeping her cool, her mind flipped back to her refusal of Jacques in the shadows of the riad courtyard the previous evening. Of course, he'd been polite enough not to mention it and as attentive as ever when they'd met over breakfast. But now she desperately wanted to unburden herself, knowing she'd left him with the impression that she didn't reciprocate his obvious attraction for her. She knew the next logical stage in their relationship was to sleep together and yet how could she? How could she even explain her actions without revealing her birthmark, the very thing she'd sought to conceal? With her few previous boyfriends, she'd spent months getting to know them on dates before she'd dropped her bombshell. But time wasn't a luxury she had with Jacques and as she considered how forthcoming he'd always been with his thoughts and feelings, guilt rose in her.

"A penny for your thoughts." As Jacques' voice dragged her back to the present, Ivy realised she'd been pondering the matter for longer than she'd thought, the rosy hues of the city having given way to muted browns and beiges of the countryside.

"They're not worth that," she commented, a little blunter than she'd meant.

"Maybe not," he shrugged his shoulders. Seeing his expression etched with concern, it dawned upon her he'd been glancing at her on and off for some time. Her obliviousness to it surprised her somewhat as her radar to detect someone's stares was clearly somehow defective with Jacques, something which unnerved her.

"You're not very good at relaxing, are you?" he observed, after a prolonged moment.

"No, I'm not," she smiled, ironically feeling calmer now he'd decided not to pursue her thoughts, "there was so much going on at the end of term and I flew to Morocco the day after we broke up for the summer holidays. It takes a while to remember where the switch off button is."

"I'm not sure I even had a switch off button when I was teaching. There always seemed to be something to worry about, something that I should have been doing niggling at the back of my mind," he momentarily glanced at her before returning his eyes to the road, "and I taught eighteen, nineteen and twenty year olds. Goodness knows how you cope with the little ones!"

"I think you just do. A lot of the time you just act on impulse, you don't have much time to consider things," she shrugged, "there's no secret to it. It helps if you get on well with children. I find them much easier to work with than adults. They are more inclined to be non-judgemental."

"Yes, you seem to have found your calling," he looked at her thoughtfully. For a moment, she felt he was going to say something more but he didn't and the silence weighed heavily in the car once more which this time she moved quickly to fill.

"But it's exhausting. Most days, you're on the go from the moment you step foot in the building to the minute you leave, making sure the kids are safe, engaged and learning and my weekends are filled with marking and preparation. It's only during the holidays I get a chance to recharge my batteries."

"Then let me help you with that," he grinned, "I've gotten far more practiced with that since I came to Morocco."

"Okay," smiled Ivy, recognising that Jacques, as well as being attracted to her, seemed to really care, too. Their conversation reached an impasse then, his concentration occupied by the road which dramatically twisted and turned as it began to climb into the mountains. In the end, Jacques opted for the high altitude Tizi-n-Test pass, the westerly and most ancient route which followed in the footsteps of tribes many millennia ago. Ivy dug into the glove compartment for a map to follow the route, a white wiggly line winding to the south of Marrakech. With Jacques taking the bends cautiously, it was over an hour until they reached the crumbling village of Tahanoute, Ivy's breath quickening as she beheld the clay houses cascading down the red rock to the green, verdant valley floor. Parking the car on a dusty, residential street, they strolled around, finding it deserted apart from the odd stray cat sheltering in shady pockets out of the sun's glare.

"This is exactly how I imagined settlements on the edge of the Sahara would look like when I was a girl," she exclaimed, glad she'd brought her trainers to change into, as even with them on she stumbled over loose rocks.

"Me too," said Jacques, giving her a hand as they negotiated a particularly uneven bit, "well, when I was a boy."

They both laughed at his quip before he grew serious again, "I imagine you were a very thoughtful child."

"Yes, I suppose I was," she paused, choosing her words carefully as she didn't want to inadvertently give anything away about her problems growing up, "maybe it was because I was an only child and I had no brothers or sisters to play with. I spent a lot of time reading in my room or else around at my great-aunt Rose's house."

"You were very close to her?" he asked as they carried on, his hand still in hers.

"Yes, because she'd never married nor had children she always had a lot of time for me. We had a lot of shared interests. We loved reading about exotic, foreign places and dreamed of one day visiting them together. Of course we never did, for some reason, but she did inspire me to come on this journey... Eventually."

"Oh, you were lucky having someone you shared so much with. When I was growing up in Toronto, I had to amuse myself. I always had my head buried in history books or else I was painting the sky, buildings or the lake from our apartment window. My mum's nursing career meant she worked unsociable hours and I often didn't see her from one day to the next and my dad didn't approve of my painting. He was a rail engineer like his father before him and I think he expected me to follow in the family trade so to speak. When I announced I was going to study art at college, he just couldn't get his head around it. I told myself his opinion didn't matter but it did. For years, our relationship was frosty."

"What happened?" enquired Ivy, as they approached a cluster of flat-roofed houses, conscious it was the first time he'd alluded to his father.

"Time passed. Then he became sick so we made the effort to get on as best we could but then he died," he paused, wiping his forehead which was beaded with sweat, pondering how to continue. "It was difficult but over the years I've reconciled myself to the fact that maybe we just weren't meant to get on, that we were just too different."

"Yes I suppose so," she agreed, not quite knowing what to say but feeling that he just needed her to listen rather than offer any comment.

He continued to talk of his father as they followed an alleyway with high walls leading to a shrine for the Prophet Sidi Mohammed El Kebir. Resting the heel of her hand on the stone wall, she felt its roughness and warmness seep through her skin. It was so quiet here she could hear the birdsong as they swooped down from the cloudless sky above. With a few more steps, she began to hear voices and chatter as the path ahead widened out onto a square, filled with a country market where people bartered over goat's milk, meat, vegetables and assorted unrecognisable commodities.

"It's as though the pictures I've seen in books and have in my head are coming to life before my eyes," she smiled up to him.

"Just lucky we came on a Monday," Jacques quipped, with a squeeze of her hand which told her he'd researched this trip meticulously so she'd have the fullest possible experience of rural Morocco. They spent some time perusing the stalls, testing everything from the goat's cheese to orange blossom scented sweets, before rejoining the road on its climb south to Moulay Brahim. After carefully cornering numerous hairpin bends, they reached

Asni, a pretty village encircled by pink walls, the odd shop selling a limited assortment of trinkets; A mini Marrakech, Ivy thought as they continued their ascent.

"That's Jbel Toubkal," Jacques pointed skywards, indicating North Africa's highest peak to the west. With its rugged, jagged edges seeming to cut into the sky, its magnitude made it even more imposing than the pictures in her guidebook. "I thought we could stop at the village of Imlil. I doubt we'll find it too busy, even now at the height of the summer holiday season."

Ivy clutched the door handle as the car rattled over the uneven surface of the road. She'd read that Imlil was well known for its walnuts, apples and cherries but surmised it was film buffs following in the footsteps of Brad Pitt in *Seven Years in Tibet,* who were responsible for the mini traffic jam they came upon as they rounded the corner.

However, this wasn't its only claim to fame as on 17 August 1995, the sleepy town of Imlil had become known around the world when it was catastrophically flooded. As Jacques recounted the tragic events which had unfolded without warning, Ivy struggled to picture the six-metre wall of water which had gushed down the valley's slopes with nothing to break its path. One hundred and fifty people had lost their lives that day, with almost eighty tourists among the dead. Ivy found herself identifying with these holidaymakers, excited to explore an exotic country as she was now. However, Jacques soon jolted her thoughts back to the locals, adding, "the disaster was only the start of people's problems here because they not only lost their food stocks but it was impossible for them to cultivate the land."

"Did the town ever recover from the flood?" Ivy asked, as they walked around the deserted streets, hoping it was the rigours of Ramadan which kept people indoors but suspecting the natural catastrophe had had a lasting effect on the village's ethnography.

"The Moroccan government was quick to help, clearing access to the village through the blocked mountain road just four days later," Jacques replied, "but to this day the village is still to return to normality. Many of their walnut trees were also washed away in the flood, each having taken up to fifteen years to mature. People here relied on selling walnuts to international companies to make an income. It resulted in many of them moving away to the cities, which is why a lot of the buildings here are no longer lived in."

"That's so sad. I suppose people are often at the mercy of things they can't control and just have to carry on the best that they can." Passing a patch of bare land she imagined would have been previously cultivated, she saw it was still littered with flood debris, "it must have been hard for the people to rebuild their lives after such a catastrophe."

"Some of them did, some of them didn't," Jacques helped her over a large stone in the road, "but that's the nature of things. Some people can get over the worst tragedy whilst some cannot cope at all."

Perspiration trickled down the back of Ivy's neck as the road's incline steepened. Continuing their walk, a *bureau des guides* was the only indication they'd reached the village's centre, around which clamoured forty or so students assembled with huge backpacks and knee-length shorts in gaudy colours. Apart from a few basic budget hotels there wasn't much else, certainly no eateries of any kind, which caused Ivy's heart to sink for the heat had made her thirsty.

"It's okay. We're stopping for lunch at Ouirgane. It's the next place," smiled Jacques, "you hungry?"

"How did you read my mind?" joked Ivy, keeping hold of his hand.

"Perhaps I should set myself up as a fortune teller in Jemaa el Fna?" he quipped and they both laughed, descending the hill companionably. The day was unfolding as Ivy had hoped it would as they'd stopped asking questions about one another's pasts to become better acquainted through enjoyed shared experiences in the present. Continuing their drive, Jacques carefully negotiated the road once more.

"Those are salt factories," he pointed to two huge, rather ugly buildings at odds with the scenery, "one traditional and one modern, that's what the locals here rely on to make a living nowadays."

"I think it's incredible how people manage to live here and bring up their families," said Ivy, thinking of Colchester and the many job opportunities available to its inhabitants, "it must be such a hard life."

"Without a doubt, more so than in Canada or the UK," nodded Jacques, "but I think that in some ways that makes everything these people achieve more worthwhile."

Ivy considered his comment on the last leg of their drive to Ouirgane which turned out to be a delightful little village nestling among trees in the valley above the Oued N'fis River. With the scorching Sahara sun a golden orb in the flawless blue sky overhead, they'd only taken a few steps before an ancient looking inn caught Ivy's eye.

"I thought we'd have lunch here," Jacques smiled as the wooden sign *Le Sanglier Qui Fume,* swung in the warm breeze. It took Ivy a moment to adjust to the darkness of the wooden interior after the glare outside. Looking around, there were mismatched tables and chairs while the walls were rustically decorated with some of the coloured pottery she'd seen for sale at the side of the road.

Following Jacques to a corner table, the place had a homely, comfortable feel which she instantly liked. They ordered meze, which filled their table when the waiter brought it – and the one next to them. As they ate they talked about everything from the French foreign legion soldiers, who according to the potted history on the back of the menu, had quartered in the inn while constructing the bridge over the Ouirgane River, to the differences between the Canadian and English language.

"Come on, we have to go," Jacques' eyes suddenly darted to his watch, "it's 2pm and we still have so much to see."

Ivy wished that she hadn't eaten quite so much as the rocky road twisted and turned to a greater degree that afternoon. Although the landscape became increasingly bare and barren, there was beauty in its starkness. Passing through a Berber hamlet, with its low-rise, cool-looking dwellings strewn along the road, Jacques pulled over to point out a commanding hilltop fortress.

"That's Kasbah Talaat-n-Yacoub," he offered his water bottle to Ivy, "just nudge me if I'm boring you?"

"Are you kidding?" Ivy laughed, conscious of his gaze upon her while she drank, "I would have paid good money for a tour like this."

"But it wouldn't have been as good as mine," said Jacques, playing the serious tour guide before bursting out laughing too.

"Modest too!" She pretended to be serious, momentarily. But she loved that they already had the ease of having known each other for years, coupled with the thrill of learning something new and unexpected at any moment.

"The Talaat-n-Yacoub," he continued, albeit unable to wipe the smile from his face, "was once controlled by the Goundafi tribe who commandeered access to the Tizi-n-Test pass until the early 20th century, when they were suppressed by the French."

"Those Frenchies, they get everywhere?" laughed Ivy.

"Hey, may I remind you that you *chose* to do a French degree whereas I just grew up speaking it because that was the language spoken by my parents?" he smiled, raising his eyebrows.

"Touché," replied Ivy, as he restarted the car and continued to curve carefully up the winding road.

"The Tizi-n-Test pass begins here," he announced, the hairpin bends suddenly sharpening, "you may excuse me for keeping my eyes on the road for the next half hour or so."

"I'd rather you do that!" Smiling, Ivy leant back, hoping her headrest would provide support as the winding rockiness of the roads jolted her neck, making her slightly nauseous. As Jacques drove on she felt grateful and yet sorry he had to concentrate on the narrow road instead of the spectacular views. Surveying the sandy plains of the Sous below, the contrast between their magnolia colour and the bright blue of the sky struck her as intoxicatingly beautiful. Reaching the top, they alighted the car and, avoiding the pleas of the owners of souvenir stalls, found a quiet spot to view the pass, a golden thread weaving its way through the rugged rocks of the low Atlas range. Ivy welcomed the bracing mountain air, inhaling deeply.

"It feels as though we are on top of the world," she sighed as the vastness of the African landscape made her feel very small indeed.

"6,861ft to be precise. I learned it in feet for the Brits because it sounds more impressive than 2,092m," smiled Jacques as she nudged him playfully.

Ivy shivered at the sudden drop in air temperature at this altitude. In response, Jacques' arms wrapped around her from behind, his chin resting gently on the top of her head. Leaning into him, she felt his warmth seep through her dress, while not being able to remove her gaze from the imposing landscape. Later that afternoon, continuing their journey towards the end of the pass, they reached a highland plateau of beautiful meadows.

"They are particularly striking in spring when the wild flowers are in full bloom. I have painted them, so many beautiful shades of blue and purple especially," he explained, negotiating another sharp bend.

"I'd like to see your pictures," she imagined him meticulously blending the different coloured paints to get exactly the effect he wanted.

"No, I don't think I've done them justice," he paused, "you must come and see them for yourself next spring."

Ivy made no comment, not wanting to think about ifs and maybes or tempt fate. Nine months in the future was a long time. Who knew what might happen, where they both would be?

Huddled within faded red walls, Taroudant resembled a quieter, calmer version of Marrakech. With deserted streets, its inhabitants no doubt enjoying their afternoon siestas, Ivy took in the low-rise buildings, sensing they owed more to the African continent and less of the Arab identity and French influences than those in Marrakech possessed. Jacques came to a stop, parking in a sun-drenched square, edged with squat, red buildings.

"Unlike almost every other Moroccan city, Taroudant was never under French occupation and doesn't possess a European quarter," he commented, reinforcing her surmising.

The Avenue Mohammed V was a modest street of food and hardware shops but Ivy couldn't stop thoughts of its grand, Marrakech counterpart whirling in her head as they strolled hand-in-hand. In her mind, she saw Louise outside the designer children's clothes shop, looking so distraught. For a moment she felt profoundly uneasy before Jacques broke into her thoughts pointing out an antiques shop and she managed to push her discomfort to the back of her mind. After spending time browsing but not buying, they stopped for iced teas in a tiny but mercifully shady cafe. Sufficiently cooled, they then ventured into the Souk Berber, buying figs and oranges which they ate, sitting on a bench beneath an orange tree, overlooking the impressive looking triple-arched Saadian gates.

Discarding the waxy peel, they stepped through them into the Kasbah where men and women were occupied with traditional Arab crafts from woodturning to weaving, each generation having refined them a little. There, Ivy and Jacques whiled away the afternoon hours, pausing here and there as one pointed out something interesting to the other.

"I have just one more surprise for you," Jacques announced, the encroaching twilight lengthening their shadows. Sheltered within the city's fortress walls, the Hotel Paris Salem possessed mesmerising, Moorish interiors which took Ivy's breath away and it was in this sumptuous setting they enjoyed a romantic dinner, watching the sun set over lush gardens. It was past midnight when they arrived back at the riad and as Jacques bade her 'goodnight' with a long, lingering kiss, Ivy felt more reluctant than ever to let him go.

28

Ivy woke at 2am, reliving their day together; the majestic mountains, the warmth of Jacques' hand in hers, the taste of his lips on hers. Her mind too animated to sleep, Ivy picked up Rose's diary, hoping to occupy her thoughts with something else other than Jacques.

"One day from the summer of '44 stands out from the rest. It was the Whitsuntide celebrations and everyone in the town came along, including the Americans from the base. We had always had a small fête with stalls, entertainment and refreshments in the fields behind the town. But that year the occasion took on a life of its own as everyone seemed desperate for a respite from the dark days of war as midsummer approached.

I chose a pretty white dress edged with lace and was accompanied to the fête by Mother, Frances and Albert. I felt my heart pounding in my chest as I spotted Ryan, so devastatingly *handsome in his uniform, leaning on the field gate. I watched as he strolled slowly towards us, my mind whirring furiously to explain to my family who he was and how I came to know an American airman. Ignoring the astonishment on my mother's face, I just stood back and watched with amusement as Ryan charmed her with his old-fashioned southern manners. I could see, however, Frances was not won over, as she gave me a disapproving look from beneath the brim of her sunhat. Albert, though, took an immediate liking to Ryan and they were soon chatting animatedly about farming, a topic in which they shared an interest.*

It was while the men were talking that Frances took me to one side to give me dire warnings that my reputation would be destroyed if I was seen going out with an American serviceman such as Ryan. She told me she'd heard women around the town gossiping about certain girls who were no better than they should be and she was not going to have that disgrace brought upon her family. I thought about trying to defend Ryan, explaining he wasn't like the other flyers, with their sometimes coarse manners, that he was kind and reliable. But seeing her displeasure, I decided against it. Nothing I could say would change her mind."

Ivy woke late to find the taste of garlic lingering in her mouth while her room was stuffy and stale. Opening a window, she turned towards the bathroom when, out of the corner of her eye, she noticed a note pushed beneath her door. Bending to retrieve it, she lifted it to her nose to inhale Jacques' musky aftershave.

Ivy,

I had the most wonderful time with you yesterday.

I was hoping to spend today with you as well but checking my emails I had one from a man who can supply me with easels for my new studio at a heavily discounted rate.

It really is too good an opportunity to pass up on. I hope I will not be too late so we can meet for a meal tonight?

Yours fondly,
Jacques.

Ivy traced her fingertips along Jacques' signature, picturing his elegant hand forming the letters as he'd thought of her. Still a tiny fraction of her considered his note might be an excuse not to see her. But then the look in his eyes when he'd cupped her chin in the courtyard returned to her, rendering the notion impossible. With their trip to Essaouira imminent, it was also perfectly reasonable he should spend time today on his new business venture. No, she smiled, folding the letter along its creases and placing it in a drawer for safekeeping, there was no doubting his growing feelings for her.

At breakfast, Ivy found a group of young, Irish backpackers planning the next stage of their trip to Gibraltar, had monopolised the courtyard. Feeling the peace of the place invaded by their loud voices, she had no inclination to linger. Instead, she gulped down her coffee and returned to her room, recalling how, at that time yesterday, she'd been sitting at Jacques' side as they'd left the city, their day together in the Atlas ahead of them.

Disappointingly, everything in her room was tidy and in order. Her clean clothes hung in the white wardrobe and sat dutifully in their drawers while her toiletries were laid out in rows in the bathroom and her books stored in neat piles on her bedside table. With no jobs to occupy her fidgety hands, Ivy felt strangely restless. Not having the inclination to read either her great-aunt's diary or a novel, she grabbed her sunhat and bag and headed out.

Avoiding the square Ivy turned down an alleyway of smart little shops, where she stumbled upon a window displaying exquisitely embroidered blouses. Knowing they were exactly the sort of thing her mother would love, she decided to purchase one for her.

"Is there anything I can help you with?" a woman in her seventies, wearing a pretty, lilac hijab, greeted her with a smile.

"It's ok, I'm just looking for a present for my mother," she smiled, drawn to some blouses embroidered with striking purple and burning orange flowers, "what sizes do these come in?"

"Small, medium and large," said the woman in heavily accented French, "I make the small ones correspond with sizes 10-12, the medium 14-16 and the large 18-20."

"You make them yourself?"

"Yes, with my sister, my daughter and daughter-in-law. We live in the mountains and split the business equally between us."

"I'll take this one," answered Ivy, admiring the way the green, gold and orange threads were woven together to create flowers, "and I'll have the green and lilac one too. It's lovely work."

"Of course a lot of people are surprised that a family of women can run a successful enterprise like this," the woman went on, with a wry smile.

"I don't mean to pry," assured Ivy. The last thing she wanted to do was insult her.

"Marrakechiyyas, we women, are having their say and taking charge of their lives like never before," smiled the woman, "let me see, I'd guess you are a nurse or maybe a school teacher?"

"Yes, a school teacher, but how did you know?" said Ivy, incredulously.

"You remind me of my youngest daughter. She wants to train to be a school teacher in the future. Schools in Marrakech are working hard to reduce female illiteracy rates as high as 60% and there are still far too many Moroccan girls under the age of fifteen who work instead of getting an education," she paused.

"I've seen some children selling souvenirs in the square," Ivy ventured, thinking how such practices would be illegal in the UK.

"Yes, but you should not buy anything from them," stated the woman, seriously, "to help keep kids in school only make purchases from adults, don't give children handouts, it encourages them to beg and shames their parents."

"I never thought of it that way. I saw a lot of tourists who probably think they are helping them when they buy their goods," sighed Ivy, glad that she hadn't succumbed more than once to those imploring brown eyes.

"How do you train to be a teacher in UK?" The woman's eyes were wide and curious.

"You can do a teaching degree that lasts four years," recounted Ivy, conscious the woman hung on her every word, "or, particularly if you want to work in a secondary school, it is more common to do a three-year degree in your subject followed by a one-year teaching qualification. That's the way I did it but I now teach seven and eight year olds."

"And you have to pay to do this?" As the woman seemed to process everything she'd heard, Ivy guessed she was comparing it with her daughter's likely experience.

Time passed very quickly as they talked. Whenever a customer came into the shop, the woman indicated Ivy should stay to continue their conversation. By the time they had compared life experiences and exchanged ideas on world events, the red-rimmed clock on the wall was striking one.

"I close until three now," explained the woman, hobbling over to lock the door, "but do you want to join me for some lunch? You're quite welcome."

"Yes, that would be lovely," Ivy consented, taken aback by the woman's kindness. She followed her through a jam-packed stockroom to a tiny but meticulously clean kitchen. Watching the woman lay out a selection of salads and breads on the table, she briefly wondered why she was breaking the fast, guessing it must be due her age or some hidden medical condition.

"Help yourself," she offered eventually and Ivy smiled in

thanks. Being invited into a Marrakechiyya's home had been something she hadn't dared to dream of and she savoured every moment, aware it was a special experience that didn't happen every day.

"As you might have seen Moroccan society revolves around the family," the woman helped herself to a cheese and herb filled pastry, "but young Moroccans are increasingly leaving home and delaying marriage to pursue careers in the cities. Mainly the men at the moment but more and more women are doing so too."

"It's been that way in the UK for decades," stated Ivy, feeling the soothing mint tea take hold.

"Have you got a husband as well as a career?" the woman smiled to reveal a perfect set of white teeth.

"No, I never met the right person," Ivy was on the verge of saying before stopping herself. She was unsure whether this woman, despite her enlightenment, would understand as she'd read arranged marriages still took place in Morocco so she added simply, "I decided to concentrate on my career. Teaching takes up all my time."

"Ah, that's sad. I believe there is someone out in the world for everyone," she sighed, bringing out some figs for dessert. They sat there companionably continuing their discussion while nibbling at the luscious purple fruit, Ivy hardly noticing the entire conversation was being conducted entirely in French.

"I don't know how I can thank you for lunch. It's so generous of you," said Ivy as they walked through the shop afterwards, "no one would ever do that in England."

"Really?" Surprise was audible in the woman's voice as

she unlocked the door, "wait until I tell my daughter. She'll want to know everything about our talk."

Ivy turned around to shake the woman's hand. "Thank you so much for the delicious food."

"You're a nice person," she said, frowning, "just one other thing I've always wanted to know, what is it like to fly in an airplane?"

The street teaming with people buying supplies to break the fast, Ivy headed back to the riad. Finding a quiet corner in the courtyard, she punched her parents' number into her mobile phone and spent the next five minutes speaking to her dad. Then he passed the phone to Ivy's mother, who wanted to know everything she'd done so far on her trip. Ivy tried her best to paint a picture of the vibrant country she was in, although she carefully omitted any mention of Jacques, still unsure where she stood with him.

29

Dressing for dinner, the anticipation of seeing Jacques again coursed through Ivy. Still trying to get her head around his attraction for her and the feelings he fostered in her, she wanted to make a big effort for him. As she surveyed the effect in the mirror, she smiled with approval as her hair tumbled past her shoulders in light auburn curls, made even glossier by the argan shampoo she'd been using for the past week while black mascara accentuated her naturally long eyelashes and green eyes.

Ready far too early, she passed the time reflecting upon her conversation with her parents, musing on the irony of being so far away at the very moment she'd realised what an important part they played in her life. She'd always admired Rose for being so vivacious and exciting and while her mum and dad brought different qualities, maybe not as exhilarating as her great-aunt, they were just as loving and enduring.

"I'm sorry I'm a bit late," Jacques joined her in the

library, his hair still damp from his recent shower. Ivy felt her heart flutter as he leaned in to kiss her before resting his forehead against hers, whispering, "I've missed you so much."

As he pulled away, she saw his expression was serious, the sincerity in his eyes, "I have missed you too. How did your meeting go?"

"Good actually," he entwined his fingers with hers. "The seller was a portrait artist, retiring to a cooler clime due to his asthma and I bought all ten easels and other art paraphernalia for a very good price. As well as opening my own gallery, it dawned on me that I could perhaps set up a class for amateur painters, backpackers maybe who are staying here for a while and want to capture their own memories on canvas?" he smiled, clearly enthused.

"I think that's an excellent idea, Jacques," Ivy smiled, looking into his dark eyes and finding herself caught up in his enthusiasm, "it marries your two talents."

"I only have two talents?" he asked, his eyebrow raised as he sat back, the sofa squeaking in protest.

"Two of your many talents, then," she kissed him full on the lips, surprising herself as it was the first time she'd initiated it. However, if he'd noticed, he didn't comment, clearly content to let it pass for normal behaviour between them. A few minutes later, they crossed the courtyard; the street outside quiet and warm as Ivy fell into his walking rhythm.

"I didn't ask about your day. How was it?" he said after a while, his hand around her waist, comforting as the souks were beginning to get busy again after the siesta.

"I met a lovely Marrakechiyya who invited me to lunch in the back of her shop. She was interested to know about my life in England," she ventured as they strolled across the Jemaa el Fna, the sunset bathing it in dusky rose, "is that usual?"

"I think the people of this city are full of life and eager to learn about other cultures, other countries and she obviously recognised you're a lovely person," he smiled, side-stepping a man pushing an orange juice cart, "just watch out for some of the men though. Sometimes they pester single women tourists, especially beautiful ones like you."

Ivy fell silent, considering. Casting Jacques a sideways glance she saw the words played on his smiling lips so nonchalantly and realised with a shock he truly believed she was beautiful. Darkness was descending quickly over the city's confined streets, an unwelcome reminder that they were already deep into August. Approaching the Ben Youssef Mosque, its green roof illuminated from within as men said their final prayers of the day, Ivy could see the appeal of living in such a city, vibrant with life 24/7. Provided you were surrounded by your nearest and dearest.

"Where are you taking me?" she enquired, intrigued as they'd already passed a whole host of busy restaurants.

"We're heading for the *Café et Maison de la Photographie.* It's not far now, I promise," Jacques smiled, admiring an opulent-looking townhouse. A couple of surprisingly straight streets later, they reached their destination. Strolling hand-in-hand down the airy, long gallery, Ivy thought it had a similarly aged ambience to the riad and wasn't surprised when Jacques said it was a renovated funduq.

"I've heard of these, didn't they used to be inns frequented by visiting merchants?" she enquired, picturing all the weary travellers who would have stopped here in bygone days en route from Casablanca or other northern cities to the Atlas Mountains.

"Yes, that's right," he nodded, as they glanced at walls bearing photos of Moroccan landscapes, kasbahs and different aspects of Berber culture, "the gallery was opened in 1960 to showcase old Moroccan photography in its original context. I come here at least once a month. Sometimes I find inspiration for my own work. I thought you'd like it here," he caught her marvelling at a 1907 vista of the Jemaa el Fna. Smiling, she thought of Jacques creating artworks in his airy studio before taking to the streets once more, searching for fresh ideas in the colours, scents and people he encountered. She knew some of her colleagues would be critical of him for having no ties at his age but she envied his daring, exciting lifestyle compared to her safe one as a teacher.

"There are over eight thousand photos here. Patrick Manac'h, a photography aficionado assembled the collection. They span the late 19th century to about 1950 and show how the city evolved in that time." Jacques led the way up a flight of white steps, "we could look at some after dinner or come back another day but this is why I brought you here," he exclaimed.

Concentrating upon her feet on the slightly uneven steps, it was only when Ivy reached the summit that she looked up. Standing on the rooftop, she gazed out over the rooftops of Marrakech and the stunning sunset which swept across the skies, bathing the pastel-pink buildings in a vivid red. Taking a sharp intake of breath, she was unable to stop tears springing to her eyes as the beauty of the scene invaded her soul.

Seeing her reaction and understanding what it meant to her, Jacques leaned into her, his arm curled around her shoulder, "I brought you here because the food is at a starving artist's price. This is just an added bonus."

The juxtaposition of Jacques' light-hearted words and his concerned expression made Ivy laugh as a young waiter showed them to a table with an unhindered view of the city's sprawl. They ordered meze starters followed by fragrant chicken tagines and creamy home-made yoghurt and strawberries for dessert. A couple of hours later, cradling her strong black coffee, Ivy stared into the infinite inky sky above their heads trying to hold on to this perfect moment.

"Well, we'd better be getting back," Jacques' reluctant voice broke through her thoughts. Although the air had grown cooler on the roof, it was barely 10pm, much earlier than their previous dinner dates had ended. Seeing confusion cloud her face, he clarified, "we've got an early start to Essaouira tomorrow."

"Oh yes, of course," Ivy smiled, hoping he didn't notice that it had completely slipped her mind, swept away as she was in the beauty of the moment.

His arm casually draped around her shoulders as though accustomed to being there, they strolled back to the riad, their exchanges and silences in between easy and natural. Nestled to his side, Ivy could no longer pretend to herself that what she and Jacques shared was a casual holiday romance. She thought it strange, having gone through all those decades alone, the tortuous teenage years when her contemporaries had experienced the joys and heartbreaks of first love, the twenties and early thirties when everyone seemingly had settled down except her, that in the end love had come so suddenly and so completely. If Rose could take a chance with Ryan in the face of the Second World War and its dangers, surely she was brave enough to do the same now with Jacques? But the chance didn't present itself that night. Instead, after sharing another passionate kiss, Jacques tenderly stroked her hair before bidding her goodnight. In her room, Ivy leaned against the cool, stone wall. Listening to his footsteps recede down the corridor, she regretted her missed opportunity with him, uncertain whether the chance would arise again.

Nevertheless, pulling on her nightdress, she was seized with the idea to test out whether her makeup would indeed transfer to her pillow in the event that he did ask her a second time. So, believing that it would have dried out sufficiently since applying it over four hours ago, she laid on the bed, resting the afflicted side of her face against the white cotton material. Rising from the still pristine pillow quarter of an hour later, she felt buoyed by the opportunities it afforded her. The excitement of her discovery rendering sleep an impossibility, she thumbed through Rose's journal to find her previous place.

30

"After the Whitsuntide fête, I didn't see Ryan for over a fortnight. He told me how busy his unit had been and I knew from gossip around town that the bombers had been operational every night. I would lay in the darkness of my bedroom, listening to the night time sounds, imagining him above the clouds, his plane flying into grave danger. I knew from my sisters' premature deaths that praying to God couldn't always help to save those I loved but talking to Him gave me a crumb of comfort. And so I asked God whenever I had the chance, at work, on the bus, walking the final stretch home and in the dead of night, to keep Ryan safe.

As spring gave way to a rather damp June, rumour of a long-anticipated invasion turned into fact. One evening I was sitting with Mother listening to a play on the radio. I remember it was rather cool for the time of year, and I had suggested we light a small fire in the hearth. For some reason I recall watching the dancing flames as they slowly consumed the logs, when the programme we were tuned into on the BBC was interrupted by an announcement that Allied forces had landed on the beaches of Normandy.

But beneath the overall euphoria of the success of the operation, other darker stories soon began to emerge, rumours of fierce fighting and heavy losses. Even though I consoled myself that Ryan was a flyer rather than with the ground forces, the week painfully wore on and hearing nothing from him, I began to fear the worst.

It was at this time that I confided in my mother about Ryan. I had felt so guilty about deceiving her, and heartened by her favourable reaction to him at the Whit fair, I plucked up courage to tell her. To my relief she gave me her blessing, saying she'd been very impressed with his courteous manners, adding perhaps now I would permit him to call for me and return me safely home! We decided, however, not to let Frances into our confidence at present, knowing how disapproving she would be. In light of this, I was forced to carry on as before at family gatherings, as though Ryan didn't possess my heart, waking thoughts and dreams. It might have been a blessing, I don't know. I got up, I went to work, I came home, I retired to bed and repeated the routine day after day, waiting for news.

By 10th June, I could stand the news blackout no longer and, after the weekly wash that Saturday morning, I headed to the airbase, knowing I wouldn't be granted admission but needing to get some news somehow to quell my rising panic. I never got there though. I made it to the end of the lane when I noticed a man in the distance. My heart thudded alarmingly as I recognised Ryan's tall, slim figure. Hazy at first in the soft, summer light, he spotted me, cap in hand, the sun shining on his golden hair. Then he was running towards me, reaching out and I felt his arms encircling me, his lips on my lips and I knew he was real. He had survived and had returned to me, as he had promised.

Our arms around each other and my head pressed against his shoulder, we walked back through the wheat fields. Ryan didn't tell me what he'd been doing or what danger he'd been in and I didn't ask. I didn't want to know, for he would soon have to return, risking death all over again. My dreams were already full of fearful imaginings any way, I didn't need them confirming. So relieved that he had come back safely, for that first hour or so, I ignored the blatant signs that he was far from alright. I chatted heedlessly on, not at first realising that Ryan was not participating in the conversation. But when I stopped suddenly mid-sentence to look at him, I noticed dark shadows under his eyes. Those same eyes, always full of enthusiasm and fun, were focused away from me as if his thoughts were somewhere else entirely. Sensing his withdrawal and wanting to bring his focus back into the present, I asked him to tell me what was troubling him. At first, he refused to say, explaining that he'd been sleeping badly the past few nights, woken by awful nightmares. I knew there was more to it than that and gently eased a little more information out of him. He reluctantly told me that several of the planes in his group hadn't returned from their missions and many of the men who had been lost, he'd counted as friends, having been with them since the early days of training in the US.

When I pressed him further, he became very irritable and refused to divulge any more. It was then that his mood suddenly changed and seeing a flash of his old smile, I realised he was *back with me. He suggested we go to the cinema and we spent a pleasant enough evening in each other's company, although, looking back, I suspect watching a film was his way of trying to avoid talking to me about traumatic events he didn't want to face.*

The following day was hot and dry. I needed to see Ryan before he left again and lingered at the lychgate after church. He surprised me by turning up in a car he'd borrowed from the base. As I glanced over to him, he looked like a movie star in his sunglasses, his hair slicked back from his face, the shadows which had clouded his mood twenty-four hours before, having dispersed. And I thought to myself, this is what Violet felt when she walked down the aisle on Frank's arm, this is why Nell tried to cling on so tightly to life. This is what love is."

31

Packing her overnight bag, Ivy couldn't help but wish it was just her and Jacques going to Essaouira. Eager to explore her growing feelings of love for him, she was sure that if he harboured anything akin to them, he too would rather it was just the two of them. Without Louise's inquisitive eyes tracking their every gesture or Patrick hijacking conversations with reminiscences, she imagined Jacques and her taking romantic sunset strolls and sharing candlelit dinners on the beach, the sea murmuring on the shore. But then again, perhaps this wasn't on Jacques' agenda at all as he seemed enthralled by the trip, with the chance to revisit all the restaurants he and his friends had dined in, which left her all the more confused.

Folding sun tops and shorts and a pretty lemon broderie-anglaise dress for evening meals, Ivy reflected upon Jacques' revelations about the death of Louise and Patrick's son. She considered the woman's carefully crafted behaviour at the dinner party in conjunction with her husband's and Jacques' obvious concern for her. This, along with her strange sighting of Louise in the Ville Nouvelle, had combined to alert her suspicions that an impenetrable darkness hid beneath the perfect image she presented to the world.

Discovering it was a profound grief, Ivy's heart went out to her. In her great-grandfather's case, the loss of his daughters had plunged him into an unfathomably deep depression, from which he had never recovered. Considering his reaction, she thought Louise and Patrick had shown an incredible resolve to build a new life together in Marrakech. Despite what Jacques had said about Louise's state of mind, she supposed it perfectly possible she and Patrick were expecting another baby but even then there was still something that didn't sit straight about it all. Zipping up her small case, she realised that her shock when Jacques had told her Louise and Patrick's son had drowned, had been heightened by the fact that she could not recall a single photo of the child in their house. But then again, Rose had never mentioned her two elder sisters' premature deaths, so deeply had the pain cut. Perhaps Louise and Patrick's heartbreak was still too raw at this moment in time? Whatever the reason, she knew their son wasn't a topic open for discussion and she must be careful not to mention it during the trip.

Checking herself in the mirror, she hoped an Aztec-print tee-shirt tucked into navy Capri pants suitable attire for the car journey to the coast. She inspected her cheek, which was becoming inflamed again as the effects of the soothing hammam wore off and the African heat continued to take its toll. Luckily she'd brought many bottles of the best camouflaging makeup available with her, the three figure price tag being worth every penny as it didn't just cover the mark but also gave her piece of mind and confidence each time she stepped out in public.

Spotting Jacques in the library, dressed in black jeans and grey short sleeved shirt, his dark hair resting on his collar, Ivy felt her heart skip but she didn't allow herself to speculate what their time in Essaouira would bring. She started to head his way but hung back when she saw he was with Mustapha, demonstrating how to draw a bird, forming the curves of its head and feathers with a thick pencil, while the little boy sat by his side, dutifully trying to mirror what his teacher told him. Every now and again, his pupil looked up for approval which Jacques gave with a reassuring smile. Ivy was reluctant to disturb them but then the handle on her bag suddenly flipped down to make a popping noise which drew their attention to her.

"Ivy," Jacques beckoned with his hand, his face suddenly illuminated by a smile, "come and join us."

She sat opposite them, Mustapha proudly showing her his drawing. "That's excellent. I love the way you have captured the feathers," she said, her French more fluent now so she didn't have to translate each and every word from English before speaking.

"Thank you, Madame Ivy," the little boy smiled, "Jacques is a good teacher."

"I've told Mustapha that we can continue this in a couple of days when I get back from Essaouira," Jacques added with a grin.

"Yes," nodded Mustapha, seriously, "I will stay in the riad until then and try to improve my drawing."

"Good boy," Jacques ruffled the little boy's hair with his hand as Mustapha giggled infectiously. Ivy pondered how the two of them looked so sweet together when her thoughts were interrupted by the impatient tooting of a car horn.

"That will be our ride," Jacques commented, before giving Mustapha quick instructions on how to proceed with his drawing, while Ivy picked up her case and headed across the foyer.

"Where are you going today?" Monsieur Hassan enquired, rearranging a sheaf of papers at the reception desk.

"Essaouira," remarked Ivy, a thrill of excitement coursing through her at the prospect of finally escaping the city heat for a prolonged period. She was on the verge of telling him of their overnight stay but didn't want him to get the wrong idea as Jacques approached them, a trace of agitation on his face. Ivy followed his gaze and spotted the source of it as Louise strode purposely across the courtyard.

"Well I'd better let you go then. It's a lovely morning for a drive," he said, as Ivy watched Louise and Jacques embrace, "I hope you have a good trip."

"Lu," Jacques kissed her on each cheek as she smiled demurely. Ivy noticed how Louise's hair was scooped back today with some oversized sunglasses, narrowing her face and making her look girlish and young. Observing Louise's outfit of a white tee-shirt, pillar-box red Capri pants and white Skechers. Ivy was reassured that she'd chosen similar attire for the journey.

"Lovely to see you again, Ivy," she breathed in her soft

Canadian accent, which was slowly becoming submersed by stronger tones of the French she spoke daily. The women then greeted each other with the customary kisses and as Jacques took the bags, Ivy realised it was the first time she and Louise had been alone together.

"And you. It's so kind of you to invite me. I didn't think I'd make it over to the coast," Ivy reined herself in, taking care not to mention Jacques' name, as she feared it would reveal a whole host of feelings she wasn't quite ready to share with this woman.

"Oh, you'll love it," enthused Louise, linking her arm as they made their way out, "that stretch is so spectacular. We try and go there every month, even if it's just for a day, especially in the summer. It's a relief to breathe the cool sea air into your lungs and hear whispers of the Atlantic, I could stand and watch it for hours, thinking how the same waters brush the Canadian coast." As she spoke a shadow fell across her face before she visibly shook herself and returned to Ivy.

"I hope you don't mind me accompanying you," Ivy cringed as her words sounded like an apology she hadn't intended.

"Oh no, we're delighted to have you come along. I can see how much Jacques thinks of you," Louise said with a sweet smile, "and it'll be nice to have some female company for a change."

Ivy couldn't help but feel encouraged by the woman's sincerity, and feeling her spirits lift determined to enjoy the break, despite the presence of two comparative strangers.

"Hi Ivy, how's it going?" smiled Patrick, unfolding his gangly frame from the small Citroën before giving her a quick hug. Since the dinner party, Ivy noticed he'd had his hair cut to within an inch of his scalp, as though ready to play a tough-guy lead in one of the action films he worked on.

"Nice to see you again Pat, I'm so looking forward to seeing the coast," she replied, noticing Jacques was having trouble fitting their luggage into an almost full boot. It wasn't a surprise to her that Louise didn't travel light.

"Hey Jacques, you're in the back with Ivy. I'm afraid Lu has volunteered to be navigator," Patrick said, winking at his friend as they all settled into their seats.

"Wake me up when we're in Casablanca, then," Jacques joked, taking Ivy's hand before leaning back and closing his eyes.

"Hey, I heard that!" Louise yelled, unfurling her map on her knee, "I don't think I should have to take this. I think we need to give these men as good as we get. Girl power, isn't that what your Spice Girls used to say! What do you think, Ivy?"

Registering Jacques' wry smile out of the corner of her eye, Ivy thought it would be fun to play him at his own game. "Isn't it well known that women have better map reading abilities and sense of direction than men?" she raised an eyebrow.

"Pat, I think we'd better keep an eye on these girls?" Jacques smiled at Ivy, evidently enjoying the banter while Patrick manoeuvred the car through a gap not even the taxi driver who'd brought Ivy from the airport would have attempted to negotiate. Within minutes they were racing through the red ramparts guarding the Kasbah, the scenery opening out as sumptuous villas of the rich and famous, encircled by manicured green lawns flew past. Feeling Jacques' hand warm in her own, Ivy felt excitement bubble in her, knowing she was in for an eventful trip with this intriguing group.

32

The road to Essaouira was one of the straightest Ivy had ever travelled on, something of a relief after the nauseating twists and turns of her trip with Jacques to the Atlas Mountains. In the close confines of the car, the conversation yo-yoed between Jacques' plans for his studio, Ivy's growing experiences and opinions of the city to Patrick's amusing tales about the film industry and Louise's current composition of a Berber mother and child in charcoal. After seemingly no time at all, Patrick pulled over to an *Afriqua* garage to refuel, a cloud of red dust kicked up in their wake.

"Jacques, will you help me stock up on cans from the shop?" Louise smoothed the creases in her trousers as she exited the car, a smile playing upon her lips.

Turning, his eyes rested benevolently upon Ivy, "are you coming?"

"I think I might just stretch my legs for a moment,"

she smiled, watching Patrick unfurl the hose from the petrol pump, "but I wouldn't mind a Diet Coke."

"You got it," he said, closing the car door. She watched as he headed off across the shaded forecourt, Louise talking animatedly at his side. Ivy discerned a slight tension between the two today and, sensing it was nothing to do with her, she hoped a few minutes on their own would give them the chance to iron it out. As Patrick operated the pumps, the smell of petrol threatened to overwhelm her in the crackling heat and she turned her attention to the turquoise sign, bold and brash in the dusty, non-descript landscape.

"You're miles away, aren't you?" Patrick commented. Standing there, Ivy noticed he was forming the beginnings of a stoop, no doubt the result of being so tall and having to constantly reach down for everything.

"It's the sign *Afriqua*," she sighed, unafraid to sound corny in this man's presence, sensing he was as non-judgemental as his friend. "I keep forgetting that in Morocco, we are perched on the edge of a vast, exotic continent. Every time I step out of the riad, I just think about being in Marrakech because the smells, the sounds, the red stones couldn't be anywhere else. I overlook the bigger picture of where we are. I know it sounds silly,"

"I know what you mean. When we first came to live here, I was fascinated by the red earth. It constantly reminded me I'd literally stepped onto a different land, so different to Canada," he agreed, "seven years on, I still feel it. Morocco is a magical place for me."

"I've never been beyond Europe before," she continued,

263

"but since I was very young I've wanted to travel to see different lands and peoples."

"Me too. I've always fancied seeing New Zealand. Spend some time there before working my way up to the Philippines, Malaysia, Vietnam, Thailand and Burma. But Lou feels at home here so I don't know if we will," he paused and, following his glance, Ivy saw Jacques and Louise approaching. A red, polythene bag containing the drinks swinging in Jacques' hand, she noticed Louise, in her pumps, fell a long way short of his shoulders. It took her by surprise as, with her slim willowy figure, she'd been of the impression at the dinner party that Louise had been much taller, a rather commanding figure in fact. But today she presented a much more vulnerable person.

"You two have been gone for ages!" Patrick relieved Jacques of his load, before passing them each an ice-cold can and stocking the cool-box with the rest. "Were you setting the world to rights again?"

"We got talking about this and that," said Louise, shooting an ambiguous smile in Ivy's direction as she got in the car.

"We've been debating the route," Jacques clarified, his eyes holding Ivy's. Despite his reassuring gesture, even with Ivy's limited experience of male-female relationships, it was impossible not to deduce from her body-language that Louise was attracted to Jacques and had perhaps taken the opportunity of being alone with him to voice her opinions about his new friendship.

"Oh, no, look at my Skechers. They are covered in earth," Louise exclaimed, breaking into Ivy's thoughts, bringing everyone's attention back to her, "I think it'll stain."

"You do insist on wearing white, honey," Patrick commented as he lifted her feet into his lap, slipping off her shoes as he might do a child's before dowsing them in bottled water. It took him a few minutes to restore them to their former state before setting off on the last leg of their journey to the coast, an uneasiness creeping over Ivy that Louise might be a potential threat in Jacques' affections. But by the time they entered the imposing city gate of Essaouira, she'd found solace in the fact that Louise had chosen and married Patrick, not Jacques.

Following the shop-lined Rue Mohammed el Qorry to the crossroads at the Medina's heart, Jacques wound down his window for them to experience the heat and aromas of the stalls, which Ivy noticed, were subtly different to those in Marrakech. No sooner had they entered the souks though they petered out, as the road unexpectedly gave way to an elegant square with a vibrantly green garden at its centre. Surrounded by pristinely white buildings, Ivy noticed people were taking advantage of the pleasant sea breeze to enjoy alfresco lunches. Out of the corner of her eye, she sensed Jacques watching her, wanting to share her delight in beholding this beautiful place for the first time.

"The journey has made me hungry," announced Louise, abruptly interrupting Ivy's daydream, "how about we check in at the riad and then follow the squawks of the seagulls down to the port for a lunch of grilled sardines?"

"That's an excellent idea, darling. Here we are," Patrick brought the car to a halt outside an elegant, white building surrounded by shady palm trees. Ivy correctly deduced this was Villa Maroc.

"Do you two want to join us or have you got other plans?" Lousie addressed them.

"I'm okay with that, if you are?" Ivy turned to Jacques, feeling, with Louise's eyes on her, she couldn't refuse.

"Fantastic," Louise cut in before Jacques had a chance to comment, having already turned to unload their overnight bags from the boot.

Ivy gazed around, enraptured by the stunning minimalism of the entrance hall, with its exposed stone arches and simple black furniture, the giant, gilt-edged mirrors its only adornment. While Jacques checked them all in at the desk, she peered into a cosy sitting room which in contrast was warm and colourfully decorated, with textiles hanging on the walls. Obviously someone with a very artistic eye had had a hand in the Villa's design and Ivy quickly saw why it appealed to Jacques, Louise and Patrick.

"Do you like it?" Jacques inquired, smiling as he ducked through the archway, to hand her a room key. "In a former life it was four separate merchants' houses and it's rather like a warren of open terraces, staircases which never lead where you expect and secluded spaces."

"I've never been anywhere like it," she smiled, thinking what a romantic setting it was. "I'll have to do some exploring later."

"Right then, shall we just dump our bags in our rooms, have a quick freshen up and then go to the harbour?" interrupted Louise, the giddiness of children on a school trip in her voice, "meet here in fifteen?"

"Fine by me, what about you, Ivy?" inquired Jacques, dark spikes of his hair standing at all angles around the sunglasses he'd perched on top of his head.

Having little choice in the matter, Ivy nodded in consent. All day, she had been desperate to spend some time alone with Jacques and the fact it still wasn't on the agenda only made her need greater. She was relieved, however, that as the corridor forked off, she and Jacques went one way to their rooms while Louise and Patrick took the other, "you're alright with the lunch arrangement aren't you?" he asked anxiously, as they stood on the threshold of her room.

"Yes, I love seafood," Ivy smiled broadly, not wanting him to think she didn't want to spend time with his friends. Besides, she reasoned, there would be lots of opportunities for them to be alone together back in Marrakech.

"Good, see you in ten minutes then," he smiled, as their door locks simultaneously released.

Ivy's room was airy and spacious, dominated by a large double bed covered with crisp white sheets and liberally strewn with wine-coloured silk cushions. There was a circular glass table and two wicker chairs at the window where soft white curtains gently billowed in the breeze. Dotted around the room were some 'amuse les yeux', quirky local art and craft pieces. After freshening up in the bathroom which was white and bright, and equipped with an array of expensive toiletries, Ivy changed from her now hot and crumpled outfit into her plain but elegant sundress. Walking to the window, she observed a large shaded terrace where she imagined reading and relaxing with Jacques. Beyond was a quiet courtyard, canopied by a purple cloud of bougainvillea which in turn overlooked the white buildings of the fishing town which eventually fell away to the infinite blue of the ocean. She lingered for a few more minutes drinking in the stunning view until she felt it was time to go and meet the others. With Jacques' arm encircling her waist, they followed Louise and Patrick and the calls of seagulls down cobbled streets to the harbour.

"It's idyllic here," breathed Ivy.

"I knew you'd like it – I think the Villa Maroc is delightful and it gives you the best of both worlds, being so close to the Medina which is steeped in history while having spectacular sea views," he beamed.

"Have you painted here?" she lowered her voice, negotiating some steep steps as he deliberately hung back from his friends, eager to afford them all some privacy.

"Yes, I've done some seascapes, although they are Louise's domain. I like to have a break and recharge my batteries here more than anything when I've just completed a time-consuming piece," he continued, helping her down the final few steps which were much deeper than the others. "The riad dates from the 18th century and, as I told you, it was formerly four houses which create the maze-like interior. I especially like the sitting rooms which are peaceful and comfortable with crackling fireplaces in winter."

Ivy smiled thoughtfully as they continued down the winding, enclosed streets before finally meeting the wide expanse of the seafront, which was populated by just a handful of new international hotels. Clinging to pockets of shade beneath blue and white striped awnings, she noticed the distance between Jacques and her and the others seemed to be growing by the second, as though it was just her and him after all.

"This takes me back to the summer I graduated, when I had a holiday in Greece with my friend," she commented as the hotels gave way to a stretch of sun-beaten blue and white buildings, a stark contrast to the warm pinks and reds of Marrakech.

"Sounds like you've always had an adventurous spirit, after all?" he gazed at her with a look she didn't know how to interpret.

"Not really. We only went for a fortnight. We visited Rhodes and had a boat trip to a tiny island called Simi where the temperature hit forty-five degrees and we spent the whole time in the relative cool of a café on the harbour front," Ivy laughed.

"But you were good friends?" Jacques turned to give her that inquisitive look of his as she realised he was blatantly fishing for details, perhaps imagining she'd gone with a boyfriend. For a moment she was tempted to tease him, but something serious in his eyes made her abandon the idea.

"Yes, we met on our first day in school and we're still friends. But Mei got married later that summer and she's got two children now and lives in North London so we only see each other a few times a year," she continued, "nowadays, I go out socially sometimes with my work colleagues but Mei's the only friend I'd confide in, the only one I'm really close to."

"I'd imagine you're a very loyal friend, too," he regarded her thoughtfully as though it was a quality he admired.

"I suppose so," she blushed, "but only the way you are with Patrick."

"Yes, I was just thinking your friendship with Mei sounded very similar to the one I share with him," he smiled before falling silent as they walked on, breathing in the refreshingly cool air.

"I've always loved it here," he stopped abruptly, looking out to the sea, "but I love it even more now you're here to share it with me."

Before she could answer, Ivy noticed Patrick and Louise stop suddenly to enable them to catch up, "I hope you're not subjecting the poor girl to one of your historical tours?" Patrick commented, the breeze whipping beneath his thin shirt.

"No, we're just having a pleasant conversation," Jacques countered his friend, while Louise looked on, her expression inscrutable, "with one or two interesting facts thrown in."

"Always did like the sound of your own voice, eh?" Patrick slapped him playfully on the shoulder, "you can always walk with us if he's boring you, Ivy?"

"Take no notice of him." Jacques winked, squeezing her hand. As they reached the sandy-stoned ramparts of the Skala du Port, Ivy mused that Jacques and Patrick sometimes behaved more like brothers than best friends and that their relationship did indeed bring out Jacques' caring nature and loyalty.

While the playful mood between the men continued, Ivy noticed Louise remained silent, her gaze focused on a dozen or so men at the beach's edge, fashioning boats from wood. With the whiteness of the silky sand and pale-blues of sea and sky contrasting with the black, silhouetted figures of the boat-builders, Ivy surmised she was probably fitting the composition of the scene into the suitability for a painting and decided not to intrude upon her thoughts. Instead, she watched the men too, their skin as brown and wrinkled as old boot leather, as they sawed and hammered, the sharp scent of sea salt slicing through the earthy mustiness of the resin.

Once more, Ivy admired the Moroccans for keeping their age-old traditions alive. Just beyond the men, tourists were sunbathing as their children took camel rides, carefully skirting around a makeshift pitch scored out in the sand where local teenagers played a game of five-a-side football before the beach shelved down to the sea, where figures bobbed up and down on surfboards in a myriad of colours. A bystander to this lively scene, Ivy marvelled at how the past and present, the old and young, the locals and foreigners seemed to effortlessly coexist here.

"This beach has become a mecca for water sports' enthusiasts in the last couple of years." Ivy detected traces of disapproval in Patrick's voice as they paused momentarily to watch the waves rush towards the sands in a foaming froth, with inexperienced windsurfers desperately attempting to cling to their boards.

"But hopefully the abundant daily catches will ensure that it remains a fishing harbour for some time. I love the old traditions. Change isn't always for the better," he continued grimly.

"Oh, Pat," Louise countered, startling Ivy as it was the first time she'd spoken since leaving the riad, "you should listen to yourself. You sound about ninety instead of forty-three. Change is exciting. It is the one thing we can all depend on, thank God. Life wouldn't be much fun without it."

Knowing what she did of Patrick and Louise's tragic loss, Ivy concluded they were clearly attempting to cope with it in different ways and refrained from commenting.

"I've had an idea," Louise continued, her tone bright as she secured her hair in a ponytail in defiance of the wind, "we'll come back here after lunch. That's when all the fun starts – when the daily catch and market arrive. The fish auction is exhilarating Ivy, you must see it!"

"It's turned into quite a tourist attraction," Patrick added, disparagingly.

"What are we, if not tourists from Marrakech?" Jacques countered as his friend nodded, disgruntled. Ivy saw that whereas Jacques embraced tourism, eager to pass on his enthusiasm and knowledge of Morocco to foreign visitors only there for a matter of days or weeks, Patrick wanted to assimilate into Moroccan life, forgetting his past life in Canada. For him, she suspected, tourists were an annoying reminder that he had been one too when he'd arrived a few years before, and in many ways, still was.

"Why don't we eat here?" Jacques suggested, indicating a smart, three-story, white-washed building on the edge of the harbour.

Sitting on the terrace of *Chalet de la Plage*, the early afternoon hours rolled by as the four chattered happily over their simple meal of freshly caught grilled sardines and salad, which they washed down with a bottle of Bordeaux. Ivy noticed Louise drank with ease and knew that if it was herself who was the pregnant one she'd take a little more care. But she decided it wasn't any concern of hers.

Afterwards, the sea breeze somewhat tempering the sun's ferocity, they climbed the port's imposing ramparts where, from her elevated position, Ivy grasped just what a powerhouse the Atlantic Ocean was as waves crashed loudly on the rocks, the fishing and pleasure boats bobbing like toys on the suddenly tumultuous turquoise waters. Casting her eyes back to the town, she recalled reading in her guidebook that its layout dated back to 1765. Apparently, its ruler had captured a French ship, hiring one of its passengers, an architect, to rebuild his port, which Ivy noticed was surrounded by a heavy defensive wall. Several ancient cannons peering out from the stonework, served as reminders of its former purpose as a fortification against invasion. While these might have proved a deterrent for invaders, she surmised they would have been easily overrun by the wrath of nature.

"I think it's these fortifications and this view that make it such a favoured place for movie crews," Louise commented, wincing as she touched the sun-scorched metal of one of the enormous cannons, "Orson Welles once filmed here."

"And *Game of Thrones* more recently," added Patrick. "They shoot here quite regularly."

"I'll stick with Orson Welles and the 20th century, thank you very much," chortled Louise, "and the early morning mist rolling along the ramparts. It is just so impossibly atmospheric."

"Speaking of Orson Welles, I'd like to visit the Hôtel des Iles again," suggested Patrick, looking at his wife, "we could have afternoon tea if you want?"

"Hôtel des Iles is where Orson Welles stayed during the 1950s when he was filming his classic version of *Othello*. Legend has it that he met Winston Churchill during his sojourn here," Jacques filled Ivy in as they reached the top of the ramparts.

"But you digress, Jacques," interjected Patrick, who, Ivy realised was a total film anorak, albeit a nice one, "Welles shot many scenes for *Othello* on the Skala while the murder of Roderigo was filmed in Hammam Pabst. Locals were drafted in as extras, earning a nice wage, some bread and sardines. How about afternoon tea then?" he unexpectedly changed the subject extending the invitation to Ivy and Jacques.

"It's a long walk to the Hôtel des Iles but it is a traditional afternoon tea so it's up to you whether you want to go or not," Jacques paused, giving Ivy one of his inscrutable looks as he left the decision to her.

"I might just give it a miss, Patrick. I'm hot and tired and it'll give you a chance to reminisce together," Ivy sighed, wiping her brow with the back of her hand, "I think I'll return to the riad, if you don't mind?"

"Not at all," smiled Patrick, a brief look passing between him and Jacques which Ivy couldn't decipher. Her gut feeling was that she'd been rude to decline and she was on the verge of changing her mind to accept when Jacques cut in.

"I'll come with you Ivy," he took her hand, before turning to his friends, "I'll book a table at Ferdeous for 8pm?"

"That would be great. See you both then," enthused Patrick. Ivy was careful to avoid Louise's gaze and was grateful as she and Jacques turned away from the glittering, golden beach, which, even with her sunglasses, dazzled, to a quiet cobblestone street lined with artisan's shops, quiet during the siesta.

They found the Villa's reception deserted, the silence magnifying the clatter of Ivy's sandals on the marble floor. Suddenly she felt Jacques pull her to a halt, their bodies almost touching, the atmosphere around them charged. Smiling at her, he gently stroked the side of her face with his hand, the desire in his eyes along with his shallow breathing leaving her in no doubt how he wished they could spend the afternoon. However much his body language betrayed his thoughts though, Ivy knew that he wouldn't ask her again, her refusal of a few nights ago evidently still weighing heavily on his mind. Something told her that if she didn't seize the moment, she might not get a third chance while in the back of her mind, she remembered putting an extra layer of makeup on that morning to combat the effects of the heat.

"Do you want a drink?" he suggested eventually as the moment lingered between them, heavy with suppressed longing.

"No, I want this… " she whispered, pulling his face down to meet hers and kiss him lightly on the lips. As he drew back a few seconds later, she saw his surprise and delight were underpinned by a desire which mirrored her own. Seeing passion burn in his dark eyes as he took her hand in his, Ivy didn't care if it was just a holiday romance, she only knew that there was no denying themselves any longer. For once, she felt nothing holding her back; she had to take a risk.

Standing in the cool of her shuttered room, Jacques' kisses were delicate but deliberate as he drew Ivy into the heat of his body. A smile briefly playing on his lips, he paused momentarily, his eyes asking her permission to continue. Gently caressing her neck, his touch then became more urgent and Ivy felt electricity-like volts course through her body as his long, elegant fingers slipped the sundress' straps from her shoulders, the light material pooling at her feet. The care he took as his hands continued on, lingering on the soft swell of her breasts, the sharp angle of her hips before coming to rest upon the curve of her buttocks, told Ivy she been correct in her assumption that he had dreamed of this moment too. Clasping her hands around his neck he then lifted her as though she was feather-light and laid her on the bed, before quickly removing his own clothes. Running her hands along his tanned and trim torso, Ivy felt him quiver with desire above her before his weight came down upon her as a soft moan escaped her lips.

Their need for each other this first time was urgent and over quickly. But for the rest of the afternoon they made love slowly, taking time to explore and enjoy each other's bodies. Behaving as though they had all the time in the world in a tangle of limbs in which Ivy wasn't quite sure where she ended and he began, they lingered over each kiss, each caress. Moving in rhythm with Jacques, she found she was able to release some of the locks and knock down walls she'd placed around herself, and for those long hours they luxuriated in each other, time ceasing to exist. When the act of love drew to its end, she clung to the heart of this man she'd so recently met but who she already knew was part of her soul.

Afterwards, they lay facing each other, Ivy careful to keep the left side of her face hidden by the pillow for the eventuality that the intensity of their lovemaking had started to reveal her disfigurement. His face so close to hers she noticed how his eyelashes were tipped with golden brown, the same colour his hair might have been when he was a boy.

"I didn't dare to hope you felt the same as I did," he smiled, still slightly breathless as his fingers tenderly brushed through her hair, strewn over the pillow.

"No, I'm good at hiding my feelings," she replied, wondering whether there'd ever be a time when she wouldn't have any need to.

As red rays of the setting sun filtered through the blinds, casting the room in a rose-coloured light, Ivy watched him as he drifted into a contented sleep, his hand lightly curled around her breast. Sometime later, while he slipped back to his room to change for dinner, Ivy took a long, cool shower, envisaging her skin to be scorched where his hands had touched her. Carefully reapplying her makeup, she reflected how her couple of sexual encounters up to this point in her life, had not come close to capturing her heart, body and soul the way Jacques had just done.

33

Smartening up her sundress with a diaphanous, grey shrug and heeled sandals, Ivy descended to the foyer early, hoping to have a quiet word with Jacques but found him already engaged in conversation with Patrick and Louise. She cringed inwardly as the level-pegging she and Louise had been on earlier in their tee-shirts and Capri pants, had well and truly been raised by her scarlet silk dress which she'd teamed with a dramatic black-fringed Spanish shawl. Complimenting her lily-white skin and glossy hair perfectly, Ivy felt diminished in her presence, despite Jacques' eyes telling her otherwise.

"You look beautiful." he affirmed, kissing her firmly on the mouth. Feeling Louise's eyes on them, she could only manage a quiet "thank you."

They made the short walk along the beach to Ferdeous' bistro. Jacques' hand warm in hers, Ivy felt tired but elated at the same time as the lights of the restaurant came into view. The thought briefly bothering her that Louise somehow sensed what had occurred between herself and Jacques in the warm afternoon hours, she soon reached the conclusion it was no business of hers anyway. At the restaurant's entrance, illuminated with hundreds of twinkle lights, a friendly woman with beautiful jet-black hair, whom Ivy guessed was the owner, greeted them. Obviously a food lover, her rounded figure didn't detract from her beauty which she'd retained well into middle age.

"Ah, Jacques, it's been a long time," she kissed him once on each cheek which indicated she knew him very well, "and you bring your friends."

Ivy noticed that she kissed Louise and Patrick once on each cheek too so her suspicions that they were all well acquainted and often came as a threesome were confirmed.

"And this is Ivy," Jacques offered. Ivy was pleased that he didn't include her under the 'friends' banner even though she was still trying to understand what had happened between them in her room earlier and the implications it would have upon their relationship.

"This is Madame Souad. She used to be head chef at Villa Maroc," smiled Jacques, as the woman gazed admiringly at him, "but then she left and set up this restaurant with her husband. Chez Ferdeous serves the best food in town."

"Enchanté, Ivy," Madame Souad pulled Ivy to her. Her skin was soft and smelt of jasmine as she kissed her once on each cheek.

"Pleased to meet you, Madame, you have a lovely restaurant," smiled Ivy as Madame led them to a quiet corner table which afforded them a wonderful view of the moonlit beach.

The place was larger than it appeared on the outside. Decorated in warm shades of ochre and pink, though, it had a cosy feel too. It was crowded with locals who Ivy guessed came every night to enjoy a homely meal at a reasonable price. On Madame Souad's recommendation she ordered a lamb tagine with dried apricots and nuts, for her walk in the sea air and her afternoon in bed with Jacques had given her a healthy appetite that evening. She polished it off with gusto, followed by a rose-infused sorbet, as the conversation revolved around Patrick's work on a time-travelling epic which, under any other circumstances, Ivy would have found interesting. But seated in between Jacques and Louise, who she noticed was picking at her food without actually eating much of it, she began to feel more and more uncomfortable as the night wore on. She was eager to be alone with Jacques, to talk to him about what had occurred between them that afternoon, certain that in every gesture and look, she was betraying what they had done to Louise. And for some reason, that notion made her feel extremely uneasy.

No sooner did they arrive back at Villa Maroc than Louise retired to bed, blaming her tiredness and lack of appetite on the journey. After enjoying a nightcap with the two men, and seeing how relaxed they were in each other's company reminiscing about the past, Ivy decided to turn in for the night herself. She left them both ordering more drinks and laughing uproariously at some shared memory of their student days.

34

Ivy left on her makeup hoping that Jacques would join her that night. Lying in bed, she relived their love-making while listening for his knock on the door, desperate for him to return, to be caressed by his gentle hands once more. Even though she'd only known him for a matter of weeks and, considering her usual caution in affairs of the heart it seemed crazy, but just as Rose had known from the beginning that Ryan was her soul mate, she sensed Jacques was 'the one' for her.

Waking to find the unfamiliar room shrouded in darkness, Ivy glanced at her clock. Registering the time, 4:20am, with a wave of disappointment she realised Jacques wasn't coming after all. Pondering the whys and wherefores, she endured a prolonged period of wakefulness, exacerbated by the chill night air. Dragging the duvet up to her chin, she rolled over onto her side to inhale Jacques' lingering scent on the pillow where he'd fallen asleep earlier. Caught in the memory once more of what had occurred between them, Ivy realised their relationship had irrevocably changed. Whether it would be for better or worse, she was unable to say but with such thoughts rattling around in her mind, she knew sleep would remain a stranger for some time. The only way she could think of to pass the remaining hours of the night was to resume reading Rose's journal.

"I thought things might calm down after D-Day but, if anything, Ryan was deployed on more ops than ever. In July 1944, I have discovered that his group were targeting German troops and artillery positions to aide British forces near Caen, gun emplacements in the west at Brest, as well as attacking refineries and communication links in northern Germany. Each time he left me by the stile, I found it harder to say goodbye to him and while he was gone, it was impossible not to think of the dangers he faced every second of every day.

But whenever he had a day's or weekend's leave between missions, we spent that time together. I'd wait by the stile and, spotting him walking across the fields in his flying jacket and boots, felt my heart pumping fiercely in my chest. Caught in our own little bubble, untouched by war, we enjoyed those warm days and balmy nights of summer. This was all an illusion, of course, as it was becoming hard to ignore Ryan's increasingly disturbing behaviour but at the time I didn't want to admit it. Whenever he spoke about the losses his group had suffered, he did it in an almost casual, callous way. Yet I could see from the unfathomable look in his eyes that his words didn't mirror what he was thinking or feeling, that he could no longer reconcile being in cosy Lavenham one day and in the skies over Germany the next.

He'd spoken of how important attending church every Sunday at home had always been to him and his family and he'd told me he often talked to the unit's chaplain. I was glad that he felt he could speak to somebody even though knowing he couldn't confide in me about what troubled him so deeply left me very uneasy. The only thing I could offer him was an escape and we sometimes ventured to the Athenaeum in Bury St Edmonds where we danced till the early hours, returning at dawn to the cottage where my mother would have breakfast waiting for us. Over bacon and eggs, my mother and Ryan got to know each other, striking up a mutual friendship, something which I'd hoped for but hadn't expected.

"You're so damned pretty. I count my lucky stars every night that I met you," he commented one night in late August as he walked me home. Our hands swung in between us, clasped together, our fingers entwined. We had spent a lovely evening in The Swan, with Ryan being the most relaxed I'd seen him for weeks, maybe months.

I commented to him that this war, which had cost everyone so much, had brought us together, giving us such happiness. He responded, with a mischievous smile that, had he stayed at home, he could have been stuck with one of those pretty, Virginia belles. I began to chide him but he just shook his head, pulling me into the warmth of his jacket. "There's only one girl for me and I'm looking right at her." He gently touched his lips to mine before pulling back; "I've fallen in love with you Rose Endicott, could you ever feel the same about me?"

Looking at his handsome sincere face I had to smile. "If

I'm truthful I fell in love with you the first moment I saw you outside The Swan."

As I got to know him more, my first impressions were proved correct. Although Ryan was charming he wasn't brash like some of the other airmen and loved to tell me tales of America. Ryan knew that he hadn't been sent to England just to have a good time; he had an unwavering sense of duty to his country and to his crew and seemed old beyond his twenty-two years. But on other occasions he just struck me as a lonely young man far from home.

"I want you to be my wife, Rose. When all this is over, I want you to come back to Richmond with me. It's such a beautiful city, you'll love it. We'll be married and we'll buy a town house where we'll raise our kids," he told me one night as we walked through the fields, filled with hayricks in the midst of the harvest.

As I accepted his proposal, I heard a car backfire in the distance. I felt Ryan tense as he held me, tremors coursing again and again through his body. I was puzzled, for someone accustomed to the loud noises of a bomber in action, it seemed an over-reaction. But after a moment or so, he brightened and continued to talk of our life together in Virginia and I forgot all about it as he swept me into his arms once more. It was only later that night, in the darkness of my room, that I recalled the incident which somehow cast a shadow over what was the happiest moment of my life.

Although Mum clearly liked Ryan, I didn't tell her of his marriage proposal, not wanting anyone else's opinion, even hers. Though concealing it from her made me feel terrible again, I needed to keep it between Ryan and me. After all I had lost, *every time he put his hand in mine, I felt endless possibilities open out before me once more."*

Spotting no sign of Jacques or Louise and Patrick on the terrace, Ivy opted for some light scrambled eggs and toast, all she could stomach from the sumptuous buffet. Sitting at a table overlooking the sweeping bay, she found the calm of the ocean conducive to collecting her thoughts. She decided not to pre-empt anything with Jacques and wondered whether what had happened between them the previous afternoon had been more meaningful to her than to him. No, surely she couldn't have got that wrong?

Looking up, Ivy spotted him heading towards her, his hair and indeed appearance, uncharacteristically dishevelled. Placing a mug of black coffee on the table, he sat down before her, managing a half smile as he rested his chin on the heel of his hand, "you don't happen to have any pain killers Ivy? I'm afraid my reminiscing with Patrick ended up with a heavy drinking session."

Rummaging in her bag, Ivy couldn't help a half smile as his hungover expression said it all. Passing him two tablets, she countered, "the friend I told you of, Mei, and I rarely get to have a proper chat anymore. It must be the same for you and Patrick?"

"It is." He swallowed the pills with a gulp of water. "We've got a lifetime of shared experiences, some good, some not," he paused, a shadow briefly crossing his face, "and it's cathartic to talk when we get the opportunity."

Ivy nodded, knowing that it would have fallen to Jacques to give his best friend the support he needed after his son's death. Realising Louise's mental state was still very fragile, Ivy surmised that while she heavily relied on Patrick for solace, she wouldn't be able to give any in return. If her guess that Louise was pregnant proved correct, it might begin to heal both her and her husband but having had no hint of this from any of the three of them, she would continue to keep that assumption to herself.

Patrick's voice cut through her thoughts. "Hey, you two." Ivy looked up and was amused to see him in dark glasses looking as worse for wear as his friend. Louise, immaculate as ever in navy slacks and a crisp white shirt sat down next to Jacques, "I hope you two feel as bad as you look," she laughed, turning to her husband, "crawling into bed at 4am."

Her cheerful demeanour settled Ivy's nerves somewhat as either she hadn't guessed or didn't seem to care whether she and Jacques had slept together. However, whenever Louise looked in her direction, Ivy was determined not to betray her feelings for Jacques with the merest careless glance or gesture. For whatever reason, she knew she had to keep them to herself, safe from the prying opinions of outsiders.

"I was reading in a brochure they serve a gorgeous afternoon tea here too. It was so lovely yesterday at des Iles, dainty sandwiches and cakes to die for," Louise turned to her husband, her voice quickened with excitement, "can we treat ourselves again before we leave?"

"We'll see," cautioned Patrick, who, like Jacques, was sticking to black coffee, "I was looking forward to Jacques' tour of the Medina and Mellah, which should keep us occupied until midnight, if we're unlucky."

"Definitely a case of the pot calling the kettle black," Jacques playfully retorted to his friend before turning to Ivy, "remember last week I didn't get back from Ouarzazate until late?"

"Yes, you missed dinner," clarified Ivy, sensing Louise's eyes on her.

"You're lucky I didn't miss the rest of your holiday as Pat gave me such a detailed insight into his current film, I felt I'd starred in it and produced it by the end." To this, all of them burst out laughing. Or so it seemed for when Ivy's gaze rested upon Louise she saw an expression on her face she could not interpret.

"Do you fancy a spot of retail therapy, Ivy? The souks here are not nearly as pushy as in Marrakech," Louise enquired, collecting herself after a few moments.

"Yes, why not?" Ivy noticed her eyes were warm and inviting now, persuading her that perhaps she'd imagined her previous expression.

"That's settled then," concluded Louise, looking pleased with herself, as Patrick and Jacques moved the topic of conversation to a film they had been discussing the previous night. While they talked, Ivy looked out to sea, tuning into the shushing of the waves as they stroked the sand, interrupted now and again by the harsh call of seagulls swooping down from the cloudless sky.

Beads of perspiration dampening the hair on her neck, Ivy was glad she'd chosen to wear her cool sun-dress again, as the group walked down Rue Mohammed el Qorry, the early morning sun hot on their backs. As in Marrakech, Essaouira's medina had been built by 18th century European colonists and consisted of a labyrinth of narrow streets. It was, however, not as difficult to navigate, being bisected by one long, straight street which began at the north gate, the Bab Doukkala, and, hundreds of haggles later, ended down at the port.

"I will never become acclimatised to these temperatures," Ivy said, momentarily letting go of Jacques' hand to adjust her sunhat to ensure its wide brim shaded her face.

"No," Jacques gave her a thoughtful look as they paused at a crossroads, "I think we'll gravitate to the shade today."

"It must be thirty-five degrees already," remarked Patrick, casually and coolly dressed in tee-shirt and shorts, turning to Ivy and Jacques. "I think we should go our separate ways now."

"But I was going to show Ivy where to pick up the best bargains," Louise chipped in, disgruntled.

"My love, last time we were here I saw some unusually cut leather belts on the far side of the Medina and I don't want to bore Ivy," he smiled, a crafty glint in his eye as he faced them, "I'll leave that to Jacques."

Jacques just shook his head, smiling, clearly accustomed to his friend's playful jibes. "How about we meet in *Pâtisserie Driss* for morning coffee then? Say 11:30?"

"Sounds perfect," Patrick pulled his wife's arm but as Louise drew away, Ivy saw from the expression on her face the arrangement far from suited her. With Jacques gripping her hand, they pushed a path through the lively food market. Ivy saw it was populated by locals doing their daily shop of fresh vegetables, fish, spices and grains.

"The Souk Jdid has got to be my favourite market in Morocco," Jacques pulled her to a stall. Ivy stood watching him as he scooped strawberries from the summit of a scarlet mound into a brown paper bag, "I love the vibe here, being surrounded by local people going about their daily business. It makes me think that life isn't that complicated if we don't make it so. It's just about having enough money and food to live and enjoying the moment."

"That's all you need, I suppose," nodded Ivy, not quite sure what he was getting at but happy to let it go as she became accustomed to his philosophical musings.

The food stalls of the Souk Jdid soon gave way to arts and crafts stalls and, after briefly browsing the ornate iron-mongering, they lingered on some exquisite woodcarving. Although her budget didn't run to one of the lovely Thuya cabinets, Ivy purchased some pens carved from the same, bartering the man to thirty dirhams a piece.

"You got a good bargain, there," remarked Jacques as she carefully slotted the pens into her handbag, thinking she would give them to her parents while keeping one for herself as a little souvenir of her trip to the coast.

"Did I? I didn't mean to." Feelings of guilt of potentially ripping off such a skilled craftsman consumed her, "I can't get used to haggling."

"No, I don't think you will," Jacques smiled, looking at her in that strange way of his. Was it admiration or something else, she thought, frustrated by his inscrutability when he seemed to read her like an open book. Leaving the stalls behind, the streets became deserted as the Medina merged into the Mellah. Reminiscent of Marrakech's alleyways during the siesta, the difference here was that people weren't sleeping on the other side of closed doors. They had long since gone.

Ivy looked around at the dilapidated and often ruined buildings, the Hebrew inscriptions still on the lintels, here and there. "Was there a large Jewish population once?"

"Yes, it flourished during the 18th and 19th centuries when the Jewish community was the most important economic group in the city," Jacques paused by a house with peeling pink paint and boarded up windows. "These streets saw extremely prosperous times up until World War Two."

Spotting a once impressive building with an ornate, wrought iron balcony in a bad state of repair, she ventured, "Did the Jewish people here manage to escape Nazi persecution?"

"Yes, they did. Most emigrated to Israel and had the chance to build new lives there. They were lucky," Jacques suddenly regressed from the role of tour guide to a mood of quiet contemplation, their feet echoing on the cobblestones as they strolled hand-in-hand, happy to be in each other's company.

Entering *Chez Driss,* which, Jacques had explained, was a famous French pâtisserie serving cakes and coffee to Essaouirians since 1928, Ivy felt herself relax in the pleasant coolness beneath the ceiling fans. Her attention was immediately drawn to the framed accolades crammed on the walls before she homed in on the reason, a huge chilled cabinet displaying a whole host of exquisitely decorated French pastries and cakes. Jacques stood patiently while she marvelled at the array of fruit-topped tarts and cream-piped gateaux before bending towards her to sensibly suggest, "how about we get a few cakes to share?"

"I think that's a good idea, unless you fancy standing here all day while I deliberate?" Seeing his grin light up his face, Ivy returned it. After some debate, they settled on a mille feuille, a tarte Belle Hélène and a gateau fraise.

Coloured stained-glass windows and yellow marble pillars gave the seating area a quirky quality, while the walls were crammed with so many framed photos of famous visitors to the pâtisserie, just a few streaks of faded magnolia paint peeped through. Sitting on red velvet chairs around a gilt-legged table, it was a little too ostentatious for Ivy's taste, who had grown accustomed to the rustic North African interiors of Marrakech's cafes and courtyards.

"It's a bit Louis XIV isn't it?" Jacques screwed up his nose, placing between them their chosen cakes which were mercifully minute, "Not really my style."

"Nor mine," Ivy shook her head, "but it's been here for over eighty years so who are we to judge?" Jacques nodded, politely waiting for her to try their selected cakes.

"I see you've ordered our cakes then?" Patrick's voice called across the café. Ivy looked up to see his beanpole body, stooped, his head grazing the tiled ceiling as the space seemed to shrink in his presence.

"Oh no! They're just for us. We were a little indecisive, weren't we?" Jacques smiled at Ivy.

"Seems about right! I'd better go get ours then," Patrick stepped back to the counter. "Just take a minute to cool down," he added as Louise appeared from behind her husband, her face red, her breathing laboured.

"Are you okay?" Jacques leapt to his feet to pull out a chair for her. Concern clouded his face as he offered her his glass of iced water. Calming slightly, she took several greedy gulps, although it was another few minutes until her colour returned to normal. Once again, Ivy toyed with the notion Louise was pregnant. But Pat obviously didn't know as he surely wouldn't have rushed her around the souks in search of a belt in this unforgiving heat. Why on earth would she keep it a secret?

"Yes, much better," Louise smiled, eventually. Despite her brave face, Ivy could see Jacques wasn't convinced, his forehead furrowed with concern for his friend. Truth to tell Ivy didn't think she looked at all well either as Patrick returned with a tray holding two coffees, two glasses of iced water, a framboise mousse gateau and an éclair. "You've cooled down a bit?" he put his hand on his wife's shoulder as she looked up and smiled wanly.

"Ahh, you've had the same idea as us, albeit on a smaller scale," interrupted Jacques, sharing the mille feuille between him and Ivy as evenly as its flakiness allowed, "did you see everything you'd planned?"

"Yes, we visited the Place Orson Welles," said Patrick. Grateful to Jacques for bringing everything back on an even keel, Ivy calmed a little, shedding some of the edginess she always felt in Louise's company as they chatted about what they'd done that morning.

Later, noticing Jacques had withdrawn somewhat from the conversation, she turned to him. His smile, previously inscrutable, was full of love for her. Or was she imagining it? Watching Louise talk animatedly now, her eyes sparkling, Ivy was struck by the rapid changes in her moods and couldn't help but remember how Rose had been concerned about Ryan for the same reason. She considered the protective instinct she provoked in both Patrick and Jacques. While she could understand the former's reaction, Jacques' attitude to Louise baffled her. Most of the time, he appeared indifferent to her and evidently closer to his friend, Patrick, but on other occasions as when she'd told him of Louise's unkempt appearance on the swanky streets of Guéliz, he'd been agitated and extremely concerned for her. But then again, maybe it was just in Jacques' nature to make people feel safe in his company as he'd done her ever since their first meeting? Seeing him smiling at her, she felt warmth rise in her once more, which overrode everything else.

To escape the heat and walk off the calorific cakes into the bargain, the group spent the afternoon in the mercifully air-conditioned Musée des Arts et Traditions Populaires, an ethnographical museum housed in the former 19th century town hall. In the first gallery, they saw stunningly colourful examples of Berber costumes but it was the Jewish costumes, sold when the owners fled to Israel after the Second World War, to which Ivy felt drawn. Examining their intricacies, she was pleased that unlike in the old Jewish area, where buildings had fallen into an irreparable decay, something of the culture of the people who had lived here for centuries was preserved in glass cases for future generations of the city to see.

Chez Sam, a wooden boat-shaped restaurant, abutting the harbour walls and seemingly poised to cast off to sea at any moment, was the perfect place for a late lunch. The maritime theme extending inside, with patterned panelling and portholes with views out to sea, Ivy felt they were floating out over the water as they dined. The conversation easy going and light fish lunch delectable, they watched boats coming into the harbour heavily laden with the afternoon's catch. Afterwards, the streets were silent, cloaked in a heat-haze as they retraced their steps to the Villa Maroc. For different reasons, each one was reluctant to leave Essaouira behind. The place where she and Jacques had come together as one, Ivy countered her sadness by looking forward to the evening when they got back to Marrakech.

"Right, I think we'd better make a move." Patrick searched his pockets for his car keys, "I want to get back to the city by dark."

"But I thought we might have a cool drink on the terrace before we leave?" interjected Louise, the sadness in her eyes reminding Ivy of a child, who having enjoyed a holiday so much, was desperate to extend it, even by just a few minutes. Feeling a wave of sympathy for her vulnerability she backed up Louise immediately before the men had a chance to refuse her. Despite eventually setting off much later than intended, the traffic back to Marrakech was light and Patrick, driving fairly quickly, managed to shave half an hour off the time their outward journey had taken.

Standing in the narrow alleyway in front of the riad, the 7pm call to prayer a mournful wail above their heads, Ivy hugged Louise and Patrick. "I would have almost certainly missed out seeing such a lovely place if you hadn't taken me. Thank you for inviting me."

"It was our pleasure," Patrick whispered in her ear, just

out of Louise's earshot who'd moved round to speak to Jacques, who was removing their bags from the boot, "and Jacques is the happiest I've ever seen him."

As he released her, Ivy saw his comment was sincere, and smiled, confident she had a champion in him.

"Ivy, I've just had the most wonderful idea," Louise sashayed round, evidently revitalised by her nap in the car on the way back, "we must arrange a trip to the Road of the Kasbahs before you return home. When is it exactly that you leave?"

"Just a couple of weeks now," she replied, somewhat unsettled by yet another strange shift in her companion's mood.

"Shall we just see how things pan out?" Jacques interrupted, diffusing both Louise and the situation. Feeling his hand rest heavily upon her shoulder, Ivy felt calm wash over her once more.

"Oh, and Jacques," Louise continued in quick, short breaths, evidently agitated by something, "you promised to show me your studio. I'd like to see what you've abandoned our gallery for and there's no time like the present."

Ivy saw Louise's eyes challenging him but he replied evenly, "Louise, I'm afraid I've other plans for tonight. I'll give you a call, tomorrow, okay?" he glanced towards Ivy, sensing her discomfort.

Seeing a look pass between Jacques and Patrick she couldn't quite read, Ivy thought it was getting a little embarrassing. Feeling sorry for Louise as her fragility manifested itself again, she smiled in thanks once more before pulling her case into the riad, leaving the three of them to sort it out in private. In her room, she kicked off her sandals before flinging open the window to let the stuffy air which had accumulated over the two days she'd been away, escape. Two days, is that really all it had been? Lying on her bed, memories of the time she'd enjoyed with Jacques at the Villa Maroc lingered in her mind. Happiness, elation, love – she alternated between these three emotions. And yet an inescapable sadness also weighed heavily upon her which she couldn't solely put down to the plaintive prayer call.

35

Changing into a rose-pink sundress, Louise's question as to when her holiday was due to end played on Ivy's mind, forcing her to acknowledge her time in Marrakech was coming to its conclusion. Desperate for the remaining days and nights to belong to her and Jacques alone, at dinner that evening, she did not enquire what, if any, arrangements he'd made for Louise to cast her appraising eye over his studio. Fortunately he didn't refer to it either and they enjoyed some light meze in the quiet confines of the riad garden, the warm air infused with the sweet scent of roses. Entirely comfortable in one another's company, they ate and talked with the new moon, hanging in the starless sky above, their only witness.

Later, in Ivy's room, she and Jacques stood inches apart, their fingers laced together, the moon casting their faces in its pale light. To begin with, they took things slowly, their kisses and caresses prolonged and deliberate. But by the time they shed their clothes on the terracotta tiles and their bodies came together on the bed, they instinctively fell into the same rhythm, each anticipating and fulfilling the other's needs. As they made love, it felt as though they'd been together hundreds of times before. Each moment was filled with such tenderness, such quiet passion, it made Ivy want to cry.

Afterwards, lying face to face while the night embraced them in its dark warmth, Jacques drew her into his arms. His face flooded with blue light from the window, he rested his forehead against Ivy's and whispered, "I love you."

Tears spilling from her eyes as she looked into his, warm with passion and love, she managed to reply, "I feel the same." She knew she had spent her life being guarded about her feelings, careful not to let anyone in as a self-protective mechanism. But then, she'd never come close to experiencing the depth of emotions she felt for Jacques. "I love you, too," she murmured, realising it was the first time she'd said those words to a lover.

"Oh Ivy, I know we've only known each other a few weeks but I feel I've been waiting for you all my life." As his soft fingertips brushed away her tears, his intent, dark eyes read her mind, "I've never felt this way before, you know. You must never doubt that."

"I won't," she trembled as he pulled her to him. Resting his cheek upon her shoulder, she found the light graze of his stubble comforting. She felt so utterly safe wrapped in the arms of this man who so astutely sensed her insecurities and yet immediately had the power to allay them. As she drifted off in the darkness, she experienced a contentment so complete, she would have been happy to remain that way with Jacques, forever.

In the weak, dawn light, she glanced over to him, his hair tousled, his face relaxed in sleep. Reaching out to gently touch his face, she hardly dared believe he was hers. But that's exactly what he was. At least for the time being, she corrected herself. Although her body felt heavy from their lovemaking, her mind was buzzing with thoughts and she knew there was no possibility of rejoining Jacques in his slumber.

She considered all the random events which had brought her to this moment, lying in bed with the man she loved: of Rose's death, of her bequest, of Mustapha's highjack of her in the street, even, sadly the death of Patrick and Louise's son. Remove one of these from the equation and she and Jacques would almost certainly never have met. Careful not to disturb him, she eased herself out of bed, tiptoeing across to the bathroom. The coldness of the tiled floor chilled her bare feet as she went to the toilet and washed her hands, peering at her reflection in the mirror. Noticing her camouflage makeup looked a little worse for wear, she carefully removed it. In the early morning light, her birthmark didn't seem as vivid as it had been and she again argued with herself whether to reveal it to Jacques or not. He deserved her honesty and his declaration of love for her should have inspired a confidence to tell him anything? She wrestled with her feelings, swallowing hard before taking a few tentative footsteps across the bathroom, her hand grasping the cold door handle…

Stepping back, she admonished herself. Bolting the

bathroom door, she acted on autopilot, unzipping her makeup bag, taking out the tubes of cream. With a quivering hand she quickly applied her base and concealer creams, watching in the mirror as her disfigurement disappeared. Her body flooded with disappointment at her cowardice, only to be instantly overridden by relief. Returning to the bedroom, she found Jacques was still sleeping so she pulled his shirt on over her slip and stealthily took Rose's journal from the pile of books. Placing the chair in a pool of light, she resumed reading for a short while. However, as Rose's description of Ryan's withdrawal grew ever more harrowing, she decided she didn't want it encroaching on her own contented frame of mind. Instead, she took her great-aunt's photo between the soft pads of her finger and thumb, holding it close to get a better look at it.

Rose looked to be in her mid-twenties in the photograph, her smile wide, her whole being radiant with happiness as she posed in a light, summer dress. As Ivy gazed into her lovely eyes, seeing past the black and white to the beautiful hazel they'd been, she realised how lucky she and her mum were to have had her in their lives. She toyed with the idea of abandoning reading the diary altogether, realising that as Rose had been so in love with Ryan, agreeing to marry him, the only logical explanation as to why they hadn't, was that he'd been killed on one of his raids to Germany. She surmised Rose had been so grief-stricken that she hadn't been able to tell her family, and had never found love again.

A part of her came to the conclusion she didn't want to know how Rose and Ryan had come to be separated, wishing to remember them as a young couple very much in love. Just at that moment, a warm wind from the street below whipped the curtain, fluttering the photograph in her hand. She watched the diaphanous material still again, the wind leaving as hastily as it had arrived. Pulling Jacques' shirt closer to her body and inhaling his musky scent, Ivy rested her head against the cool wall. She felt herself drifting off to sleep when Jacques' voice pulled her back.

"No, don't do that," she detected agitation in his tone. Flicking her eyes open, she saw that he was clearly still asleep but the peaceful expression on his face before had been replaced by a stormy one, his hands crushing his pillow into a ball.

"Hey," she whispered, sitting on the bed, taking hold of his hands to still him. After a few moments he opened his eyes, initially clouded with confusion before focusing on her, "hey, I think you were having a bad dream," she soothed, stroking the side of his face as she might a small child.

"Yes, I believe I was," he nodded, sitting up against the pillows, wiping beads of sweat from his brow. Leaving him to compose and collect his thoughts, her eyes were drawn to his lean, tanned torso and to distract herself, she poured some water from a bottle into a glass for him. Handing it to him, she felt his fingers brush hers, desire quickening in her once again.

"You even save me from my nightmares," he smiled, taking a few sips before placing the glass on the bedside table. Drawing her back into the warmth of his body, her skin tingled as he eased his shirt from her shoulders. Sometime later as dawn broke in the eastern sky, they fell into a deep, contented sleep in each other's arms.

36

By mid-August, the city's rhythm of life had become sluggish as the mercury surpassed one hundred degrees by some distance. With the sultry atmosphere unbearable in the enclosed warren of the souks, Ivy began accompanying Jacques to his studio, helping him decorate in preparation for his first exhibition, which he'd planned for the fall. Secure now in his love for her, she relaxed in his company as they got to know each other more intimately with each passing day. It was only when he had meetings with interested potential customers that she felt in the way, having little in common with wealthy tourists who thought nothing to spending thousands of dollars on a painting. Realising the esteem people held Jacques' work in reinforced the fact that he could certainly make a good living from his art in a city where she was just a tourist passing through.

To prevent herself from pining like a lovelorn teenager on the days Jacques was occupied with other things, Ivy fell into a routine. She alternated between two cafés – the Café du Grand Balcon, whose uninterrupted vista of the unfurling activities on the Jemaa el Fna made it her favourite morning coffee stop. For a leisurely lunch, she preferred the quieter Marra-Book Café, where she'd relax on the cool, cushion-strewn terrace overlooking a peaceful, walled garden. Afterwards, she'd return downstairs to browse the English and French paperbacks in the shop, where she became acquainted with the shop assistants, Simone and Elise, art students from Marseille, working there to finance their summer in Morocco.

Over coffee and pastries or a chicken salad sandwich, Ivy continued to document her time in Marrakech and her growing love for Jacques in her brown leather-bound notebook. She sensed it was important to record her experiences and feelings for him just as Rose had done with her romance with Ryan in the summer of '44, as spending time on her own made it inevitable that doubts concerning the future invaded her thoughts. In her eyes there were so many obstacles for her and Jacques to overcome if they were to be together on a long term basis. Unable to foresee they would have the happy ending denied to Rose and Ryan, she hoped that reading about her own love story in the future would at least bring it back to life for her.

The Muezzin's evening call echoing over the tiled rooftops soon became her signal to return to the riad. Jostling through the overcrowded streets, she felt excitement build in her at the prospect of dinner and the passion-fuelled hours of the night ahead with Jacques. Being apart from him during the day only heightened her anticipation of enjoying an intimate meal with him before they retired to her room. Wrapped in his arms each night, the cares of the outside world forgotten until the following morning, she was able to push her doubts about their future away.

Every evening, in between showering and changing and meeting Jacques, she found she had an hour's interlude. Spending this time reading and writing in the riad library, it didn't take Mustapha long to work out her routine. With his cheeky grin, he'd plonk himself on the sofa opposite her, an English novel on his knee, his expression expectant. So, instead of working her way down her pile of novels, she read *Treasure Island* and *Robinson Crusoe* to her attentive audience of one. It was a pleasure rather than a chore as the little boy always seemed so engrossed in whatever she read, wanting to act out the scenes with her as the characters embarked upon thrilling adventures.

As well as being the model pupil, Mustapha always proved himself the perfect host. After she'd been reading for twenty minutes or so he'd excuse himself only to reappear a short time later, precariously balancing a tray of pastries to share along with a lemonade for her and a giant glass of orange juice for himself. Ivy wondered whether his father knew Mustapha was giving free food and drink to one of the riad guests but she suspected not. With each meeting, his conversational English improved as he possessed a serious inclination to learn everything she could teach while his impish sense of humour could reduce her to tears of laughter. As they spent more time together, Ivy couldn't help thinking what a dear child he was. She found herself beginning to really care for his welfare in a way she didn't permit herself with the children in her class, and she realised how much she would miss their funny conversations on her return to England.

Although she avoided the stifling souks, there were still a few sights she wanted to see and one slightly cooler Thursday afternoon she ventured to the Agdal Gardens, just within the southern limits of the ancient city wall. Enduring a long, exposed walk, Ivy was exhausted by the time she spotted the Royal Palais in the distance and almost turned back. Vindicated for continuing on, she was greeted by a peaceful orange grove, olive plantation and vineyards and orchards of pomegranates and figs, which were all linked together by a maze of picturesque pathways.

Designed in the 12th century, she felt she'd literally stepped back into the city's past as the heat of the sun-drenched, ancient stones burned through the soles of her sandals. Enclosed within high walls the oasis felt seemingly many miles away from the city's bustle instead of on its doorstep. At the garden's heart, she took some time to sit by the large pool, reflecting how, in 1873, Sultan Mohammed IV had drowned while boating with his son. As she sat staring into its blue waters, a sudden breeze rippled across its surface causing her to shiver as she imagined Louise, inconsolable by a lake shore, Patrick grabbing her jacket to prevent her going in after their son. Is that how it had been? She would never know but reaching the riad an hour later, her breath burning her throat, Ivy still hadn't got the image of the grief-stricken mother out of her mind.

"Hello, Madame," Mustapha shouted her over to the desk on her arrival back, "I have note for you." He scrimmaged through a pile of papers, eventually extricating a cream-coloured envelope. "Jacques left it for you on his way out."

Carefully opening it, she noticed his writing was messier than usual as though he'd been in an awful rush.

Ivy,

Patrick is sending a group of Americans round to the studio to view my art tonight. I'm really hoping I'll be able to make a few sales. Americans think nothing to shipping large artworks home while Brits prefer something small enough to fit in their suitcase! I'm so sorry, our evenings together are very precious and special to me. I should be back around one.

Leave a note under my door to let me know what you want to do,

Toujours, Jacques.

"I hope everything's okay, Madame Ivy?" Mustapha added, his big, brown eyes brimming with concern.

"Yes, thank you for remembering to give it me." Despite her most reassuring smile, she feared she couldn't mask her profound disappointment that her evening plans with Jacques were to be curtailed, if not cancelled.

"Are you eating here tonight, Madame Ivy?" Mustapha ventured. Sometimes he seemed old beyond his years to her.

"Yes, I am," she brightened, nodding as his father emerged from his back room to answer the shrill telephone.

"Do you want an early meal?" he offered, his sensitive eyes seemingly understanding her situation, the role of comforter fitting him like a glove.

"Yes, if that's no bother. I'm not terribly hungry, so a simple herb omelette and salad would be fine, thank you."

"Can I have the same, father?" Mustapha implored, his eyes as big as saucers as he reverted to being a little boy, "I could eat it with Madame Ivy and keep her company?"

"Mustapha, Madame Ivy might want some peace and quiet," his father spoke in rapid French, his deep forehead furrowed with a frown.

"No I would love to have a dinner guest," pressed Ivy to Mustapha's obvious delight, "if that is alright with you?" Seeing his father's face break into a smile, Ivy felt relief flood through her; she wouldn't have to spend the evening alone, after all. So, at 6pm, she and her diminutive companion took their places at the table for two next to the trickling fountain. With amused looks from other early diners, Mustapha tucked his serviette into his shirt as they toasted each other with Diet Coke.

"Thank you," Mustapha smiled as his father set down two omelettes, served with French fries and salad, in front of them.

"Anything else you want, Sir, just let me know?" his father winked, his eyes warm as he left them.

Over their meal, Ivy talked about all manner of things with Mustapha who was particularly fascinated with what children in the UK liked to eat for their school lunches, how many times a week it rained and what it felt like to dip your toes in the sea. Presently, his father brought their lemon mousses.

"Have you enjoyed your evening?" he smiled, topping up their wine glasses with a fresh can of the fizzy drink.

"Very much," replied Ivy, winking in Mustapha's direction, "delicious food and lovely company. I've learned a lot about Moroccan schools, very interesting." She saw Mustapha smiling with pride.

"Umm," he said, looking doubtfully at his son, "well it's this young man's bedtime."

Disappointment flashing over his face at having the role of obedient son thrust upon him once more, Mustapha dutifully got up and encircled his arms around Ivy's neck. "Good night, Madame Ivy, you lovely lady," he managed in English, kissing her softly on the cheek.

"Thank you, Mustapha," replied Ivy, taken aback by his affectionate display, "for such a lovely meal and conversation."

A wave of exhaustion engulfing her as she climbed the stairs, she considered Mustapha. Thinking of the children in her class, many of whom had plenty of opportunities to travel beyond the boundaries of their town and often country, she wondered whether the gentle boy would ever venture beyond the red walls of the city or whether he would be hemmed in these narrow alleyways for the rest of his life.

37

It was with a heavy heart that Ivy slipped a note beneath Jacques' door, saying her walk in the scorching heat had left her dizzy with tiredness and she didn't think she'd be able to wait up for him. With night cloaking her room in utter darkness and lulled by the oscillations of the fan Jacques had insisted she have, her decision was vindicated as, no sooner as her head hit the pillow, she drifted off into a sound sleep.

Snapping her eyes open, she was conscious a noise had dragged her from her dreams. Then she heard it again, a faint rap on the door. "Coming," she called, softly padding barefoot across the cold, tiled floor. Despite her hair falling across her face in a bird's nest of tangles, she could tell the room was filled with light. Clicking the key in the lock, she opened the door, just an inch.

"Jacques!" she exclaimed, adrenaline coursing through her as the fact she was wearing no makeup hit her square in the centre of the chest with the force of a fist, winding her. Instinctively, she trained her hair over her birthmark, her brain whirring into overdrive to avoid disaster. The last thing she wanted was to tell him like this.

"I'm sorry if I woke you but I couldn't wait any longer to see you," he began, his face furrowed as he picked up on her anxiety or maybe she was overthinking it and he was just tired. "It's almost lunchtime to be fair," he grinned.

Her stomach twisting with panic, she unlatched the door before stepping away in a swift movement to prevent him catching her in his arms. "You'll have to excuse but I've just woken up and I need to use the lavatory. I'll be with you in a moment."

Not hanging around for his response, she hot-footed it to the bathroom, guilt surging through her that she still couldn't find the courage to tell him. Panic pulsed through her as she considered the possibility Jacques might have already glimpsed the rough, red skin through her hair. Her heart leaping in her chest, she edged towards the mirror, where she saw that her auburn hair, made bushy by sleep, thankfully covered the entire port-wine stain. Exhaling a sigh of relief, she applied her foundation and concealers as quickly and neatly as her shaking hands permitted.

"Are you okay, darling?" Sitting by the open window, she noticed Jacques was dressed in his smart navy suit and crisp white shirt, his damp hair resting on his collar and she realised he must have just showered before coming to her room.

"Yes, just a call of nature," she forced a smile. Seeing the concern in his eyes as he scooped her onto his knee, she reproached herself bitterly for her continuing dishonesty.

"I missed you yesterday," he whispered, pulling her to him so she could feel his warmth through her cotton nightdress as he kissed her long and hard.

"I can see that," she giggled, kissing him back. Her laughter was a release of the stress of the past few minutes. His eyes holding hers, she saw his consternation had dispersed too, leaving only love.

"I'm sorry about last night," he went on, placing his arm around her shoulders as they sat down on her bed. "But the Americans bought three pieces of art from me and I've just had a call to say they want to bring their friends around tonight before they move onto Agadir. I didn't have any choice but to say 'yes'."

"I understand," she took his hand in hers, his skin warm to her touch. "It's how you make your living, you don't have to apologise."

"It doesn't leave much time for us, though," Jacques stated, regretfully shaking his head as his hair flicked down over his forehead.

"No, I suppose not," Ivy paused, the silence stretching out as they both looked at each other, considering.

"Which reminds me, Pat called to say he and Louise are looking forward to taking us on the Road of the Kasbahs tomorrow," he drew her closer running his fingers through her hair.

"It completely slipped my mind," Ivy murmured, momentarily disconcerted.

"I'll phone him to say we're pulling out," his tone brightened, as he stroked her face with the back of his hand, "and we can go someplace alone?"

"No, it's all arranged," she shook her head, remembering Louise's excitement for the impending trip. To back out now and let her down would seem churlish. No matter how much she craved time alone with Jacques, she couldn't do it, "I just don't want to disappoint anyone."

"I know you don't," Jacques nodded, searching her eyes for a different answer. When it didn't come, he took her face in his hands to kiss her long and deeply once more, almost persuading her to change her mind.

"I've an idea," he started, his face suddenly animated as he pulled back, "the Americans aren't due at my studio until seven which means we could go some place this afternoon together?"

"Where?" Ivy asked, excitement bubbling up in her.

"That's for me to know," he kissed her again, a crafty smile pursing his lips, "and for you to find out. All you need to do is change into your best dress."

"Why?" Piqued with curiosity, her eyebrows arched, "where are you taking me?"

But Jacques just gave her his enigmatic smile and releasing her, he turned his attention to focus on the daily drama unfolding in the street below. Peering into the dark depths of her wardrobe, Ivy saw her choice of 'best dresses' was becoming increasingly limited. Luckily there was a sweetheart-necked, full-skirted scarlet tea-dress still unworn. After putting on clean underwear, she stepped out of her nightdress, sensing Jacques' attention was no longer occupied by the comings and goings of their neighbours.

"Hey there, no peeking," she ordered, turning towards

him to pull a funny face to see he was indeed viewing her with an amused expression.

"I was just admiring the view," he smiled but she noticed that he didn't look away. Fastening her bra, she realised that although her skin wasn't quite as firm as it had been in her twenties, she was still slender and relatively cellulite-free. Far from minding him watching, she knew that in his eyes, she was beautiful and that meant everything to her.

Having already done her makeup, she teased her hair into loose curls, noticing the sun had produced some lovely strawberry-blonde highlights amongst the natural auburn. It had grown a little too, falling just past her shoulders while her frequent use of argan oil made it shine like silk. Even she had to admit that it looked lovely as she realised that if she saw such a girl on the street, she'd have to agree with Jacques that she was pretty and nowhere near her late thirties. After a lifetime of low self-esteem this realisation came as a shock.

"Do you think they'll let me in now, wherever it is you're taking me?" she smiled as she moved towards him, coquettishly twirling the material of her dress.

"Maybe, maybe not," he reached for her, zipping her dress as she stood before him, his warm hands coming to rest on either side of her ribcage as he smiled at her, "on second thoughts we could just stay here all afternoon instead? It is still unbearably hot today, and I won't be around this evening… " He lightly kissed her on the lips, a teasing promise.

"Nice try. Ten minutes ago I would have said 'yes' but now I'm dressed up and ready to go," she grabbed her bag and his hand, "come on."

"You can't blame a guy for trying," he smiled, shrugging his shoulders as he followed her out of the door.

The grounds of the Mamounia Hotel, just a stone's throw away from the animation of the Jemaa El Fna, were by contrast a haven of tranquillity. As they approached via its majestic, sweeping driveway, hand-in-hand, Jacques filled Ivy in on its history. Built in the 19th century, it had originally been the crown prince of Morocco's palace. Then, in 1923, the French had converted it into a hotel and it had been welcoming the rich and famous ever since. As Jacques talked, Ivy considered this was just the place her great-grandmother would have stayed in all those years ago with Violet and Nell, if they'd made it beyond Paris and the battlefields of the First World War to Morocco and she felt a twist of sorrow for them once more.

"Sean Connery, Catherine Deneuve and Bill Clinton have all been guests here," remarked Jacques, the delightful gardens, surrounded by the city's red-ochre ramparts, stretching before them on the left. "But of course Winston Churchill is the Mamounia's most celebrated visitor."

The opulence of the building's exterior left Ivy lost for words as they approached it. Jacques told her how Churchill had stayed at the hotel on a few occasions, spending the mornings penning his memoirs before painting in Marrakech's extraordinary afternoon light. He said the British prime minister had even met Jacques Majorelle during his stay in 1946 and had persuaded the Mamounia's management to commission a mural for his painter friend.

"In a letter to his wife Clementine, Churchill wrote: *This is a wonderful place, and the hotel is one of the best I have ever used.* Two of the signature suites are named in honour of Churchill and Majorelle," stated Jacques before trailing off, lost in thought. Whether it was about her, the former prime minister or the painter, Ivy couldn't guess.

Reaching the entrance, a man in a maroon uniform held the doors open for them, while Jacques whispered, "if my finances ran to it, I'd book us a room for the night in the Churchill suite as it overlooks the gardens where he used to paint. It also contains artefacts from the 1920s, including his pipe."

Standing in the foyer, Ivy was mesmerised by the architecture which effortlessly blended the Arab-Moorish tradition with the outrageous decadence and artistry of times gone by. It was truly stunning. "I love this," she whispered as Jacques took her hand, ushering her into the extended lobby. "Look up."

There, on the ceiling, she beheld the most incredible octagonal mural etched in deep, forest-green and bold, sunshine-yellow. As they strolled around the public areas, Ivy liked the way the architects had blended Art Deco with Moroccan motifs, seeming totally in sync with one another. Stepping beyond to the formal gardens where well-manicured paths led them between pools and flowerbeds, they reached a central pavilion where the lunchtime buffet was being served.

In the low white building, brushed by palm trees on either side, Jacques led her to a table overlooking the scalloped swimming pool. There, they enjoyed a sumptuous array of fresh seafood, smoked salmon, unbelievably exotic salads and the most amazing display of French pâtisseries she had ever seen. Sitting in her lovely dress opposite Jacques in his smart suit, it was the most perfect lunch Ivy could ever imagine.

"Here's to you, Ivy," Jacques clinked his champagne flute against hers, "thank you for the most beautiful afternoon."

"I think it's me who should be thanking you, for all this," she took in the buffet and the gardens with a sweep of her arm, "this really is something special."

"I think so too," nodded Jacques, a light breeze ruffling the pristinely-pressed, white table cloth, "I've wanted to come here for years but never have and never thought I would," he swallowed, considering for a moment, folding his napkin. "I wanted to share it with the right person."

Ivy smiled wistfully, realising this experience meant as much to Jacques as it did to her. Time seemed to stand still that afternoon as they alternated between chatting and falling silent with their own thoughts, both entirely at ease to do so. With him there beside her Ivy was able to put her anxieties to one side, musing that while she'd been coming to terms with the fact that she'd never meet anyone to love, Jacques had been on the other side of the world, waiting for her all the time.

"Well, we'd better be getting back to the riad," he sighed reluctantly as his watch nudged towards 6pm. Retracing their steps back through the foyer, Ivy noticed the date, 18th August, displayed in huge letters behind the reception desk. The discovery seemed like a physical force hitting her hard in the chest as it meant only a week remained before she would be forced to leave Marrakech and return home. Would these carefree days spent with Jacques then just fade to a pleasant memory?

At midnight, Ivy reluctantly turned off the lamp. Drawing her duvet close to ward off the growing chill in the air, she acknowledged that she'd been waiting for Jacques, even leaving her foundation on this time. Laying dispirited in the darkness, she knew that with Louise and Patrick accompanying them to the mountains the following day, she and Jacques were unlikely to steal any time alone together. She was deeply disappointed, as it was all the little reassurances from Jacques in private which made her feel so loved and made her want to open her heart to him. She closed her eyes and was poised on the edge of sleep when a gentle tapping dragged her back. Relieved she'd followed her instincts to keep her makeup on, she flew to the door.

"I managed to finish early," Jacques smiled, his face glistening and his breath short as though he'd run from his studio to be with her. Before he could go on, she stopped his words with a kiss.

38

Ivy woke to find the white curtain billowing in the breeze of the open window. Shivering, she snuggled into the warmth of Jacques' body and, studying his face as he slept, she noticed nuances she hadn't previously picked up on: his long, perfectly straight nose, how his bottom lip was just a fraction fuller than the top, a tiny, white scar just above his left eyebrow. Moving her hand to his bare chest, she felt the rhythm of its steady rise and fall and thought she would be quite happy to spend the day in bed with him.

Returning from the bathroom, Ivy saw that he had rolled over into the centre of the bed, his arm laid across his bare chest, his still face in peaceful repose. Remembering he'd volunteered to share the driving with Patrick on their trip to the mountains, she resisted the urge to climb back in with him and disturb him from his slumber. Instead, wrapping a white, fluffy bathrobe around her, she ensconced herself in the wicker chair by the window where she resumed Rose's diary, a suitably silent activity to occupy her time before Jacques stirred.

"*Ryan and I continued to meet whenever we could throughout harvest time. One day as we strolled across a field full of ripening wheat, the sky aflame with the most spectacular autumn sunset, he stopped in front of me. His demeanour serious, I thought something significant had occurred on his raid over the Netherlands the previous day. Knowing he never welcomed discussions about any of his missions I waited in trepidation for him to speak. To my surprise he took my hand in his, and smiling that beautiful slow smile of his, slipped a lovely gold ring onto my finger.*

My eyes brimming with tears, I commented how pretty it was, with its two tiny gold hands clasping a heart, beneath a gold crown. Ryan explained it was a Claddagh ring he'd found in the antiques shop on the high street. He told me his mom and grandmother both wore these traditional, Irish engagement rings and he wanted me to have the same. It was beautiful and unusual, encapsulating all the things we felt for one another."

With a shock, Ivy looked down at the ring she'd been wearing out of sentimental attachment to her great-aunt. The same ring Rose had worn until the day she died. It wasn't merely an unusual and beautiful ring, it was Rose's engagement ring borne out of traditions Ryan's family held dear. Her tears flowed as she gently touched it, knowing she would treasure it even more now.

"I wore Ryan's ring on a chain around my neck, the warm metal against my skin a constant reminder of our promise to one another. Hiding it beneath my clothes, I still wasn't ready to share our news with anyone, even my mother and least of all, Frances, as I knew her disapproving views on servicemen in general, let alone an American one. As the leaves browned and fell from the trees, the winter frosts beginning to bite, Ryan and I met in country pubs away from the village. Nestling by cosy fires, he whetted my appetite to move to Richmond with him, causing me to almost forget there was still a war to survive.

And yet the war was the glue which held us together. Without it, its death and sacrifice, Ryan would have been finishing his Engineering degree while I would have stayed at home with my mum, making jams and pies and being courted by village boys. It sounds selfish but I thanked God for bringing Ryan to England, to me, even as I prayed for an end to the war, our strange Cupid.

The run-up to the sixth Christmas of the war brought seasonal optimism that it would all be over by this time next year. I couldn't quite put my finger on it but there was definitely a shift in the mood in Lavenham that December. Everyone seemed just that little bit more cheerful and hopeful than in the previous few festive seasons. The streets bustled as people did their Christmas shopping and went carol singing once again, albeit without their lanterns shining due to the blackout. For me, however, it was different. Whether it was because, as always, Christmas was the time of year when I most missed my father and sisters, I don't know, but as the days shortened and the nights darkened a feeling of dread seemed to curl its freezing fingers around my heart.

Ryan's mood also turned downbeat. He hated the snow and shivered involuntarily as he told me of conditions in his corrugated metal Quonset hut, where he woke each morning to find frost formed on the inside wall. The cold seeping into his bones, even wearing his padded flight suit did not bring him comfort anymore. Although there was an army stove at the centre of the hut, as coal was rationed to a couple of shovels a day, he said the men waited until the evenings to light it, so often in the afternoons they'd sit there utterly cold and miserable. His sleep also suffered as he was often woken daily between 3am and 4am and given just thirty minutes to get ready. After bolting down breakfast he would head to the briefing room to learn where he was going and what to expect from the enemy before takeoff at around 7am.

The mornings I sensed Ryan was on a mission, I also woke early. Knowing I'd be unable to find sleep again, I dressed hurriedly before racing down to the airfield where I spotted the tell-tale green flares which told me takeoff was imminent. I stood there, beyond the perimeter fence, temporarily deafened by the roar of the engines as the huge planes gathered up speed on the runway. Watching them soar upwards before disappearing into leaden clouds, I sent up a silent prayer to God to keep Ryan safe for me.

On the evening of the 22nd of December, we'd arranged a rendezvous in The Swan, as Suffolk was in the grip of a particularly harsh winter and it was too cold to meet in the open air. It's strange but I still recall the fire blazing in the hearth, I remember the heart-shaped locket he gave me for my Christmas present, I can still see Ryan's cheeks, ruddy from the freezing fog outside, and, of course, the fear in his eyes. But I *don't recollect anything we said to each other that day. Maybe what happened afterwards made it all irrelevant anyway."*

As Rose's writing came to an abrupt stop, Ivy carefully unfolded the fragile newspaper article taped to the next page. Looking at the faded photo of the handsome soldier with his dark eyes, she recognised it as the one which hung on the wall of *The Swan*, General F.W. Castle, Medal of Honour. Proceeding to read the article, Ivy took time to decipher the words caught on the creases.

"It was before daybreak on Christmas Eve 1944 that Brigadier General Frederick Castle took off from Lavenham at the helm of the largest Eighth Air Force mission of the war. 2000 bombers, escorted by over 800 fighters set off with instructions to bomb eleven German airfields east of the Rhine, thus destroying the German Air Force's air cover provision for their troops during the Battle of the Bulge.

The bombers' take off, however, was delayed due to a long briefing that morning. After encountering inclement weather conditions, they arrived fourteen minutes late to the place they were due to pick up their fighter escort and were forced to proceed towards Babenhausen unaccompanied. Over Liège, the bombers encountered a group of sixty German planes and with no fighter jets to protect them, they were attacked. Four were shot down while five more badly damaged aircraft were forced to make emergency landings in Belgium. That day, 56 American aircraft were lost, including General Castle's B-17, in an action for which he was posthumously awarded the medal of honour. Refusing to jettison bombs to gain speed when one of his engines failed, General Castle ordered his crew to bail out while he and Lieutenant Harriman remained on board. Their plane hit, gasoline tanks caught fire in the right wing, tearing it off and causing the aircraft to plummet in a spin before exploding in mid-air.

His citation reads as follows: "He was air commander and leader of more than 2,000 heavy bombers in a strike against German airfields on 24 December 1944. En route to the target, the failure of one engine forced him to relinquish his place at the head of the formation. In order not to endanger friendly troops on the ground below, he refused to jettison his bombs to gain speed maneuverability. His lagging, unescorted aircraft became the target of numerous enemy fighters which ripped the left wing with cannon shells, set the oxygen system afire, and wounded two members of the crew. Repeated attacks started fires in two engines, leaving the Flying Fortress in imminent danger of exploding.

Realising the hopelessness of the situation, the bailout order was given. Without regard for his personal safety he gallantly remained alone at the controls to afford all other crew members an opportunity to escape. Still another attack exploded gasoline tanks in the right wing, and the bomber plunged earthwards carrying Gen Castle to his death. His intrepidity and willing sacrifice of his life to save members of the crew were in keeping with the highest traditions of the military service."

Ivy's heart became heavy with dread. Her throat constricting, she guessed Ryan had to have been in one of the planes shot down, certain he and Rose would never have let anything separate them if they could have helped it. Glancing over to Jacques who still slept soundly in her bed, her insides contracted in pain at the prospect of ever losing him. Hesitantly, she turned back to the page where Rose picked up the story.

"On Christmas Eve, despite the heavy-falling snow, the church was packed out during midnight mass. Everyone had so been looking forward to Christmas but in that freezing, candle-lit church the mood was sombre, the fate of the missing US airmen occupied all our minds as we prayed for them. As my mother stroked my hand, my heart filled with such pain, I thought it would break in two.

When we emerged on what was now Christmas morning, the snow had stopped. I peered up at the stars, shining brightly in the clear, frosty sky. Homing in on the brightest, I prayed again for Ryan's safe return even though I knew it was probably already out of even God's hands. My boots crunched on the newly frozen snow as I walked down the church path into the darkness, leaving behind the candlelight glow through the stained glass windows. It felt a sham to celebrate peace and goodwill on earth and as the graveyard enveloped me in its endless darkness, I knew for certain that Ryan was dead.

That Christmas Day was so cruel. How could I contemplate celebrating when my world had crashed down upon me? I knew my mother was missing Violet, Nell and my dad but in my raw grief I was unable to offer her the comfort she needed. I'd experienced so much loss and pain already in my young life, I simply couldn't bear it again. On Boxing Day, Frances and Bert came around for a warm-up dinner, but instead of lightening the atmosphere it soon became clear some kind of disagreement festered between them. After washing up, I sneaked out of the house, knowing Frances wouldn't confide in me, and made my way up the lanes, now treacherous with frozen snow and ice. My heart already broken, I had to know what had happened to Ryan or I feared I would go mad with grief.

I found the airfield eerily quiet, lying beneath its blanket of snow. It looked abandoned and yet, if I'd even attempted to scale the perimeter fence, I would have been in grave trouble. This was hopeless. I cried in frustration, realising there was nothing to be done, except go home. But how could I return there, still not knowing what had happened to Ryan? I don't know why but I turned towards the woods, where I had played with my sisters when we were children, and where Ryan and I had spent so many happy hours in the sun-dappled shade of the beech trees the previous summer. As I drew closer, I noticed a movement in the bare trees. I saw it was a man, standing motionless and slightly hunched over. My first instinct was to think it was a tramp, or worse and I felt my stomach turn over with alarm.

Caught with the urge to run away from there, something kept me from moving. Slowly the man stepped forward and, as he lifted his head, it took me a moment to recognise him, his blonde hair unkempt, his handsome features now haggard and drawn. No sound came from my lips as I ran towards him. And then he was right before me. It was Ryan's face, his hands, he was real; he'd come back. He wasn't dead, after all. But the joy I felt was brief, as looking into his shadowed, blue eyes was the most bittersweet moment of my life for I knew then that not all of him had come back to me.

I remember he spoke only one word – Rose – as he

stretched his arms out towards me and in a split second I was wrapped up in them as we collapsed to our knees onto the frozen ground. We remained kneeling silently for some time until I started to feel chilled from the cold wetness of the snow seeping through the edge of my coat. My teeth chattering, I heaved Ryan to his feet, noticing the dark rings which circled his eyes while pale stubble covered his chin. His skin had a grey pallor to it and yet somehow he was more handsome than when I'd pictured him in my prayers those past few nights. He put his arm around my shoulders as I led him down the lanes to an outlying barn on Sophie's farm where her father stored last summer's dried hay.

We stayed in the warmth of the sweet-smelling barn for the rest of the day. When Ryan took me in his arms I didn't realise that this was not only our first time, but only one of three precious times we would make love. Over the years, I've relived that day many times with both joy and sadness, thinking how it should have been the beginning of a lifetime together."

Ivy's fingers flipped through the remaining pages of Rose's notebook, her stomach lurching with profound disappointment on discovering they were blank. Sobs rising within her, she fathomed her great-aunt must have found it too painful to continue, that Ryan had almost certainly been killed on one of his missions during those final months of the war. After everything they'd been through, it was too much for Ivy to bear.

"Hey, what's wrong?" Naked and his hair tousled by sleep, Jacques crossed the room and knelt before her, enveloping her in his warm arms. His brow creased with concern, he whispered, "you're shivering and why are you crying?"

"I was reading my great-aunt's diary again. You remember I told you that during World War II she met an American flyer? They were so much in love, Jacques, until fate stepped in and parted them forever." Tears were falling down Ivy's cheeks, "the worst thing about it all is Rose lived out the rest of her life never finding love again, and never speaking of him." Calmly, Jacques tightened his grip and comforted her for a few minutes, her cheek resting upon his chest until her sobs subsided.

"There's something else, isn't there?" he stroked the side of her face, brushing tendrils of hair behind her ear, his eyes intent and concerned.

"I'm fearful that something similar will happen to us. That I'll go home next week and we'll drift apart. Aren't you?" she asked, her voice barely a whisper. It seemed crazy to think that in just a few weeks he'd become the most important person in her life, that she couldn't envisage being without him.

"No, I'm not," he smiled, cupping her chin in his hands, "because I've never felt this way for anyone and I have no intention of letting fate step in."

He then kissed her deeply before taking her in his arms and carrying her back to the warmth of their bed. The sun streaming through the windows as they made love once again, every part of Ivy wanted to believe what he'd said was true.

39

"Come on, you two, hurry up!" Casually dressed in khaki combats and tee-shirt, Patrick strode purposely across the riad courtyard. "What time do you call this? We said 9am!"

"You know me and timekeeping, Pat," Jacques stood up to greet his friend, brushing stray croissant crumbs from his navy slacks, "never did go together!"

"No, I seem to remember you missed an entire semester of Monday morning lectures in our second year of college." Joining them at the breakfast table, Ivy thought, despite his apparent good-humour, Pat's face seemed strained, his usual laid-back demeanour absent today.

"You'll have to watch him, Ivy," he continued on in a forced jovial manner. "I've calculated that so far I've spent an entire month of my life waiting for Jacques. His tardiness is something you'll have to factor into your life, somehow."

"I will, don't you worry!" she smiled. Considering

Patrick's words, she realised he saw them as a couple and wondered what messages he'd picked up from his best friend to formulate such an opinion. Realising Jacques was watching her, she felt herself flush.

"Are you ready to go?" he asked her, attentively bending to kiss her. Smiling in assent, Ivy noticed Louise standing serenely behind him and could have sworn she saw the ghost of a sad smile pass her lips.

"Come on then Jacques, we can't wait all day," Louise interjected, her tone and expression once again inscrutable to Ivy. Following her and Jacques to Patrick's Citroën, Ivy thought Louise looked tired and unhappy, her clothes pale and washed out rather than their usual vibrant colours. However, she wasn't unkempt in the way she'd been when she'd spotted her in Guéliz, having taken great care to plait her hair while her makeup was picture-perfect. Taking her place on the back seat next to her, Ivy reflected her light-coloured attire was in fact a sensible, cool choice as the forecasted temperatures threatened to boil the mercury once again.

As the Medina's narrow streets opened out onto the wide, white boulevards of the Ville Nouvelle, Louise's animated mood returned. She pointed out her favourite cafés and boutiques, advising Ivy on the 'in' places to eat and shop. Having been concerned about Louise's mood earlier, Ivy welcomed the easy, girly talk, especially as the traffic noise filtering through the wound-down windows, cut her off from Jacques in the passenger seat. Presently the buildings hemming in the road on either side, became sparser before disappearing from view entirely as they joined the highway's south-westerly route to the Atlas Mountains. The landscape became ruggedly barren as the road twisted in the steep rise to the Tizi-n-Tichka pass and even though Patrick was taking the hairpin bends as sedately as he could, Ivy felt her stomach flip over with each turn. As nausea rose in her so did the prospect of showing herself up and being ill in front of them all and she closed her eyes to concentrate on regulating her breathing.

"Are you two girls okay, back there?" Patrick enquired, on a long downward curve, which brought Ivy welcome respite.

"Yes, we're fine." Her tone tense, Louise answered for both of them. Ivy looked over to meet her eye but saw she was staring wistfully at the dry, desert-like landscape, their chatter having dried up since leaving the city.

"If you carry on south, you'd reach the Sahara in a couple of days," Jacques commented after a while, his eyes meeting Ivy's in the rear view mirror on the passenger seat's sun visor. Seeing Louise was dozing, he broke off his conversation with Patrick and proceeded to tell her all about Telouet Kasbah, where they were headed. Ivy realised with gratitude that he didn't want her to feel excluded, even for a moment.

"Once it belonged to the Glaoui tribe who ruled all of southern Morocco in the early 20th century but then it was abandoned for nearly half a century and much of the structure is dangerous and crumbling. We can visit the reception hall, which is very ornate and the rooftop terrace, if you want."

"Yes, I'd like that," demurred Ivy, reaching out to place

her hand on his shoulder. As they passed through some walnut groves on the approach to a village, she noticed a Berber farmer, in an ankle-length coat and blue turban, leading his flock of sheep. Further along were two Berber women, each with a donkey carrying a pile of wood strapped to its back.

"It's almost as if we've time-travelled back a century or more. How many Berbers live in Morocco?" She noticed that women in the countryside wore dresses and headscarves in more muted shades than the vibrant colours popular with the Marrakechiyas.

"There are actually twelve or thirteen million, which is 40% of the overall population. They're a very ancient culture living in North Africa, mainly in Morocco and Algeria. For many centuries they continued to speak the Berber language but over time they have acquired other languages," he continued, as they took a particularly sharp bend.

"What do you do every night, Jacques?" Patrick interjected, "read your encyclopedia before you fall asleep so you can dream about its contents?"

"Not every night," he joked, smiling at Ivy again in the mirror. Sensing Louise stirring beside her, she was powerless to prevent a blush suffusing her neck and face.

"I think it said in my guidebook that today over half of Moroccans speak a Berber language," Ivy stated to leapfrog the awkward moment, hoping that Jacques would take the bait.

Thankfully he did, going on to describe the migratory lifestyle of shepherds in such an inhospitable landscape. The road becoming marginally straighter, he told how Berber men took care of their livestock, following the natural cycle of grazing, seeking water and shelter while the women raised their families and made handicrafts to sell in the city's souks.

"Breaking you off, Jacques," Patrick intercepted as they drove through another dusty village, "but isn't the feminine collective here in Taddert?"

Passing a handful of rustic-looking houses, he abruptly pulled over in front of a low-rise, cream-coloured, slightly ramshackle building. Ivy stepped out of the car, the full force of the dry, desert heat hitting her so she could barely draw a breath.

"Are you alright?" Jacques enquired, his face full of concern.

"Yes, fine. I wasn't expecting it to be quite so hot," she smiled, feeling rather silly as Louise breezed into the building before them.

"Me neither," he took hold of her hand and led her slowly down the cool passageway, "I'll make sure we keep indoors," he gave her a reassuring smile. Her eyes taking a moment to become accustomed to the muted light, Ivy focused on the four Berber women she estimated to be somewhere between their late twenties to early forties, sitting cross-legged on the blue and white tiled floor. The blue, pink and purple wall-hanging behind them complimented the vibrant colours of their gowns and scarves. Bent over, they were peeling shells off what appeared to be nuts, discarding the various parts into the large baskets which surrounded them. Ivy felt Jacques draw nearer in the semi-darkness to whisper. "These women are mainly widows, although some have escaped arranged marriages and abuse. They live and work in the collective, making products from argan oil to support themselves and the group."

"But they seem so young," Ivy said, as the woman wearing a jade green headscarf, who didn't look thirty, smiled at them.

"Yes, many of them, if not all would have married much older men," Jacques explained, stopping before a woman in a blue headscarf and lilac gown. She was vigorously grinding the nuts with a pestle and mortar to extract oil.

"Peux-je?" Jacques smiled and she passed him the bowl of sticky, golden oil. As he tasted it, another woman in her early fifties, emerged from the shop with a plate of unleavened bread.

"Here, try some," Jacques tore a piece in half, dipping it in the oil before handing it to Ivy. Savouring its delicious nuttiness, she smiled and nodded enthusiastically to the delight of the woman. In the shop, she purchased hand and body creams, liking the idea that whenever she took a shower for the next few months, she would be reminded of these brave women who nurtured their new-found independence making such lovely soaps and creams.

Leaving Taddert behind, with every twist the road steepened a few degrees, the drop on Louise's and Patrick's side ever more precipitous. Even though Ivy knew Jacques was a competent driver, she flinched as he took on one sharp bend after another and felt relief flood through her when he pulled in at some stalls stacked with brightly painted tagines at the roadside, welcoming a breather.

"This is the highest point of the pass. 7,415ft if I recall," he smiled, putting his hand protectively in the arch of her back as they stepped out of the car. While the stalls, in particular ones selling colourful rocks, which when broken revealed glittering crystal formations within, diverted Louise, the view commanded Ivy's undivided attention. The muted brown shades of the rock with the road twisting and turning through it like a grey snake, might not have been prettily picturesque but it was undeniably spectacularly beautiful. She thought of the Berbers and other nomadic people, who for centuries had been travelling this road en route to the Sahara and, not for the first time on her holiday, she felt as though she was a part of something much bigger than herself.

"We'd better be going. It's still a long way to Ouarzazate, and if we plan to visit Ait Benhaddou first… Where's Louise?" Jacques asked, a sudden panic shadowing his face.

"She's just over there, at the other side of the stall," replied Ivy, Jacques' hand steadying her as they retraced their steps on the loose-stoned path. Glancing up, she saw Louise suddenly emerge, hot and flustered before them, Patrick bending to whisper something in her ear.

"What have you been buying, Lou?" Jacques asked as they caught up with them. Ivy noticed her skin glistened with sweat despite the cool air at that altitude.

"Nothing, I don't think the house needs anything more," laughed Louise, but Ivy detected a hollowness in it, which resounded in her ears as they resumed their journey.

As the road continued downwards, Louise and Patrick dozed off, leaving Ivy wishing she'd joined Jacques upfront so they could chat while he drove. It was an interminable forty minutes before he pointed out their lunch stop, which was a remote guesthouse, its red building dwarfed by the dramatic, surrounding landscape. Following the rest of the party up a narrow flight of stairs to the rooftop restaurant, Ivy sneaked a peek into the empty guestrooms. The epitome of simplicity with just a bed and wardrobe, they each had the feel of a retreat, far away from Marrakech, the distance not merely measurable in miles.

It was indeed an idyllic spot, the rustic restaurant overlooking stunning views of the Atlas Mountains which extended as far as the eye could see. Settling around a low, oak table on soft scatter cushions, Ivy noticed how the golden sunlight streamed in, counteracting the heaviness of the rich upholstery of the settees while picking out the red hues in Louise's dark hair. A grey-haired man in a flowing cream robe brought out dish after delicious dish of traditional Berber food as they enjoyed cumin-infused chicken, saffron potatoes, steaming bowls of fluffy couscous, washed down with glass after glass of refreshing iced tea, followed by water melon for desert. As they ate, Ivy noticed Louise seemed pale and withdrawn, barely touching her food while staring wistfully at the mountains beyond the flung open windows. But then she suddenly looked up, smiling brightly, causing Ivy to put her lack of appetite down to queasiness after the twisty journey rather than heaviness of mood.

"After all that driving, I'm going to have a sleep," Patrick announced, lazing back on the cushions, "wake me up when you're ready to go."

"And I'm going to explore this place," Louise picked up her bag, slinging it casually over her right shoulder. Ivy's eyes followed her across the restaurant, the breeze catching her white blouse and loose harem pants, which billowed like the wings of a dove in full flight.

With Patrick gently snoring and Louise gone, Ivy was grateful to have Jacques all to herself for the first time that day. Leaning against patterned cushions, the fan circulating cool air above their heads, they stretched out on the settee where they lost track of time, making tentative plans for Ivy to visit Marrakech again in the October half term.

"But it would only be for a week." These four-and-a-half weeks having raced by, Ivy imagined one would pass in a flicker of an instant.

"Or," Jacques leaned into kiss her in their new-found privacy, "I could come over and visit you in Colchester? The tourist season here has tailed off by then until Christmas so I could stay for a month. What do you think?" he regarded her seriously.

"Yes, I'd like that," she interlinked her fingers with his, her heart aflutter with not just the prospect of seeing him again but also the fact that he was prepared to travel hundreds of miles to be with her.

"I'm already looking forward to it," he mused as Ivy rested her head on his shoulder, suddenly sleepy in the heat, "yes, I've always wanted to visit England, see your thatched cottages, enjoy a pint in an old pub, watch a football match. Now I have the perfect excuse."

Ivy looked up to see his eyes glinting with mischief. "You!" she gently nudged him in the ribs.

"And see you, my love," he smiled, his voice sincere. *His love* – the concept seemed simultaneously both strange and new and yet familiar and established. The next hour or so passed pleasantly as they talked and laughed until, with their plans all but finalised, Jacques leaned in to kiss her once more.

"Hey, you two lovebirds, we'll have none of that here!" Wiping the sleep from his eyes, Patrick glanced down at his watch, "Gosh, it's gone four. Where's Lou?"

"She said she was taking a look around," Ivy straightened, her back aching from sitting in one position for too long.

"But that was nearly two hours ago!" Patrick shouted in panic, before leaping to his feet and disappearing down the stairs.

Picking up on his alarm Ivy glanced in consternation towards Jacques. "Wait here," he warned, raising his hand, his strong features set with determination. But as he stood up, his face hovered momentarily in front of hers and she could have sworn she detected fear in his eyes. As Jacques followed his friend, she tried to collect her thoughts and found that in spite of the mountain range in front of her, sturdy and still, she suddenly felt as though she was on a ship, pitching and tossing at the mercy of devastating waves. Memories flashed through her mind adding up to more than the sum of their parts – images of Louise outside the swanky baby shop in the Ville Nouvelle, her hyper-excitability at the dinner party, her withdrawal into an uncommunicative state in Essaouira, the tone of Jacques' voice when he'd told her of the death of Louise and Patrick's son. But it was the terrible look in Patrick's eyes a few minutes earlier that made her disobey Jacques and hotfoot it after them.

Enlisting the help of the owner, Ivy searched every room of the guesthouse. When it proved fruitless, she stepped outside, the merciless late-afternoon sun rendering the landscape hazy and indistinct as she stumbled along blindly, calling out Louise's name over and over. The sun's rays felt like fronds of fire, licking the exposed skin of her face, threatening to devour it whole. But such was her fear, for the first time in her life, Ivy was unconcerned about her birthmark and, disregarding the damage the sun could do, she pushed on. Eventually, she caught sight of Jacques' and Patrick's blurry silhouettes in the heat haze.

"Have you found her?" she cried, not thinking how frightful she might look.

"No, I think we'd better call the police," muttered Patrick, fighting back tears, "it feels like it did in Toronto."

"She's gone missing before?" Ivy's breaths were short and sharp now.

"Yes, she made an attempt to take her life," stated Jacques bluntly, his emotions clearly spent. Hearing his words, the fear gripping her stomach combined with the sun's ferocity, threatened to overwhelm Ivy as she felt herself on the verge of fainting.

40

Staring at their smeared plates, crumpled serviettes and leftover food, Ivy pondered how their feast, so sumptuous when the waiter had laid it out, had been reduced to something so unattractive in such a short space of time. She lifted her eyes to Jacques and Patrick sitting opposite her, their faces grey with worry as the full comprehension of what was unfolding around them, sunk in.

"Louise Morris disappeared between three and four, this afternoon?" repeated the police officer, making careful notes in his leather-bound book. With a boyish face and slight frame, Ivy guessed he was no more than thirty despite his dark hair greying slightly over his ears as she sat on the periphery of the conversation, not a bystander and yet not quite involved either.

"Yes, she did," nodded Patrick, his face flushed from the exertion of his frantic search in the searing heat, "I dozed off after lunch and didn't notice she had gone." His voice broke with anguish, "I should have been watching her. She's been suffering from depression for some time."

"She has a history of psychological illness?" clarified the police officer, his brow furrowed. At this point, Patrick broke down into convulsed sobs, unable to answer so Jacques spoke for him. "Yes, a decade ago she made an attempt on her own life after her son died in an accident in Canada."

"And what relationship have you with Mrs Morris?" the policeman clarified as a sudden breeze picked up, ruffling his notepad so he lost his page.

"I'm a close friend of both Mr and Mrs Morris," Jacques stated evenly, attempting without success to keep his voice steady. "We've known one another for twenty-five years since we met at college."

Sensing Patrick needed some physical comfort, Ivy shuffled around to sit next to him. She noticed his face had assumed a ghostly, grey pallor as she took his clammy, cold hand in hers. Floundering and failing to find something comforting to say, he nevertheless smiled in gratitude for her effort. She sat holding his hand while having half an ear on Jacques' account of Louise's depression to the police officer, the panic which had consumed her during her fruitless search subsiding as it gave way to a hollow, anxious feeling of dread, which was infinitely worse.

"I must get out again and search for her," Patrick stood, fighting to hold back the tears, "I've got to do something. I can't just sit here while Lou's out there."

"We'll all go," announced Jacques, resting a comforting hand on his friend's shoulder as the policeman continued to write.

Patrick then took Jacques' arm and led him away into a quiet corner as several more police crowded into the restaurant. One, in his early twenties, with an immaculate uniform, sat down with Ivy to take a short statement. As she stumbled through the confused events of the afternoon in French, her attention was inevitably drawn back to the two friends, who were talking conspiratorially just out of her earshot. From their body language, Ivy discerned they were having some sort of disagreement although she couldn't imagine what it was about.

Her version of events completed, the police officer thanked Ivy before moving on to the restaurant owner, who, she guessed, having helped her explore every room of his establishment, was unlikely to be of further help. After a few minutes, Jacques and Patrick returned to the table, their grim expressions telling Ivy they were prepared for the worst.

"This is no place for you. It's no place for any of us, God knows," Patrick hugged her, whispering in her ear. "Please take Jacques back to the city. He'll go with you. I need to deal with this in my own way. Please." His eyes downcast with desperation, he reluctantly released her.

"Alright, I'm so sorry," muttered Ivy, not understanding why he wouldn't want his best friend's support during his darkest hour but not questioning it either. Instead she moved back to Jacques, slipping her arm around his waist and saying in her calmest voice. "Come on, let's go. There is nothing more we can do here."

"I'll call you if there's any news," Patrick affirmed before he and Jacques hugged each other, wordlessly.

"Bye," whispered Ivy as Patrick folded his arms around

her once again. He held her tightly for a brief moment before following the policeman down the stairs. Glancing back, he managed a half smile which nearly broke her heart. Taking Jacques' hand, she tried to avoid the desolation in his eyes as she led him back to the car.

"I may as well carry on to Ouarzazate." Jacques' voice was hollow, as he adjusted his rear view mirror, "from there we can cut back a quicker way to the city."

"Okay," Ivy nodded as he started the engine. Realising it was the first time he'd spoken directly to her for over an hour, she fought in vain for a reply. Although carefully negotiating the winding road, when it came to straight stretches, Jacques broke the speed limit by a significant margin, his jaw tense with concentration. As the mountains eventually gave way to a hot, bare plateau, Ivy's mind swam with a hundred and one questions about Louise. But despite numerous attempts, she failed to catch Jacques' eye, giving her the impression that any intrusion on his thoughts would be unwelcome.

A substantially sized town, Ouarzazate was sleeping soundly in the late afternoon sun. Entering via a majestic gate through the red walls of the Kasbah, Ivy had a strange feeling of watching a film set to slow motion. She barely registered the quiet, shuttered houses they passed or the half-deserted streets with the occasional stray dog sleeping in the shade. The few people she did notice seemed to be meandering along with no particular destination in mind: young women, carrying baskets of herbs trudged along while men sat on shaded terraces, drinking mint tea as they waited out the heat of the day. Seeing these people going about their everyday lives oblivious to the potentially horrific tragedy unfolding in the lives of her friends, served to intensify the fearful agitation Ivy felt as they roared on. She tried to calm her breathing as a wave of nausea threatened to engulf her, before being jolted back to reality by the speed Jacques was driving as they approached a red light.

"Slow down," she heard herself scream out as she felt the thrust of the brakes and the screech of the tyres beneath her. As he pulled over, she noticed Jacques' hands had turned white in his vice-like grip on the steering wheel.

"Oh God, are you hurt? Ivy, I'm so sorry. I could have…" he put his head in his hands as she heard a rasping sob escape from his throat.

"But you didn't," Ivy soothed, pulling him to her, so that his chin rested on her shoulder. Wordlessly she stroked his hair in an effort to console him. "Let me drive?" she suggested quietly, aware that she would need to get a move on before darkness fell.

Without speaking, Jacques got out of the car and walked around to the passenger seat and they changed places, Ivy adjusting the driver's seat to accommodate her smaller frame. Hearing children shrieking and laughing, she looked up to find he'd pulled up by a playground and in that moment it all seemed too much to take, their innocent happiness in bitter contrast to Louise's and Patrick's desperate suffering. Pushing these thoughts from her mind, she set off driving, relieved to have something to concentrate on as Jacques gave succinct directions on the fast road back to Marrakech. After a few miles, Ivy noticed the low, pink buildings of the Atlas Corporation Studios running alongside them to the left.

"Are these the studios where Patrick does much of his work?" she enquired absently, wanting to fill the long silence with some conversation to stop either of them thinking.

"His first film here was in 2009," Jacques answered tonelessly, staring at the impressive entrance gate with its ten feet tall golden sphinxes guarding it on either side.

"Is that when he and Louise came to live in Morocco then?" Ivy asked, wanting him to talk on so she could concentrate on her driving.

"Yes, they came looking for a fresh start after Louise's attempted suicide in Toronto," he paused and Ivy sensed him looking at her. "In hindsight I suppose I should never have followed them."

"Why not?" asked Ivy, apprehension rising in her as she looked briefly towards him.

In that single glance she registered the pain in his eyes, "Because it was me she was trying to get away from. From her past, that is," he whispered slowly, brushing his hair from his forehead which glistened with sweat. Ivy cast her eyes down to her hands which gripped the hot steering wheel, the sense of Jacques' words cutting through her. Feeling her insides contract, she let him continue uninterrupted.

"When you hear the whole story, you will understand why Patrick insisted I leave earlier. It was his way of sparing me more pain and God knows I never wanted to inflict any on you." Seeing his eyes were deep hollows of hurt, Ivy stood at the edge of the dark precipice, willing Jacques to take her over it with him.

"Louise, Patrick and I met at art college. We attended the same courses, we had the same tastes in art. Patrick was our friend but it was Louise and I who became a couple. We were young and so in love, she was the most beautiful girl I'd ever seen, and I was totally smitten. Looking back she was, even then very unpredictable, her moods swinging suddenly and wildly. At the time I put it down to her artistic temperament, for she is extremely talented, way more than either Pat or myself. Truth is we have always been in awe of her work, she eclipsed us and every student in our year, she could become a really great artist if she wanted. The day after our graduation we married, just a quiet wedding with a few witnesses and we bought an apartment in a quiet suburb of Toronto. We made a living selling our artwork, hers always selling for considerably more than mine, I must confess," he laughed, hollowly. "I only got a proper job at the university when Louise discovered she was pregnant. We'd tried to have a child for years and were on the point of losing hope but then Luc came along and... He was the most beautiful child you ever saw," he choked back tears, experiencing the rawness of grief again.

Ivy couldn't recall anything shocking her quite so much in her entire life as the words Jacques had just uttered. She felt numbed to her very core, as though she'd morphed into a robot and her thoughts and actions were no longer hers. She considered pulling over but sensing Jacques' need and hers for him to finish his story, she thought it better to continue driving so he could carry on without her platitudes of pity.

"He had blonde hair and beautiful brown eyes. He was just three when... He was so inquisitive. He loved playing with his toy cars and in the snow. He was such a lively little boy, endlessly running around and exploring," he smiled faintly as they finally left the sprawling studios in their dusty wake.

"Lake Ontario is dotted with tiny islands. It happened on a crisp Sunday afternoon in January when Louise, Luc and I took the ferryboat to an island. After a walk in the park, we went down to explore the shoreline and Luc, of course, was full of beans as always, playing snowballs. I can see him now," he closed his eyes for a prolonged moment, "his little yellow jacket a burst of sunshine against the grey of the winter lake and sky. He was scampering about when he let go of Louise's hand. It happened so fast after that. One minute he was laughing, the next he had somehow run onto the ice which was thin at the edge. I shouted out his name but before I could move there was a loud crack and I saw Luc go under. I tried to save him but by the time I managed to pull him out… He'd been in there too long… " he faltered.

"Oh, Jacques," Ivy found herself unable to put any thoughts into words. So profound was her shock at his revelation, her overriding emotion was one of intense sorrow so she waited patiently until he was ready to continue.

"The moment I held my son in my arms I knew he'd gone. I don't think that feeling will leave me as long as I live," he looked directly at her. "I tried to bring him back but it was hopeless… Everything I've done in the years since has been defined by that day. You forget life was ever normal, I don't know how to explain it. You just survive each day at a time," he paused, his gaze on the point where the road disappeared into the distance.

"Louise and I blamed ourselves and each other until we reached the point where our grief was tearing us apart and we could barely stand to be in the same room together. On the six month anniversary of Luc's death, I woke to find a note on her pillow, telling me she was going to join him." While Jacques fought back tears, Ivy finally comprehended Louise's state of mind and the men's behaviour towards her. Not comprehended, she thought, she simply knew the reason for it. Not having children of her own, she would never really understand what either had endured.

"Luckily an early morning jogger spotted her walking into the lake in her pyjamas and pulled her out. Afterwards she got the psychiatric help she needed while she turned to Patrick for the emotional support and love that she was unable to accept from me," he wiped tears from his eyes, "or, if I'm honest, that I was no longer capable of giving her."

Concentrating intensely on her driving, the pieces Ivy had been puzzling over for a few weeks finally fell into place and yet the bigger picture still seemed hazy. In fact, if anything, Jacques' explanations had created far more questions, which she dared not ask, let alone hope for coherent answers from him now.

"Just a year-and-a-half after Luc's death, we divorced. Soon after, Louise moved in with Patrick, and I gave them my blessing, hoping she could find some happiness again. Louise had talked about leaving Toronto ever since Luc's accident and when Pat was offered a transfer to the Atlas Studios, she jumped at the chance to begin a new life in Morocco," he cursed beneath his breath, "I should have just let them be."

"What made you move here?" Ivy asked, feeling it was an intrusive question but, at the same time, wanting, no needing to know his explanation.

"Patrick and Louise invited me over for a holiday. Even though she was still taking anti-depressants, I could see the North African life suited her and she'd even started painting again, something she hadn't done since Luc died." He paused to consider how to continue. "Anyway, by that point, I was disillusioned with my lecturing job and, having lost direction with my own artwork, I found inspiration in Marrakech with all its colours, smells and tastes. This country seemed to have healed Louise in some way and selfishly I suppose, I hoped it could do the same for me. On my return to Ontario, I painted a few pieces from my sketchbooks and I managed to sell them. I asked Patrick and Louise if it was alright if I moved here for a short while… "

"And so you came to stay at the riad?" Ivy said, noticing as darkness fell, the city lights in the far distance.

"Yes, I chose to rent a room there because I never wanted to make the move permanent. I always knew that one day I would leave," he trailed off, a shadow passing over his face as he blamed himself once more.

"But Louise and Patrick, they have made a new life here for themselves, haven't they? Louise has so much to look forward to," Ivy began, recalling her sighting of her in the Ville Nouvelle. "She's pregnant, isn't she? I saw her shopping for baby clothes."

"She often believes herself to be pregnant," Jacques shook his head, "but the truth is after trying for so long to conceive, Luc's birth was difficult and she can't have any more children." Jacques closed his eyes, indicating the conversation for now was at an end. Sensing he needed some space, Ivy was left alone with her own thoughts for the final part of the journey.

As the familiar night lights of Marrakech greeted them, she considered all that had happened since she'd seen them just twenty-four hours earlier and found it too much to process. The riad courtyard was cloaked in darkness as they walked through it, Jacques checking his mobile for seemingly the fiftieth time since they'd left, his face lost in the shadows of the night. She longed to take him in her arms and give him the solace he needed in the dark hours before the dawn. But as they reached her room, he wearily brushed his hand across his eyes, saying, "I need to be alone tonight, Ivy. I'm sorry."

Turning, he retreated to his room, the night stretching before him to be filled with memories and bad dreams.

Ivy closed her door to the outside world. Glancing around her room, she noticed the red dress she had worn for their lunch at the Mamounia Hotel the previous day, casually flung over the back of a chair, Rose's diary resting on her bedside table. Everything the same, everything changed. Removing her makeup, her birthmark was as red and inflamed as she'd ever seen it after her exposure to the sun that afternoon, as if that mattered any more. She stood in the shower until she was stone cold, the water mingling with her tears. As she slid into bed in a white towelling robe, she shivered violently, the shock of Louise's disappearance and Jacques' subsequent revelations finally catching up with her. In the darkness she cried for Luc, Louise, Patrick and Jacques and for everything they had lost until eventually her sobs lightened as sleep rescued her from the nightmare of the day.

41

Ivy was standing at her bedroom window when the eruption of an argument in rapid French in the street below broke into her unhappy thoughts. Due to the background noise of a cart's wheels on the cobbles, however, she was only able to pick up fragments of the young couple's disagreement about the cheapest mode of travel to Casablanca.

Casablanca. The word hit her like a thunderbolt as she remembered the last time she'd heard it. Recalling Jacques' goodhearted teasing about Louise's navigational skills as they'd set off to Essaouira almost three weeks ago, Ivy felt herself plunge into a bottomless pit of darkness once again.

It had been five days now since she'd opened her bedroom door to find Jacques standing on the other side, still wearing his crumpled shirt from the day before. Ashen-faced and his eyes red-ringed, he'd virtually collapsed into her arms, his breathing ragged with suppressed sobs.

Swallowing hard, he'd collected himself to tell her, "Patrick called me to say the police have discovered Louise's body at the foot of a steep precipice behind the restaurant. They found a note in her pocket saying she couldn't live without Luc anymore." His voice had cracked as he'd mentioned his late son's name, tears flowing steadily down his cheeks.

Holding him, Ivy had recalled her last sighting of Louise, a slight breeze lifting her loose-fitting white clothes, which had brought to mind a dove in full flight. She knew the image of Louise falling to her death, her light blouse and harem pants fluttering around her like wings, would be etched into her memory forever. Wordlessly Ivy had gently brought her hand to Jacques' face, wanting to take away his pain, but having no idea how.

"My only prayer is they are together at peace now," his eyes had searched hers desperately for confirmation as they'd perched on the edge of her bed. Ivy had felt that if that was to be his consolation she would go along with it, even though she sometimes questioned her own belief in an afterlife.

"I'm sure they are Jacques," she'd taken his hand gently in hers. "She's where she has wanted to be for so long, with Luc."

"I just keep thinking it's my fault. She left Canada to start over with Patrick but I had to follow them to pursue my art, didn't I? Seeing me every day had to have reminded her of Luc, of what she'd lost." He'd pulled out a photo from his wallet of himself smiling down at a beautiful boy, wrapped up in a red snowsuit, his blonde hair falling in curls over his forehead, his deep, brown eyes unmistakably his father's. A cheeky smile lighting up his face, tears had sprung to Ivy's eyes as she'd thought how Louise's and Jacques' hearts must have been broken at the unbearable loss of such a precious child.

"And now Louise has gone too and Patrick is a widower. Maybe if I had just stayed in Toronto, she would have been able to recover and move on?" his voice had cracked once more, "oh God, I can't bear it."

"Jacques, nobody is to blame," she'd wiped away his tears with the back of her hand as he'd exhaled deeply, "least of all you. Life is just cruel sometimes. Louise found herself locked in a circle of grief from which she couldn't or didn't want to move on, that's why she did what she did, not because of you."

"But why didn't she come to me or Pat and tell us how she felt? Why didn't either of us realise the desperate state she was in?" Looking beyond her towards the window she'd realised he was asking himself the question rather than her.

"I don't know and we'll probably never find out," Ivy had said, "people just deal with grief in different ways. Sometimes it just gets too much and overwhelms them and they can't find their way out of the darkness."

Lying fully clothed on top of Ivy's bed, Jacques had spent the next few hours telling her quietly about the events of the proceeding years which had culminated in Louise taking her life. As he'd tried to come to some kind of understanding of the depths of desperation his ex-wife had plummeted to, Ivy had just let Jacques talk, saying what he'd needed to. She'd been relieved to be able to reach him in his sorrow, welcoming the role of comforter now the tables had turned.

"Thank you for being here for me," he'd said, his thoughts reaching an impasse as the Muezzin announced lunchtime prayers, "there is no one else in the world I could say these things to."

Over the next couple of days, Ivy hadn't seen much of Jacques. While he'd busied himself, supporting Patrick in his grief as well as with the practicalities of the inquest and the transportation of Louise's coffin to Canada for burial, she'd found herself with time on her hands which she'd spent dwelling on whether there was something, anything she could have done differently. What upset her most was she'd always been a sensitive soul, in tune with people's emotions and yet she'd failed to spot Louise had been perched on the edge of something so terrible with no safety net to catch her. With hindsight bearing heavily upon her, the warning signs had been there but she'd failed to act upon them.

Perhaps the problem had been that since the moment she'd met Louise, she'd been in awe of her, thinking how beautiful, how elegantly dressed and talented she was, accepting without question the confident picture she had presented of herself to the world. Choking back the tears, she felt like a hypocrite. She had done exactly what she hated people doing to her; she had judged Louise by the way she looked without really trying to get to know what sort of person she was. And now it was too late.

Her only respite from her guilty reflections were her light-hearted meetings with Mustapha every lunch time. Although he hadn't been acquainted with Louise and, of course knew nothing about Ivy's situation with Jacques, he seemed to possess a sixth sense that Ivy was hurting in some way. With Jacques occupied with Patrick and the arrangements for Louise, they soon fell into a daily routine. After sharing meze they played games together which gave Ivy comfort and took her out of herself, if only for a short time.

One afternoon, when Ivy's thoughts were with Jacques, she'd suddenly felt Mustapha's tiny hand on hers. "You sad, today, Madame Ivy?" he whispered.

"Yes," nodded Ivy, unable to speak for fear of breaking down in front of him.

"Sometimes, I'm sad," he smiled, "but it won't last forever."

Ivy smiled, "good advice, Mustapha, thank you." They played the rest of the game without talking, at ease in each other's company.

42

Making her way to the courtyard late one morning, it weighed heavily on Ivy's mind that since Louise's death she and Jacques hadn't made love. As they'd set off on that fateful day, she had felt so secure in the depth of his feelings for her. But now, every night just before falling asleep, she was unable to get the image out of her head of a nineteen year-old Jacques falling in love with the mysterious, willowy girl in his art class. Entranced by her beauty and intelligence, and so sure of his feelings, he had married her the day after their graduation. Picturing Jacques and Louise setting up house together and imagining their joy of becoming parents, she saw how wrong she'd been to think of him as an artistic loner.

Having been on the receiving end of Jacques' tender and caring nature, it was obvious now he'd known a deep love in the past. However, while falling in love with him, Ivy had willingly seen him as a man searching for something, who'd found a unique connection with her, his soulmate. She rebuked herself now, seeing that she'd got too caught up in Rose and Ryan's young love and had unwittingly transferred their feelings to herself and Jacques. Their stories had nothing in common. If Jacques truly loved her, why had he hidden something as important as having a wife and son? Before that thought could take root, however, she castigated herself for hypocrisy as the careful concealment of her birthmark from him came to her mind.

She found Jacques sitting in the library that morning. Approaching him, with the fountain trickling gently in the background, her mind rewound to the first morning when she'd sat down to read a book and a cultured, Canadian accent had asked what she was doing in Marrakech. As his tanned face had emerged from the shadows of the shelves, he'd smiled, catching her heart and holding it ever since. How far they had travelled together in the intervening weeks! Taking the leather seat opposite him now, she noticed his skin was pale, his unruly dark hair in need of a cut. His grief for Louise laid bare.

"Ivy," he smiled sadly, "I've just got back from Pat's. I wasn't sure whether you'd gone out or not."

"No, it's far too hot for me today," she smiled, trying to hide her anguish at his forlorn appearance, "how is he?"

"I'm afraid he's in bad shape at the moment. It's just starting to sink in for him. He just can't imagine Lou not being in his life," Jacques trailed off and Ivy's heart went out to him, realising that yet again in a time of crisis and grief, he had to be strong for someone else.

"I wish there was something I could do." Moving next to him on the sofa, she slipped her hand into his.

"You're here. That's what matters to me," Jacques' dark eyes held hers. Sitting in silence she dug deep within herself for that inner calm which had always got her safely through difficult times, hoping she could provide him with the comfort he so needed.

"I don't suppose you'd come round to Pat's with me tonight?" Jacques asked after a time, clutching her hand.

"Of course I will. But wouldn't you prefer it being just the two of you?" Ivy replied, wondering whether her presence would stir up memories of the dinner party, reinforcing that it was just the three of them now, instead of four.

"I want you to come, please," he tightened his grip. Seeing the burden Jacques was carrying, she couldn't refuse.

"Then, yes, I will," Ivy realised that, for someone who always cast himself in the role of protector, it must be difficult to admit he was vulnerable and needed her support.

"I know Pat would appreciate seeing you before we go," Jacques gave an audible sigh of relief, "I know he thinks a lot of you."

"Go?" Ivy swallowed, panic pulsing through her.

"To Canada," Jacques confirmed, "Pat was waiting for the police to release Louise's body and now they have, we can travel back in a couple of days. He wants to take her home and start planning her funeral. He's made the decision to put their house here up for sale and return home. It was for her, after all, that they came to live in Marrakech. Without her, there is nothing to keep him here. He's so good at his job, he'll easily find work in Toronto."

Ivy found it difficult to breathe as the full force of Jacques' words hit her. The fog of grief which had enveloped her during the past days suddenly cleared as the reality dawned on her that they had just two days left before their time together would be over, to be separated beneath a cloud of tragedy, just like Rose and Ryan. It was almost unbearable. A host of questions whirled in her mind, none of which at this moment had an answer.

43

"I'm so glad you could come," Patrick wrapped his arms around Ivy; a desperate plea for solace she felt unqualified to give. "I'm sorry… " she began, but he had already turned away as he led her through the passageway cleared now of Louise's paintings, Jacques looking uncomfortably on.

Jacques fixed their meal, affording Ivy some time alone with Patrick. Sitting with him on the sofa, the lamps and furnishings packed away in boxes at their feet, Ivy listened to his stories, hearing the depth of his love for his late wife in the timbre of his voice and seeing it in the expression in his eyes. So vivid were his recollections, she almost expected Louise, striking in a brightly-coloured dress, to breeze into the room announcing dinner was ready.

Suddenly, Patrick lowered his voice, "Jacques mentioned he'd told you about him and Lou." As Ivy nodded slowly he continued, "I don't want you to feel resentful or threatened by Lou and him once being married. I've known them both for so long and they obviously still cared deeply for each other because of what they'd shared together. But their love changed forever the day Luc died and I know Louise came to love me. I was the rock she needed. Sadly, it just wasn't enough, in the end. Ivy, Louise was never a threat to you, but because she cared so deeply for Jacques, she wanted him to find someone who could make him happy again. When we were in Essaouira, she confided in me that she knew he had, and she was glad."

"Thank you for telling me that, Patrick," she drew him into a tearful embrace, sadly wishing that she'd known about all of this sooner.

"Hey you two!" Jacques called, "dinner is ready."

As the three of them sat down to a simple spaghetti meal the conversation soon stalled. Ivy reflected that Patrick's move back to Canada coupled with Jacques' admission that he'd cancelled his lease of the studio and flat meant it was unlikely either of them would ever return to Marrakech. Continuing that train of thought, while it was just a few hours' flight time from Morocco to London, she realised the prospect of Jacques and her taking frequent transatlantic flights to see each other, was not an option.

Watching Jacques' measured movements as he ate his pasta and listening to his controlled tone as he spoke, Ivy found herself comparing his behaviour to Patrick's. One minute Patrick was animated, talking about Louise and the funeral, but the next he stared silently into his barely-touched food. She shared concerned glances with Jacques, whose sorrow she realised, was for his friend and the mother of his child. Although his grief was raw, she hoped that time would heal him once more. There was something haunted, however, about Patrick. He was drowning in grief for his beloved wife, from which he wasn't looking to be rescued. The evening eventually drew to its close, but reluctant to leave, they lingered in the hallway, Patrick drawing her into his arms once again.

"Louise was a remarkable woman. I'm glad I had the chance to meet her," Ivy smiled as Patrick stooped to kiss her on the cheeks. It felt strange that she'd shared so much with this man, knowing him during the most painful period of his life but that in all probability, she would never see him again.

"Just remember Jacques loves you so much," he whispered, "I know you could make each other so happy, if you give yourselves the chance."

Wending their way down the winding, dark streets to the riad, Ivy caught Jacques looking at her with a wistful smile. As they stood in the courtyard, the scent of the late summer roses filling the air, he kissed her gently, pausing for a moment as his eyes searched hers before he took his leave. Watching him walk away, Ivy couldn't interpret what he was silently asking. She knew it wasn't sexual tension emanating from him but something else, that she had disappointed him in some way. Feeling hurt and confused she retreated into her room, alone.

After breakfast, Ivy found Jacques working on his laptop in the library. Sitting beside him, she noticed he'd taken more care with his appearance than in recent days. With his wavy hair lapping the collar of his blue shirt and his square jaw set, she tried to quell the desire rising in her. Leaning in, he kissed her chastely on the cheek, although his eyes told a different story as he commented, "you've only two days left in Morocco?"

"You too. Are you spending today with Patrick?" Ivy enquired, desperate for a little time alone with him before they left.

"No, he is saying goodbye to some friends before we leave," he shut down his computer to cast his attention solely upon her.

"Oh," Ivy replied, nonchalantly, attempting to disguise the hope flooding through her body as Jacques took her hands in his.

"Ivy, before Louise died," he stumbled over his late ex-wife's name before collecting himself, "I planned to take you to the Cascades d'Ouzoud. It is the most beautiful place I've ever been and I booked us in at the riad there, thinking we could spend your last night in Morocco overlooking the waterfalls. I don't suppose you want to go now, after everything..."

His eyes downcast, Ivy detected the despair in his voice, assuming she'd say 'no'. Part of her wanted to make a clean break so that when she got home it would be easier to shake it all off as a failed holiday romance. But she knew it would always be much more than that, that the events of the past few days had only deepened her feelings for him.

"I want to come," she affirmed, finally, lifting her hand to stroke his cheek. Seeing a smile pass his lips, relief swept over her as she managed to reach him in his suffering, bringing a crumb of comfort. Knowing that she'd be pushed for time to get to the airport on their return from the Ouzoud

Waterfalls, Ivy made her final farewells to Mustapha that night in the courtyard.

"Safe journey home, Madam Ivy," the little boy held out his hand as she tried to commit his beautiful, white smile and wide, dark eyes to memory.

"Thank you. Is it my imagination or have you grown taller since I arrived?" asked Ivy, not wanting a tearful goodbye which it very easily could become if she let it.

"I think so," Mustapha's attention flipped to his father and then back to her, "I'm going to miss you, Madam Ivy. Thank you for playing games with me and teaching me English."

"My pleasure, which reminds me, I have something for you," she smiled, reaching behind her back for a box she'd wrapped in some blue tissue paper.

"Ah, le jacquet," he ripped back the paper, enthusiastically "I always want a new one!"

Ivy smiled at the simple pleasure he took in it, explaining. "In English, we call it backgammon. I thought your old board was looking a little worse for wear." She watched him scurry off into the back, the game carefully slotted beneath his arm. She had an idea he'd succeed in persuading his father to play.

"Thank you for keeping my boy occupied," his father bowed his head to kiss Ivy's hand, "and out of mischief."

"I loved every minute of it," smiled Ivy, looking around the courtyard, trying to commit the details; the light, the bird song, the scent of roses and jasmine, to memory. "I'll really miss this place."

"Then you must return. It's been such a pleasure having

you here," he stated, "for once my son's mischief paid off and brought you to us."

"He's such a sweet boy and he's brought a lot of fun to my stay here," Ivy agreed. Before she could continue she was interrupted by the shrill ringing of the phone at the reception desk. With an apologetic smile Khalid hurried to answer while she took the opportunity to return to her room and finish her packing.

Ascending the spiral stairs, she realised that no matter what happened now between her and Jacques, one twist of fate had changed her life forever. She remembered how reluctantly Rose had accompanied Sophie to *The Swan* that evening in the spring of '44, the evening she had first met Ryan, and reflected that, in the same way, if Mustapha hadn't led her to his father's riad, she would never have met Jacques. It seemed unthinkable now, even though she had no idea where their story would end.

44

The Ouzoud Waterfalls were a two-and-a-half hour drive to the east of Marrakech on the dusty road to Fez. They set off just after ten, stopping for lunch at a Berber village on the way. For most of the journey, they sat silently side by side as they skirted the foothills of the Atlas, content for the moment just to be in each other's company once more, each lost in their own thoughts. On their arrival, Ivy took in the traditional style guesthouse, a jumble of pink buildings on different levels. Jacques was right, it was the loveliest place she'd ever seen.

"Thank you for bringing me here," she smiled as they strolled down picturesque paths which wound through graceful gardens.

"Just one thing," he stopped, turning to her, hesitantly, "I made the booking a week ago before… and I got us a double room. If you want I can ask them to change it," he paused, the silence awkward between them.

"No, don't do that," she replied, meeting his eye and

feeling rather disconcerted. Normally so in tune with Jacques she felt confused by these mixed signals he was giving her now. Since Louise's death he had seemed reluctant to spend the night with her and she wondered whether this trip was just his way of saying a final goodbye? Heartbroken by such a possibility, she tried to console herself that maybe it was for the best. Since telling her he'd fallen in love with Louise's beauty when they'd been students, Ivy had found herself slipping back into her shy shell, afraid to reveal her birthmark to him for fear he'd be disgusted by it. For one last night together, she could keep up the pretence and return home tomorrow, her memories of their holiday romance intact and untarnished forever.

The centrepiece of their room was a beautiful ceiling painted in a myriad of blues and silver in fair imitation of a starry night sky. The walls were in neutral cream as was the bed, strewn with soft green pillows which matched the shade of the glass wall lights. A small table and soft upholstered chairs in one corner and a cream chest of drawers and wardrobes completed the decor. Ivy unpacked her remaining clean clothes into the drawers before dotting her toiletries around the state-of-the-art green bathroom, the pretty room in its idyllic, calm surroundings at odds with the turmoil she felt. Jacques disappeared into the bathroom and, having changed into a fresh, checked shirt, he lingered hesitantly in the doorway, looking as though he was about to say something before changing his mind. "Come on, I want to show you the waterfalls before dinner. I don't want you to miss a thing," he said instead, taking hold of Ivy's hand.

After a short steep climb, they paused at the top of

the cascades, taking in the village below where little huts sheltered around a dozen small watermills, some still in use, grinding wheat into flour. The soothing splashing of the water invaded Ivy's senses, her newfound calm ruffled only by the quick movement of a large, black creature in the trees. "What's that?" she turned to Jacques, intrigued.

"A Barbary ape and those are pomegranate trees I think," Jacques took hold of her hand. "The apes often come down to drink in the river before nightfall."

The setting sun soon cast everything in its rosy glow and as they made their way through the olive grove, Ivy thought the place possessed a timeless quality. Being in the midst of such beauty made it easy to forget everything else. As they sauntered along the path which wound its way downhill, they admired the rainbows arching over the falls in a myriad of colours. Ivy closed her eyes, feeling fine drops of spray cool her face.

As they reached the bottom, an amphitheatre of waterfalls descending into pools in a lush valley, appeared at the last moment. It was a scene which in many senses fulfilled Ivy's idea of paradise. In the basins below the cascades, a procession of boatmen rowed tourists to the main pool but Ivy didn't want to share the moment with other people and Jacques didn't suggest a trip, evidently feeling the same. For Ivy it felt like it had before Jacques's revelations: that he was hers and she was his. As the sunset gave way to a starry night she almost believed it to be true, that this was the beginning for them rather than the end.

"I should change for dinner," stated Ivy as they reached the terrace, noticing her shoes were streaked with red earth.

"You go ahead," Jacques smiled, pulling up a chair, "I'll just wait here for you."

Ivy nodded, appreciating the fact that he intuitively understood that for the moment she needed her space. In their room, she stripped off her clothes, sweaty from the journey and walk. She showered quickly before drying her hair into a straight bob and dressing in a cream sundress, which she was glad she'd saved until now as it accentuated her end-of-holiday tan beautifully.

The citronella candles flickering on the tables helped create a suitably romantic ambience on the terrace. Walking past and exchanging smiles with other couples near the entrance to the restaurant, Ivy spotted Jacques seated at a table at the far end. As Hicham, the riad owner, led her down some white, stone steps, she was glad to be away from the other diners, cut adrift with him. There, they enjoyed a quince and lamb tagine followed by orange blossom crème brûlée, speaking little, content to let the peace of their surroundings overwhelm them.

Later, they stood awkwardly in the middle of their room, their shadows thrown onto the pale walls by rose-scented candles flickering in jars. "You were very quiet tonight," Jacques gazed down at her with a slight frown, his hair flopping over his forehead, making him appear much younger and somehow vulnerable.

"I know, I'm sorry," Ivy felt tears pricking her eyes and quickly looked away, "it's just after all that has happened in the past few days… and now this will be our last night together."

"Why would you say that?" As he lifted her chin upwards, she saw his eyes were full of hurt.

"Because I'm returning to England and you're going back to Canada. We'll be an ocean apart," she swallowed, averting her eyes to the stone-flagged floor to momentarily avoid his gaze, his pain, "I don't see what future we have, do you?"

"Yes I do see a future for us, because I love you," his hands came to rest on her shoulders as a cloud darkened his face, "unless you don't feel the same about me anymore?"

"Of course I do," she momentarily felt affronted he could even begin to doubt her feelings but this subsided as she saw his expression calm, "it's something else."

"I'm in love with you and you feel the same," a weak smile nudged his lips upwards as he tightened his hold on her. "What else is there? Apart from details?"

"You're not making this easy for me," tears spilled down her cheeks as she wondered how to put what she had to tell him into words; how it was those very details which to her seemed insurmountable.

"Is this about Louise?" his hands moved up to cup her face, his expression determined as he pulled her to him, "Ivy, I loved her once and with hindsight I wish I'd told you about her and Luc. I was going to in time but I honestly thought it would have no bearing on us, on what we have together. Louise and I had the kind of love young couples have, intense like a flame but it soon burnt itself out. What I feel for you is so much deeper, so much more.." his eyes brimmed with tears, "I can't imagine my life without you."

"I understand, Jacques," Ivy shook her head, determined to stop herself crying and find a way to tell him.

"What is it, then, my love?" His brow still crinkled with

confusion, he gently kissed her tears away, "don't you see, I want to spend my life with you?"

"I do too, but," with a deep intake of breath, she pulled away from him, "I haven't been fair with you, Jacques. There's something I need to show you."

Wordlessly, she led him into the bathroom and, turning to the mirror, her hand trembling, she slowly removed her makeup. She watched him, standing motionless by her side, his expression unchanging as the ugly redness of her birthmark appeared in her reflection in the mirror. Her eyes brimmed with tears once more as the silence stretched between them for an interminable moment.

Then, the warmth of his hand on her bare shoulder, Jacques slowly turned her round to face him. As he lifted her chin with his fingers she had no option but to meet his eyes, and it was then she saw that wonderful smile of his. Wiping her tears away with the back of his hand, he bowed his head, gently kissing her face, his lips lingering on the rough, redness of her birthmark. "You're not… " she started but didn't know how to finish the sentence as her pain was overcome with the tenderness she felt for him.

"I've always known about it, I'm an artist remember." He caressed her cheek, smiling as he traced the outline of the birthmark with his long, elegant fingers, "to me, it looks like the imprint of a beautiful red rose, it's part of who you are. And who you are, Ivy, is the woman I love."

"I'm sorry I doubted you," Ivy felt relief flow through her before noticing a subtle change in his expression as he pulled away from her.

"It was more than doubting me, Ivy. You've diminished

my feelings for you if you think all I care about is how you look. I thought we'd connected on a deeper level than that," his hurt was audible in his voice, "I've felt your insecurities and knew that you'd only tell me about it when you'd learned to trust my feelings for you. I've waited so long for this moment. The truth is I fell in love with you the moment I saw you pouring over that huge travel book in the riad library."

Trembling with emotion, Ivy could only mutely shake her head as Jacques gathered her into his arms once more, kissing her hair. "Don't cry, my love. I realise how much courage what you just did took."

Composing herself, Ivy whispered. "It's because I love you so much that I was afraid of losing you. Forgive me for being so stupid."

Jacques nodded and then his mouth found hers, hastily and hungrily. Tasting the saltiness of his skin on her tongue and feeling his mouth move down to her throat, Ivy's body tingled. Sensing an urgency in his kisses she'd never felt before, they hastily undressed each other before stumbling to the bed.

Unlike their first time in Essaouira when she'd allowed Jacques to guide her, it was Ivy who took control now. Tentative and a little self-conscious at first, she quickly felt empowered by the confidence Jacques's passionate caresses gave her. After revealing to him the thing she'd kept hidden to the world and which she'd allowed to define her whole life, she held no part of herself back and cried out in relief and joy as he willingly took it. As darkness fell, plunging the room in a purple light, they made love again, before talking long into the night, unwilling to lose in sleep the precious hours left to them.

The roads were quiet so they arrived back in Marrakech before lunchtime. Ivy retired to her room to complete her packing, her joy that Jacques wanted them to spend the rest of their lives together tinged by the sadness of their parting. Wheeling her suitcases through the riad courtyard later, she spotted him sitting by a vase of red roses, nervously drumming his fingers on his knee. As he stepped towards her she studied his face, taking in his long angular nose, the laughter lines around his mouth and eyes, his love for her apparent in his expression. Choking back her tears, she attempted to commit all these details to memory.

"I want to come with you to the airport," he folded her into his arms as his dark eyes searched hers, their imminent separation now laying between them no matter how close they got.

Ivy shook her head, "I'll be fine." She had already made the decision to go alone, the truth being that saying goodbye to him was going to be one of the hardest things she would ever do and she wanted to get it over as quickly as possible.

"Are you sure?" His forehead furrowed as his eyes continued to plead with her.

"Yes," she swallowed a lump in her throat, "and besides I want to remember you in this beautiful courtyard…." she added, pointing to the fountain to detract from her breaking voice.

"Alright then," he leaned back, still holding her, his arms protesting against letting her go, "I'll keep in touch regularly but please don't worry. It may take some months for me to sort things out. Pat's in a bad place at the moment and I want to see Louise's family again. With my parents dying when I was young, I grew very close to my in-laws so I'd like to spend some time with them, help them get through this."

Ivy found she couldn't speak as her composure finally broke and the tears she had been trying so hard to hold back spilled over.

"We'll find a way my love, I promise," he held her face in his hands, "Je t'aime." And then he looked long into her eyes before kissing her softly. Closing her eyes, she breathed in his scent.

"I have to go," she pulled away from him, grabbing hold of her suitcases, "I love you."

"Au revoir!" He shouted behind her as she briefly turned back, managing a half smile. At the desk, she paused briefly to say a final goodbye to Mustapha's father before looking back again to see Jacques standing where she'd left him. After a moment she stepped out into the street beyond and into the taxi which would take her away from him.

45

Ivy's eyes flew open. Coming to focus on the familiar, flowery wallpaper of her bedroom, memories returned to her of the plane's descent through thick, grey cloud and its bumpy landing on the rain-shiny runway of Stansted Airport. Recalling a brisk taxi journey on pre-rush hour roads back to Colchester, she felt sick with the thought that every mile had taken her further away from Jacques. Hugging her warm pillow, she pictured him on his transatlantic flight to Toronto, dozing or else talking to Patrick, and felt hollow at the prospect of the weeks and months ahead without him.

So this was the other side of love. Now she'd enjoyed the intense rapture of falling in love, she was forced to endure the wretched pain of separation, just as Rose had. She wished she could speak to her now to ask for guidance on how to get through it, how to stop her heart hurting. Dispirited by the grey, late August weather, she mooched around her flat, opening windows to release the shut-in smell after so many weeks laying empty, before making tea and toast to silence her growling stomach. For the remainder of the morning she was glad to lose herself in the dozen menial tasks which presented themselves one after the other, welcome distractions from thinking of Jacques. Unpacking her suitcase was her priority, loading the crumpled, soiled clothes into the washing machine and binning almost-used toiletries. Then she turned her attention to what was left, sorting her guide books, leaflets and souvenirs into piles on the carpet before finding places for them in the regimented rows on her shelves.

Cradling a mug of tomato soup, she then curled up on the sofa to read the well-thumbed anthology of Canadian poetry Jacques had pressed into her palm as she'd left him standing in the riad. Noticing his mother's loving inscription on the title page, she realised just what it meant for him to give her such a prized possession, and she felt guilty for ever doubting the depth of his feelings for her. That afternoon as she ironed each item of her clothing, memories flitted to her like late-summer moths: her lemon sundress conjured up the bedroom in Essaouira where she and Jacques had made love for the first time, her red-flowered dress with its full skirts caused her to relive their lunch in the sumptuous surroundings of the Mamounia Hotel, while the simple cream dress brought back the moment at the Ouzoud Waterfalls when she'd finally found the courage to lay herself bare and Jacques had accepted and loved her for who she was.

That evening, after nipping out for fish and chips, she called her mum. Deciding to say nothing about what had happened in Marrakech on the phone, she arranged to meet her at their favourite forties themed teashop in Colchester the following afternoon. Exhaustion creeping up on her, she then settled down on her sofa with a box of chocolates, to watch *Hideous Kinky*, filmed in Marrakech. Barely taking notice of the story, she concentrated on each street Kate Winslet walked down, trying to discern whether she'd done so with Jacques. Seeing Marrakech on screen unleashed a whole host of different memories and, as the credits rolled, she knew she'd watch it many more times in the coming months. Later, she snuggled into her bed, half-harbouring a hope Jacques might have contacted her and, logging into her email account, she discovered he'd been true to his parting words.

Ivy

I hope you had a safe journey home. I've just touched down in Toronto after a quiet flight. Thinking about all the miles separating us as I travelled west, I actually believe that we've spent our lives moving towards each other.

Arriving back in Canada felt strange and I know that seeing all the old places will reopen my old wounds. Luc is everywhere here and it feels like yesterday again that I lost him.

The dream of being with you again, whenever that may be, gives me the strength to get through this.

Je t'aime,
Jacques.

Reading his heart-lifting yet heart-breaking words, tears flowed down Ivy's cheeks. Quickly, she typed an email back, telling him if there was anything he needed, all he had to do was ask. She signed off sending her love before closing her eyes to escape into dreams of him.

"You look well," Ivy kissed her mum outside the tearoom secreted away in the Little Wynd. With a newly-cut graduated bob, highlighted by the summer sun, she looked trim in a pale-pink pencil dress, "how's dad?"

"He's fine. He's probably climbing a tree as we speak! Oh Ivy I've missed you... You look... " her mum pulled back, her brow furrowed in concentration as she studied her daughter's face, "... different... good. I can't quite put my finger on it."

"Come on. It's looking busy in there already. Let's get our order in and I'll tell you all about my holiday." Ivy linked her mum's arm, leading her past a group of Japanese tourists enjoying afternoon tea, to a quiet table in the far corner of the café.

They decided to treat themselves to afternoon tea too, brought to them on a three-tiered cake stand by a young waitress dressed in keeping with the wartime theme of the teashop. With her chestnut-brown hair pinned up in an elegant chignon, full-skirted blue and white polka dot dress and red lipstick, something about her reminded Ivy of Rose. She was on the point of mentioning it, her recollection providing her the ideal in-road to launch into telling her mum about Rose's diary. But watching her pour their tea into mismatched, flowered china cups, Jacques stepped to the forefront of her thoughts.

"While I was in Marrakech I met a man, an artist called Jacques and we fell in love." The ease with which the words tumbled out of her mouth shocked Ivy, but she supposed that part of the story really was that simple. Her mother's open-mouthed expression as she continued to pour into an already overflowing cup sent Ivy into a fit of giggles, "I'm sorry that was a bit abrupt," she smiled, soaking up the spilt tea with her serviette.

Recovering after a few seconds, her mum took hold of her daughter's hands across the embroidered table cloth. "Oh, Ivy, I'm so happy for you. When are you going to see him again?"

"I don't know. Jacques is French-Canadian and he's returned to Toronto for the time being," she faltered, her eyes brimming with tears.

"What's wrong, sweetheart?" Her mother's hands warming hers, Ivy launched into how she and Jacques had met and all the wonderful times they'd spent together, before moving on to Louise and the ensuing tragedy which had unfolded.

Her mum sighed, concern for her daughter etched on her face. "Oh my God, those poor people, what a dreadful thing to happen to them but also to you Ivy, when you had just found such happiness… " her voice faltered.

"It was dreadful. One minute, we were enjoying a day in the mountains and the next, she'd just… gone. Looking back I think Jacques and Patrick suspected straight away what had probably happened because she'd attempted it before but I… " Ivy began to tremble. "You should have seen her, Mum, she was so beautiful, so talented. There were times when I felt envious of her and suspected she had designs on Jacques. Other times though I felt she was trying to reach me and if I'd been thinking less about myself, maybe I would have been more receptive to her cry for help?"

"It was a tragic waste of life, for sure. But don't feel guilty, Ivy. If the two people who loved her most couldn't comfort her, it sounds as though the poor woman was beyond any human help." She gave her daughter's hand a reassuring squeeze.

"Maybe," Ivy answered unconvinced and for a few minutes, they just sat there in silence, drinking tea and collecting their thoughts.

"What are you going to do, now, sweetheart?" her mum said eventually, the enormity of what Ivy had just told her starting to sink in.

"Nothing at the moment. Jacques is grieving for his former wife and mother of his son and supporting his best friend. He says he wants a future with me but who knows? Situations evolve, feelings change." Ivy choked a sob, unsure how she would bear the separation. Taking out her BlackBerry, she scrolled through her photos to find one of her and Jacques together. Gazing at their smiling faces and windswept hair against the backdrop of the beach at Essaouira, she handed it to her mum, "this is Jacques."

"I can see what you see in him! He's certainly good-looking, but he has kind eyes too," smiled her mum, intently studying the screen. "You must do whatever you think is right, but don't leave it too long. You have to let Jacques know that while you are there for him when he wants you, you need him too."

"I will, Mum, I promise," she averted her eyes to the yellow rose in the centre of their table, thinking how forlorn it seemed alone in its vase. They ate their sandwiches, and as the waitress brought a fresh pot of tea, Ivy braced herself yet again, attempting to think of the gentlest way she could broach the subject of Rose.

"Have you any idea how Aunt Rose spent the Second World War?" she managed finally, glancing at the gramophone and wartime memorabilia adorning the walls of the tearoom.

"She worked as a typist in Colchester Magistrates' Court?" Her mother poured more tea, which was strong and brown, into their dainty, flowery teacups, "something like that."

"It's just that she writes about some of her experiences during that time in this diary," Ivy rooted the green book from the depths of her handbag, its pages committed to her memory.

"I remember you telling me about it before you went on holiday, but I've never seen this," remarked her mum, flipping through it, "what does she say?"

"Take it home and read it," murmured Ivy, deciding in the end to let her mum get her head around Rose's revelations and come to her own conclusions, alone and at her own speed. As strains of *I'll be Seeing You* wafted around the teashop, Ivy couldn't help but be affected by the song's poignancy, thinking of Rose's American airman, wondering again what had become of him.

As they moved on to the scones heaped with jam and clotted cream, their conversation reverted to Ivy's experiences in Morocco. Her mum sat enthralled, eager to hear of the city's sumptuous palaces and bustling souks, the majesty of the Atlas Mountains and the ruggedness of its coast. "It sounds like everything I've ever read about it magnified by 100%," she commented as her daughter drew to a close.

"It was. I just wish Rose could have seen it. I know she visited lots of European capitals but Marrakech was something else... So exotic, so intoxicating," she paused, her emotions threatening to get the better of her again.

"I think it's so fitting you used some of her legacy to visit. I know she'd have been thrilled you fulfilled an old dream," her mum smiled. "It's as though you went there for the both of you."

"Yes, there were a lot of times when I felt exactly like that," Ivy nodded, draining her teacup, before helping herself to a mini custard slice while her mum opted for the éclair.

"I'll pay the bill, my treat. I thought maybe we could go shopping or at least window shopping, if you've got time?" her mum smiled as they finished off with chocolates.

"Of course I have. I've missed you too, you know?" Ivy linked her mum's arm as they strolled past the eclectic clothes and jewellery shops on the Long Wynd. Never one to indulge in retail therapy, Ivy found it surprisingly relaxing after the hot hassle of the souks.

The town centre fashion shops already stocked their autumn ranges, this year in luscious shades of plum and burnt orange. To-ing and fro-ing between the usual high street stores, Ivy picked up some jeggings and long sleeved and short sleeved tops in these muted shades which would suit both the Indian summer predicted for September as well as layering up when the weather turned colder in October. They saved their favourite haunt, a market housed in a deconsecrated church, until last. With stalls selling antique cutlery and furniture and everything in between, while her mother made a beeline for the second-hand bookstall, Ivy perused the vintage clothes stall.

Leafing through the rack of forties-style outfits, their flimsy, silky materials soft to her touch, Ivy picked out a whimsical swallow-printed, iris-blue dress. Unsuitable for school, she didn't have a clue where she'd wear it but sensed it would suit her. As she paid for it, she thought of the anticipation Rose must have felt as she put on similar dresses ready to spend the evening with the man with whom she was falling in love.

Of course Ivy no longer had to imagine how being in love felt, thanks to Rose. She'd not merely been instrumental in her going to Africa but her romance with Ryan had inspired her and had led her to give herself to Jacques, heart, body and soul. She wanted to believe they had a future together and yet, despite his reassurances, Rose's and Ryan's story had taught her that no matter how much two people loved each other, sometimes it just wasn't enough. Over the next few days, Ivy made a conscious effort not to think of it, instead immersing herself in the finer touches to her planning for the autumn term. In fact, she was glad to put the summer holidays behind her as the new school year fast approached.

46

With the unappealing prospect of spending the bank holiday weekend moping around her flat alone, Ivy hastily arranged a trip to North London to visit Mei. Knowing she'd be less inclined to travel up there once winter set in, she also wanted to leave the October half term free for the eventuality that her plans to see Jacques again might come to fruition. So, that lazy, late summer Thursday afternoon she took the train to the city, excited at the prospect of catching up with her oldest friend after her eventful holiday.

"You look amazing, Ivy. Your hair has grown so long," Mei drew her into a hug outside Belsize Park's red brick tube station. Her friend's compliment made her glad the late heat had permitted her to wear her swallow-printed dress for the first time, teaming it with a lemon cardigan and pumps.

"You do too," Ivy took in her friend's effortless grace, her chin-skimming ebony bob perfectly complimented by her pale-pink dress, cinched at the waist by a wide, black patent belt. She looked as though she'd stepped right off the stage of a production of *Jersey Boys*.

"Morocco obviously suited you!" Mei released her, scrutinising her face.

"It was everything I dreamed it would be," she began, seeing two pairs of brown eyes fixed on her. "Hey you two," she addressed Ruth and Harry who were dutifully holding their mum's hands tightly as suited city workers swarmed past, "how did you enjoy your summer holidays?"

"Lots," replied Ruth, her beautiful ebony hair in a French plait. "We went camping in France. We had the best time ever, we stayed near a river and every day we had a baguette and Nutella for breakfast. And we went swimming in the pool and met a nice French boy called Laurent."

"That sounds brilliant. And what did you enjoy Harry?" Ivy smiled at the little boy standing in his sister's shadow, his big eyes blinking.

"We did kayaking on the river and there were competitions in archery and table tennis," continued Ruth, more and more excitedly, "Harry won the competition in…"

"Ruth, honey, why don't you let Harry tell Auntie Ivy?" Mei butted in as a man with a newspaper beneath his arm stepped around Ivy looking at her with annoyance, before descending the steps to the tube station.

"I was good in archery," stated Harry, with a grave smile, "I won ten Euros."

"Wow, how cool is that? Remind me not to enter a competition with you then?" Ivy exclaimed, at which the little boy laughed an infectious giggle which rippled through the group.

"He's really looking forward to starting school next week, aren't you Harry?" Mei smiled at her son.

"I am," nodded the little boy, "I'll be with Ruthie."

"That's right, you'll see your big sister at playtime and dinnertime," smiled Ivy, looking at Ruth before back to Harry, "you'll really enjoy school, I'm sure."

"I'm going to look after him," Ruth took hold of his hand as the little boy looked adoringly up to her.

Golden leaves, a prelude to autumn, skittered at their feet as they crossed the tree-lined high street. But beneath the yellow and white striped awnings of *Pierre's Pâtisserie* locals were making the most of the end of summer mini heat wave. However, with two little ones in tow, Mei headed into the stylish cafe and Ivy followed, grateful they weren't eating al fresco as she still hadn't yet acclimatised to the steep drop in temperature since her return from Morocco.

The children ordered their favourite ham and emmental cheese croissants followed by warm tartes aux pommes and whipped cream for dessert. Ivy opted for the leek quiche which she'd developed a liking for during her semester in France followed by tarte Belle-Hélène which inevitably took her back to her time with Jacques, Louise and Patrick in *Chez Driss* in Essaouira. With the lunchtime rush in full swing now, they were lucky to find a table in the window away from the queue which snaked its way along the counter.

"Can I try some?" smiled Harry, regarding Ivy's tart with interest while having great fun pulling gooey strings of cheese from his croissant. His cheeky grin and jet-black hair put Ivy in mind of Mustapha as she wondered whether he'd found someone else to play his board games with, now she'd gone.

"If you stop messing with that, young man, then maybe Auntie Ivy will be kind enough to give you a small piece to try," Mei replied with a half-smile.

"Okay, mummy," the little boy did as he was told, before embarking on a conversation with his sister just beyond Ivy's earshot.

"I've got some news," Mei leaned over to Ivy, her voice hushed, "I begin my nursing training next month."

"Wow," Ivy spluttered, gulping down her Diet Coke, "so you took the plunge?"

"Yes, I completed my application form after our conversation in May. You made me realise that if I kept putting it off, I'd never do it. " Ivy saw excitement glittering in her friend's eyes, "I can't tell you how excited I am, if a little scared to death."

"Oh, Mei, I'm thrilled for you," Ivy drew her friend into a hug, inhaling her familiar citrus perfume, "you were born to be a nurse."

"Thank you so much for giving me the kick up the backside I needed," she looked at her intently, her eyes wide. "Which reminds me, you haven't told me about your trip to Morocco?"

"Auntie Ivy," the little girl cut in with her most charming smile, having eaten all of her croissant apart from the slightly scorched top which she'd broken into bits to create a smiley face on her plate, "Harry and I were thinking you might like to go to Camden. We could have ice cream?"

"Yes, that would be nice but I don't think we'll have time to see everything there today," Ivy showed Ruth her watch which was nudging towards two. "Why don't we get up nice and early and go tomorrow instead?"

The four of them spent the afternoon collecting conkers and playing in the park. On their way home, at Ivy's request, they called in at *Atticus Books,* a bibliophile's paradise on the high street with its dark, secret corners hiding undiscovered treasures. Perusing the shelves crammed with huge, hard-backed books, dust hanging in shafts of sunlight, Rose's library came to her mind, closely followed by the riad's reading room where she and Jacques had spent so many happy times. With twilight enveloping the streets they made their way to Mei's house.

"Wow! I love the way you've decorated," Ivy exclaimed as they entered the sitting room. It wasn't merely a change of wallpaper or a lick of paint, though, the whole style and feel of the room was different. Gone were the muted beiges and creams Mei had always seemed to like in favour of an over-sized, flowery sofa, a wood burning stove and a large, oak coffee table strewn with toys, well-thumbed books and magazines interspersed with jam jars holding freshly cut flowers. "It's a lot like your room was when we were teenagers."

"Yes," Mei laughed as the children took their precious hoard of conkers and leaves upstairs, "I looked around one day and decided it was uninviting and lacked character so I thought I'd ring the changes."

"Well you've certainly done that! It suits you." Ivy kicked off her pumps, curling her feet beneath her on the sofa, "how is Phil?"

"Good, he's been so accommodating with my course," smiled Mei, lighting the scented candles in the hearth, "and we make sure we do something as a family most weekends. We have our arguments, plenty of them. Who doesn't? But he's been so supportive, altering his working hours to fit in with the kids and I. I couldn't ask for anything more."

"That's wonderful," smiled Ivy, recalling the routine she'd got into with Jacques in Marrakech for a few short weeks, supposing it was the same give and take for married couples. She missed him so much now she was back at home, even their little disagreements. "You definitely seem a lot happier than when I saw you last."

"I am," smiled Mei, "one step at a time but I'm getting there."

For tea, they enjoyed spaghetti bolognaise, accompanied, much to Harry's delight, with garlic bread. After washing up, they settled down to watching *Garfield*.

"Come on, you two, off to bed." Mei announced at nine. The children then kissed Ivy before Mei ushered them upstairs, giving Ivy a chance to check her emails. To her relief, there was another from Jacques.

Ivy

Today was Louise's funeral and, as you can imagine, it was a very difficult day for us all. Patrick held it together very well but I can tell he's broken inside. For me it brought back memories of Luc's funeral which is still, even after all this time, so raw and painful I can hardly bear it. Ivy, I just want you here with me. I'm sorry this is very brief but I can't write any more just now.

Je t'aime,
Jacques.

Feeling helpless being so far away, Ivy tried to find some words of comfort in her instant reply, resolving to send him another, more considered one, later when she was alone. "So, tell me all about your holiday in Marrakech," Mei kicked back on the couch in silky, black pyjamas, cracking open a second bottle of Cava.

"It was eventful," Ivy said, enjoying the cool sharpness of wine on her tongue, wondering where to start.

"You shady lady! You met someone didn't you?" Mei slapped her hand on her knee, "I knew there was something different about you. I just couldn't quite put my finger on it."

Energised by regular top ups of wine, Ivy spent the next hour or so relating the unabridged version of her relationship with Jacques, the one she couldn't tell her mother. It felt a relief to share it with someone, reliving it all rather than the fantasy she slipped into during quiet moments alone. It made it feel immediate and real once more.

"Wow, that has more twists and turns than an episode of *Downton*," Mei sighed, as Ivy related Jacques' parting promise to her. Flicking on the lamp as dusk descended into darkness outside, she added, "but I must say, it sounds like Jacques is 'the one'."

"I think so, too," Ivy blinked in the bright light, feeling woozy as the wine went straight to her head.

"Then why aren't you with him now, instead of sitting on my sofa?" Mei laughed pushing her fringe out of her eyes, "not that I'm ungrateful, mind."

"Well?" her friend persisted, dark eyes gleaming when Ivy hesitated.

"I just told you," she leaned over for the wine bottle to replenish her glass.

"Err, no you didn't," Mei wagged her finger in a way Ivy imagined her doing with the kids, "oh come on, Ivy. You love him, he loves you. The rest is just details."

"Funny, that's what he said. He says he loves me. He might even believe it but as time goes by… " she swallowed not wanting to voice her greatest fear.

"Do you believe he loves you?" Mei looked serious as they got to the crux of the matter.

"Yes," Ivy shifted uncomfortably, knowing her friend's no-nonsense attitude would stand her in good stead in her nursing training. "That is, I did when he told me after the first time we slept together and then when I showed him my birthmark, anyway."

"Well, you must hold onto that then! Don't allow doubt to creep in," Ivy detected exasperation in her friend's voice, realising what a gentle ride her mum had given her in comparison.

"Yes, but… " Ivy rested her head back on the sofa, "even if Jacques gets over what happened to his son and ex-wife, we come from different worlds and I'm not sure things will work out between us."

"None of us do. That's why it's called 'falling in love'. You have to let yourself fall and hope the other person will catch you, take the risk of getting hurt. And as for coming from different worlds, well haven't you noticed Phil and I could say the same? We had to overcome a lot of disapproval, especially from his family," Mei drained her glass. "Besides, I think you were always destined to be with someone a bit out of the ordinary. If you haven't noticed you're rather quirky yourself."

"I'm not quite sure how to take that. Is that good or bad?" Ivy smiled at her friend, resting her chin on her hand.

"Good, of course! Would I have a boring best friend?" Mei laughed, hitting her with a cushion, "but honestly, I think you just need to give Jacques some time and space to make his next move."

"That's what I was thinking," Ivy nodded, suddenly feeling sleepy.

"Well, maybe just a few months," Mei countered, "because I don't want you sitting around on that dusty shelf, forever."

After, they settled down to watch back-to-back episodes of *Charmed,* an American drama series they'd first enjoyed in the long summer holidays home from university. The story of three sisters who were also witches who fought evil warlocks and demons on a daily basis, it always did the trick of putting their lives and problems into perspective.

"Philip might work late some nights but at least it's in an office and he's not morphing into a demon," Ivy chuckled, feeling rather drunk now, "as far as we know."

"And Jacques may be helping his friend through his loss but on the bright side he's not an angel whose job it is to help the rest of mankind with its woes," laughed Mei.

"I suppose we should be thankful for that," Ivy replied, hearing the front door open and close. A moment later, Philip poked his head through the door, his blonde hair greying over the ears. Smart in a sharp black suit, he was holding his briefcase in one hand while balancing a pizza box in the other.

"Ivy, it's good to see you. You look so well," he took the seat beside her. Even though he looked incredibly tired he spent the next ten minutes asking about her summer holiday whilst sharing some funny stories about the kids. When he finally excused himself to reheat his food and get a glass of wine, Ivy glanced across at Mei. "You've got a good man there, you know that, don't you?" to which her friend nodded.

As predicted the good weather extended through the bank holiday. Taking advantage of it, Ivy, Mei and the kids spent Friday morning in the garden, sunbathing and cooling off in the paddling pool before venturing out to Hampstead Heath to explore its untamed woodlands and ponds and enjoy a deli picnic amongst the wildflowers. On Saturday morning, Camden Market was already thronging with activity when they arrived, the water in the lock gleaming blue in the late, summer sunshine. With two excited kids in tow, the old friends mused around the clothes stalls, wondering whether or not they were looking at the designers of the future before they became household names. They then crossed over the canal bridge to the Lock Market to explore the exotic foods and arts and crafts section with its hundreds of stalls of bric-a-brac, candles, prints and period clothing.

It was while strolling through this area that something about the sounds of bartering, the smell of street food and the vibrant colours of the clothing transported Ivy to the markets of Morocco and more specifically to the one in Essaouira where she and Jacques had enjoyed that heady afternoon exploring the alleyways together before returning to the Villa Maroc to make love for the first time.

"We'll leave it up to Ivy," she tuned back into the conversation between Mei and the kids, "after all, she is our guest."

"I'm sorry, what are you leaving up to me?" Ivy returned to the present with a jolt.

"We're trying to decide where to have lunch," replied Mei, by now loaded down with bags.

Ivy turned to the children, "what would your choice be, kids?"

"I fancy going to the pizzeria but Harry wants to go to that pub with the paddling pool filled with plastic balls. He likes the double cooked chips," Ruth pulled a face, "very unhealthy, if you ask me," she pronounced in a grown up way which brought a smile to Ivy's face.

"I think pizza sounds the best bet, today" said Ivy, seeing disappointment sweep over the little boy's face, "and then we'll go to Girellis. I've heard they do the best ice creams in London."

"Nice one, Auntie Ivy," the little boy grinned, jumping up to high five her.

"Don't even ask where he learned to do that," Mei rolled

her eyes as they followed the throng of bank holiday crowds through the market.

"I wish you didn't have to go home," moaned Ruth later that evening, her head lolling on Ivy's shoulder in rhythm with the jolts of the tube heading back to Belsize Park, her little wrists rubbed red raw by the handles of cheap shopping bags.

"Me too, but we all have to go to school later this week," reminded Ivy, which made the children giggle.

"But it's so sad when summer ends," Ruth replied, sounding a lot older than her seven years, "I hate the dark and the cold."

"Umm, I'm not too keen either," Ivy nodded, "but what about all the other exciting things that take place in the autumn?"

"What things?" Ruth narrowed her eyes.

"Well, I've always loved autumn with all the beautiful colours in nature, the leaves, the harvest, Halloween, Bonfire Night and then there's Christmas to look forward to at the end of it," Ivy said as the tube slowed on their approach to the station.

"See, didn't I tell you? And now Auntie Ivy agrees you have to believe it!" Mei took her daughter's hand as they stood up while Ivy guided Harry safely to the exit. As they waited for the doors to open Mei moved her mouth to Ivy's ear, "promise me you'll contact Jacques soon to let him know where you see things heading?"

"Let's just see what the autumn brings," Ivy replied in a low voice, as much to herself as to her friend, as they stepped off the train.

47

A dramatic thunderstorm broke the short heatwave as the calendar flipped into September. However, for a time the weather was unpredictable and Ivy constantly found herself wearing the wrong clothes. On cool, overcast mornings, she'd set off to work armed with her coat and umbrella, only to find herself hampered with them walking home in the late afternoon sun. On sunny mornings, she'd wear her sandals and light jacket only for the heavens to open when she left work as late summer and early autumn fought it out amongst themselves.

At school, Ivy found it difficult to settle back into the swing of things. Feeling she'd been away for months rather than weeks, she struggled through the inset day preceding the start of term, unable to remember her computer passwords or where she'd put her marking schemes, little things she usually took for granted. After the staff meeting, Ivy spent the rest of the morning locked away in her room trying to get her head around new directives, her colleagues popping their heads around her classroom door for quick chats every now and again. Kate seemed equally reluctant to be back in school as she regaled tales of her American trip to Ivy, but Sara and Naomi related the thrilling details of their Greek island holiday while buoyed by waves of enthusiasm for the new school year. Clare was the only one who seemed genuinely interested in Ivy's Moroccan trip though and they shared a lengthy conversation over lunch about the Jemaa el Fna, the souks and Ivy's trip to the Atlas Mountains, although she was careful to omit all mention of Jacques, Louise and Patrick. When her teaching assistant Amber and the children started back the following day, Ivy gradually began to find her way. Soothing playground tears, explaining her expectations for the year ahead and introducing her new class to the delights of column addition and conjunctions, the weeks passed in a whirlwind.

At home, however, it was a different story. Every night, once she'd got her tea and lesson planning out of the way, she found herself longing for Jacques. His melodic voice, his reassuring smile, his gentle touch. They soon fell into a routine of being online at the same time, 10pm her time, 5pm his, to engage in an email conversation while, every other day they talked on the phone. Ivy gauged by his tone he was relieved to get Louise's funeral out of the way as their chats regained the same easiness they'd had before those revelations of the final few days. He remained upbeat they would see each other again soon, although concrete plans, never his strong point, weren't made. For her part, Ivy tried to keep up her new-found French fluency, delving into her old novels each night in the light of Rose's Tiffany lamp. Words she'd once known by heart returned to her like old friends as she immersed herself in Camus. *Aujourd'hui maman est morte, ou peut-être hier.*

On the final Friday of the month, Ivy took advantage of escaping playground duty to finish her Maths marking in order to free up her weekend when Amber breezed into the classroom on a cloud of *Rive Gauche*. "All set for tonight, then?" she enquired, her smart blue shirt tucked into a navy pencil-slim skirt. With her honey-blonde hair swept up in a chignon, she reminded Ivy of a glamorous air steward, albeit with a fraction of the makeup.

"Tonight?" Ivy replied, suddenly feeling frumpy in her long, rather shapeless red tunic over serviceable black leggings.

"The staff meal at *Oriental Times?* To celebrate surviving September and finally having some money in our bank accounts?" Amber busied herself, tidying piles of exercise books.

"You don't mind if I give it a rain check?" she sighed, putting down her pen, "to tell you the truth Amber, I'm bushed. I was planning an early night with a DVD and a box of salted caramels."

"Of course not. There's always next month," Amber regarded her, her forehead suddenly wrinkled with worry lines. "Are you alright though, Ivy? You look a bit peaky."

"A bit tired," she reached for the final exercise book, "it's just taking me some time to get used to all the new intervention procedures but I suppose everyone else is in the same boat."

"You need to relax Ivy, this is a long and busy term, pace yourself is my motto," Amber's voice was laced with concern, as she perched on the small, blue chair opposite her, "have you heard from Jacques?"

"Yes, we spoke just last night," Ivy paused, reluctant to elaborate further after having explained the situation to Amber at length one evening over drinks.

"He's obviously missing you and thinking of you?" she kept her tone optimistic, her red-lipsticked smile bright.

"Yes, I suppose," Ivy hesitated, "but as the weeks go by, the time we spent together and our feelings for each other become more and more distant. As for a reunion, I just don't know."

Following a few moments of contemplation, Amber's manicured hand took hold of Ivy's, "It must be hard for you. I count myself lucky Jamie and I live in the same street. You've just got to hang in there and if you're meant to be together, you will be," she smiled, as Ivy recalled Amber telling her once that she believed in fate and romance and star-crossed lovers, notions Ivy had given up on during her teens.

"Well, I'm an old hand at getting on with things," she said. After a few ticks and a 'well done', Ivy closed the exercise book, pleased that her afternoon art lesson wouldn't generate any more marking, "have you anything planned for the weekend?"

"Just the usual: a lie-in tomorrow recovering from tonight, then I'll spend the afternoon preparing for my date with Jamie. He says he's booked some fancy restaurant although he won't tell me where," she grinned impishly, "followed by karaoke."

"Sounds like he's serious about you," Ivy smiled, recalling Amber had been going out with him since they'd met at a Roman themed weekend at Colchester Castle in the spring. Working with her for the past three years, Ivy figured out six months easily tripled the average duration of her relationships.

"He is and vice versa," Amber beamed, "my mum reckons we're too young to settle down but when you know, you just know!"

Ivy was about to reply when blonde twins, Ellie and Esme, appeared in the doorway, their faces tear-stained, knees bloody, "oh girls, what's happened?"

"We fell over," Esme, with green ribbons, began before her sister, with purple ones, took over, "we were playing on a barrel and when it rolled we fell off and cut our knees."

Seeing they were on the verge of bursting into tears again, Ivy smiled, "I know you do everything together but I think this is taking it a bit far. Come on, let's get you both cleaned up."

"I'll sort them out. Come on you two," Amber led the compliant girls to the door, "let's leave Miss in peace to get on with her work so she can have a nice, relaxing weekend."

Walking home at 5pm, the autumnal breeze gently stroking her face, Ivy's legs felt as heavy as lead. Feeling ravenous but with no inclination to cook, she took advantage of being unencumbered by bags of books to pick up a banquet-for-one at the Chinese takeaway at the end of her street. Its name, *Moon and Stars and Fortune Cookies*, in orange and yellow neon always produced a smile from her even at the end of trying days.

399

Comfortable on her sofa, she tucked into spring duck lettuce wraps, vegetable spring rolls, sweet and sour chicken and prawn crackers while catching up with Mei on the phone, listening to her best friend regale her son's first month in school with excitement and pride. Dusk was already setting in as she finally rang off and, drawing the curtains, Ivy settled down to watch *Suite Française*. The second time she'd seen the film since returning from Marrakech, she lost herself in the romance between a married local woman and a German officer during the Nazi occupation of France. There was something about the actor playing the German that reminded her of Jacques, not so much in looks but in the story behind his eyes. As the credits rolled, she swallowed a sob, quickly collecting herself as her phone vibrated again on the occasional table.

"Ivy." Hearing his voice, his Canadian accent unmistakably stronger, she closed her eyes, imagining he was sitting beside her on the sofa.

"I was just thinking about you," she smiled, picturing his dark eyes, his hair, his smile.

"Were you?" she heard the amusement in his voice.

"Yes, I'm watching a film called *Suite Française* about the Nazi occupation of France and the lead actor who plays the German officer has more than a passing resemblance to you," she crunched a salted caramel.

"Oh, okay," Jacques chuckled, "I'm not too sure how to take that."

"Don't worry, he's the romantic lead, a sympathetic character," she laughed.

"Well, that's okay then. I was getting a bit worried there,

Ivy." He laughed again as she imagined the crinkles around his eyes whenever he did so.

That night, they chatted for over an hour, interested in hearing about the other's day before reaffirming their love. By the time she hung up, despite her fatigue, Ivy felt reenergised and closer to him than she'd done since they'd parted. Afterwards, perusing the bulky photo album she'd put together to document her holiday, she studied each photo of him. Although some had been taken by other people, like the first one of their smiling faces surrounded by the verdant plants in the Majorelle Garden, there were mainly selfies of Jacques and her against dramatic backdrops of the coast at Essaouira, Atlas Mountains and Ouzoud Waterfalls. Cataloguing their time together, she saw their relationship easily surpassed the few stolen moments of the lovers in *Suite Française* and her fear Jacques was slipping away, was wide of the mark.

48

"Rose never gave any hint of a romance with an American airman and yet the way she writes about him, they were obviously deeply in love," Ivy's mum looked puzzled as they strolled down the quiet lane that Sunday afternoon. It was early October and they'd wrapped up in warm puffer jackets and scarves as the autumn chill began to bite. "Did she ever mention anything to you?"

"Nothing, although once when she took me for afternoon tea in *The Swan*, she talked for ages to two elderly veterans over here for a reunion. I seem to remember them saying they were from New York though, not Virginia," Ivy stopped to pick a cluster of luscious blackberries she'd spotted amongst the green in the hedgerow, "and I don't recall her speaking of Ryan."

"I wonder whether he ever returned to *The Swan* after the war?" her mum dug a plastic bag from her pocket for the fruit.

"We can't be sure that he survived it, Rose's diary cuts off so abruptly at the end of '44. But I agree with you, they sounded so in love," she paused, yet again considering the parallel with her and Jacques, "for me, unfortunately the most logical explanation is that Ryan was killed during the spring of '45."

"I'm inclined to think that too," nodded her mum, moving on to the next purple patch of fruit, "but if that was the case surely Rose would have confided in someone? She couldn't have kept it bottled up inside all these years?"

"But who would she have told?" Ivy licked at the juice on her fingers, "certainly not Grandma Frances as she seemed so judgmental about everything Rose did."

"No, she definitely wouldn't have found a sympathetic ear with Mum," Erin smiled ruefully, "I can testify to that. We know my gran knew she was courting, but she never mentioned it to me. Maybe if Ryan was killed, it was to spare Rose's feelings that they never spoke of it?"

"Perhaps Sophie knew what happened to them? She seemed a good friend... Unless," Ivy stalled, picking some particularly fat berries, "she married Luigi and went to the US?"

"No," her mum shook her head, "Sophie was around when I was growing up. She married a farmer, a big, burly man, if I recall. I guess everyone got back to normal when the war ended and the Americans left? Whenever Mum took me to Rose's, Sophie always seemed to be there. Looking back, I don't think her marriage was the happiest but I liked her because she always brought her son, Robert, with her. I remember bossing him around, he being two years younger than me."

"How come I never met Sophie?" Ivy picked more fruit, before stopping again to lick the purple juice from her fingers.

"She was only in her late forties when she died. A heart attack, I think," her mum stepped back from the hedgerow, deciding they'd collected enough, "she was so pretty though, full of high spirits and fun, very much like Rose. The two of them must have had some good times together when they were young. I remember Rose was so upset when she died, another link to her past gone, I suppose."

"That's so sad," Ivy bit her lip, "oh, it's so frustrating! I could kick myself for not asking Rose about her youth, although there's no guarantee she'd have told me of course. I suppose we have to be thankful she kept a diary."

"Possibly, but why leave it unfinished?" her mum asked, to which Ivy shrugged her shoulders.

"Look, we're going around in circles. I think we just have to face the fact that it is too late," her mum concluded, peering into the full bag, "these are beauties. I'll make a nice crumble for you to take back tonight. Get some vitamin C into you as you're looking a bit pale."

"Yes, I can't wait for the half term break to put my feet up. Doing nothing for an entire week sounds like bliss," Ivy rubbed her back, which was aching after bending for so long.

"I thought Jacques was supposed to be coming to visit you?" Her mum linked Ivy's arm as they resumed their walk.

"He mentioned it in Morocco before everything happened with Louise," replied Ivy carefully, "but he hasn't brought it up again. I know Patrick is still in a bad way though, and of course Jacques is trying to get a job back in Toronto, as he doesn't want to return to Marrakech. "

"Oh Ivy. I know it's difficult and I'm really not sure how to advise you. But if you really have found such happiness together don't let him drift away… " her mother faltered as they reached the first thatched, pink cottages at the edge of town.

"I know. It's just so complicated, the dreadful events in Morocco, the timing, the distance between us," Ivy sighed partly in frustration that they couldn't be together, partly in fear that she was unsure she'd be able to make Jacques happy if they were.

They took the scenic route through the town, the autumn sunshine burnishing the Suffolk pink buildings so they almost appeared to glow. Passing *The Swan,* Ivy was seized by a sudden impulse to take a closer look at the memorabilia in the Airmen's Bar. While her mum was ordering them a cafetiere of coffee, she stepped into the cool, stone-flagged room and stood looking closely at the walls, which she saw in a different light now she'd read Rose's diary. The plaster yellowed with age, every inch of them was covered with the signatures of the American airmen who had served at the nearby base during World War II. Her thoughts inevitably turned to Ryan as she scrutinized them, recalling how Rose had always done the same. She focused on the framed, faded newspaper article remembering General F.W. Castle who had led the Eighth Air Force and had been awarded a posthumous medal of honour. Staring at his photo, her eyes were drawn to his conventional chiselled features, descending to the lapels of his smart uniform pinned with medals, the reflection of her own face ghost-like on the glass. But looking into his eyes, she saw they were focused on something far beyond her.

Returning to the scribbled signatures, she attempted to decipher the most faded ones written during the war which were now protected behind clear glass: Denny Thompson 839th, Clarke E Yocum 839th, Bombordiez 'Bucky' Buxton 857th, Larry Jalowicz 839th, Jim Hyland 836 B.S. Navgtr, Ray Wisdom 100 CR5 and Dick (Salvo) Saveien, 95th Bomb Group bringing up the rear. Totally absorbed in what she was reading, she didn't hear her mother return with their coffee.

An hour later, on their way out, they passed a wall of names with their bomber groups and ranks with the dates beside them stretching right up to the eighties and nineties. This prompted a distant memory in Ivy of watching the old men dressed in baseball caps and trainers writing their names on the wall with marker pens, her great-aunt in quiet conversation with them.

"Why end her memoir so abruptly?" mused her mum as they came to Rose's cottage, "unless… "

"Unless she wrote a second one?" Ivy finished her mum's sentence excitedly, her pulse quickening.

"Let's go and have a look," her mum rummaged in her bag, "I have her house keys somewhere in here."

Ivy hastily followed her mum up the path, careful not to knock Rose's dahlias, in full bloom on either side. Ever the florist with an artist's eye for colour, she'd planted them in swathes of delicate white and pastel pinks graduating to the deeper lilacs and blues. Mother and daughter spent the next hour and a half rooting down the backs of shelves and cupboards for something they hoped existed, before reluctantly admitting defeat.

"This means we'll never know what happened," sighed Ivy later as she sprinkled the crumble topping on the purple fruit, succulent sweet smells wafting all around her mum's kitchen.

"Maybe we're not supposed to," her mum replied, cutting three triangles of Victoria sponge she'd filled with her own raspberry jam, "call your dad from the garden would you?"

Ivy strolled across the lawn, where autumn leaves spread out like yellow and bronze starfish, inhaling the woody aroma of smoke issuing from her dad's bonfire. Beyond the crackling flames, she saw him, in his old clothes, black marks in his hair, his face ruddy from being out in the open since lunch. It wasn't hard to imagine him as a scruffy child, always planning his next escapade. However, now he'd hit seventy, she saw that climbing trees and making fires might not be the most suitable pastimes and understood why he infuriated her mum sometimes. But as he gave her a cheeky wink, she wished she'd inherited a little of his daring and devilment.

"Did you have a nice walk with mum?" he linked her arm as they walked back to the house.

"Yes, we had a lovely chat," smiled Ivy, the aroma of charred wood hanging heavily in the air. As they stopped in the porch for her dad to take his wellies off, Ivy contemplated bringing up Rose's war diary with him but then, deciding he wouldn't be able to shed any light on matters either, she dismissed the idea. It seemed destined to remain a frustrating mystery.

49

The spectacular show of autumn leaves in fiery russets and golden browns tempted Ivy to take the longer route through the park on her walk to and from school. In the mornings, she enjoyed its tranquillity while in the evenings she began to strike up conversations with regular dog walkers over marshmallow-topped hot chocolates in the café housed in the old orangery, overlooking the ornamental lake. These interludes soon became a feature of her working week, giving her time for quiet reflection, a welcome contrast to the turmoil she often found herself in when her thoughts strayed to the events of the summer.

Seemingly no longer content with a phone call every few days, Jacques began to ring her every night just after 10pm. Their conversations continued as effortlessly as they had in Morocco as they often lost track of time, chatting about everything and anything. The one thing they never mentioned was the future, perhaps because the previous time they'd made embryonic plans about a reunion during the October half-term had been the day Louise had taken her own life. One evening, Jacques told her of Patrick's decision to find an apartment within commuting distance to the film studios where he had resumed working after informing his former boss that he had moved back to Canada to stay. Noticing he avoided any mention of his own plans, in her characteristic way, Ivy fought shy of asking.

Having reviewed Amber's tasks that Friday lunchtime, Ivy set aside her unappetising cheese sandwich and sighed.

"Chin up, Ivy. Only a week to go until half term," Amber dug enthusiastically into a wedge of cream cheese covered carrot cake, "my end of week blowout, do you want some?"

"No thanks," Ivy waved it away, "I've been giving into chocolate far too much recently and I really should shed a few pounds before my winter comfort eating kicks in."

"Vitamins, that's what you need to boost your immune system if you're not going to pick up every bug going," Amber's ice-blue eyes glittered beneath her blonde fringe, "and Manuka honey. My mum swears by it."

"Isn't it expensive?" Ivy sorted her papers into order in her lever-arch file.

"Yeah, but there's a sale at the *Walkman's Wholefoods* this weekend," Amber straightened her pristinely-pressed, pale-pink shirt, "I'd get down there, if I were you. Stock up!"

"I'll have a look tomorrow," laughed Ivy, thinking if Amber ever wanted a career change, she'd make a smooth transition into the world of sales, "are you doing anything nice tomorrow?"

"I thought you'd never ask. Jamie is driving me to London tonight. We're staying in a beautiful boutique hotel in Kensington," she cooed, scrolling through her iPhone to show Ivy photos of a sumptuous cream marble foyer and rooms with four poster beds and their own private hot tubs.

"It sounds like things are getting serious between you," Ivy paused to take a bite of an apple.

"Yes, they are. I've known him less than a year but I think I'm in love with him. We've talked about moving in together. Of course, Mum is still putting the dampeners on things a bit, warning us to slow down. She reckons we're too young but I am twenty-four and Jamie is twenty-six. My parents were married by then, for heaven's sake," Amber rolled her eyes, making her appear significantly younger.

"But when you know, you know, right?" Ivy smiled, remembering Amber's previous words on the subject, before briefly wondering what would have happened if she and Jacques had met in their early twenties.

"Exactly! Which brings me to that gorgeous Canadian of yours. What's the score, Ivy? Have you taken your own advice? Or are you applying your usual caution?" Amber swallowed a huge mouthful of cake.

"Well," replied Ivy, "the truth is, he never mentions the future and I don't want to pressurise him with everything he's been going through." All she knew was that with each passing day, she yearned for him a little bit more.

Waking early on Saturday morning, Ivy still felt off colour. But the sunlight streaming through her bedroom curtains told her it was going to be a glorious day she didn't want to miss, so she pulled on a forest-green tracksuit and scraped her auburn hair into a ponytail. Then she applied her makeup, light and natural, having abandoned the heavy camouflage creams she'd been using since her teens. As she did so, she realised that, following Jacques' reaction to her birthmark, she'd been unfazed if people gave her a second glance. Buoyed by the thought, she made herself coffee, a bowl of porridge and some granary toast, having read that a healthy breakfast was an important step to losing weight.

Deciding she wasn't in the mood for jostling with shoppers in town, she followed the road to the park, the crisp air keeping her cool as she fell into a slow jogging rhythm. She found the park deserted apart from a few dog walkers she exchanged pleasantries with and whose pets greeted her with a friendly wag of the tail, or, in the case of a small terrier, a jump up onto her knees as she bent down to stroke its woolly, sheep-like fur.

"Bess just likes a friendly face," smiled her owner, a portly man in his mid sixties.

"She's lovely," remarked Ivy, the dog's fur coarse beneath her fingers. She chatted to the man for a few minutes about his dog and the weather before recommending a restaurant to take his wife to for her birthday the following day. As he walked off, or, more accurately was dragged away by Bess, who'd found something far more interesting in some flowerbeds, Ivy mused how much more confident she'd felt chatting to strangers since her return from her holiday. Before, she would have probably averted her eyes and just walked past Bess and her owner, missing out on the friendly interaction she'd just enjoyed.

Feeling a low grumble in her stomach, on cue the white pavilion of the orangery café peeped out from among the trees. Ivy skirted half a dozen metal tables where walkers were enjoying their morning coffee al fresco, their dogs lapping water from bowls at their feet, to duck inside where the scent of frying bacon hung heavily in the air. Unable to stomach the strong smell, she hastily ordered tea and a toasted teacake before finding an outside table.

Presently, the terrace grew quiet, in the lull between morning coffee and lunch. Buttering her teacake, Ivy looked out over the swathes of trees to the children's playground where a blonde boy and girl, about three and five, were playing in the pirate ship, raising the flag and shouting 'ahoy!' Watching them, a slight breeze comfortingly stroking her face, she realised there was something so innocent, so easy about being a child, free from all the hang-ups people gained as they grew up. As she sat there, she recalled not only the hardships she'd endured through her childhood years but also the easy pleasures she'd enjoyed, her park picnics with Rose, days out to the seaside with her mum and dad and playing on the swing in her back garden with Mei.

The warming effect of the tea fading, Ivy suddenly felt chilled as a breeze swirled the fallen leaves around her feet. Depositing her empty mug and plate inside the café, she hurried down the hill, the gusts of wind weakening as she neared the bottom. Trying to catch her breath, she paused to watch a squirrel collect a small nut in its tiny paws before it scurried off to bury it for the winter, its oversized, grey tail bouncing behind it. It was then, out of the blue, that Ivy was floored by a wave of nausea. Realising she wouldn't make it back to the café toilet in time, she bolted into the nearby trees. Her body shaking with violent retches, she brought back everything she'd consumed that morning. After a while, her stomach calming, she leaned against the cold bark of a tree until she was positive her vomiting episode was over. Her breathing normal again, she dug into her handbag for a mint to take away the bitter, bile taste before resting on a nearby empty bench as her legs had turned to jelly.

Her first thought was she must have picked up the stomach bug sweeping through school. But then she recalled suffering a similar sickness episode on Wednesday morning. At the time she'd put it down to a dodgy curry she'd eaten the evening before but as she sat shivering, another idea began to formulate in her mind. Trying to recall when her last period had been, she realised she hadn't had one since her arrival back from Marrakech, seven weeks ago. Her stomach twisting with something other than sickness, she hurried out of the park gates, fervently clinging to the hope that all the upset surrounding Louise's death and being separated from Jacques must have sent her cycle spinning off kilter.

Stopping herself from thinking one way or another, she rushed to town, her concentration focused on crossing the roads safely. She headed to the nearest pharmacy, her hands trembling as she took a pregnancy testing kit down from the shelf. Back in her flat, she ripped away the cellophane and the box, calming sufficiently to carefully read the instructions as the last thing she wanted was to botch the test.

She needed to know, one way or the other. Unwrapping the testing strip, she perched on the loo, consoling herself with the knowledge that Jacques had always been so meticulous about using birth control. But her sigh of relief was instantly cut short by a sudden flashback to their final night together at Ouzoud when, caught in the urgency of their feelings for one another, neither had stopped to consider the potential consequences. Her insides contracting, she picked up the stick and watched as the blue line appeared, faint at first before becoming strong and clear.

Her eyes transfixed on the line, she felt her body shake as fear and happiness threatened to overwhelm her. She had never imagined she would be a mother, had always thought she'd have to be content teaching other people's children. But she instantly knew that in spite of all the difficulties which undoubtedly lay ahead, she wanted this child more than anything in the world. Her child. Jacques' child. Their child.

Telling him, however, was another matter entirely. She certainly didn't want to approach the subject by email or even by phone. Not being able to see his reaction to her news would mean that even if he accepted the child and her as his partner, she might never know whether he truly wanted to be a father again or whether he felt under obligation for the predicament in which he'd put her. Then there was the unthinkable possibility that, still feeling blame for Luc's tragic accident, he might not be able to cope with the painful memories having another child would inevitably unearth.

Later that afternoon, after much deliberation, she blandly responded to Jacques' email in which he mentioned that

Patrick had found a loft apartment in need of renovations. Anxious to get his best friend's life back on track, Jacques was moving in with him to help with the work. Composing a friendly reply, knowing that he needed this time to help Patrick, she decided to give him some space. She reasoned he had enough to deal with for the present and didn't want to burden him with any other worries. She wasn't that far into her first trimester anyway and, realising she was considered old for a first time mum, she concluded she needed to know whether things were progressing normally before she even broached the subject with him. After all, she knew her mum had suffered a few miscarriages before she'd had her and she had been so much younger than she was now. Coupled with her grandma Fran's miscarriages before she'd had Erin, her family medical history on that score wasn't exactly encouraging. But nevertheless that evening while watching T.V., she absently caressed her flat stomach with her hand, barely able to contemplate the new life growing within her.

50

Fatigued with constant nausea, Ivy battled through the final week of the half term. Calculating she was just over two months pregnant, her doctor had arranged her first scan for mid-November. As she struggled through each day, she longed to tell Jacques but each time she composed the perfect email in her head or thought of dialling his number, she considered the increased prevalence of Down's syndrome and other birth defects among older mothers. No, she would go with her instincts to postpone telling him until after her three-month scan, unable to contemplate what she'd do if something untoward showed up

By Friday night, she was dead on her feet. Arriving home, all she had the energy to do was snuggle on the sofa with a takeaway pizza while watching *Hocus Pocus,* a Halloween treat she indulged in every year. However, the opening scene with the Sanderson sisters approaching Salem by broomstick had barely unfolded when Ivy's mobile bleeped.

"Ivy, you'll never guess." Her mum sounded breathless on the other end of the line, "we've sold Rose's house. We've been astonished at the interest it has attracted. Apparently cottages like this don't come on the market very often, and when they do they get snapped up in no time. Of course we still have to get the survey done and dusted but the Redmonds seem very keen... "

"I just didn't think it would be this soon," Ivy felt her stomach lurch which she knew had nothing to do with the morning sickness she'd been experiencing, "the Redmonds, wasn't that the retired police inspector and his wife you told me about?"

"That's right! They live in Ipswich but they've always wanted to move to Lavenham. They have a daughter nearby who has a young family of her own," her mum went on, sensing Ivy's doubts, "it really couldn't be in safer hands Ivy, I'm sure Rose would have approved."

"I know," Ivy swallowed hard, desperately trying to banish thoughts of this new family living in Rose's cottage, "but our final link with her will be broken."

"Sweetheart, I know how upset you are but it's out of our hands. They are after an early completion as they've already sold their house and want to move in before Christmas, so when the survey's completed... " her mother broke off to let her digest her words.

"Christmas?" Ivy felt panic fluttering in her chest.

"Ivy, why don't you come over on Sunday?" her mother's voice was soft, steady. "We can have a quiet look around, say goodbye?"

"Yes," she murmured, wiping away tears which had

417

spilt down her cheeks, "I think I need to."

Some small talk later, Ivy hung up the phone, having dismally failed to pave the way for breaking her pregnancy news to her mother. Resting her head on a cushion, she tried to imagine what Rose's advice would be to her. With a rueful smile, she heard her slow Suffolk vowels insist, "*Get on with your life, Ivy. That's all any of us can do.*"

Driving down the country lanes late that Sunday morning, the autumn sun glinting on the touch of frost on the shaded grass verges, she pushed the sadness of visiting Rose's house for the final time to the back of her mind. Instead she focused on the fact that today was the day she would tell her mum and dad they were going to be grandparents.

She noticed her parents' car was already parked outside Rose's cottage. Walking up the path, she observed with regret how unkempt the garden now looked, with weeds left to flourish in the once immaculate herbaceous borders. However, a few of her great-aunt's beloved rose bushes still held their late summer blooms and tears sprang to her eyes as she pictured Rose, secateurs in hand pruning away deadheads. She only hoped the Redmonds were keen gardeners who considered it sacrilege to destroy her great-aunt's work in favour of flags, gravel and wooden decking.

Nudging open the front door, Ivy found the hall completely empty now, the wallpaper sun-faded, except for where her great-aunt's much loved Constable prints had hung. There, the colours in the flowered patterns were as vivid as the day Rose had decorated decades before. The heels of her boots clattering on the bare floorboards, Ivy followed her parents' voices to the living room where she found them sealing large cardboard boxes with brown tape.

"Sweetheart," her mum got to her feet, holding out her arms to embrace her, "how are you? You look tired." Ivy closed her eyes, breathing in her mum's familiar perfume, and feeling as she had done as a child, safe and comforted.

"Oh, you know – I'm always a bit run down by the time I reach a holiday," she attempted a light-hearted tone. Glancing around, she noticed everything was packed away, neatly labelled. There was nothing left for her to do. "You've been busy since I was last here."

"You know your mum! Once she gets a bee in her bonnet, there's no stopping her," her dad pulled one of his Les Dawsonesque faces, which made Ivy laugh out loud, "now girls, it's coffee time."

"But I thought the electricity was off?" Ivy said, puzzled.

"Who needs electricity when you've been a boy scout?" he flashed her a broad grin before disappearing into the kitchen only to return a few seconds later with a cardboard box. Opening it theatrically like a magician, he produced a primus stove, small kettle, three mugs, coffee, milk, sugar and a packet of digestives.

"I wondered what you were up to in the garage this morning!" Ivy's mum laughed, rolling her eyes.

A couple of hours later, her dad pressed the keys to the cottage into Ivy's hand. "Well, that's about my lot. After all our hard work, I think we all deserve a nice meal at *The Swan,* save your mum cooking and me the washing up!"

"Okay," Ivy hesitated, not quite ready to leave yet.

"Your dad and I will go on ahead. We'll see you down

there," her mum added knowingly, "no rush, take your time."

She silently thanked her parents for their diplomatic exit to give her some time alone to make her final farewell to the house which held so many loving memories for her. Walking from room to room, the silence resonated in her ears and although she'd harboured the possibility of finding a second diary, she saw the place was entirely empty and everything that had been Rose, already gone. So in the end, locking the front door behind her and walking down the garden path for the final time, wasn't quite as difficult as she'd feared.

The spirit of Halloween had inveigled its way into every cobwebbed nook and cranny of *The Swan* as pumpkin and witch decorations brought splashes of orange and black to the neutral colour scheme. Ivy and her mum sat beneath the commemoration to the American commanding officer, G. W. Castle, while her dad got in the drinks and ordered their Sunday roasts. Ivy was quiet, thinking of all the memories she'd left behind in her great-aunt's house and, seeing her mum's faraway look, she knew instinctively she was experiencing a similar sense of loss.

"What have you been up to this week?" Ivy's mother enquired when they had finished eating.

Seized by the presentiment that if she didn't tell her parents now, she would lose her nerve and head back to Colchester later, kicking herself for missing the opportunity, Ivy drew a deep breath.

"Mum, dad, there's no easy way to say this. I'm pregnant." Her stomach twisted as her announcement was met by the stunned silence she'd envisaged all along.

"Oh, Ivy, are you sure?" her mum took hold of her hand.

"Yes, the doctor confirmed I'm about two months pregnant," Ivy replied, trying to discern something from her parents' bewildered expressions.

"Is the father the man you met in Marrakech?" her father queried, the quiver in his voice betraying his shock and suppressed anger for a man he had never met.

"That's right, his name is Jacques. And before you say anything, Dad, it wasn't a holiday romance," Ivy's eyes glistened with tears. "We love each other but after what happened with his son and his ex-wife, I just don't know…" she broke down, sobs wracking her body.

Her mother pulled Ivy into her in her arms, rocking her as she had done when she was a small child, whispering, "don't worry my love, you know we will always be here for you, whatever you decide."

Her tears subsiding, her dad reached out and took hold of her hand, the anger in his voice now replaced by heartbreaking concern. "Your mum's right, Ivy. We'll do all we can to help you."

As her mum gently wiped away Ivy's tears, she looked up at her, "you know mum, I never thought I'd have a child or imagined what it would be like, but now, I want this baby more than anything."

"Oh, sweetheart, I know how you are feeling for that's exactly how I was when I had you."

The waiter collected their dirty plates and glasses, before replacing them with coffees and mints. Outside dusk was falling, and feeling emotionally and physically exhausted, Ivy decided to drive straight home afterwards.

In the car, she felt relieved that she'd shared her news with her parents at last and that their response had been so reassuring. It was only now she realised what a heavy burden she'd been attempting to bear on her own. On the day she had said goodbye to a significant part of her past, she was now looking forward to what the future may bring for her and her unborn child.

51

An upbeat email from Jacques countered the emotional exhaustion Ivy felt as she arrived at her flat that evening. He talked enthusiastically about Patrick's new apartment in a converted warehouse in Cabbage Town, an arty and up-and-coming neighbourhood in Toronto. Ivy was heartened that it was Patrick's endeavour, as Jacques made it clear he was helping his friend renovate and decorate rather than putting down roots again himself in his hometown. Buoyed by this and her parents' support about the baby, she once again allowed herself to hope that things would work out.

Pouring in the last of the fragrant jasmine oil from Morocco, Ivy luxuriated in a relaxing bath. The water ebbing around her she noticed, for the first time, her stomach was slightly rounded. Stroking it, she recalled the loving words of Jacques' email and suddenly it felt he wasn't thousands of miles away at all but in the room, with her. Later, in her pink fleecy pyjamas, she settled on the sofa with a soothing cup of camomile tea and phoned Mei to tell her of her pregnancy. Their conversation lasted over an hour as her friend shared in her excitement while urging her to tell Jacques at the first opportunity.

As Ivy hung up, despite having a warm feeling inside, as much down to her parents' and friend's reaction to her news as the tea, it still irked her that she hadn't discovered a second diary at Rose's cottage. Feeling sure her great-aunt had carefully put the first notebook in a place she knew she'd find it, Ivy came to the conclusion that, no matter how heartbreaking it was to write her story, Rose would have found a way to finish it. Her stomach plunged at the notion the Redmonds might discover the ending and discard it or that it might remain in its hiding place, beneath a loose floorboard or else slotted in between the chimney bricks, forever.

Seeking a distraction from this rather depressing train of thought, her eyes rested on the novels she'd brought back from Rose's earlier in the summer. Stepping towards the shelf, she ran her fingers along the spines until they hovered over the beautiful, blue, leather-bound edition of *Jane Eyre*, Rose's and her favourite book to read on wintery, Sunday afternoons while toasting crumpets or muffins on the open fire. She slipped it from the weight of the others, envisaging hearing Rose's soothing voice in her head as she read it one more time.

As she opened it, it released a musty smell and she was taken aback to find an envelope sellotaped to the inside cover. Easing it away with her thumb nail, her puzzlement turned to astonishment as she read her own name in Rose's elegant hand. Fetching a knife, she carefully slit it open.

Sunday 14th February 2016

Ivy swallowed hard. Rose had written it just a week before her death.

My dearest Ivy,

I hope you found my journal. I knew you'd be the one to sort through my books and that you would remember where I always placed it. I could never bring myself to complete my story then, but now I know I have little time left, I want you to be the first to know something that should have been told many years ago. It affected all the family and I'm sorry that my actions caused pain to those I loved. So, read the end of my story, sweetheart. I know you won't judge me harshly and I'll leave it to you to decide what to do.

As 1945 dawned, Ryan's group continued to fight in the Battle of the Bulge, and sometimes days would pass when we didn't see each other. But the talk of the town was the war was in its dying throes and I hoped that Ryan would stand by his promise of marrying me. That remained a distant dream, however, and I spent my days and nights in constant fear for him, as he was still involved in the thick of the fighting. I think, though, that those missions over Germany gave him the release he needed to fight back after his friends' deaths the previous Christmas Eve.

As the green shoots of spring sprouted in the countryside, Ryan's unit undertook numerous bombing raids to support Allied troops as they crossed the Rhine and made the final push into Germany. In between missions, we were desperate for some time alone together but the only place that afforded us any privacy where we knew we'd be undisturbed was the disused barn and we managed three further rendezvous there. Each time I saw Ryan, however, he appeared ever more withdrawn and disturbed by his experiences and I grew fearful for his well-being. As he wouldn't confide in me what was going on in his head, all I could do was hold him in my arms, his body shaking with suppressed sobs. The only comfort I could give him now was physical, and as we made love I was happy that, for a time at least, the darkness in him seemed to lift a little.

It was actually becoming difficult to hold a conversation with him and whenever we met at The Swan he'd just sit morosely, staring into space, cradling his glass. I noticed that he was drinking more too, which in turn made him irritable and his anger would explode at the most trivial things. One evening, this erupted into a sudden flash of violence over an incident of no importance. We'd just entered The Swan when another airman holding two drinks accidently backed into us, spilling a small amount on my shoe. Ryan seemed to lose control completely, and eyes blazing, he punched the man so hard that he fell to the ground, his nose bleeding profusely.

What happened next made me realise that this wasn't an isolated incident. Ryan's friends moved in quickly before he could inflict any more injury to the man and gently took him outside. I could only watch, *trembling with fear, not able to comprehend what had just happened to provoke such an over-the-top reaction in the gentle, sensitive man I loved. Through the open door, I saw the others talking quietly to him before one of them waved me to come out. The wild anger had gone from his eyes now as he stood dejected and forlorn. I took hold of his hand as Luigi told me they were taking him back to the base and they would look after him. I watched as they walked away down the street, their arms around Ryan's shoulders, his head bowed. I still hold that image in my heart, the last one I have of him as they took him away from me, forever.*

I think I once told you that on VE Day we had a huge street party on Lavenham High Street? Everyone was singing and dancing and full of joy. Everyone except me. I recall looking around all those happy, smiling faces for the one that would make my heart sing but Ryan was nowhere to be found. In fact, I hadn't laid eyes on him for almost three weeks. With no way of contacting him, I'd been to The Swan every day to see if any of his friends were there but they never were. Amid the celebrations that afternoon, however, I bumped into Luigi who told me Ryan had been confined to the hospital wing since the night he'd floored the airman. He said Ryan was in very bad shape and, after being assessed by a psychiatrist at the base, he was being repatriated early to the States with others who needed immediate medical treatment. With a paper and pencil from the bar I wrote Ryan a note telling him how much I loved him and that I would always wait for him.

At the beginning of June, Luigi and the rest of the airmen returned home too and a couple of weeks later I missed my period. I had been so consumed with worry for Ryan that the implications didn't hit home at first but I soon realised, with a stab of fear, the terrible dilemma I was now faced with. After a few weeks, I plucked up the courage to break the news to Mother. Things were different back then, Ivy, unmarried mothers and their illegitimate children were considered a disgrace, and I truly felt that I would bring dishonour to my family, a family who had always been so respected in this town. I wanted Ryan's child with all my heart, but I had no means of finding him, and didn't know if he would ever recover enough to try and find me.

Having no other choice I agreed that Frances and Bert could bring up my baby as their own. I knew that, after her miscarriages, my sister could never have the child she desperately craved so it seemed like the right thing to do. I reasoned that this way I would at least be able to still see my child albeit as its 'aunt' instead of having it adopted by strangers and lost forever. Of course I didn't know then that Fran would exert a terrible punishment for my 'sin'. For the months leading up to giving birth I stayed at the farmhouse with my sister, supposedly helping her during her pregnancy, and since neither of us were seen out in public it was a simple thing for her to pass the child off as her own. My daughter was born in the evening of January 3rd, 1946 and that night I kept her close to me, weeping as I thought of Ryan who would never have the chance to hold his baby girl. Then as dawn broke, Fran came in and took her from my arms, making me promise that I would never tell anyone I was her mother. I was to distance myself from my beloved child and only visit when I was invited. The one thing I insisted on was that they called her Erin, after Ryan's mother, my way of dedicating the child to her father and the land of his ancestors – Élrinn or Ireland. Even though Fran thought it an outlandish name, unfit for a Christian child, she had to concede defeat.

I always kept my promise to Fran and have lived with that heartbreak all my life. So she became Erin's mother while I was her Aunt Rose. Of course I had deep reservations as much of the time I hadn't seen eye to eye with Fran. But she was a decent person and I could tell Bert doted on Erin as her real father might have done, if I hadn't denied him the chance. From the moment she was born and every day since, when I look at your mother I see Ryan, those cornflower blue eyes and hair the colour of ripening wheat. I was always surprised that no-one ever appeared to notice how different her colouring was to anyone else in the family.

Do you remember Ivy, whenever there was a veteran's reunion in the Airmen's Bar at The Swan, I'd go and talk to them? Well, now I can tell you I was trying to find out if anyone knew Ryan or what had happened to him. But I never had any success. In 1945, he completely disappeared from my life and I never found out if he'd managed to put his bad memories behind him and move on. I hope, with all my heart that he recovered to find happiness again, even if it was in another woman's arms.

A short while ago, I read a newspaper article on Post Traumatic Stress Disorder, which I now recognise to be what Ryan was suffering from at the end of the war. Nowadays it is treated in a very sympathetic manner and, in severe cases like Ryan's, with medication and counselling. During World War II, however, such cases were classed as mental patients and one of the treatments was to administer sodium pentothal which forced the soldier to relive his dreadful battlefield experiences. In some instances, this would make the condition even worse and the man would end up institutionalised. I can only pray that this wasn't Ryan's fate.

The airfield finally closed in 1948 and over the years I saw it gradually revert back to farmland. Sometimes, on summer evenings at sunset, I still walk down there, lost in my thoughts of what might have been. Of course most of the runways have disappeared in the long grass but the hangars, pump house, mess hut and the gymnasium are still there, falling into ruin. Whenever I look up at the control tower, I ponder how Ryan would've seen it from the sky each and every time he came into land, as it guided him home, back to me. Over the years I've never stopped thinking about what happened that summer, and how those events irrevocably changed all our lives. Ryan and I were pulled apart by circumstances beyond our control and denied the happiness that should have been ours. I gave my daughter to my sister and her husband because I couldn't remain in Lavenham as a single mother and inflict that stigma on Erin. It was only with the passage of time I realised my terrible mistake. I soon saw that Fran had only taken in Erin to save her family from disintegrating into scandal, and never gave her the love she deserved. As the years passed, I witnessed my sister's strictness and coldness towards Erin. Perhaps with her overly pious nature, she resented her illegitimacy or just didn't want her to grow up with my perceived loose morals. Maybe watching her grow from a pretty child to a beautiful woman released that kernel of jealousy I always sensed she felt towards me. I don't know. Whatever the reason, she was far from being a doting mother and constantly kept me apart from Erin when I yearned to hold my child and hear her call me mummy.

In August 1957, Bert died and, when the farm was taken over by new tenants, Frances and Erin came back to live with Mother and I. I think the next few years were the happiest in my life, having my daughter under the same roof. When Mother passed away one morning in early September 1965, her final thoughts were of Violet and Nell, and it gave me much comfort over the following months to think that she'd been reunited with the daughters she'd outlived by over thirty years. When Erin married Daniel five months later, I bought my cottage from the money I had made from my floristry business, and offered Frances a home with me. It was a strange irony that I was left with the one person in my life with whom I'd never been able to form a close bond. When Fran succumbed to breast *cancer five years later, Erin clung to me in her grief for a mother who had never been able to reciprocate her love. I realise now that this was a missed opportunity and that I should have told Erin about her parentage. But I wasn't brave enough, I was fearful that your mother would be so angry with me that she'd reject me and I couldn't have borne that. So I took the coward's way out and concealed the truth. And then you came along, my beloved grand-daughter, I could hold you and shower you with all the love I'd never been openly able to show to your mother.*

Wiping away the tears which streamed down her face, Ivy turned to the final page.

And yet there hasn't been a day gone by when I haven't thought about Ryan and what might have been. I regret being so easily persuaded to give my baby away, and taking the coward's way out, too frightened of what people would think. You know all of my story now, Ivy dear, and the mistakes I carry with me to my grave. I'll always regret giving up my daughter and if there's one, final word of advice I can leave you with, it's that you should always follow your own heart and hold onto those you love and never let them go, whatever difficulties are put in your path. My story is yours now Ivy, my dearest, to do with as you choose.

My love always
Grandma.

Placing the piece of paper carefully between the pages of the novel, Ivy buried her head in her hands and sobbed as if her heart would break. She cried for Rose who had lost her only love and was denied being able to acknowledge the child of that love. She cried for Ryan whose dreadful experiences had destroyed him as surely as any weapon of war. She cried for her mum, brought up by a taciturn, unfeeling mother while her real mother adored her from afar. Finally, she cried for herself, as she'd never got to call the woman she'd idolised all her life, 'grandma'.

She recognised she now had a difficult decision to make, one Rose had put off for seventy years. Her initial thought was of course she would share Rose's revelations with her mother, who deserved to know who her real parents were. But then she began to consider the implications more deeply. She knew her mother would be devastated, knowing Rose had abandoned her to Frances who had been a cold and unloving mother and feared her anger might turn into bitter resentment, meaning that she would never forgive Rose. The promise she had been forced to make to Fran to keep her distance explained why her mother had always felt Rose was too preoccupied to give her the attention she craved. Recalling her mother saying that she and Rose had recently become very close, she didn't want to destroy those memories for her. She also realised that Rose was a wise woman who clearly had good reasons for acting the way she did. Ivy sensed that by leaving her diary incomplete and then addressing the letter to her granddaughter alone, Rose hadn't intended Erin to know. Twisting Rose's claddagh ring on her finger, she came to the conclusion that it was all too late in any case and would serve no purpose now.

"I've made the decision. This has been your burden for all these years and I'm so glad that you've shared it with me," she whispered to the quiet room around her, "but I always sensed the special bond between us and looked upon you as my grandma anyway so your secret will remain mine as I feel that's what you would want. I love you, grandma."

52

November blew in with an icy blast, winter clinging to its coat tails. Waking up to leaden skies which portended snow, Ivy spent her half-term holiday burrowed in her flat's centrally heated warmth, recharging her batteries and preparing her lessons up to Christmas. As her pregnancy progressed, her energy would inevitably diminish and she needed to keep her weekends work-free, providing recovery time in between the hectic weeks.

On the first day back, she told her colleagues of her news during the morning break, both for health and safety reasons but mainly because she couldn't keep it to herself any longer. After initial, tentative enquiries about the father's identity, everyone seemed thrilled for her, especially Amber who immediately set up sweepstakes on the baby's sex and name. Ivy's baby news was also greeted with excited gasps among the children in her class, although a group of girls became a bit teary when she explained to them they'd be having a different teacher for the summer term. With everyone sharing her happiness, a burden Ivy hadn't realised she'd been carrying was lifted as the first fortnight back hurtled by in the flicker of an eye.

"What have you come as?" Amber greeted her at the school's main entrance, wearing a too-sexy-for-school cat costume and brandishing a yellow collection bucket.

"Come as?" Ivy said, blankly. Feeling slightly lightheaded, she was pleased to have reached Friday so she could recharge her batteries over the weekend.

"For Children in Need?" Amber clarified, jiggling the money in her bucket.

"Oh, it completely slipped my mind," Ivy slipped a ten pound note into the collection bucket, "I didn't realise being pregnant would make me so tired or forgetful."

Amber swished her tail dramatically but unfortunately her assistant's good humour didn't have its usual effect of lifting Ivy's spirits, as she headed into school feeling sluggish and heavy-headed. That morning, she found herself to be irritable with the children who were understandably distracted by the fancy dress costumes they were wearing. Normally Ivy would have made allowances for this and joined in the fun, but today all she wanted was to get to 3:15pm so she could go home for some peace and quiet. By the morning break, her head pounding, she sought a quiet corner of the staffroom, hoping a strong coffee would perk her up sufficiently to get through to lunchtime. Slowly, she closed her eyes...

"Well, it's time to go back into the fray," Amber's squeaky

voice jolted Ivy from her catnap. Startled and disorientated she jumped up from her chair, barely having time to register her graceful plunge into black nothingness.

"Ivy, Ivy," Amber's voice penetrated the darkness, pulling her back to consciousness. Opening her eyes, her colleague's pretty face hovered over her, her ice-blue eyes brimming with concern.

"What happened?" Ivy murmured attempting to lift her head, but thinking better of it as the room began to spin once more.

"You fainted," Amber soothed, catching a tendril of Ivy's hair that'd worked itself free of her clip, to tuck it behind her ear. Peering from behind her assistant, Ivy noticed Naomi's and Sara's worried faces bearing down upon her too, "just lie still for a moment before you sit up."

When she was ready, Amber and Sara grasped Ivy's arms, helping her back to her chair. "Here, drink this," Kate pressed a glass of water into her hand. Sipping the water slowly it suddenly occurred to Ivy that she'd never fainted before in her life and her free hand resting on her stomach, she was seized with panic. "What if something is wrong with my baby?" As soon as her unspoken fear was out, she felt tears welling in her eyes.

"Don't worry," Clare soothed, flustered from having rushed from her office, "it's quite normal to faint at this early stage of pregnancy."

"It happened plenty of times to me," added Kate, her jolly, red face peeping from behind Amber's worried, white one, "I fainted in the classroom once and when I came to, I had twenty-five faces bearing down on me. Some of the

437

girls were in floods of tears while one of the boys solemnly announced that I'd died!"

Despite her head still whooshing with wooziness, Ivy couldn't help but laugh.

"All the same, I'd get it checked out," Clare added, "just to make sure everything's okay. I'll take your class for the rest of the day." Ivy nodded in gratitude, realising her head teacher was willing to sacrifice her Friday afternoon's work on the school budget for her. But still it wasn't enough; she wanted, no needed, Jacques.

"I've got some free time too this afternoon," Kate said, "so don't worry, Ivy, we've got your class covered. All we need is someone to run you to the hospital."

"That'll be me," Amber announced, slinging her handbag over her shoulder.

"Aren't you forgetting you're wearing a catsuit which clings to all your curves for dear life?" Kate pointed out to Ivy's young assistant with a wry smile, "you don't want to be responsible for distracting all those handsome doctors from their duties in A&E, do you?"

"Miaow," purred Amber, "I can think of worse ways to spend a Friday."

In the car, Ivy phoned her mum, assuring her the hospital visit was just a precaution. In A&E the triage nurse assessed her as a non-urgent category three before disappearing down the corridor, her white rubber-soled shoes squeaking as she pursued a pressing emergency. Luckily, in the waiting room, there was only a teenage boy who'd trapped his finger in a car door and Ivy's bottom had barely touched her chair when she was called.

"Ivy, are you alright?" her mum gasped as she emerged back into the waiting room on Amber's arm twenty minutes later.

"Mum, calm down. I'm okay," she took her mum's hand as she sat beside her, "but you're shaking like a leaf."

"I drove like the clappers, probably got a speeding ticket. Thank God you had Amber to look after you," she eyed her catsuit dubiously but offered no comment. "You said you fainted? What did the doctor say?"

"That it's just low blood pressure. He explained that I blacked out due to the dramatic changes the cardiovascular system undergoes during pregnancy," Ivy saw her mother's concerned look. "Don't worry, it's nothing serious. And I must confess I felt so nauseous, I didn't manage much breakfast today."

"Ivy, you must try to eat, even when you have morning sickness," her mum's forehead furrowed with worry lines, "when did the doctor say your blood pressure would start increasing?"

"Around about the mid-point in my pregnancy. So, in January, it should start to go back up, returning to its normal level by the end," smiled Ivy, noticing her mum's expression was unchanged, "honestly, I'm fine, mum. Tired but fine!"

"I'd better get back to school. Clare will be wondering where I am," Amber hugged Ivy tightly, "just make sure you have a proper rest this weekend and don't worry about our class this afternoon. I'm ready for anything now I've met the dishy Dr Lowry."

"Amber! You're incorrigible!" Ivy exclaimed as her

assistant walked away, swishing her tail provocatively behind her to any passing doctors who might notice.

"Why was she wearing a catsuit?" her mum enquired as they steadily made their way through the hospital car park a few minutes later, "it's rather unsuitable for school, isn't it?"

"We're raising money for Children in Need," Ivy pointed out, feeling suddenly very tired, "to be honest, I'm not sure it's appropriate attire for school either but she's so sweet, she gets away with it," to which they both laughed.

Pulling out of the car park, her mother turned to Ivy, "I'm taking you home with me for the weekend and that's non-negotiable."

They stopped by Ivy's flat to pack an overnight bag before continuing on to Lavenham. On Ivy's previous visit home, the trees had still worn their orange and yellow autumn dress but now their branches were bare and black, their dried up dead leaves clustered beneath the hedgerows. A feeling of melancholy pervaded, with spring, summer and autumn gone for another year. Yet as Ivy looked up to see the stark, spindly branches silhouetted against the leaden sky, they were undeniably beautiful, too.

"Ivy, how are you feeling?" her dad greeted her at the front door, his face etched with worry.

"Just a little tired," Ivy felt his warm arms wrap around her, "low blood pressure is very common at my point of pregnancy, no big deal."

"She needs to take it easy," her mum explained, her concerned expression slightly mellowing, "and if Ivy won't, we'll make sure that she does, won't we Dan?"

"We certainly will." Taking his daughter's hand, he led

her into the living room and sat her down in his armchair, draping a blue blanket snugly over her legs.

"It must be serious if I get to sit in *the armchair,*" Ivy laughed, feeling like a child once more.

"It's only for VIPs," her dad winked, hovering over her until sure she was comfortable.

Her dad made them all chicken salad sandwiches and cut up some fruit for lunch. Two hours later, he brought in some tea and slices of salted caramel cake as Ivy and her mum watched their favourite Second World War/romantic movies; *Shining Through, Charlotte Grey* and *Enigma* back to back. Ivy was struck that the theme of each one was love conquering all under the most dramatic circumstances. As the credits of the final film rose, she couldn't help but think that this rarely extended to real life, that Rose's happiness with Ryan had been cruelly curtailed by tragic events coupled with a responsible decision. Later, Ivy felt ravenous and so, for tea, her dad got his way to have fish and chips although her mum insisted they eat them with the kitchen window wide open to prevent the greasy smell from permeating the house.

"This is such a treat," Ivy tasted the salt and vinegar on her tongue. "It takes me right back to my childhood when it was our Friday ritual."

"That's right." Her dad tucked into a jumbo haddock and chips. "It was always a great start to the weekend!"

"Now then Dan, don't start getting any ideas. Remember, this is just because Ivy is here and it's been a tough day for all of us. It's back to your healthy diet tomorrow," her mum cast him a warning look, "lots of vegetables and hearty casseroles now winter is upon us."

They settled on the sofa with their coffees as *Children in Need* was warming up with a performance from *One Direction*. By eight thirty, however, Ivy was finding she could barely keep her eyes open and, being told by her parents to go to bed, she smilingly obeyed. Lying in her old single bed, the walls around her plastered with now-peeling *A-ha* posters, Ivy thought of the kids' stories she'd just watched on T.V. and thanked God her own childhood had been filled with love, from Rose and from her parents. As she drifted towards sleep, she prayed she could provide the same for her child. She just had to put her fears to rest and get through the scan…

53

Fat flakes of snow fell the following Friday afternoon as Ivy waited by the school gates. Since being a young child, she'd always loved watching snow drift down from the sky, transforming the most mundane scene into something breathtakingly beautiful. Now, she held out her hand before her, capturing snowflakes and studying their intricate patterns of crystals before they melted to nothing on her warm skin. Hoping the snow was too slushy to settle, she spotted her mum's car emerge from the whiteness and gingerly negotiated the frosted pavement.

"Sorry, I'm a little late. It took me a while to de-ice the windscreen and then the traffic was horrendous coming into Colchester. Seems everyone is using their car today; I should have given myself more time," her mum remarked as Ivy eased herself into the passenger seat beside her.

"It doesn't matter, don't worry about it." Ivy smiled, calming a little as she pulled her seatbelt over her stomach.

Her mum looked at her, putting the car into gear, "ready?"

"As I'll ever be," Ivy bit her lip, twisting her hands nervously in her lap. The risks of having a first baby in her late thirties came to the forefront of her mind now, despite her attempts all morning to suppress them.

"You'll be fine, you and the baby. I'm sure of it," her mum assured, seeking to quell her daughter's apprehension. As they pulled away from school, with the windscreen wipers working furiously to push away the snow, Ivy prayed her mum's instinct was well founded. To avoid getting stuck in heavy traffic, her mum cut down a series of side roads, meaning that despite her slight tardiness in picking up Ivy, they still arrived in the hospital car park forty-five minutes before her scan appointment.

"Do you want to go straight in?" her mum fiddled in her purse for change for the parking meter.

"Not just yet," Ivy handed her the two pounds parking fee. "I think I'd rather listen to the radio, try and take my mind off it. I've never liked hospital waiting rooms," she added, recalling the many times she'd spent in them as a child before appointments with various dermatologists. Her mum nodded and switched on the radio, already getting into the Christmas spirit with *Driving Home for Christmas*.

"I think November 22nd is a bit early for that, unless you're driving from China or South Africa?" laughed Ivy as her mum pulled up her hood before heading through the snow, falling even faster and more furiously now.

"The snow is starting to settle," her mum shivered as she returned a few minutes later, leaning over Ivy to attach the parking ticket to the dashboard. "It's a bit slippery too so we'll have to be careful."

Their arms clasped tightly together, they progressed slowly across the car park, which had taken the appearance of a skating rink, although mercifully the snow was mostly powdery rather than slippery at this stage. In the absence of an umbrella, snowflakes stung their faces and settled on their shoulders as they walked. But their priority was reaching the gritted path safely which they then followed, a little less anxiously, to the Outpatients entrance.

"Thanks mum," Ivy paused in the busy foyer, the cloying antiseptic smell familiar to her nose, "and thanks for being here with me today, no matter what happens."

"Don't think about ifs and maybes," she clasped Ivy's cold hand in her glove-warmed ones, "let's just find out what the scan shows, okay?"

In the antenatal waiting room there were six other women, wrapped in thick coats, all younger and in more advanced stages of pregnancy than Ivy. She noticed too they were all supported by the men in their lives and, as she waited, she tried to push from her mind images of Jacques sleeping soundly in Toronto, oblivious to the fact that she was carrying his child. To calm her nerves, she drank from her bottle of water while her mum distracted her with plans to call in at a garden centre tearoom on their way back to Lavenham.

"I think the Christmas shop will be open by now," her mum suggested, "I could do with a few more baubles."

"Haven't you got enough?" Ivy remembered her mum had bought a fourth Christmas tree in the January sale to accommodate her burgeoning collection of decorations.

"You can never have too many tree decorations." Her mum's firm reply was interrupted by a young nurse, calling Ivy's name. Following her down a white corridor, the smell of fresh paint invaded Ivy's nostrils and, despite her concerns, she felt her heart soar. She was going to see her baby for the first time.

In her late forties, the sonographer was a pleasant-looking woman with a chin-skimming blonde bob. After checking Ivy's details and summarizing what her doctor had already explained, she looked up from the notes and smiled. "Now, if you just want to get on the bed, pull up your jumper and ease your leggings down a bit, we'll take it from there," the woman turned to face the scanning screen to give Ivy a degree of privacy. Once in position, the sonographer handed her some paper towels to tuck into her waistband. "Right, I'm going to put some gel on your tummy first and I'm just warning you, it's cold."

"Okay," Ivy smiled at her mum. It soon turned to a slight wince, however, as the woman spread the icy gel over her abdomen, "sorry," the sonographer said, "it's so I can get a good contact between your skin and the transducer."

Ivy then began to feel some pressure as the woman moved the device over her tummy. Lifting her eyes from her stomach, she focused on the black and white screen humming at her right side. At first all she saw was a collection of fuzzy dots but then suddenly a clear image of her baby's head emerged from them, followed by its body, arms and legs. "Oh gosh," she gasped, her eyes transfixed on the moving image. Turning to her mum, she saw she had tears in her eyes too.

446

"Yes, everything seems to be fine. Your baby has a strong heartbeat," assured the sonographer, clicking computer keys, "let's just take a few measurements… yes, that's well within the range and the anatomy of the baby is fine. There's the head, the brain, the heart, the stomach, bladder and bowel. And here are the arms and legs." As she pointed out what they were seeing, Ivy felt bubbles of excitement explode into pure joy.

The snow had largely melted away by the time they left the hospital. With the light already fading, they found the garden centre tearoom quiet apart from a group of elderly couples discussing the implications of Brexit over coffee and cake. Ordering a pot of tea and spiced toasted teacakes, Ivy and her mum headed to a corner table overlooking the walled garden. So deep into November, the bare flowerbeds and leafless trees gave the view a rather sad, forlorn look, relieved only by stacks of fir trees waiting to be given a home and beautified for Christmas. The thought gave Ivy the little thrill she always felt as the festive season got underway.

"Are you alright?" asked her mum, clicking open the tiny pot of raspberry jam, "only you've hardly said a word since we left the hospital."

Ivy had used that time to formulate her thoughts and now they hastily tripped over one another. "It's just… I still don't know how to tell Jacques about the baby. I know I said that I would tell him if the results of my scan were okay. But it doesn't feel right somehow to do it over the phone and with everything that happened with Louise and Luc still so recent, I just don't know what his reaction will be… "

"I realise it's difficult but you have to give Jacques a

chance. I'm sure he loves you darling and wants to start afresh with his life too…" her mum smeared her teacake with the jam. "You both deserve to be happy."

"I know," Ivy sighed deeply. "Oh, mum, at the moment I'm just so relieved everything seems to be alright with the baby. To be honest I haven't thought much beyond today, didn't want to tempt fate I suppose. But now I have to make a decision."

"Yes, you do, sweetheart. But from where I'm sitting it doesn't seem as difficult as you believe," her mum smiled to which Ivy nodded.

"Why did Rose and I fall for men who live half way around the world?" Ivy asked, just as much to herself as her mum.

"That's just the way life is Ivy. None of us can help who we fall in love with," her mum stated, simply. As they finished their tea, Ivy reflected yet again how lucky she was that her parents had been so supportive. She would never have to face the terrible dilemma which Rose had met, and the heartbreaking decision she had been forced to make. As dusk drew in over the garden centre, they chatted excitedly about the coming baby, deliberately leaving the more mundane arrangements of maternity leave and childcare for another day. With *Away in a Manger* playing softly in the background, it was a time for hope and dreams of a new life. Afterwards, as her mother disappeared behind curtains of tinsel, lost in bowls of bright baubles and boxes of fairy lights, Ivy bought a small, simple, wooden nativity carved in Bethlehem, to forever remind her of this afternoon when she saw her baby for the first time.

"Let's see the picture of my grandson then. I wonder if he'll be as handsome as his old granddad?" beamed Ivy's dad as they arrived home later. "First thing I'm buying him is a baby-sized Ipswich Town shirt," he joked.

"Well, you'll have to put that idea on hold as we didn't find out the sex, dad," Ivy squeezed onto the sofa next to him, slotting the grainy photo into his hands, "look, that's the head, an arm, a leg," she pointed out delightedly.

While her mum was preparing tea, Ivy made quick phone calls to Amber and Mei, to tell them of her scan results and that her pregnancy was progressing normally. Amber's was a rather rushed call as she was getting ready for a night out with Jamie whereas Mei pleaded with her yet again to tell Jacques, before moving on to her nursing course and her children's schooling, both of which seemed to be going well, as far as Ivy could tell. Later, over their sausages, mash and gravy, Ivy and her parents chatted about the baby, whether they could fit a fifth Christmas tree into the hall and what Ipswich's chances were of reaching the play-offs at the end of the season, although that principally constituted a monologue of Ivy's dad without much informed input from either his daughter or his wife. After washing up, he settled in front of the T.V. to watch his beloved Town live on Sky Sports, while Ivy's mum brought out a brown, battered photograph album.

"I found it at Rose's house a few months ago. At some point she'd spilt some tea on it so I want to transfer the photos into this one," she announced, picking up a huge album with trademark Emma Bridgewater coloured spots breaking out like a rash over its cover. They spent the next couple of hours carefully removing the black and white and sepia photos from the soiled album, those welded down with yellowing Sellotape proving trickiest. Some had names and dates helpfully scribbled on the backs while others, Ivy recognised from the photos she'd found in the back of Rose's diary, were of Frances, Eleanor and Violet.

"Yeeeesssss, get in," her dad's voice echoed loudly from the living room. Through the crack in the door, Ivy saw his fist punch the air and she and her mum exchanged smiles. "Sounds as though 'Town might be about to break their Sky duck this season?"

"Still plenty of time to go yet," her mum raised her eyebrows, sticking a photo of Rose in the new album, writing her name beneath it for future generations of their family to read, "she was beautiful, wasn't she?"

"Very," smiled Ivy, looking at her glossy hair, her pale skin and wide, luminous eyes, "how old do you think she is there? Twenty-three, twenty-four?"

"Yes, around that age," her mother nodded. "It's hard to imagine why she didn't get married. She couldn't have been short of suitors but she obviously never got over Ryan. It's so sad."

Unable to reply honestly without divulging the truth, Ivy left the comment hanging in the air. The next photograph her mother handed her was dated 1932 and was of the four sisters. Studying it, she thought that Violet and Nell, with their tall, slender figures and light-blonde hair could easily have been taken for twins while Frances, whom she'd always believed to be her grandma, peeped out shyly through her glasses, her dark curly hair unsuccessfully controlled by a large bow. Lastly, there was twelve year-old Rose, already blossoming into the lovely young woman she was to become.

"My dad was the most loving, gentle soul. I absolutely adored him. I just wish I could have had him a bit longer," her mum handed her a photograph of a couple, him very tall with white, bushy hair, her the mousy sister with glasses Rose had never seen eye to eye with. "I suppose it was hard for Mum bringing me up after he died, I can understand why she was strict with me," she said. Watching her mum wistfully stare at the photo, Ivy knew she'd made the right decision not to tell her they weren't her biological parents, realising that it would be a secret forever-kept. The remaining photographs were of family weddings, days at the seaside and picnics in the park. As she sorted through them, handing them in turn to her mother, Ivy's eyes lingered on one, her pulse racing. Turning the photograph over, she read the inscription on the back, penned in Rose's fine hand. *Whitsuntide Fair, 1944.*

Rose's description of that day coming to mind, Ivy recognised her kindly-looking great-grandmother sandwiched in between Frances and Albert. But it was Rose, or rather the figure standing next to her, who caused her heart to somersault. A tall, young man in an immaculate American Air Force uniform. As she peered at his handsome face she knew for certain, even though it was a black and white photograph, his hair would be the colour of wheat and his eyes cornflower blue, the same colouring as her mother. The resemblance was too striking for her to ignore. She noticed how young and happy Ryan looked, just a boy really. Out of sight of the rest of the group, she saw that his fingers lightly laced Rose's and felt a wave of sadness overwhelm her as she reflected on his fate, hoping with all her heart that he had recovered enough from his illness to find happiness again back in the States. Seeing that her mother was busy sticking in the previous photo and was paying no attention to her, Ivy slipped the photo into her pocket, intending to place it in Rose's journal where it rightfully belonged.

54

As twinkling Christmas trees started to appear in the windows of the houses she walked past on her way to school, Ivy came to a decision. Seeing her baby's image on the scan and feeling a gentle fluttering like butterfly wings inside her, had intensified her determination to protect her unborn child. Increasingly tired with all her responsibilities at work and with the sale of Rose's house dispelling her financial fears, she brought forward her maternity leave from spring to Christmas.

Telling Jacques, however, was a matter over which she continued to procrastinate, the habit of a lifetime she would never shake off. Originally, she'd convinced herself she was awaiting the scan results before giving him her news and yet something still held her back. Walking to school one frosty morning in early December, she recalled her first instinct on reading Rose's letter was that she should have been braver and tried to contact Ryan to let him decide whether he was ready to be a husband and father, instead of being persuaded to give her baby to her sister. She felt hypocritical now she was guilty of the same. She was still pondering this dilemma as she lined up her class for assembly when Amber, in her gingerbread man covered Christmas jumper derailed her train of thought. "Where do you want to go for your leaving do? You need to decide soon because everywhere is getting booked up for the festive season. Do you fancy *Romanos?*"

"Oh Amber, I don't want a big fuss. You know I don't like being the centre of attention. I was thinking more of a Jacob's join at lunchtime on my final day."

"Okay, I can arrange that," Amber smiled, mischievously. During her morning break, Ivy discovered two lists on the staffroom notice board, one entitled *Staff Christmas Party at Romanos,* the other; *Ivy's Jacob's join.* As she added her name to the lists, Ivy couldn't help but admire her teaching assistant's craftiness.

Ivy and Amber had the task of organising year three and four's contribution to the Christmas production as Naomi didn't have a musical bone in her body. Called '*The Christmas Child*', it was a twist on '*The Little Match Girl*', a Christmas fable which had always been a favourite of Ivy's since Rose had first read it to her nearly thirty years ago. The school's version was about a boy who sold Christmas ornaments on the streets of modern day south-east London and while some people bought the angel decorations from him or gave him cups of tea and hot pies, others rushed by, caught up in their own business and too busy to notice him. Then on Christmas Eve, he disappeared, never to be seen again, but good fortune reigned over all the kind people who had helped him as their Christmas wishes came true. It sounded simple but when you added two classes of seven, eight and nine year olds it was anything but.

"Alright, year three, can we have some quiet please?" Ivy raised her voice half an hour into their seventh rehearsal, "thank you. Now, Sophie and Carl, can you say your lines again?"

A hushed silence descended on the hall as the blonde twins went through them without a hitch.

"Perfect," Amber clapped her hands, "except, Carl you're an angel so, on the night of the show, can you try not to pick your nose?"

"No, Miss," came the squeaky voice as Ivy stifled a laugh. After school that evening, Ivy found herself joining the throng of Christmas shoppers making their way into Colchester city centre. In need of sustenance first, she headed to the Christmas market where she enjoyed German sausages and sauerkraut washed down with non-alcoholic fruit punch. Reenergised, she spent the next hour or so strolling around the wooden chalets, browsing the array of seasonal goodies on offer. Loudspeakers churned out seasonal tunes and twinkling fairy lights suspended in trees created the festive vibe, while the intoxicating blend of spices from the mulled wine stalls instantly transported Ivy back to Marrakech's night market. Jostling past loved-up couples, her heart suddenly ached with longing to have Jacques by her side.

Luckily, she had her Christmas present mission to divert her from feeling downcast as she followed the flow of crowds to the high street shops. She managed to get her dad's gift done and dusted in *W.H. Smiths*: with the new *Guinness Book of Records*, a James Bond box set and a model airplane construction kit that would occupy him on Christmas morning until summoned for his turkey carving duties. As well as her favourite French perfume, Ivy bought her mum a lovely bottle-green, forties-style cabled jumper. Gathered in at the waist and embroidered with Christmas-red flowers, Ivy initially baulked at the three figure price tag before deciding to push the boat out to show her how much she appreciated and loved her after her difficult year.

Next, she visited *Bygone Books*, a musty, dusty second-hand shop where she'd spotted a pristine first edition of Albert Camus' *Le Premier Homme* the previous Sunday. The novel on which she'd written her final dissertation at university, it had a special place in her heart and, set in Algeria, she knew it would appeal to Jacques and his love for North Africa. Laden with her purchases, she headed back to her car, conscious of one notable absence on her Christmas gift list this year.

She'd always seemed to know instinctively what to buy Rose whether it was a pretty pair of leather gloves, one of those embroidered tablecloths she favoured or some expensive scented candles. Returning home without any of these emphasised the fact she'd never see her again and she realised how difficult it would be to enjoy Christmas without her.

The next day, she mooched around her flat in her pyjamas wrapping her purchases from the previous evening in holly-sprigged paper, before making herself a simple omelette for supper. Sunday dawned bright and clear as Ivy drove to meet her parents at *Ye Horns Inn*, an ancient pub a few miles from

Lavenham and their favourite haunt for lunch. Beyond its Suffolk pink walls and latticed windows, Ivy doubted the interior had changed much since World War II, and wondered if Rose and Ryan had visited on one of the occasions he'd managed to borrow a car from the base. Sitting by the roaring fire, the air infused with pine needles from the huge tree, Ivy enjoyed a three course lunch rounded off by treacle sponge, not giving a thought to the calories.

"This is nice," Ivy's dad observed as they finished off with coffee and mints at a cosy table in the snug, "just me and my girls."

"It won't be like this for much longer. In a few months we'll have our grandchild with us," Ivy's mum gazed reflectively into space.

"I doubt our grandson will be eating roast beef followed by pudding and custard anytime soon, Erin!" he laughed, covering her hand with his own.

"Oh your dad thinks he's so funny!" her mother rolled her eyes.

"Why are you convinced the baby will be a boy, dad?" Ivy said, having purposely not asked the sex of the baby at her scan.

"No reason other than wishful thinking," said her mum, raising her eyebrows as she looked at her husband, "I keep telling him we come from a long line of women but will he have it? He's even got a name picked out! You ask him!"

"Erin!" he reddened slightly, looking at his daughter, sheepishly. "You said you wouldn't!"

"Wait for it, Ivy," her mum persisted, failing to keep a straight face.

"Okay," her dad held up his hands, "it's Kevin. And before you say anything about Harry Enfield, my grandson would be named after Kevin Beattie, the most successful Town player in the history of the club."

"Right," Ivy shifted uncomfortably in her chair, seeing he was in earnest, "I'll bear that in mind, dad. Thanks for the suggestion." As her parents' good-humoured banter continued, she realised whatever happened with her and Jacques, her baby would be fortunate indeed to have these two as grandparents.

Ivy was writing her Christmas cards that evening when her baby gave her a gentle kick. Resting the heel of her hand on her stomach, she waited and, after a moment, came a second, more powerful one. Tears pricked her eyes as this, far more than a grainy image on a scan photo, brought it home that she was carrying a new life inside her. Mindful of Rose and Ryan's lost opportunities, she knew she must give Jacques the chance to be a father again. It seemed unfair to keep delaying telling him. Buoyed by her grandma's exhortation to hold onto those you love and never let them go, she typed an email, imploring him to come over for Christmas. She knew that if he loved her, he would be on the first plane to England.

The Christmas concert rehearsals paid off as the children's performance was met by rousing applause from the proud parents packed into the school hall. Ivy's class, in particular, were pitch perfect in their ensemble and afterwards, she mingled with the kids and their parents over celebratory mince pies and non-alcoholic mulled wine. With news of her impending maternity leave having spread on the school grapevine, Ivy received a stream of good wishes and, walking home that Monday night, she was buoyed by them even though it niggled her that Jacques hadn't replied to her email.

55

Ivy woke early on 21st December hardly able to believe her final day in school had come around so quickly. Part of her just wanted to get through it so she could enjoy Christmas before putting her feet up to concentrate on preparing for her baby's birth, but she also felt sad that she'd be saying goodbye to colleagues and children who were such an important part of her life. Even though she reminded herself it was only a temporary state of affairs and she'd be back at school in the autumn, her pregnancy was playing havoc with her emotions and she knew she wouldn't get through the day without shedding some tears. The shrill ring of the phone cut through her thoughts.

"Hello, birthday girl!" she heard her dad's cheerful voice.

"Thanks for the lovely card and beautiful bracelet," she looked down at the amethysts nestling in a gold band encircling her wrist.

"Oh, your mum chose it," he chortled down the line, "she wouldn't trust me with anything like that."

"That I believe," smiled Ivy, knowing the only cards or gifts he'd ever bought down the years, had been for his wife, some of them of distinctly dubious taste.

"The other thing I wanted to ask is, do you want to go to *The Swan* on Christmas Eve? If so I'll book a table for 6pm?"

"Of course dad, I love that tradition of ours," Ivy replied. Remembering it had started at Rose's suggestion many years ago, she wondered now whether perhaps it was so she could feel close to Ryan once more.

"That's great, I'll get the reservation made right away. I'll just put your mum on. Don't work too hard today and have a lovely evening with your friends. Bye darling." Ivy heard the phone rattle and then her mum's voice, wishing her 'Happy Birthday' before they briefly refined their plans for Christmas. Even though she realised memories of Rose would be ever present this year, Ivy was determined to follow her example and enjoy Christmas as she had always done.

The crisp, clear air heralded a frosty night as Ivy drove home with goodbye cards and Christmas cards and presents nestling on the passenger seat. Despite having managed to refrain from crying, unlike many of the children in her class, especially the girls, Ivy felt drained after what had been an emotional day. Arriving at her flat, she kicked back on the sofa with a comforting cup of hot chocolate and a mince pie in an attempt to regain enough energy to see her through the staff Christmas party.

After showering and teasing her newly tinted chestnut-brown hair into soft curls, Ivy had to face the problem of what to wear. Her wine-red 'party' dress with its close fitting skirt which she always wore to such occasions was out of the question this year while her maternity wardrobe of baggy sweaters over leggings was clearly inappropriate. She eventually settled on a deep-blue, tunic dress, which she'd mistakenly bought in a size fourteen in an *Oasis* sale, teaming it with festive sparkly tights and high-heeled pixie boots which accentuated her slim legs.

"Happy Birthday," everyone shouted as Ivy entered the restaurant, multi-coloured strands of paper from party poppers shooting up to the ceiling, "and sorry you're leaving."

"I thought I had my leaving do at lunchtime?" Ivy looked in Amber's direction as *Celebrate Good Times* began to play loudly.

"Sandwiches, crisps and cake?" mocked an already merry Amber in a silver-sequinned mini dress which left little to the imagination. "You didn't honestly think I'd let you get away with that when you've been with us for zillions of years? It's low-key, you have to admit."

"Hmmm, maybe for you," Ivy replied, but Amber just smiled her sweetest smile as she led her to the head of the table, which was decorated in the red, green and white of the Italian flag but which also managed to look extremely festive.

"We'll have to meet up for coffee every week," smiled Sara, who'd obviously been to the same shop as Amber to buy her dress, although hers was a gold version.

"Definitely," beamed Amber, looking at Ivy, "catch you up on all the excitement you're missing at St Mark's."

"And Ivy can fill us in on what it's like to be a lady of leisure," quipped Naomi, who was already looking worse for wear. Evidently failing to keep up with the drinking pace of her companions, Ivy wondered just how many bars the three of them had visited en route to *Romanos*.

"That sounds like a good plan," smiled Ivy, suddenly realising how much she'd come to rely on her colleagues' support and friendship over the past months. "I'd miss you all too much, otherwise."

"Ivy, don't start me off," said Sara, fanning her moist eyes with her hands, "do you know how long it took me to do my makeup?"

For starters, there were mozzarella balls, sundried tomatoes and olives, which everyone fell on ravenously. Conversation and laughter flowed as they moved on to garlic breads, followed by pasta and pizza main courses before ending with a selection of mouth-watering Italian desserts.

"Thank you for arranging this for me," Ivy squeezed Amber's hand over coffee and mints, "I couldn't have got through all this without you – you're the best teaching assistant I've had and, more importantly, a good friend."

"I don't know what I'm going to do without you," Amber drew her into a perfume-infused hug, "I'm gonna really miss you."

"For goodness sake, I'm not leaving for good, Amber," laughed Ivy, "I'll be back in September."

"All the same, I wanted to tell you, just in case." Releasing her, Ivy nodded as her emotions threatened to overcome her. The meal concluded, the waiters cleared the tables to the edges of the room to create a small dance floor.

Predictably Sara, Naomi and Amber were the first ones up and the last ones to be dragged away at midnight, while Ivy ensconced herself in a quiet corner, checking to see if Jacques had responded to her email. Disappointed he still hadn't, she welcomed the distraction of the steady stream of well wishers which gravitated to her. Hearing her colleagues' complimentary sentiments, including Kate's tearful and somewhat drunken speech, made Ivy apprehend just how well respected she was, their affection clearly genuine. She realised that over the years she'd allowed her insecurities about her appearance become a barrier to her forming close relationships with anyone. But since opening herself up to Jacques that summer, she'd got much better at letting people in. Sitting poised on the brink of motherhood, she was determined to take her new found confidence into the next phase of her life.

"Ivy, what'll I do without you?" Clare sat down beside her, her thick dark hair brushing her bare shoulders in corkscrew curls, "it would make my job a hell of a lot easier if all my teachers were like you."

"I'll be back in the autumn," Ivy reassured, yet again, a little confused as to why everyone assumed she wouldn't return to work after her maternity leave.

"As much as that is music to my ears, just wait and see how things turn out," Clare's eyes twinkled in the candlelight, "I was going to come back after my first pregnancy but in the end I waited until after Cheryl."

"I don't think you need to worry about that with me," Ivy smiled as *Last Christmas* made way for *Time to Say Goodbye*.

"This isn't very Christmassy," remarked Clare, hugging

Ivy to her substantial bosom which was perilously close to falling out of her black velvet bodice.

"No, but I know exactly who is responsible," Ivy hesitated, searching for Amber's blonde head in the crowd before being drowned out by the booming DJ. "This song is dedicated to Ivy. Where are you, Ivy? Come and join me."

Ivy sheepishly got up and walked across the dance floor where Sara, Amber and Naomi were waiting, "this is low-key?" she shouted as the volume ramped up a gear.

"Oh, Ivy, you know I don't do low-key," laughed Amber, damp strands of hair starting to become detached from her beautiful, blonde chignon. The four women then joined hands and swayed in time with the music, in the middle of the dance floor, the spotlight on them, the centre of attention. And for once, Ivy didn't care.

By half past eleven, Ivy was dog-tired and dialled a taxi. Leaving the restaurant to a rousing, if somewhat drunken, rendition of *For she's a jolly good fellow*, she saw that the predicted frost had started to take hold, covering everything with a sparkling mantle of white. Worried the pavements were already becoming treacherous, she made sure the taxi driver dropped her at the front door of her flat. Finding the lock already iced up, she fumbled her key with freezing fingers, trying to get it to turn. "Come on," she urged as a man muffled in a long, dark coat and cap came up behind her.

"Here, let me get that." Hearing his soft, melodic voice again, the memory of when she'd first heard it in the riad library, sunlight spilling onto the spines of the books, flashed into her mind. Her heart pounding, she turned to check whether she was dreaming but seeing the golden light from the streetlamp fall on his familiar face, she saw she was not. He had come.

"Jacques?" she managed to say before his lips fell onto hers.

56

"I can't believe you're here," Ivy whispered in amazement as they stepped into the warm hallway, his arm comfortingly curled around her shoulder. Realising that within hours of asking, Jacques had travelled across the Atlantic Ocean to be with her, allayed some of the fears which had troubled her in the past few weeks.

"I wasn't going to miss my best girl's birthday, now was I? Happy birthday, my love," his eyes filled with tears as he pressed his forehead to hers before kissing her softly again. For a long time they just held each other wordlessly, the physical presence of the other all each of them needed for now.

Eventually he drew back, holding her at arm's length to gaze into her eyes. "All this time I've kept the image of you in my head, but it doesn't come close to the reality of seeing you, of touching you." He traced his fingers down the side of her face, "and without thoughts of you, these long months would have been unendurable, Ivy. As I told you at Ouzoud, I want to spend my life with you. I love you with all my heart and if you feel the same… "

"I do, Jacques," she smiled, seeing his expression relax. Over the past few months, she'd dreamed of seeing him again so often but now he was standing before her, it hardly seemed real. His cold fingers entwined in hers, she led him into her flat, busying herself for a moment switching on lamps and Christmas tree lights. Returning from the kitchen with matches to light the wood burner she found Jacques slumped on the sofa, still wearing his thick coat and scarf which were sprinkled lightly with melting snowflakes. His eyes closed on the verge of falling asleep, she thought how vulnerable he looked and in that moment it hit home that he needed her as much as she needed him. She saw that for once, she wasn't the one with the frailties and this in turn put their relationship on an equal footing in her mind. She also knew Jacques had succeeded in bringing out a strength in her which had always been there but which she hadn't perceived until recently. As he opened his eyes, her remaining doubts disappeared and she knew she must follow her heart and do what Rose had never had the chance to.

"Oh god, I'm so sorry," he laughed, the corners of his eyes crinkling as he combed his long fingers through his dark, thick hair, which was standing up in all directions, "that's what a transatlantic flight does to you."

In the end, the words she'd not known how or when to say to him just tumbled out as she sat down beside him, stroking the side of his face, "Jacques, I know you'll never get over losing Luc and that nothing could ever replace him."

With confusion clouding his eyes, he straightened up, smiling at her, "Ivy, what are you trying to say?"

"That I'm pregnant." Silence pervading the space in between them, Ivy felt her heart hammer in her chest as she seemingly waited an eternity for him to speak.

"Ivy," his eyes were wide with wonder as his smile became even brighter, "why didn't you tell me before? I would have come straight to you."

"I wanted to," she whispered, her eyes filling with tears as he drew her into his arms, "I just didn't know how to. I suppose, deep down I wasn't sure whether you'd want another child. I'm sorry," she stopped, her voice catching in a sob.

"My love, on the plane over here, I thought of how I wouldn't be alone anymore because I'd have you," he paused to formulate his thoughts, "and now I discover you're pregnant with our child, I couldn't ask for anything more. You've given me a future I never dreamed was possible."

Nestling in each other's arms, at his insistence, she related each and every detail of her pregnancy from her morning sickness to her scan, "I'm sorry you had to go through these past months alone. I won't leave you again," he said as she finished, "ever."

She smiled, snuggling into his warmth and closing her eyes. "Hey, don't fall asleep on me!" he soporifically stroked the side of her face, "haven't you forgotten something?"

"What?" she looked up at him, confusion knitting her brow.

"To show me the scan photo of our baby," he whispered in her ear and in that moment, she knew everything was going to be alright, after all.

57

That Christmas Eve, the Airmen's Bar was crowded with families and friends enjoying a festive drink together. At the table where she and Rose had always sat, Ivy's mind drifted away from the conversation Jacques and her parents were enjoying to the extraordinary turn of events over the past six months. She remembered her grandma, whose death and diary had given her the courage to take a leap of faith to pursue her long-forgotten dreams. She thought of the cruelly curtailed lives of her great-aunts', Violet accepting her fate with grace while Nell had angrily fought against hers right up to her dying breath. Even though she'd tried to convince herself otherwise, she had a gut feeling things had not ended well for Ryan either, his love for Rose being such that he'd surely have made contact with her if he'd been in a position to do so. When she'd shown Rose's letter to Jacques, he'd agreed with her that telling her mum the truth about her parentage would only cause them both unnecessary heartache. And yet, who was to say Ivy wouldn't feel differently when her own child was born?

Looking up at the angel atop the Christmas tree, she said a silent prayer for Louise and Patrick and all they had lost. She hoped Patrick would find happiness again one day. Shared happiness, she smiled, which was finally in her grasp after all those years believing she was destined to live without it. Conscious the conversation around her had halted, she looked up to find Jacques and her parents watching her.

"I have something for you," Jacques smiled at her, his green and navy tartan scarf muffled beneath his dark overcoat. Although he'd only been in Suffolk a few days, it already felt he belonged there, with her.

"What is it?" Ivy smiled, her eyes drawn to the little red velvet box he removed from his inside pocket, "a Christmas present?"

"Not exactly," he smiled his eyebrow arching quizzically as he went down on one knee. Snapping open the lid to reveal an emerald ring, his eyes held hers, "Ivy, will you marry me?"

"Yes," she managed to say through salty tears. As Jacques slipped the ring onto her finger seemingly everyone in the bar looked on and applauded as for the second time in three days Ivy didn't mind being the centre of attention at all. "Just one thing," she whispered as he held her in his arms, "I sent your Christmas present to Canada."

But he just shook his head, smiling, "I have everything I'll ever want right here."

Later as Jacques and her parents became better acquainted, Ivy's attention focused on the framed newspaper report on the adjacent wall, detailing General G.W. Castle's fatal crash on Christmas Eve 1944. Staring at his handsome face, it suddenly struck her that tonight marked the anniversary of the tragedy and she reflected that, only last Christmas, Rose had been here with her, grieving for her lost love with no one to share that burden with. If only she'd known…

Ivy moved her attention to the flyers' scribbled names. Faded yet still legible, she wondered whether the airmen, with a presentiment perhaps that they would not return from their missions, had wanted to preserve their names for future generations to remember them. She skipped down the list; *Ron Wisdom, Danny Thompson, Dick Nolan, Ryan O'Connell,* her gaze faltering on the last name. *Ryan O'Connell 489th.* It couldn't be, could it? But the 489th was Ryan's unit and Ivy realised the looping signature was directly above the seat Rose had always occupied. Although she'd never mentioned Ryan's surname in her diary, Ivy knew that his family were of Irish descent. Could it be that her grandfather's name had been on the wall all these years, waiting for her to discover it? She would never know for certain of course but it comforted her that this spot would act as a little memorial to him, lost as he had been in mind, if not in body, like some of the other names which surrounded his.

Later, walking through the freshly-fallen snow to her parents' house as the Christmas bells pealed, Ivy clasped her hand around Jacques' arm for support. Seeing her emerald engagement ring sparkle next to Rose's Claddagh ring, she felt there truly was magic in the crisp, cold air.

Epilogue

Despite Ivy's concerns in those early months, her pregnancy had been pretty much plain-sailing after her reunion with Jacques that Christmas. They'd spent the cold, winter months of her maternity leave confirming everything they'd felt for each other during those sun-soaked days in Marrakech and had enjoyed a quiet wedding in Lavenham church in mid-February, the first snowdrops peeping among the gravestones. Pausing for the first time as man and wife by the lychgate, Ivy had plucked two white roses from her bouquet to lay them on the seat to remember where her grandparents had often met, hoping they too were happy together, somewhere.

May 2018

Ivy sat in the cottage garden, breathing in the heady scent of the summer's first roses, the table laden with left-over sandwiches and jelly from her daughter's first birthday party. She looked at her little girl, pretty in a pink smocked dress, her unblemished face and cornflower blue eyes framed by her honey-coloured curls. The image of her grandmother Erin and her great-grandfather Ryan. It was hard to believe that a whole year had passed since she'd held her newborn in her arms. But in other respects it felt she'd already had her for a lifetime.

Just after Jacques' arrival at Christmas, the Redmonds' purchase of Rose's cottage had fallen through after a survey had revealed some issues with the building which needed resolving. Unwilling to take a project like that on at their age, they'd reluctantly withdrawn their offer. A week after their wedding, Jacques and Ivy had moved in, with Jacques buying out Erin's share of the house and Daniel calling in a favour from a builder friend to do the repairs for a reasonable sum. They'd then decorated and furnished the rooms with their belongings, recreating the library with their own books and Rose's favourites which had become keepsakes. They hadn't planned on living in her cottage and yet somehow, it felt right. Jacques, freed from his painful memories in Morocco and Toronto, had taken a part-time job as an art lecturer at the local college. Teaching young people as well as having sufficient time to pursue his own painting, had given him a new lease of life, his happiness completed by having a wife and daughter upon whom he doted.

"Present time," Ivy's dad announced, scooping his chubby granddaughter into his arms as she ripped open the pink spotted paper to reveal a tiny blue Ipswich Town shirt.

"Oh, for goodness sake," Ivy's mum rolled her eyes while

the little girl occupied herself playing with the wrapping paper.

"Gotta start 'em young," Ivy's dad winked, tickling his granddaughter's tummy so that she squealed with laughter.

"I agree," smiled Jacques, who had been more than happy to exchange his loyalty for the Toronto Blue Jays to his father-in-law's football team. After attending a few matches in the spring after his arrival in England, he'd bought a season ticket that summer and now accompanied Ivy's dad to every home game as the two struck up a deep friendship.

"I think she needs a change," Ivy's dad grimaced, "what on earth have you been feeding her, Ivy?"

"Healthy food, dad," laughed Ivy, resting the little girl on her hip, as she pointed her tiny fingers in the direction of the huge pink and white birthday cake.

"It's okay, sweetie," Jacques kissed his daughter on the top of her head, "I'll bring you some cake."

Ivy retreated into the shady coolness of their cottage, her little girl contentedly sucking her thumb. During the months after her birth, they had all noted how she had Jacques' temperament, quiet and thoughtful. However, the more time she spent with her grandfather, Ivy could see his cheekiness rubbing off on her. For her part, Erin was pleased that her granddaughter had inherited her cornflower blue eyes, Ivy and Jacques being the only ones to know that they had been passed down through the generations from Ryan. Every time Ivy looked at her daughter she was reminded of him. Walking through the hallway now she passed Rose's Constable prints and two portraits painted by Jacques. He'd presented the first one to her on their wedding night, and as she looked at it now, she saw herself through his eyes: beautiful, her skin flawless and radiant.

"I didn't realise this is the way you see me," she'd said as they'd snuggled in the warmth of the four poster bed in the Honeymoon Suite at *The Swan*.

"It's not. This is the way you are," he'd smiled, pressing his lips to hers and as time went by, she came to believe it more and more.

Ivy stopped before the second portrait, startled as ever by the skill with which Jacques had captured the twenty-four year-old Rose from the creased photograph she'd given him. The little girl smiled, pointing up to the familiar painting.

"Yes, sweetie, that beautiful lady is your great-grandma," Ivy whispered, as she beheld Rose's lovely face once more. "One day I'll tell you her story, Rosie."

Acknowledgements

Roses of Marrakech gave me the chance to write about two places I love visiting – Morocco and Lavenham. While most of my characters are entirely fictional, Violet and Nell's stories are based on my great-aunts, Gladys and Ivy Dook. My character Ivy's struggles to come to terms with her birthmark are loosely based on my own experiences with cerebral palsy.

I want to express my deep gratitude to my dad, Peter, brother, Gareth, my aunts Pat, Jenny and Carolyn and my uncle Paul for your unwavering support over the years.

Thank you also to Andy, Nicola, Liz and Jane for your encouragement and enduring friendship and to my lovely colleagues: Sue, Maeve, Sarah, Elizabeth and everyone at St Mary's Catholic Primary School for all your kindness. It's a joy to work with you all.

Most of all, thank you to my mum, Pamela. Your belief in me has given me the courage to achieve so many things in my life I never dreamed would be possible. I love you.

Further Reading:

"Off the Runway: Memories of Wartime Life in and around Lavenham, England" by Lisa Parnell. Copyright 2013 Lisa M. Parnell.